HOODWRITTENS PUBLISHING
PRESENTS

REDEMPTION

I0553046

A NOVEL BY BOBBY DENNIS JR.

PUBLISHED BY HOODWRITTENS PUB.
PROMOTIONS BY HWP ENTERPRISES
www.hoodwrittenspublishing.com
hwpublishing@gmail.com

REDEMPTION, *A HoodWrittens Production*

For information on how individual consumers can place orders, please write to, e-mail, or visit us on the web.

HoodWrittens Publishing Inc.
119 Platte Street
Winder, Ga. 30680
E-Mail: hwpublishing@gmail.com
Internet: www.hoodwrittenspublishing.com

For orders other than individual consumers, HoodWrittens Publishing allows a discount on the purchase of (10) ten or more copies of a single title order for special markets or premium use.

For orders purchased thru the above named affiliates. We offer a 50% discount off the sale price for orders being shipped to prisons including, but not limited to federal, state, and county. We truly feel y'all pain.

PUBLISHED BY HOODWRITTENS PUB.
PROMOTIONS BY HWP ENTERPRISES
www.hoodwrittenspublishing.com
hwpublishing@gmail.com

Other Large Print Editions by J.E. Terrall

Western Short Stories
    The Old West
    The Frontier
    Untamed Land
    Tales from the Territory
    Frontier Justice

Western Novels
    Conflict in Elkhorn Valley
    The Valley Ranch War

Other novels by J.E Terrall
    The Return Home
    Sing For Me
    Return to Me

* * * * * *

"What's going on, Mr. McKenna?"

"Oh, hi, Mary. It seems we have a Peeping Tom in the neighborhood."

"Did you see who it was?"

"No. I didn't get a good look at him. It's too dark. He sure took off in a hurry when I yelled at him, though," he said with a slight chuckle in his voice.

"You might want to keep your windows locked and your drapes closed at night," he suggested.

"I'll do that, and thank you for running him off."

Mr. McKenna just smiled, waved and then went on his way. Mary closed and locked the window, then closed the drapes. She felt uneasy knowing that someone had been watching her. It sent a cold chill down her spine. She couldn't understand why anyone would be interested in her and what she was doing. She tried to put the uneasy feeling aside, but it was difficult for her.

* * * * * *

REDEMPTION

"Kane Family Saga Series"

A NOVEL BY BOBBY DENNIS JR.

PUBLISHED BY HOODWRITTENS PUB.
PROMOTIONS BY HWP ENTERPRISES
www.hoodwrittenspublishing.com
hwpublishing@gmail.com

REDEMPTION, *A HoodWrittens Production*

Note:
Sale of this book without a front cover may be unauthorized. If this book was purchased without a cover it may have been reported to the publisher as "unsold or destroyed." neither the author nor publisher may have received payment for sale of this book.

This novel is a work of fiction. Any resemblance to real people, living or dead, actual events, establishments, organizations, and/or locales are intended to give the fiction a sense of reality and authenticity. Other names, characters, places and incidents are either products of the author's imagination or are used fictitiously, as are those fictionalized events & incidents that involve real persons and did not occur or are set in the future.

Published by:
HoodWrittens Publishing Inc.
119 Platte St.
Winder, Ga. 30680
www.hoodwrittenspublishing.com
hwpublishing@gmail.com

Library of Congress Catalog Card No: To be supplied
ISBN: 978-0615457390
Copyright: 2011© Second Print (Revised)
All rights reserved by HoodWrittens Publishing for Bobby Dennis Jr.

BLOODLINE CREDITS:
Story by Bobby Dennis Jr.
Edited by Ausha Rogers
Text formation by Ausha Rogers
Cover work by Patrice Jamison pjamison85@gmail.com
Printed and pressed by on demand presses.

Dedication

First and foremost I want to give thanks to "Yahweh" who is ruler of my life! I dedicate this book to the loving memory of my Father; Bobby "Breeze" Dennis Sr. who was responsible for introducing me to the lifestyle I write about and lived. To my Earth; Ann "Betty" Dennis who loved me when I thought I didn't deserve to be loved, and who has supported me but never condoned the lifestyle I lived.

To my Ace and C.E.O of HoodWrittens Publishing, Ausha Rogers; without whom this work would have never made it to this stage.

To our in house typist, editor, critic, technician, and designer, Thanks for wearing so many hats {LOL} Trice! Our other typist and editor who have been instrumental in our progress, Dee-Dee, keep up the good work. To all of my supporters; Carl, Guy, Carlo Wilson, Tony @ Real or Nothin, London's Seafood, RogersThat Inc., Rahman and Nelray Ali of the Y.I.E.L.D Foundation, and everyone I missed on role call who have been there for me and supported me, to my brothers and sisters, " We Preciate Ya"

Don't think I done forgot the naysayers and future haters…. Y'all must be done forgot the word………"I TOLD YA!!!!!"

YOU GOT DAT!!!!

5

REDEMPTION

"Kane Family Saga Series"

A NOVEL BY BOBBY DENNIS JR.

BOOK TWO OF
KANE FAMILY SAGA SERIES

REDEMPTION!
1992, Jacksonville Fla.

On a warm April night, Berean Kane found himself in Theo's base house. He wasn't a baser he was a recreational drug user. He was in a room shooting up a speedball, a potent concoction of heroin and cocaine. He was interrupted by Will, who was a crack dealer from somewhere in Georgia. He had set up shop in Theo's house.

"Check this out Bro." Will said smiling, "I got a deal for you. I'll give you these two fat boulders for twenty dollars."

"I ain't into the stones." Kane said looking at Will, trying to get him to leave so he could take care of his business. Will persisted in trying to get Kane to buy his product.

"I done told you I ain't in to that shit. So step the fuck off!"

"Damn dog, you ain't got to trip I'm trying to give you a deal."

Kane looked at him with no nonsense in his eyes and Will turned and walked from the room. Kane finished doing the dope and walked to his younger brother Tony's house where he had left his car. Tony only lived a block from Theo.

Tony was sitting on his porch broke as usual; he had smoked up his paycheck on rock. Tony didn't see himself as a baser since he only smoked in cigarettes, and not off the pipe or a can.

"What's up Tee?" Kane asked looking at his brother's long face.

"Ain't shit Bro," Tony said despondently. "I need you to float me a loan until next payday. I done fucked up again and Lu gonna kill me when she get home."

"You ain't paid me back the money I gave you last week. And now you expect me to throw good money after bad."

"Awe man, don't do it like that Bro. I need you man."

"Fuck!" Kane exclaimed. "Dig this Tee, there's a nigga down in Theo's house serving; I'm go knock him off. Nigga named Will."

"Who's Will?"

"He from somewhere in Georgia, don't nobody know him. I asked a few people and they say the nigga just popped up out of the blue with a bomb, and started slanging."

"I'll roll with you then." Tony said rising from his seat.

"Naw, I got it." Kane said raising his hand to stop Tony, "I'll break bread with you when I get back."

"Sure you don't need me to roll and get your back?"

"Ain't but one nigga, I got it." Kane walked back to Theo's house and knocked on the door and Theo's voice floated out.

"Yeah, who is it?"

"This Kane, dog!"

Theo came to the door, opened it and let him in.

"Where's that dude that was serving? I wanna get a twenty."

"Gimme the money and I'll go get it for you." Theo said with his hand held out.

"Nigga, you know I don't give a muthafucka my money to cop for me. Just take me to the nigga and I'll handle it from there."

Kane and Theo grew up together and he knew Kane's rep, though he didn't think Kane would pull a caper in his house. He took Kane upstairs, and knocked on the door to one of the rooms. Will's, muffled voice came thru the door.

"What's up?"

"I got a cat that wants to cop a twenty!" shouted Theo, his face close to the door.

"Come on in dog!" Will shouted.

Kane followed Theo into the room, and saw that Will was tricking with Chell, a fine, brown skinned woman he knew well. Will and Chell were in bed naked. Theo rented out rooms to the whores in the area that needed a place to trick.

"Where's the dope?" Kane asked Will, who was looking at him closely.

"Ain't you the same nigga I tried to look out for earlier?"

"Yeah I'm that nigga. What my money doesn't spend now since I turned you down?"

"Hell yeah your money spend." said Will rising from the bed naked and walking to a dresser in the corner. He moved his clothes and pulled out a big bag of rocks.

Kane pulled his pistol from his back pocket, a compact 380. "Let me get all of that." He said, pointing the gun at Wills face.

"Aw man, you ain't got to go out like that!"

"Shut the fuck up nigga!" Kane said, and snatched the bag of rocks from Will's hand. He walked to the dresser and searched Will's pockets. Pulled out a fat roll of money and slid it in his pocket. "Get your shit and get from around here, and don't let me catch you round here again."

He led Will from the house naked. He pushed him down the short flight of steps, where Will sprawled and lay in an untidy heap with his clothes clutched tightly to his chest.

"Get your ass up and get moving." Kane said threateningly pointing his pistol at the frightened man.

8

Will rose, and loped off naked down the street.

Kane stepped back into the house, where Theo stood in the hall shaking with fear.

"Damn Kane that was fucked up. You could've waited till the nigga left before you touched him. You ain't had to jack the nigga in my crib!"

"Nigga please, I asked you did you know the nigga! You said you didn't, so what the fuck difference does it make where I touched him?"

"The difference is that now niggas is gonna think I set him up, and won't wanna come round here and serve. That's how a get my little bread and smoke for free, because it ain't like you gone come round here and break bread every day."

"Dig this Bro don't let your mouth overload your ass, it ain't like you just met me. You know what I do, and if I catch another nigga in here that nobody don't know, he gonna get the same treatment!"

Theo looked at Kane with words on the tip of his tongue, but he decided to keep them to himself. He knew Kane was a serious cat, and would resort to violence if he kept pressing. He decided the best thing for him to do was to hold his peace. Even though they had been raised together, he knew Kane would snap on him.

Kane pulled the big bag of rocks out of his pocket. He reached in the bag and gave Theo a hand full of stones.

"I bet that's more than that nigga was gonna break you off."

"Bet that up dog." Theo said, looking at the rocks and counting them up.

Kane walked to the big French doors that separated the living room from the hall. He opened them, and saw that it was about eight basers inside. He gave Chell five of the big rocks, and then broke off all the other basers a little something to smoke.

A fine young woman named Becky, walked in from the other door; she had been in the bathroom. She had cocoa brown skin, was 21 years old, and facially she resembled a young Anita Baker. She was 5" feet tall, and wore about 115 pounds. She had nice firm breast, a slim waist, and a fabulous ass. She was from Detroit, and had moved to Jacksonville a few years ago, and lived with her grandma. She was new to the crack game, and was a part time whore. He had his eye on her for a minute, but never tried to catch her. Kane walked over to her, went in the bag, and gave her about ten big rocks.

She looked up at his smiling face, and said. "Bet that up, what do I owe you?"

"That's on me Lil Momma so go on and get off." he said smiling as he turned and walked away.

9

She watched as he walked back thru the French doors and into the hall. She saw Theo sit next to a female named Lois, and load up her pipe. Lois was Theo's on and off woman, a heavy set pretty light skinned woman.

Becky went into her purse, and pulled out a small pill bottle. She dropped all of the rocks in it but one, and grabbed a glass stem and small mirror. She sat on the sofa, cut the rock in half, loaded it, lit it, and took a long drag.

*   *   *   *

Kane stood in the hallway, and served some of the rocks for about an hour and a half. He heard a car pull up outside, so he stood where he could see who it was. He saw Will get out on the passenger side, and another guy get out on the driver's side. He turned out the lights in the hallway, and hid in the recess underneath the stairs and waited.

There was a loud knock on the door, and Theo came from the front room where he and Lois had been smoking. He thought Kane was gone and in his drug induced state, he looked right pass where Kane was hid in the shadows.

"Yeah, who's there?" he asked walking to the door.

"It's Will!"

Theo looked out and saw Will with another man, and thought they were coming to retaliate against Kane. "We'll there too late now he's gone." Theo thought.

"Where's that nigga that robbed me?" Will asked.

"Man that nigga been gone." Theo said opening the door. Theo was an opportunist, and had no compunction about going out on Kane if he could get something out of it.

"This is my partner Dave." Will said introducing the other man. "Dig this dog. I ain't sweating that little shit dude took, hell that wasn't nothing I got plenty more."

Kane, standing under the stairs heard every word, and stepped out with his gun raised. "Nigga, since you got plenty more you don't mind me getting that what you got!"

"Damn dog, you gonna rob me again?" Will ask incredulously,

"Hell yeah! Now let me get that."

Will tossed Kane the dope, and Dave said. "Man fuck that!" And turned to the door, and fumbled with the latch.

"Fuck nigga don't move!" Kane shouted, as Dave continued to nervously attempt to open the door.

Kane dropped his aim and squeezed the trigger. The sound was deafening in the confines of the hallway as the bullet crashed into Dave's

10

right buttock. The force slammed him into the door as the round exited in a spray of blood, flesh, and cloth. Dave crashed thru the flimsy screen door and fell halfway out the house. He turned to Kane, pleading and moaning in fear and pain. "Oh lord, please don't kill me mister, please!"

"Don't kill us man, please don't kill us." Will begged.

"Shut the fuck up!" Kane yelled, and the two men ceased their wails.

"Damn!" said a voice behind Kane. He spun to the sound, his pistol at chest height. Becky stood there staring down the barrel of the .380. "Oh shit!" she said.

She had walked out of the living room at the moment Kane shot Dave and witnessed the entire scene.

Kane saw who it was and slacked up on the trigger. "Lil Momma you damn near got shot." he said disapprovingly. He turned back to the men, pointed the gun at Dave, and said. "Give it up, keys and all!

Dave hurried and pulled out a fat roll of bills, and tossed them to him along with his keys.

Kane swung the pistol on Will. "Get that nigga, and y'all get the fuck from roun' here. I see y'all again I'm shooting to kill!"

Will helped Dave to his feet, and they stumbled off. Kane turned to Theo as the men hurried into the night.

Theo was scared shitless. Even though he knew Kane and had heard the tales, he had never witnessed the gunplay first hand. Kane opened the bag of rocks he had just taken from will, and gave Theo two hands full. "Let's go Lil Momma." he said to Becky, who stood rooted to her spot. "Come on!" Kane said authoritatively.

She followed him from the house, and they got in Dave's car and drove off. Kane stopped in front of Tee's house, and yelled. "Yo Tee, check this out!"

Tony jumped from the porch rail, and ran to the car. "What's up Bro?"

Kane tossed him the keys to his car. "Follow me!"

Tony caught the keys and ran to Kane's car; he pulled in behind Dave's car as Kane pulled off. Kane hit I-95 north and got off on Church Street. He headed towards Uptown, found a dark secluded spot, and pulled over. He and Becky got out of the car. He walked to his car, told Tony to pop the trunk and grabbed two rags. He gave Becky one, and instructed her to wipe her prints from the car. After they finished they got in the car with Tony. Becky sat in the middle of the two men, as Kane said. "Go up to Perks Place."

*   *   *   *

Kane got out of the car and walked up to Perk's Place. Perk's was a bar and lounge, that was frequented by all of the players and dealers in the area. Kane was well known Uptown, because one time his father Bishop had the whole area on lock. The Kane's had a long line of history in what was once known as LaVilla, almost a hundred years. Generations of Kane's, had been instrumental in the growth and prosperity associated with the area. LaVilla had also been the death of quite a few Kane's.

"What's up my nigga?" A man named Sly asked Kane as he walked inside. Kane stopped right inside the door, and slowly panned the room. He had made very few friends, and a slew of enemies, so he was always on guard. He looked to the voice and saw Sly.

"What it is Sly?" he asked smiling.

"It's all gravy baby. What brings you thru this late?"

"What brings me thru every time?" Kane replied with a smile. "Is Dirty Harry in pocket?"

"Yeah man, he in the back holding court; I got some of that work though, if you need it."

"I need to holla at Harry." Kane said, and walked to the lounge section. He looked to the back corner and saw Harry at his regular table, and walked over.

Dirty Harry looked up and saw Kane, and his face broke into a big smile. Dirty Harry was a young cat who had idolized Kane's father Bishop, and liked Kane. He knew Kane was a gunslinger, and a serious dude. He had respect for him, because Kane didn't live on the laurels of his father. He made a name for him in the underworld, and was both respected and feared in certain circles. Dirty Harry sold him heroin and powdered coke, and Kane was good for at least $400 dollars a week.

"What's up Kane?"

"Just chilling dog, Let me get a yard of girl and a spoon of boy."

"I got you dog." Harry said rising from his seat. "You must of hit a decent lick, you spending $350."

"I'm straight, and that ought to take me thru the weekend."

"Yeah it should," Harry said. "Dig this, why don't you just mail that bread to your daddy, and let him know I sent it."

"I'm cool with that."

"Yo Darlene, check this out." Dirty Harry said looking at a pretty dark skinned young lady.

The woman got up and came over. Harry wrapped her in his arms and whispered in her ear. She nodded her head, broke their embrace, and walked to the restroom.

"So, you got Sly on the clock now. You must've hit a good lick yourself?"

"Yeah, I'm doing alright." Harry said preening. "I gave the nigga some work cause I got tired of him roun' here with that penny ante juggling. I could use a nigga like you if you wanna get some money."

"Naw dog, I ain't cut out to play second fiddle, so I'm straight."

Darlene came back, looked at Kane and wrapped her left arm around his waist. She drew him close and slipped a package in his pocket. He looked at Harry who smiled. "Holla at me if you change your mind, cool?"

"That's a bet." Kane said, giving Dirty Harry some dap. He patted Darlene on the ass and walked away.

"You gone dog?" Sly asked as Kane headed for the door.

"Yeah dog I'm out." Kane said without breaking his stride. "I'll holla." He got in the car, and pulled out the two bags of rocks he got from Will from under the seat. He counted out a hundred rocks, and gave them to Tony. Then pulled out the two rolls of bills, counted off $500 dollars, and gave that to Tony also. "Don't try to smoke it all nigga, serve some and put some money in the house. Can you get a ride from here?"

"Yeah Bro, I'm straight."

Kane got out and walked to the driver's side, as Tony got out. He hugged and kissed Tony. "Go and drop at least four of them bills to Lu, before you do anything else. I'm gonna call you in the morning alright?"

"Alright Bro.," Tony said, and walked over to Perks place and went in.

Kane got behind the wheel and drove to I-95, and headed north to Dunns Ave. He went to Motel 6, and rented a room for him and Becky.

She had been silent the whole time, a little scared because she had witnessed the whole scenario. She knew Kane, had heard about him, but they had never really talked. She almost felt like a kidnap victim, because she didn't know what to expect. She was also somewhat excited too, so she just followed his lead. He sat her on the bed, sat next to her, and asked in a concerned voice.

"You alright Lil Momma?"

"I guess I'm just a little scared."

"You ain't got to be scared I ain't gonna hurt you, or force you to do anything. After we talk, if you want to leave it's cool. I'll take you anywhere you want to go, alright?"

"Okay," she said puzzled, at the rapid change he had made emotionally.

Tenderly he took her hands, and turned her so that she was facing him. "I been checking you out for a minute and I know your rep. I know

13

you do a little trickin', and I know you smoke that shit. I know you been living in the rooming house on Price Street, so I've been doing my homework on you. The reason I've put in so much work trying to find out about your pedigree, is that I had planned to step to you. I didn't want you to vaguely assume that I was a trick. Some of the cats that have been trying to catch you have told me how independent and sassy you are. I see that the little incident tonight could be used to my advantage, so I took the opportunity. Hopefully I used it wisely. Like I said, I checked on you because I wanted to make sure you had the necessary credentials and qualities to be on my team. This ain't no game so I'm gone be real with you off the top, cause I want you to be down. You probably heard a lot of shit about me, some true some bullshit. Now you saw me in action, so you know what I'm all about. There are some things you don't know, but I'm gonna pull your coat and see where we stand after that."

My wife's name is Leslie. If you decide to get on my team I'll let you see what she looks like, so if you see us together you'll know how to conduct yourself. See I ain't bout playing games, or trying to get you to change the way you live. I believe we all have our reasons for doing the things we do. I ain't trying to pass judgment or tell you being down with me gone be a fairytale because I ain't living that way. I'm looking for someone who is out here like I'm out here. Who I can have fun with, and be my whole self with, both good and bad. I choose you, but the decision is yours. I can tell you this; being down with me gone boost your rep, plus take some of the pressure off when niggas try to step. When they find out you down with me they gone back off, because they know I don't play games and down for gunplay. By the same token, that won't give you license to be disrespectful."

"If you conduct yourself properly and when some shit goes down; and I know it wasn't on you. I won't hesitate to have your back and I'll expect you to have mine. Like I said, I know you trick and what not and I ain't asking you to stop. That's one of the qualities I like about you. Knowing you will go get yours, and not lay around and wait on a muthafucka to give you something. Don't get it wrong, I ain't trying to pimp you and I ain't about you pimpin' me either. I'm talking about us being down for each other. I look out for you, you look out for me. Sometimes my paper gets flaky and if you strapped lookout, because I got you. I don't want you selling pussy just to get high. I haven't heard you get down like that and I don't ever wanna hear it. I'm gonna do my best to make sure you stay straight. I don't want you out there chumping yourself, and that's whether you down with me or not. I know I can make you happy, and keep you that way. The choice is yours, so what's up?"

She squeezed his hands, looked in his eyes, and said. "I dig where you're coming from and you did your homework well, but still there are blank spaces that need filling in. I left Detroit and came down here because I was getting in a lot of trouble. I was in a gang and that's where the trickin' started. I had dibbed and dabbed with coke but it wasn't anything serious. Then I got here and moved in with my Granny, you probably know her, Essie Smith?"

"Hell yeah I know her." he said surprised. "That's my Granny's dog. You know Esther Johnson?"

"Oh yeah, I know her! Anyway, I moved in with her and she was very strict. Telling me when to come and go and I just couldn't deal with it, so I got the room. I still keep most of my shit there and I go by every day, but shit works better with me living in the rooming' house. I ain't got to answer to nobody, but me. I like being my own woman because I don't have to put up with too much bullshit. I done kicked it with a couple of cats since I been down here, but I ain't ready for that housewife shit I'm still young.

By the way, I was checking you out too. I heard you be jacking, but I use to see you in the hole with Chris and his crew. I thought you were down with them; you dress like a dope boy so I just assumed you were one. I never copped from you, but occasionally when I swung thru you were down there. Always with a big pistol in your hand, so what was I supposed to think?"

"I feel you, but I just kick it with them cats, we cool and everything. We smoke weed and shit together, but I ain't down with their set. I've known them since they were youngsters."

"I can dig that," she said with a smile. "I use to see you in all the hot spots, kicking' it with the ho's who hung out there. Seemed to me you always had bread. I never seen you actin' all big headed like you the shit. I wondered what your game was, but couldn't quite figure you out. Sometimes you would just disappear, and I wouldn't see you on the set for a week or two. Then you'd pop back up, so I started asking people about you. What's up with Kane and shit like that? Everybody said you were straight. I talked to Chell and she said the same thing, but she said you were crazy. Shit that's what they all said. Neicy said you didn't play, and all the ho's say you a freak. I asked myself "why he ain't holla at me?" after I heard all that. Remember three or four days ago when I saw you at the Bootleg House and asked you to buy me a beer?"

"Yeah I remember," he replied.

"I wanted to get with you then, but you didn't pursue it. You just brought me a beer and dipped. I know I was looking good, but you had me thinking something was wrong with me. Other niggas was trying to catch, but they weren't talking about spending no cheese and I ain't with that. I knew Tony was your younger brother and we cool. I hope you ain't one of them jealous niggas who beat ho's up, because I ain't wit that shit. I might see a nigga I like and wanna fuck, just a fuck thing. How you feel about that?"

"Hold on a minute Lil Momma," he said halting her. "Your business is your business. I ain't the type of nigga to trip on a woman she does what she wanna do, and I ain't into beating women. If a woman puts her hands on me, she gone get the same treatment that anybody puts their hands on me gets. I ain't jealous, but I got standards. That's your pussy; if you wanna bless me with it I'm happy. I would prefer that every dude you fuck pays for it and I be the only one get it for free. I ain't gone be riding around checking up on you, I expect you to be real with me. We don't have to sneak or keep secrets if we real with each other."

"I'm cool with that," she said.

"Dig this. I ain't into all those labels and shit, but I do want you to be my little lady. You can do all the shit you been doing, but when I call set all of that shit aside cause it's time for us. Think you can live with that?"

"I can live with that," she said smiling. "And I can live up to your standards as long as you don't try to control me. I'm your girl or little lady as you put it."

"Alright, let's do this since we are staying here tonight. Let's go to Wal-Mart and get a few things we gonna need, like toothbrushes and shit. In the morning I'll pay the room up for a couple of more days, and we can chill and get to know each other a little better." said Kane smiling.

They rode to Wal-Mart and did their shopping, then rode thru Helena and bought a few bags of weed. They stopped to Jax Liquor and bought a bottle of Hennesy, a Jax Pack, and a case of Bud before going back to the motel.

Kane went to the bathroom and did a speedball, and she smoked a few rocks. They had a few drinks, smoked a joint and talked.

"Come on Lil Momma let's take a shower," Kane said.

They walked to the bathroom; he sat on the toilet and watched her undress. "Damn shorty finer than I thought." he said to himself, as she removed her shirt and bra. He saw that her breast stood high and firm, even without the restraints. They had dark chocolate, silver dollar sized areolas. Her nipples stiff, the size of pencil erasers. He saw the smoothness of her flat stomach and noticed a thin trail of hair leading from the top of her jeans to her navel.

She looked at him as he admired her and caught his eyes. She looked into them deeply as she pulled her jeans down.

He saw the faint shadow of her vagina and the spray of hairs springing from the sides of her panties, and felt his penis starting to rise. She knew she had him entranced with her little strip tease, so she decided to stretch it out. She hooked her thumbs in the waistband of her panties and watched his reaction. Slowly she swung her hips from side to side, easing her panties down. She shook her breast in a rhythm only she could hear. Inch by agonizing inch, she continued to slide her panties down her beautiful cocoa skinned thighs.

He got a glimpse of her hairy pubic, but when she bent over to finish removing her panties she blocked his view. She stood quickly and turned, giving him a great view of her perfectly rounded ass. He could see the puffy, pouting lips of her cunt thru the gap in her legs. She pulled the shower door open, looked over her shoulder at him, and closed the door.

"Damn, shorty playing me," he said to himself, "and the shit working too," he couldn't help but smile.

He undressed and joined her in the shower, his penis rock hard and throbbing. "I got something for her; I wanna see if she can deal with what I'm gonna put on her ass." He thought to himself.

*   *   *   *

After making deliciously good love he kissed her deeply, and they lay there breathing heavily. He rolled over and pulled her on top of him. She rose up, looked in his eyes and asked. "Damn, what you trying to do, make a bitch fall in love with you in one night?"

"Why not; tomorrow ain't promised to muthafuckas who live like we do."

* CHAPTER 2*

About 6:30 p.m. that Sunday Kane and Becky left the hotel. They were on I-95 south, headed towards town.

"So when will I see you again?" she asked, looking at him as he drove.

"Probably Wednesday or Thursday about nightfall," he replied. "I've told you my situation and the way I handle things. Now it's time for you to see if my absence makes a difference in your life."

"So you're cool with me going back to doing all the stuff I did before we hooked up?" she asked seriously. "I mean, even after all we've said and done this weekend?"

"Dig this Lil Momma. I told you from the get go what I wanted, and what I was prepared to accept. If there are certain things you do or did to make ends meet, and I call myself your man. Then if it displeases me, I should make sure you don't have to do those things. I don't want you selling pussy, but it's your choice. I won't be able to make all of your decisions for you. I'm gonna try to put you in a position where you don't have to do it, but if it's in you to ho then there's nothing I can do."

"So your saying you gonna take care of me so I ain't got to be in the streets?" she asked.

"I'm gonna try to," he answered. "I got this dope and we should be able to make five or six grand off it. I'm gonna give you half the dope, and some money for your pocket. If you use your head, you can get us some money and get high. If you sellout get with Tee and have him to call me, and I'll give you the rest. If you fuck it all up ain't no sweat, but I'll know I can't trust you to look out for us without me being on top of you."

"So this is a test then?" she asked.

"Naw, it ain't a test," he said firmly. "Only test for us is the test of time? You made the grade when I chose you. Time will tell if I judged you correctly."

"I ain't gonna let you down baby," she said sliding closer to him.

"You can't let me down you can only let yourself down."

"Believe it or not, I'm gonna miss you the next few days." She said, as she molded her body to his.

"I'm gonna miss you to Lil Momma," he said honestly.

She kissed his cheek as he pulled off the expressway, and drove to the rooming house. They got out of the car and walked to the door, the door opened and Chell walked out.

"Hey Kane!" she said excited. "Those niggas brought the police to Theo's house the other night, but ain't nobody tell them anything. Shit, by the time they came back most of the people that were on the set were long gone, so shit cool. Damn Beck, you been with this nigga all weekend? Sherrie came thru looking for you, but ain't nobody knows where you were. Now I know, so what's up with y'all? It's got to be something, because I've never known this nigga to kidnap a bitch all weekend."

Becky put her arm around him possessively and smiled broadly. "Yeah me and this nigga done hooked up. I'm his Lil Lady as he calls me."

Kane and Chell laughed.

"I guess I won't be getting any more of that good dick then?" Chell said laughing. "Kane I was just about to go holla at Chris and spend thirty dollars. You wanna get this little money?"

"Naw Chell," he said smiling. "Becky will though, she gone be doing a little something. As for you missing the dick, it ain't got to be like that."

Becky punched him in the shoulder and said. "Y'all ho's had y'all shot; now this my nigga and I ain't gone tolerate no disrespect."

"Girl I was just joking, damn." Chell said, seeing the look in Becky's eyes.

"Hold on for a minute," Kane said. "We got to go and take care of something then Beck gonna serve the thirty."

Chell nodded and sat in one of the chairs as Kane and Becky went inside. Kane gave Becky 250 big rocks, and $200 dollars. "If you work this right, you'll have some money for us when I come thru later on this week. Now go on and take care of Chell."

Becky rose and left the room, stepped to Chell and gave her two big stones. "Bring me some business and I will break you off every trip."

"Bet that up." said Chell, passing her the $30 dollars. "Was the nigga everything I told you he was or what?"

"Hell naw!" Becky said. "The nigga is that and a whole bunch more. I ain't had a nigga put it down on me like that, and I ain't even talking about the sex. Shit girl that nigga got a rap game for a bitch ass, and when he put down his sex game I was sprung. I'm feeling the nigga in my heart already!"

"I told you the nigga was tight girl!" Chell said. "Ain't no secret I wanted the nigga. Hell, I done bought dick from the nigga but he schooled me on what he was about. For some reason we decided we should just be friends. The nigga must see something in you for him to choose you; he ain't never done no shit like that before."

"That's what he told me, and I wanna be all he wants me to be." Becky said.

"The nigga dangerous though, and don't forget that girl." Chell cautioned her. "I'm gonna spread the word that y'all down, so none of them niggas won't trip."

"Do that girl." Becky said, as she turned and walked back into the house. She walked into the room and Kane was lying back in the bed smoking a joint. "So what time you leaving?" she asked.

"In a minute, you straight, need anything before I pull up?"

"Yeah I do," she said.

"What you need?"

"Enough of that dick to last me till I see you again," she said smiling.

"I got you." He said laughing, and getting undressed.

    *   *   *   *

After they made love he drove home. Kane was a father of four; Berean Kane Jr., who was 15 and called B.K by his family and friends. He was the spitting image of his father, same lanky build but with the promise of getting big and nearly as tall as his father. He had the same deep set brown eyes, bushy eyebrows, and fun loving attitude. His father had enrolled him in martial arts school when he was five, and he was a second degree black belt now.

His second son Jamal was built along the same frame as his father and brother, but his facial features was a combination of both his parents. You could see his father in his brows, nose, and the shape of his head. Where his father and brother were cocoa complexioned, he was a shade lighter than them. He had high cheek bones that showed signs of his Native American ancestry, and his eyes were slightly slanted. He was usually very serious, especially for a boy of 13.

Then there was Anika, the apple of Kane's eye. She was a 12 year old mixture of his mother and his wife. It was like when she was with her grandmother they bore a strong resemblance, but when she was with her mother she was Leslie's spitting image. Anika was a red skinned girl, lighter than her mother with the same Asiatic slant to her eyes as her mother and brother. Her personality was a combination of both her parents. She could be both shy and outgoing according to the circumstances, but she was surely spoiled.

The baby was Damon, who looked just like his father. The same face, but he had his mother's skin complexion. He was extremely perceptive for a boy of 11, and could read moods easily. He too was a serious as well as inquisitive young man, he questioned everything.

Leslie was beautiful, a combination of African, Native American, and Caucasian. She was also Kane's high school sweetheart. After the birth of four children she had gained considerable weight, and she had always been a thick strong woman. She stood 5'5", and wore 215 pounds. She wasn't exactly fat; she was voluptuous, big full breast, a small waist for a woman her size, wide hips, big pretty red thighs, and a nice fat ass. She had cut her hair and now it fell to her shoulders. She had Asiatic eyes, high cheeks, a slim nose, full lips, and a beautiful smile and loving personality. She was the type to go out of her way to help friends and family in need, and the first to visit or call them.

Kane sat at the dinner table with his family. The kids were glad to see him, as he hadn't been home in several days. They were all trying to get his attention, but Leslie was strangely silent. Sensing her mood, he knew a storm was brewing.

Even though Leslie was a kind soul, she was by no means weak. She had a quiet strength that he depended on to keep his home straight. He waited, because he knew she wouldn't be put off, and she would never voice her displeasure in front of the children. Damon perceptive as ever knew something was up, but not what. He kept looking from his mother to his father.

After dinner he played with the kids. They watched a little television then he sent them to bathe, and get ready for bed. All the while Leslie stayed in the background, and smiled at the way he interacted with the kids. She just wished he'd stay home more.

After the kids were put to bed, they lay in bed. He rolled over, looked at her and asked. "Baby what's up? I've seen the way you've been looking all evening. I can tell something is on your mind so come clean."

"Damn honey," she said. "Am I that easy to read?"

"To me you are. So what's up?"

"I been thinking bout going back to work," she replied.

"Hold up!" he said. "You got a job, taking care of the kids, the house, and me. That's the only job you need."

"I need more honey," she said seriously. "You just don't know what it's like being cooped up in the house all day. I love my kids, I love my home, I love you, but those children drive me crazy some time. Then you, you're not home as much as I would like for you to be to help me. You're out in the streets doing God knows what. I'm here trying to be the perfect housewife, not knowing if my husband is lying in the street shot or dead. I don't have a way to contact you to check and see if you're alright. You just don't know; you stay gone two or three days at a time and you don't even call to tell me if you're alright. Pearl and Paul Washington told me you be robbing people and shit."

21

"They told you what?" he shouted with anger.

"They said you are robbing people and you know how nosy they are. They stay down the street from Lucinda so I asked Lucinda about it, and she said she didn't know anything about it."

"It's obvious Pearl and Paul needs me to talk to them," he said still angry. "They ain't got no business telling you shit like that. You should've asked if they ever seen me do it, or are they going by some shit that was told to them. You ain't got no business letting nobody tell you nothing bad about me anyway. I'm your man, what are they to you?"

"Naw baby," she said. "It ain't like that. It's just when you're gone a day or two, every time the phone rings I jump. I'm afraid to answer for fear that someone is on the other line with the news you're dead. It's so bad I let the kids answer the phone when you're not home. I just can't stand the not knowing baby. I figure if I go back to work, I won't have as much time to worry. I'm telling you I'm about to have a nervous breakdown. It ain't like I'm trying to get in your business, but I love you and I don't think I could go on if something happened to you. Do you understand?"

He reached over, gently touched her face, and said. "It's not really about you getting out of the house, or going back to work. It's all about me and the way I've been handling shit. Sweetheart, I've never considered your thoughts or how you think when I'm not here. I can see from what you said that I was dead ass wrong in neglecting to do certain things to insure that you have peace of mind. I promise I won't leave you to wonder if I'm safe ever again. I'll even go as far to say, I won't stay away from home as often as I have.

We've been through so much together, good and bad. Regardless to what I do when I'm not with you, the love I have for you is always in my heart. I won't say your fears are needless because I do be out there fucking up. I try to be careful as I can, and not do shit where people know it's me and try to come back at me. It ain't like I can't make a mistake but I damn sure try not to. Les, you're my heart and nothing or no one is going to change that. I hope what I've said will help to ease your mind. I ain't gonna feel like no chump for checking in with you either, with yo slick ass. I know this was designed so you can keep tabs on me, but I ain't mad at you."

She looked in his eyes and smiled. "You sure know how to twist some shit around, and make it seem like I'm trying to make you look pussy whipped."

"Baby you been pussy whipped me," he said laughing. "Why you think I'm still with your fat ass?"

She laughed, and said. "But you love this fat ass!"

22

"I damn sure do. Now come on and give Daddy some sugar." She rolled into his arms and kissed him passionately.

"Damn girl!" he exclaimed. "The way you just kissed me make me think your little coochie's hot?"

"What do you think; you ain't taken care of her in three or four days?"

"Well I'm going to fix that right now." He said, as he pushed her on her back, climbed over her and kissed her passionately.

After they made love she grabbed the sides of his face, lifted his head, looked in his eyes and said. "I love you baby."

He kissed her lips tenderly. "I love you too."

They lay there for a few more minutes then he rolled off of her, and she went to get something to clean them up with. They lay in the bed in the afterglow of love, and went to sleep.

CHAPTER 3

Kane wasn't just a gangster or a thug, he was a man truly torn between two worlds. He held down a 9 to 5 as a machine operator, and made decent money. Enough to take care of his family and enjoy a few of the finer things, but secretly he hated his square job and only kept it to please Leslie. Kane loved women, and had fucked just about every woman that worked at the plant. As a matter of fact, he was working on his latest conquest; an older woman that had the hots for him, since he started working there. She was fine as hell, with a body of a woman nearly half her age.

Emma was 50 and frisky, about 5'3", and 130 pounds. She had apple sized breast, a nice trim waist, flat stomach, flaring hips, and an ass that was shaped like an upside down Valentine. She wore her hair in the short cut that Toni Braxton and Halle Berry had popularized. She was cute and, from looking at her you'd never believe she was 50 years old. He had been playing hard to get with Emma, because the dude's on the job had told him she was a black widow. She had sucked a few young guys that had worked there dry, and cast them to the side. They acted like fools, and soon left to find employment elsewhere.

Kane had no fear, but he wanted total control where she was concerned; so he went thru the young freaks that worked there. He dicked them and dismissed them yet there was never any animosity, because they still got together every now and then for a little fun and games.

For the next two days all he did was go to work, go home and hang out with his family. That Wednesday after work, he went home and ate dinner, bathe, and kicked it with the kids. After he helped them with their homework, he hung out with Leslie for a few then got ready to hit the streets.

Kane stayed strapped, but he kept most of his major arms locked in a big red toolbox. He kept it in his trunk when he was in the street; and in his garage when he was home. He always kept a snub nosed .38 or a .380 on him; even at work he was armed. At home he would hide it, but it was always at hand.

He got his toolbox and put it on the floor of the passenger side, got in and looked at the door where Leslie stood. He waved, blew her a kiss, and then pulled off.

*   *   *   *

REDEMPTION, *A HoodWrittens Production*

Kane arrived on the set at around 9:30 p.m. He rode around to all the hot spots to see if Becky was on the scene. When he drove thru the hood he saw Tony with two young men that he vaguely knew, by the names of Sonny and Tracy. He knew they lived in Mixon, and he also knew they got a little money serving. They were up and coming dope men. They had the rides, the gear, and a little rep. They went to school with Kane's youngest brother Alvin, who was killed in a gun battle with the police a few years earlier at a jewelry store robbery.

Kane pulled over and got out of the car, and walked over to where they stood. He hugged and kissed Tony, then gave the other men some dap.

"Tee break bread."

Tony reached in his front pocket, pulled out a nice roll of bills and asked. "What you need Bro?"

"I just wanted to know if you had some cheese in your trap," Kane said smiling. "What y'all cats up to?"

"Actually we were waiting on you to show," Tony said.

"I got something I wanna run by you!" Sonny said excited.

"They came and got me, and put me up on a lick." Tony said. "I know how you feel about me going on capers, so I asked them to wait till you swung thru. That's why we're standing here. If you hadn't come by 10:00, I was gonna call you."

"Alright, dig this. Let's go to my girl's room so we can talk in private," Kane said. "I don't want all these niggas round here in our business."

They walked to his car got in, and he drove to Becky's room. They sat down and begin to talk.

"So what's the deal?" Kane asked Sonny, and Tracy.

"This nigga we know name Jermaine is strapped," Tracy said. "He got west 21st. streets sewed up. He served the whole area up to 45th street, but his main spot is an apartment right behind Pearl's Place. They usually keep a bird or so on hand. They serve both hard and soft, plus they got boy. He usually ain't there, but he got two young broads serving. They ain't packing heat, so I guess the nigga feel like they can't be touched."

"I feel you," Kane said. "But I wanna know why y'all ain't knocked them off yourself, if it's so easy?"

"The ho's know me and Tracy," Sonny said. "They don't know you and Tee. It's an easy lick, and you can throw us whatever once you take it off."

"The shit sounds sweet," Kane said interested. "Before I hit it, I wanna check it for myself. If it looks straight I'll hit it, but if it looks fucked up I'm gonna back off. I ain't using my car and Tee ain't going in with me."

25

"That's cool," Tracy said. "We can use the car I got, it's a rental."

"I'm cool with that, but I'm going in solo. When we get there let Tee drive, y'all stay in the car. If shit gets flaky I don't need to be hesitating when I start capping. Everything I see outside the car is fair game, so stay in the ride. Y'all got gats?"

Sonny and Tracy nodded, but Tony spoke up. "Naw I ain't packing."

"Y'all chill for a minute," Kane said and left the room.

He came back with the big red tool box, and a tote bag. He opened the tote and pulled out a Dickie jumper and a Raiders cap, both black. He pulled the Dickie on over his clothes, put the Raiders hat on then slipped on a pair of black driving gloves. He opened the tool box and pulled out a sawed off, pump shotgun. He took a lightly greased rag from the tool box, and wiped the shotgun down. He pumped the shotgun five times, and each time a bright red shell jumped out. He pumped it again to make sure it was empty then he wiped each shell and reloaded the gun. He sat the shotgun down and pulled out an Army issue .45 automatic. He racked the slide a couple of times then wiped it down. He dropped the clip, wiped it and the shells then reloaded it. He pulled out a 9mm, did the same thing, and passed it to Tony.

Tony took the gun from Kane, and smiled at him.

"Remember what I said Tee, stay in the car." Kane said.

"Damn Bro, we done did this enough times for me to know what you always say by heart." Tony said smiling. "I got it Bro."

"Alright and you can give me back my nine, before I drop your ass back off."

"Nigga I ain't gone sell yo shit," Tony said laughing.

"You did it before," Kane said laughing.

"Aw man that shit dead."

"Don't sweat it Tee." Kane said, rising to his feet. "Come on let's roll."

They walked out got in the rental, and jumped on I-95 north. They got off on 20th St. expressway, and drove down to Myrtle Ave. and made a right. They drove up two blocks and made a left on 21st St. Sonny pointed out the apartment, and Kane said.

"It's looking good so far."

Tracy drove on down the block, made a right, and parked by the beauty salon that sat on the corner.

Kane pulled his cap down over his brows, zipped down the Dickie jumper, and slid the .45 in his waist. He grabbed the shotgun and said, "One of you niggas give me twenty dollars."

"What you need twenty for?" Sonny asked.

"How am I gonna buy a dub rock without a dub?" Kane asked. "I ain't gonna use my money. I need to be able to see inside the crib. Plus when they see the money coming to them, more than likely that's all they'll watch."

Sonny gave Kane the money, and he got out of the car. He walked quickly down the street, with the shotgun riding close to the side of his right leg. He walked to the door and knocked. He had his body turned to shield the shotgun, and the twenty dollar bill in his left hand.

A man's voice said. "Yeah, who is it?"

"Yo it's Black," Kane answered.

The door cracked open and the man asked. "What's up Black?"

"Let me get a dub dog." Kane said, passing the man the money. As the door begun to open Kane saw that the dude held a pistol in his hand, and he sprang into action. He kicked the door with tremendous force, and it crashed into the center of the man's face. It broke his nose and smashed his lips, knocking out several teeth. His head snapped back, as blood gushed from his nose and mouth. As he fell back, the pistol flew from his hand in his feeble attempt to break his fall. He landed hard on his ass then rolled on his back. The momentum forced his head back, and it slammed into the floor with a sickening thud. He was dazed, and he raised his head up slowly as Kane quickly stepped thru the door. He glanced around the room swiftly, his shotgun up panning the room. He saw two young women, one on the sofa, and one curled up on the love seat. They were smoking a blunt and drinking wine.

Kane lashed out with the heel of his boot, and kicked the dazed man in the face. He grabbed the door and closed it. Kane aimed the shotgun in the area where the stunned young women sat, with their mouths hanging open in shock.

"Don't scream! Don't make a fucking sound! I want the dope and money now!" he shouted.

The women looked at him in shock, as still as marble statues. The entire incident was over in a matter of seconds. He talked to the women in his normal tone of voice.

"I ain't got all night, so don't trip and start all that screaming and shit. Just give me the shit I asked for."

One of the women got up and got a big bag that sat on the table, and brought it to him. He looked in the bag, and saw that it was filled with small Ziploc bags of rocks.

"There's some powder and boy under the seat cushion, with the money we done made today." The woman said, her voice trembling.

"Let's go get it." He said, as the woman turned and walked back to the sofa. She moved the cushion and pulled two more big bags, and a small bag out. He looked in the three bags, and saw that everything she said was there.

The other woman just sat on the love seat watching him, and the fear that was once in her eyes gone replaced by anger. Her eyes shot daggers at him. He walked over to her, dropped the bags on the table, and viciously back hand slapped her. Before she could recover, his palm lashed into the other side of her face. Her head snapped to the side, and blood trickled from the corner of her mouth.

He gripped her chin, turned her face to his, and looked in her fear filled eyes and said.

"You trying to memorize my face, don't? If I ever suspect you of pointing me out to anyone, I'll find you and I'll kill you. Understand?"

Tears streamed down her face, as she nodded her head.

"Now where is the rest of it?" he asked.

"I'll show you," she said in a tremulous voice.

The woman that cooperated was stunned by the sudden outburst of violence. She had stumbled back and fell on the sofa crying. He released the woman's chin, and walked to where the man's pistol lay. He picked it up, and slid it in his waist near the .45.

"Let's get the rest," he said.

The woman he slapped said. "It's in the back," and pointed down the hall.

Kane pointed to the unconscious man and said. "Get your partner. Y'all grab an arm apiece, and drag dude to where the rest of the shit at."

The women followed his instructions, and drug the man into a room in the back.

As soon as the women grabbed the man, Kane locked the door. He slid the security chain on then rushed to catch up with them.

"Y'all sit on the bed. Don't move, because I don't wanna have to really hurt y'all."

He started opening dresser drawers until he found what he was looking for, some stockings. He called the girl who had so far cooperated and said. "I want you to take these stockings, and tie your girlfriend and dude up. Tie their hands behind their backs, and make sure you do it right!"

She tied them both.

"Now I want you to tie dudes ankles, and hook them and his wrist together."

She did as he said, then stood waiting on his next order.

"Now let's get the rest of the stuff."

She walked to the closet with him close behind her. She went to the clothes rack and pushed them aside, then reached up to where a second rack was. She twisted it then pulled it from the wall. She stuck her finger in the flange that the rod had set in. He heard a click then a small panel opened.

Kane saw that someone had built a sizable compartment.

"The dope is in the metal box." she said, stepping back and pointing.

He grabbed her arm gently but firmly, and led her back to the bed. He tied her loosely, but right. Then he tied the two women together, and checked the man's bonds. He walked back into the closet, pulled the metal box out, and saw a money bag and tote bag. He pulled them out and noticed the metallic clinking in the tote. He saw it contained guns and ammunition. He put the metal box and money bag inside, and zipped it closed. He quickly searched the house, and found a jewelry box filled with jewelry. He took the jewelry from the women and the man then put it all in the big tote bag.

Kane got the woman that helped him, and took her from the room. When they got in the front room, he put the bags of dope and the shotgun in the bag also. He reached in the bag of money, and took out a fat wad. He removed the rubber band, and spread the money out flat. He pulled the woman to him by the waist band of her jeans, undid the top of her button, and she whispered.

"Please don't hurt me."

Kane zipped her jeans down, pulled them past her hips then pulled her panties down. She looked at him with tears streaming down her face. He grabbed the stack of money; put it in her panties like a pad then pulled her panties and jeans back up. He looked in her eyes and whispered.

"That's for you. Keep it on the low."

He kissed her cheek then led her back to the room, where he loosely tied her to the other woman and headed back up front. When he walked in the front room, he heard a knock on the door. He looked out the peephole to see who was there.

Standing there fidgeting, shifting from foot to foot, was Tony. He unhooked the chain and snatched the door open, and Tony's nine was right in his face. Kane's head and hand moved with lightning quickness, as he snatched the gun from Tony's hand. He couldn't help but smile.

"Put this shit up," he said handing Tony the pistol.

He tucked the .45 back in his waist, got the tote, slung it over his shoulder, and they left.

"Damn Tee, I thought I told you to stay in the car?"

"Shit, you were taking so long I thought you might have been in some trouble, so I stepped." Tony said. "Tracy and Sonny wanted to come too, but I told them to stay in the car. I know you didn't wanna leave bodies if you didn't have to."

"Good looking out Bro." Kane said, as he punched Tony on the shoulder and laughed.

When they got back to the car, he and Tony got in the back seat. He pulled off the cap and jumper, and stuffed them in the tote. About ten blocks away he said.

"Tracy, stop at the next phone booth you see. I got to make a call."

A few blocks latter Tracy pulled over. He jumped out and punched in his home number. Damon answered the phone, and Kane asked.

"Boy, what you doing up this time of night?" It was nearly 12:00.

"I was going to the bathroom and I heard the phone ring, so I picked it up."

"Okay, get your momma for me."

The next thing Kane heard was Damon's voice yelling. "Momma! Daddy on the phone!"

He heard Leslie's voice yelling. "Boy you better stop all that hollering in here!"

Leslie picked up the phone in their room, and said. "I got it."

"I love you Daddy." Damon said.

"I love you back Dee."

Damon hung up, as Leslie's voice asked. "You don't love anybody else?"

"Girl you know I love you. I'm just calling to let you know I'm alright, and I should be home in about an hour and a half. If it takes me longer, I'll call and let you know."

"Alright honey, I love you."

"I love you back baby," he said and hung up.

He jumped back in the car, and Tracy pulled off and asked. "Where we gonna go?"

"We could go back to my girl's spot, but too many eyes and I don't wanna do that."

"We can go to this chick's house I kick it with, if y'all want to?" Sonny said.

"Is she cool?" Kane asked.

"She down, all we got to do is break her off."

"She got her own ride?" asked Kane.

"Yeah, she got her own shit." Sonny said.

"Alright let's do it like this. When we get to her house go in and holla at her. Give her a yard, and tell her to step off for an hour and a half. I don't want her to see me and Tee, so we'll drop you off. When we see her leave, we'll come to the crib and handle our business."

"That's cool," Sonny said.

They pulled up to the woman's house, and Sonny jumped out and went inside. Tracy parked down the street, and they sat and watched the house. When the woman came out, got in her car and left, Tracy pulled in her driveway. The three men went inside, and Kane sat the big tote bag on the floor.

The men looked at Kane who sat down next to the tote bag, and they all sat on the floor. Kane opened the bag, and started pulling out its contents. He sat his stuff to the side, then pulled out the bag of money and sat it in front of him. The other money bag he left in the tote, because he planned to split it with Tony not the other men.

He took the guns out of the tote next. There was a .357 Magnum, three .38's, four 9mm, two .380's, a .25 automatic, and ammo for all of them. Kane took his pick and passed the others out then they spilt the shells. Kane counted the money, and it was $18,000. He gave them $4,000 apiece, and he kept $6,000. He thought to himself.

"That girl I gave the money too got to have at least four or five grand. If she kept it to herself she will be straight for a minute."

When they split the jewelry, Kane picked his first and kept the most. He got up and went to the kitchen with the metal box, found a screwdriver and busted the lock on the box. Inside was a key and a half of coke, and about a quarter key of heroin.

"Y'all come on." Kane said, and led them back to the kitchen. He looked in the cabinets, and found a box of big zip lock freezer bags. He grabbed a big enamel serving platter, and sat it all on the table. He busted half the key down in three parts, and gave them to Tony, Tracy, and Sonny. He kept the other half of key for himself.

He broke the Quarter key of heroin in half then made three piles out of one half. He gave Tony, Tracy, and Sonny the three, and kept the other half for himself. After they divided the rest of the drugs, Kane asked. "Y'all straight?" While making eye contact with each man.

They all nodded with bright smiles.

"Hell yeah we straight!" Tracy yelled, and gave Kane some dap.

They gathered up their stuff and left.

*   *   *   *

Tracy and Sonny dropped Kane and Tony off at Kane's car.

"If we hear something else, how can we reach you?" Tracy asked.

"Get in touch with Tee," Kane replied. "He knows how to contact me, or just swing thru and chill. I'll come thru sooner or later."

"Alright, but we gone leave our beeper numbers just in case you wanna holla." said Tracy.

All the men shook hands and they drove off.

Sonny looked at Tracy and said. "That nigga the real deal dog."

"That he is," Tracy said shaking his head. "I done heard bout the nigga, seen him a few times, but I didn't really think the nigga was all that. The cat seem like he got his game tight."

"No shit!" Sonny said, laughing. "The nigga fair as fuck too cause ain't a way in the world I would have broken a nigga off like he broke us off. A grand or two yea, but that nigga looked out!"

"We need to keep our ear on the vine. See if we can't find another lick like this or better." Tracy said.

"You got that right," Sonny said laughing.

Tony and Kane sat in Kane's car. Kane had the tote bag in his lap. He reached in it, and fished around until he found the money bag. He pulled it out and Tony's eyes grew wide.

"Slick ass nigga. What you got there?" Tony said, smiling.

"Hell if I know." Kane said, reaching over in his glove compartment, and pulling out a folding knife.

Kane split the bag from the bottom, stuck his hand in, and pulled out a handful of big bills. He came up with $25,000 after he counted it, and Tony whistled. Kane gave him $10,000, and kept the rest.

"What you gonna do?" Kane asked Tony.

"I'm gonna hang out for a few," Tony said smiling.

"I feel you, but you better give me some of that shit to put up for you. And give me back my gun before I forget."

Tony started laughing. "You done made a good as lick, and you still worried about this raggedy ass gun?"

"It's mine. So give it up."

Tony gave Kane the gun, laughing.

"Check this out Bro." Tony said, as he counted out 200 rocks, 100 bags of powder, and 50 bags of boy. "Give this to Becky and tell her to hold it for me." He gave Kane all the dope, the 9mm, and the .38. He kept the .380 and .25 automatic. "Tell her to break herself off, and drop this fourteen grand off to Lucinda for me." He said, passing Kane the money. "Tell her I'm gambling or something. I don't need no money cause I'm gonna work some of this."

"I got you Tee," Kane said hugging and kissing him.

Tony got out of the car, put one gun in his waist and the other in his back pocket. Kane blew his horn, and pulled off.

*   *   *   *

Kane looked for Becky in route to Tony's house, and no one had seen her all day. He spotted Chell on the corner of Magnolia St., and pulled over. She strutted over to the car and leaned in the window.

"Hey baby." she said, and kissed him on the cheek.

"I'm cool," he said. "I'm looking for Becky, have you seen her?"

"Not today, she has been rolling since Sunday night, so she might be somewhere getting some rest. Baby girl was pushing those stones! You got a real money getter, but I believe I'm just as qualified."

"You are that," he said laughing.

"Tell me daddy, why did you choose Becky not me? I showed you how much I wanted to be on your team."

"It has to do with intangibles baby," he replied. "I don't want you to take my words the wrong way, cause that ain't how it is. See, you set in your ways and I don't believe you could submit to me without resistance. Much as you would wanna follow my lead, your past and the experiences you've had with other men would dictate that. I'm not, nor ever will be the men you've dealt with. There are certain things I won't tolerate, and disobedience is one of them. I dig you, but in order to be on my team you have to unlearn a lot of shit. I ain't saying you couldn't do it, but it would be too time consuming for both of us. Becky can be molded into what I want, but with you I would have to break the mold of what you already are and start from scratch."

"You probably right," she said. "I'm also a selfish, possessive bitch, and that alone means drama."

"You might be all of that baby, but you also real." He said, smiling.

"You still gone give me a little bit of that dick every now and then?" she asked, with a lusty twinkle in her eye.

"Yeah baby, when I can find the time," he said. "Hold up for a minute."

He leaned over, and unzipped the tote. Found his bag of rocks, got a good handful, and gave them to her. "Get money baby." he said.

"Thank you sweetie, see you later." She said, taking the rocks, kissing his cheek, and stepping back from the car.

He blew her a kiss then pulled off.

Kane drove to Tony's house, got out and knocked on the door. Lucinda came to the door, saw who it was, and let him in. He hugged and kissed her.

"Tee in the hole, busting them niggas heads with them craps. He told me to drop this off, so if his luck runs bad at least he knows the house is straight." said Kane.

She looked in his eyes, as she took the bag of money.

"Damn this is a nice piece of money. How much is it?"

"I don't know, I didn't count it," he answered.

"By the way, you need to holla at Paul and Pearl," she said, "They all up in your business. Lez, asked me about you robbing and shit. I told her I didn't know anything about that."

"You alright money wise? She said. "You can get some of this, if you need it."

"I'm straight." he said pulling her into his arms. "I'm gonna go straighten Paul and Pearl tomorrow about that shit."

"You need to," she said.

Lucinda and Leslie could've been twins. They had the same facial features, same build, except Lucinda was two inches shorter and twenty or twenty five pounds lighter. And, she was two years younger than Leslie.

"Well, I got to get back round there and try to get some of my money back." he said and kissed her. He rode to a couple of spots asking if anyone had seen Becky, and no one had. He drove to his grandmothers' house where he had a room at, and went inside. His grandmother was asleep, so he went to his room, and there was Becky in his bed asleep.

She had on one of his T- shirts, and a pair of red French cut panties. She was lying on top of the covers, hugging a pillow to her breast. The T-shirt had rose above her waist, and he could see her ass cheeks hanging out of her panties, and a darker shadow between her legs.

He felt himself getting aroused, but he fought to curb it. He sat on the bed and rubbed her ass, ran his hand between her legs and felt the heat radiating from her cunt. She moaned in her sleep, so he patted her ass, and called her. "Becky, Becky, wake up."

She rolled over on her back, released the pillow, and stretched her arms out to him. "Come here baby, I missed you."

He leaned into her, and kissed her lightly. "How long have you been here?"

"I been here all day." she replied. "I hadn't seen you and I missed you, so I came around here to feel close to you. I kicked it with our grannies for as few, walked my granny home then came back. After a while I decided to stay. At first your granny was a little reluctant, but after I told her you were my man it was straight."

"I'm cool with that." he said smiling.

"Hold on baby." she said. "I got something for you."

She got out of bed, and he watched the way her beautiful ass swayed as she walked to the dresser and grabbed a small purse, and came back. She sat next to him, opened the purse, and passed him a knot of money.

"That's three grand," she said. "I probably could've made more, but I didn't want to break the stones down too much. Let me go brush my teeth right quick."

He watched her as she walked from the room, and shook his head. "Damn, I forgot how fine she was." he thought.

She came back into the room and he said. "Tee wants you to do something for him. You can do it from here, just as well from the room."

"What he want me to do?" she asked.

"Keep this stuff for him." he said giving her Tony's dope.

She opened it up, saw all of the dope, and said. "Damn! Where Tee get all this shit from? Guns in here too!"

"You don't need to know all that." he said smiling. "He just wants you to hold it for him. He told me to tell you to break yourself off."

"I damn sure will." she said.

Kane laughed, went in the closet, and got a lock box he kept there. He dumped the tote and got his packages.

"Damn! You got more than him!" she said.

He counted out 500 rocks, and 200 bags of powder. Got $1,000, and put it with the three she gave him, and said. "This for you; handle it like you wanna. It's all yours, none for me."

She looked at him with wide eyes as he walked to the dresser. He opened the drawer, pulled out a key ring, and showed it to her.

"This small key goes to that box. When you run out and want some more, just go in there and get it. Don't tell anyone else about it, but if you go in it, tell me so I will know." he said. "Whatever you do don't lie to me about this kind of shit. I don't give a fuck if you use it all up, but be real with me about it. Don't ever give my shit to any nigga, I don't care who he is. If you want to get some of it and get your girls off or whatever that's cool, but don't bring them here. None of your friends need to know you come here, so keep it on the down low."

"Baby you ain't even got to worry about none of that. I ain't going out like that. Where am I gonna put this shit for tony?"

He went and got a big shoe box from the closet, and gave it to her.

She put the stuff in the box then asked. "How much should I get?"

"He said break yourself off, so go on and break yourself off."

She got up and went to the kitchen. She came back with a plate, spoon, and three sandwich bags. She opened the big bag of powder and got six spoons full, and put them on the plate. She counted out 200 rocks, and 100 bags of powder. She put that with what Kane gave her in one of the sandwich bags. She put all of her rocks in one, scooped up most of the powder off the plate and put that in the last bag. She put hers with Tony's, put the lid on the box and slid it under the bed. "So, what are you up to?" she asked.

"I had planned to go home after I checked on you." he answered. "Wait a minute! I got something else for you." He grabbed the tote, opened it, and pulled the jewelry out. "Get some of that."

She got two thick gold chains, three gold and diamond rings, a diamond tennis bracelet, and four gold bangles.

He put all of the jewelry on her. "I want you to use some of that money to buy something pretty for yourself tomorrow."

She threw her arms around him, and kissed him. "Can't you stay with me for a little while tonight? You ain't made love to me since the weekend."

"Hold up a minute, I got to make a call." he said reaching for the phone. Leslie's sleepy voice answered the phone. "I'm gonna be a little later than I thought, so go ahead and get some sleep. I got something for you when I get home."

"Alright baby, I love you." Leslie said.

"I love you back." he said and hung up the phone. When he looked at Becky she had a funny look on her face. He knew what it was, so before it got out of hand he wanted to check it.

"Come here Beck." She moved close to him. He grabbed her shoulders and turned her to him, looked in her eyes, and asked. "Are you alright?"

"Yeah I'm cool." she said sadly.

"Girl don't bullshit." he said. "Remember what I said about us being real with each other? So tell me, are you okay?"

"Naw," she said. "I'm a little hurt." She looked at him with tears glistening in her eyes. "I thought I could really handle the situation, but when you called and told her you love her and all of that in front of me... I guess because I've never seen you with her or heard you talk to her before, it didn't seem real to me that you had a wife. Shit was so special over the weekend that I somehow dismissed that part and was dreaming it was just you and me. Then the reality of the situation stepped in, and I found I couldn't handle it as well as I thought I could. I'm sorry baby. I wanna be that strong, down ass bitch you looking for, but I don't know if I can. We've been together for such a short time, yet it seems like it's been forever. Five days you've been a part of my life, and it's almost like I can't remember a time when I didn't have you. I ain't had a man to love me so totally in my life. Look what you've done for me already, money and jewelry. You the one made me dream, you made me feel like there was no one else. Your words weaved the spell that trapped my heart. I hate to be the one to say this, but I know I love you. I don't wanna lose you. I wanna be with you, but damn if what just went down didn't scare me."

"Lil momma I never meant for that to hurt you." he said sincerely. "If I had known in advance that you would respond the way you did, I would've made the call in the other room. I told you the deal from the start. I never tried to paint you a bullshit picture like I was unhappy at home, or going thru marital strife. I realize you're young, and that you might allow your emotions to get involved. Hell my emotions are involved too. I had hoped that because our relationship was in its infancy, we would forge a bond that would help us endure when problems arise. I never anticipated they would arise so soon. We made an agreement when we first started this, but I never expected us to follow it to the letter. Certain things yeah, but I knew we'd have to fill each other out. As time goes on we would develop a greater affection for each other. I knew after that, things would change. Do you think I want you out there doing what you do, or smoking that shit? Of course I don't, but I'm not trying to make or force you to change who you are. I accepted you as who you are, and what comes with it. If you change I want it to be because you want to, not because it was an expectation or stipulation that I placed on you. What I'm trying to say is this. Don't change for me, change because of me. I wanna be instrumental in giving you all the things you've never had no matter what they are. Do you understand me?"

"Yeah I do," she said.

"I remember you said you weren't into that housewife shit, so don't get all domestic on me."

"I'm cool." she said getting up.

She went into the bathroom, and he could hear water running in the tub. He sat on the foot of the bed, and wondered how he was gonna handle her getting emotionally attached.

She walked into the room, stood in front of him, put her hands on his shoulders, and said.

"It's gonna be alright. I know you're gonna make sure everything works out for us. I just got a little scared because I don't wanna lose you. It seems I've waited my whole life for a man like you to come along. For a minute it seemed that as soon as I found you I was gonna lose you. Baby I'll do anything for you, all you got to do is say it and I won't hesitate, believe that!"

She took off his cap, grabbed the bottom of his shirt and pulled it off. She dropped to her knees, took off his boots and socks then massaged his feet. Then grabbed his hands and pulled him up and removed his pants and boxers. She went to the closet and got his robe, then helped him put it on. She slid his slippers on his feet then led him to the bathroom where she took off his robe and helped him into the tub. He eased into the warm water as she removed her t-shirt and panties then got in the tub and grabbed a washcloth and soaped it up.

"Stand up baby", she said.

He stood and she gently washed him. She washed his face, his upper body, stomach, pubic hair, and his legs all the way down to his feet then turned him around and repeated the process on his back. As she washed him she reached between his legs and cupped his heavy balls, squeezing them gently. She reached for his penis and stroked it slowly. She dropped the washcloth and with her free hand squeezed his ass. She spread one cheek then ducked her head forward and ran her tongue up and down his crack occasionally pressing her tongue against his anus. Using his manhood as a handle, she turned him so he was facing her then she licked at his penis. Her tongue swirled all around the crown before she sucked him down deep. Patiently she took her time and loved him orally. Suddenly she stopped, pulled him from her mouth, looked up at him and smiled, then rose to her feet, wrapped her arms around him and asked," Did you like that Daddy? "Yeah I did," He said holding her in his arms. She broke the embrace and quickly bathed then they dried off and quickly went to the room. She sat him on the foot of the bed with his feet on the floor and spread his legs then she kneeled between them and started kissing and licking his inner thighs.

After they had made love he reached over and pulled her to him and kissed her. "If you gonna be sexing me like that I'm gonna call her in front of you more regular," He said and laughed.

She pulled away and punched him playfully." Nigga don't try me," She said laughing. "Daddy are we gonna be alright?" She asked seriously.

"Lil Mama don't worry," He said," Everything's gonna be alright as long as you know what to expect. As long as you conduct yourself by the rules we set, stay on top of your game and be honest with me shit gonna work out. We gonna ride this for as long as it last. If it comes to an end; one thing we'll know is that it was straight love while it lasted. Don't let jealousy rear its ugly head because what you have to understand is this; even if I have 100 women when I'm with you you're the only one! Don't ever forget that. I'm gonna always satisfy you cause I'll do whatever it takes to keep you satisfied. We gonna have our bad days because it's impossible to have a perfect relationship with two imperfect people. As long as we keep honesty and trust we can work it out. I don't have any reason to lie to you and you don't have to lie to me. As long as you remember that and abide by it we gonna be straight. You know I have obligations elsewhere but I won't ever neglect you!"

"Damn Baby you make it sound so easy," She said.

"Naw it ain't easy," He said seriously. "But it's the hand we chose to play!"

CHAPTER 4

Kane didn't make it home that night. He woke up early the next morning and tossed Becky a fuck, showered and dressed for work.

When he arrived on the job Emma was waiting on him at the loading dock platform. He always parked in the back lot of the plant and entered from the rear loading area. Emma was a supervisor at the plant and had been budging him to transfer to her section. Of course he resisted because he didn't want Emma to be in a position where he was under her and she held control.

She stopped him as he reached the deck of the loading dock. "Kane I've always wanted to ask you a question."

"Go ahead, ask away," he said.

"What kind of name is Berean?"

"Berean is derived from the city of Berea somewhere in the middle east. There were a group of people that followed the teachings of the Messiah and they were called the Berean's. My mother blessed me with that name. I think it's rather fitting don't you, an unusual name for an unusual man."

"It is kind of cute and unusual," she said smiling.

"Emma what's really on your mind?" He asked looking in her eyes. "Cause I just know you ain't been waiting here to ask me what kind of name is Berean. I feel like there's more that you wanna say. So what's up?"

"You're right," she said. "I wanted to know if you've considered transferring to my section."

He cut her off before she could go any further. "Hold up Em. Why don't you cut the bullshit and get to the heart of the matter. You're too old to be acting like a moonstruck school girl with all of that stammering and fake ass small talk. The first thing you need to know about me is that I don't play any games; I don't have time for them. I believe in being honest and upfront with people unless my life is in danger because other than that it serves no useful purpose. I'm very blunt but I do know when to hold my peace. If you wanna holla at me on a serious level regardless of what aspect, just be real."

"Damn Berean!" She said stunned. "That was a mouthful. I really do wanna talk to you about something but we don't really have the time right now and you're never at work early enough for us to sit down and talk. The only time I see you outside the job is if someone throws a get together. Then all you do is speak and keep stepping you don't ask me to dance or nothing. You speak and bullshit but other than that you act like you don't even see me. I really want us to sit down and talk. Tell you what, why don't you let me buy you lunch today then we'll have time to talk?"

"Do you really want to do that?" He asked. "You know how these niggas around here be talking. I would hate to ruin your reputation?"

"I really wanna talk to you," she said.

"Alright I'm cool with that," he said. "You wanna take my car or yours?"

"We can take mine if that's cool with you," she said.

"No sweat, he said. "I'm alright with that."

The whistle blew signaling that it was time to punch the clock. He went in and punched his time card then walked to his work station. He started filling his orders. He worked steadily from 7:30 to 9:30; took a 15 minute break then went back to work until 11:00.

He walked to the front of the plant then to the parking area where Emma stood at her car waiting. She had opened the doors and turned on the air conditioner to cool the inside of the car down.

"What's up babe?" He asked smiling.

"It's you Berean," she said smiling nervously. "You ready to ride?"

"Oh yeah," he answered.

"So where do you wanna eat?" She asked.

"I don't eat everything and I ain't no hamburger and fries type of nigga. So all that McDonald's and Burger King shit is out," he said. "Dig this; let's go to Captain D's its right up the road and we'll have time to eat and talk."

They got in the car and headed to Main St. which was only 4 blocks from where they worked. It only took 4 or 5 minutes to get to Captain D's. She parked, they left the car and he held the door open for her. She looked at him shocked because the last thing she expected from him was chivalry. She could see that he was hard but there was also a mysterious quality that she couldn't quite put her finger on, she also knew she was drawn to him like a moth to a flame. There was a little fear involved too and that thrilled her. He didn't approach her or respond to her like most men and she wanted to see what was up with this young nigga who seemed so confident and sure. They went to the counter and ordered. She paid for their order; he grabbed the tray and took it to a table in the back.

"Damn there's more to this nigga than meets the eye," she thought.

They sat down and he started eating. She just toyed with her food, nibbling. "You know I dig you," she said tentatively. "I like your style and like I said earlier I had been trying to attract your attention but you looked

41

right thru me. I said to myself, damn I know this nigga ain't gay because he creeping and fucking all them silly ho's at the plant. What've they got that I don't besides their youth? Cause I'm fine and better looking than all them ho's. What is it that turns this nigga off on me? Am I too bold in making myself open and available to him? Or does he like to chase instead of being chased? I asked myself these and many more questions because I didn't know what the deal was. I didn't know if you like strong willed women or weak passive women and that kind of fucked me up because most of the dudes I've fucked with were chumps and suckers. They pursued me, but you're different and I just didn't know how to come off to you."

"First of all I don't creep," he said looking in her eyes. "I'm a man and I don't do shit I have to hide and do. I believe in being discreet; as often times it protects my lovers and their integrity but I don't do no creeping. I do freaking! And if you think for a minute that I didn't notice you then you're sillier than those other women that you labeled ho's. See I might be young but I've had the opportunity to learn a great deal about women and their ways. I knew what your game was from the beginning. But see I also know that you've been fine as fuck and good looking all your life. I know you're use to niggas running behind you and I wasn't about to fall in your trap, and you put me in the same category as all the other chumps and suckers you fucked with in the past. One thing I know is this. You're fine, good looking and the average nigga would be head over heels to stick his dick in you and sport you on his arm. I ain't your average nigga! Some of them would even consider you a status symbol; an older woman fine as fuck, independent, and strong. They'd be glad to give you all of their money for a little bit of your time. But tell me this; what can you give me besides some pussy? And remember this. I can get some pussy when I can't get a plate of food."

She stared at him with her mouth open not knowing what to say. She closed her mouth, looked at her food and said, "Damn! If I didn't know any better I would've swore that you just ran Mack on me from the old school. The shit must be working because I really don't have an answer to that question."

"I know you don't," he said. "And that's because you're not looking to the future. If we fuck all I am is another notch in your belt. Another mission accomplished. What you need to see is that I'm more than just a fuck. I have principles and standards that I live by. To be a sex object just because you wanna make another conquest is not in line with what I believe. Would I fuck you? I answer damn right I would and I would find great joy in it. But, I would fuck you only on my terms and on my time. I know you're used to having things your way so there would be a conflict. You don't know how to be submissive because you've been so

42

dominant in your past relationships. I'm sure you could play the role for a while but eventually your aggressive nature would win out. I love strong women, aggressive women, a woman with a will of her own but I don't like a disobedient woman and I'm sure your age and experience would dictate that you be in control. You're almost 20 years older than me and what that means is you'll occasionally feel that you're wiser than me simply because of my youth. In some cases that may well be true but when it comes to the mechanics of engaging in a relationship I believe my wisdom far exceeds yours. You may disagree and I don't have a problem with that. I'm not looking for a sheep but a lioness. Fiercely strong but understanding her place in the scheme of things. Do you understand?"

"Some of it," she said in awe at his words. "I'm finding it difficult to absorb because I've never had a man to sit me down and talk to me this way."

"Perhaps that's because you've never had a man period! See most of them were afraid they might blow their shot at getting in your panties so they let you get away with using your feminine wiles on them. The difference between me and them is this. I would love to fuck you but it's not one of my first priorities. If I never fuck you, what have I missed expect a piece of pussy?"

"You didn't have to say it so nasty," she said. "But still I get your point."

He finished eating, leaned back and asked, "what's up baby have you got the answer to my question?"

"To be honest I haven't had the time to think about it or at least to concentrate on it because of all the other things you've said. Believe me I don't think the answer is simple and I don't wanna blow my shot to get in your pants."

He looked in her eyes and started laughing when he saw that she was dead serious.

"Could we finish the conversation over dinner at my place tonight?"

"Damn girl!" He exclaimed. "Did all of the shit I just said go in one ear and out of the other?"

"No," she replied. "But I just had to see if you meant everything you said."

"I didn't just mean it. I live it," he said looking at his watch. "We got 15 minutes. What you wanna do?"

"Nigga you know what I wanna do," she said smiling. "Just sitting here listening to you got my coochie wet. Believe me it's been a while since I felt like that bout a man."

"Damn you a freak," he said.

"You better believe it!" She replied.

He stood, grabbed her hand and pulled her up. "Come on let's go."

They got in her car and she said, "Berean you're a hell of a guy so I'm gonna sit back and see what we can come up with."

"You do that," he said pulling a joint from his shirt pocket. "Mind if I smoke?"

"It's cool as long as you pass it," she answered. He laughed and fired up the joint.

They rode around until they finished the joint then went back to work.

He finished off his production sheet, put up his tools and cleaned his work area.

"What's up my man?" The supervisor at his section asked.

"I'm cool," Kane replied.

"I wondered when you would get around to Emma," the supervisor said laughing.

The supervisor's name was Archie Meadows a big, dark skin brother who had worked at the plant for nearly 25 years. "It ain't like that Arch," Kane said.

"Bullshit," Archie said laughing. "See I know Miss Emma and she had her eye on you since you started working here. I wondered how long it would be before she drew you in. Be careful cause you in the big league now!"

"Dig this Arch," Kane said. "First of all I ain't the type of man that kisses and tells. One thing you need to know is that I mind my own business. You have never seen me participate in the gossip that goes on around here and you won't. I don't want people running up in my face asking me all those silly ass questions. Whatever Emma and I do is our business and no one else's. I know how shit was when I first got here and shit hasn't changed that much but I don't need to be the topic of every conversation. Don't take this the wrong way because I'm not trying to be hard, I'm trying to be private."

"My bad," Archie said. "I didn't mean any harm."

"No harm done," Kane said smiling.

He gave Archie some dap just as the whistle blew. He went and stood in the long line and waited to punch his time card.

After he punched his time card he headed out back to his car. When he got there Emma was leaning on his car looking lovely even after a day of work.

"When are we gonna get together again?" She asked.

"Tomorrow for lunch," he replied. "As a matter of fact we can eat lunch together every day because we got a lot of ground to cover and I'm still waiting on you to answer my question."

"Alright," she said smiling and moving close to him.

"Can you cook?" He asked her.

"Hell yeah," she said inching ever closer.

"Good," he said. "You can make us a lunch and we can go sit in the park and have a picnic. I don't eat any pork or pork filled products. I don't eat any kind of seafood except fish, the ones that have both fins and scales."

"Okay baby," she said standing mere inches away looking up into his eyes.

He grabbed her by the waist, pulled her to him and gave her a deep passionate kiss as she melted in his arms. He broke the kiss, traced her lips with his tongue then slipped his tongue in her mouth. In and out, in and out he plunged his tongue in her mouth.

She sucked at his tongue greedily and started to grind slowly against him. He pressed his erect penis tightly between her legs. She spread her legs and arched her pelvis so his cock was pressing against her clit.

She broke the kiss and moaned out softly, "Oh God ... Oh my God."

His hands slid down to her ass and pulled her against him tighter. She hunched against him faster.

There was no one else around and he pumped his stiff rod against her.

"Oh Berean..." She moaned softly and shuddered. "I can't believe it ... I'm cumin...oh my God...!

She held on to him tighter as her orgasm washed over her, gently he kissed her then pulled away. Her hand shot down to the big bulge in his pants and caressed it. "My God it's so big and hard," She whispered.

He moved her hand, and unlocked his door. He led her to the passenger side, opened the door and let her in. She sat there looking at him as he closed the door and walked around the car and got in.

"Never in my life has that happened to me," she said looking at him with wonder in her eyes. "I mean never ever. By the way I've got the answer to your question."

"Give it to me," he said turning toward her.

"You gave me the answer in the beginning," she said smiling. "You asked what I could give you besides pussy. I knew off the top it wasn't money, so I wrecked my brain all afternoon but when you made me

45

cum it came to me. Truth, honesty, and devotion, that's what I can give you besides this pussy."

"You're very perceptive," he said smiling and reaching over to caress her cheek. "And you answered the question but the next question is this. Can you give me all of those things knowing my time with you will be limited?"

"All I want is the opportunity to show you I can give you the question's answers," she said seriously. "I won't be unreasonable about time."

"We'll see about that!" he said. "I'm inclined to give you that opportunity, but I'll expect you to live up to the words from your mouth."

"No doubt," she said. "What about the girls at the plant?"

"What about them?" He asked. "You know like I know that when they saw us go to lunch they automatically assumed that we got something going on. I have never taken any of them to lunch so more than likely they think I'm your man. They gonna back up, watch and see. They probably gonna give me the cold shoulder. I don't know how they'll respond to you."

"And you gonna be cool with that?" She asked.

"I didn't make them lay-up with me," he said. "And if the urge arises they'll try to give me the goods behind your back. Don't sweat it because I'll let you know. Remember, I don't do no creeping. When I bring it to you I don't want you tripping or confronting them about it. You'll know where you stand with them from there."

"Alright baby," she said as he cranked the car and drove her to the front lot next to her car. "I think I can live with that."

"Can you come by my place tonight?"

"No," he answered. "I got business to tend to, but tomorrow after work we'll go to your place and see if we're compatible."

"Damn baby," she said. "I can't wait; you know how long I've wanted you?"

"If you really want too, take the day off and I'll swing by and we can lay in all day." he said.

"Now that's what I'd really like," she said smiling broadly.

"It's done then," he said. "Give me your number and I'll call you first thing in the morning."

She wrote her number down and he gave her another deep kiss. Everybody had left and they were the only ones in the big parking lot.

"I want you to at least touch it for me before you go," she said wistfully.

"Girl you gonna get yours," he said laughing.

"My coochie is just throbbing," she said lustfully. "Please do that for me, it'll hold me till in the morning."

"Alright sugar," he said.

She quickly loosened her pants, raised her ass from the seat and pulled her pants and panties down to her ankles. He looked at her cunt. It was covered in hair, the lips fat and puffy.

"Reach over on the side of your seat and pull that lever," he said.

She pulled the lever and her seat lay back. He put his hand between her legs and cupped her fat cunt. He leaned over and kissed her as his middle finger parted her lips. She was hot and wet, and his finger slipped in.

She moaned deep in her throat, "ummmm....ummmhmm..." as his finger pumped in and out of her and slid back and forth over her stiff clitoris.

He broke the kiss and with his free hand opened the buttons on her blouse and spread it wide. He lifted her apple sized breast from her bra, dropped his head down and sucked her nipple into his mouth and flicked his tongue over it. She hunched his finger and moaned softly, "ummm...ummm....umm..."

He sucked her breast and fingered her, his penis hard as steel. She hunched his finger faster as he worked it in deeper and kept pressure on her clit. Lightly he bit her nipples and she moaned, "Oh....oh...oh...."

Her hands reached up and pressed his head tighter to her breast then suddenly she shivered and moaned, "Oh...God...I'm cumin... oh yes....yesss..."

He fingered her for another minute then pulled his finger from her and slid it into her mouth. She licked and sucked at his finger until he pulled it out and kissed her. He backed away and said, "Straighten out your clothes."

She fixed her clothes, threw her arms around him and kissed him. "I wanna see it," she said looking in his eyes. "Let me see it baby." She reached down, rubbed his bulging cock then unzipped his pants. She reached in and tried to gently pull it out. He was rock hard and she couldn't get it out. She loosened his belt, undid his pants and freed him.

"Oh my god you'll kill me with this...It's so big," she whispered as she slowly stroked him.

She ducked her head and wrapped her lips around it and sucked him in deep. She bobbed her head up and down on it and he moaned, "Damn girl... You know what you're doing...."

He let her suck it a little longer then pulled her head up. "Why did you stop me?" She asked puzzled.

"Cause if you keep that up we'll be fucking in the car," he replied. "That's enough. Now go on home, and I'll see you tomorrow morning."

She kissed him and hopped out of the car. He watched her get in her car and leave, and then he pulled off.

*　　　　*　　　　*　　　　*

Kane stopped in Brooklyn on his way home. He parked a couple of houses away from Paul and Pearl Washington's house. He walked to their house and Pearl was sitting on the porch drinking a beer. "Hey Kane," Pearl said as he approached. "What's up?"

"You and your man," he replied.

Pearl was a fine dark skinned woman, cute, big breast, wide hips, and a fat ass. She had been trying to sneak and give Kane some pussy but he knew if he fucked her Paul would soon find out, because they argued and fought all of the time. They always ended up telling each other about their indiscretions and he didn't want any part of that.

Paul called himself a dealer and he was, but not on a major scale. They were somehow related to Leslie and Lucinda; which one of them he didn't know.

"Where's your man?" Kane asked as he walked thru the gate.

"He in the house," she replied.

"I need to talk to y'all." he said, as she got up and lead the way into the house.

He had went in his tool box and got a big .38 special and tucked it into his waist and pulled his shirt over it.

"Paul!" Pearl screamed. "Kane's here to see you!"

Paul came from the back bare chest wearing long shorts and a pair of black Reebok classics. He stood about 6'3 and wore a muscled 225 pounds. He was big, where Kane was only 5'11 and 185 pounds.

Paul and Pearl were notorious gossips. They kept their business in the street and everybody else's too.

"What up Kane?" Paul asked.

"You and your woman's mouth, that's what's up," Kane said calmly.

"Nigga, what the fuck you talking about?" Paul asked angrily.

"I'm gonna tell y'all one time and one time only," Kane said firmly. "You need to give me your undivided attention. I want y'all to mind your own business when it comes to me. Don't be telling Leslie shit about what happens in the street. That shit about me robbing people and shit. Keep my name from crossing your lips. If she tells me one more time that y'all done told her anything I'm gonna forget y'all family!"

48

"Nigga you gonna come in my house and make half ass threats to us?" Paul said with venom. "You might have a few niggas spooked cause you down with gunplay but you ain't the only nigga got a gun and I ain't scared of you. So get your punk ass out of my house before I throw you out!"

Kane reached under his shirt with lightning like speed and pulled his pistol out and asked, "Where's your gun Paul?"

Paul saw the gun and his eyes filled with fear because he knew for a fact that Kane would shoot. He raised his hands and pleaded, "Now hold on a minute."

"I done said all I'm gone say," Kane said ominously. "Y'all know I don't play games. Paul you may not be scared of me but if I ever see you on the street anywhere near me and I even suspect you got a gun you better be shooting, cause I'm a be shooting mine. If I have to come back and talk to y'all bout your mouths it's gonna be the last time we talk and I promise you that. Paul I came to you like a man but you called me a punk. Now I'm gonna let that slide this time but don't make the mistake of believing your words. You've been warned. Everything that happens from this point is on y'all, and ain't no hard feelings far as I'm concerned. We cool despite Paul's slick ass mouth."

He slid the pistol back in his waist and looked at them and said, "All I'm asking is that y'all don't tell my wife anything about me good or bad. Stay out of my business cause I stay out of yours. Can y'all live with that?"

They both nodded their heads and he turned and walked from the house.

When he walked out of the gate he saw two women sitting on the hood of his car. He couldn't tell who it was from the distance plus their backs were to him. He walked to the car and heard Becky's voice.

"What's up little momma?" he said to her back.

Her head spun around and he saw that her hair was freshly braided. She jumped off the car and he saw that she had on a new outfit, sky blue Capri pants, matching blouse, and sky blue and white Nike running shoes.

"Hey daddy!" She said and flew into his arms.

"Damn if it doesn't look like your glad to see me," he said wrapping her in his arms. "Hey Chell what's up?"

"Ain't nothing playa," Chell said smiling. "Look like you got my girl nose wide open."

Kane kissed Becky lightly and asked, "How was your day?"

"It's been cool," she said. "I took Chell to the mall with me and bought her a couple of outfits. We were serving at the rooming house. I got a little something for you."

49

"What you got for me, sweaty?" He asked.

"Two Grand I made today," she answered.

"I told you that was for you", he said. "I'm straight baby. Go on and stack your paper. When you finish working yours we gonna work what I got; Cool?"

"No it ain't," she said firmly her arms wrapped around him.

"We in this together, those your words not mine. What kind of money you got in your pocket?"

"I got a couple of bills," he answered.

"Well you got two gees to go with it!" She said firmly. "I done took everything you gave me because you wanted me to have it, now I want you to have something and you turning me down. In your own words, eat the fruit from your own mouth daddy. I don't want it to be a thing where you keep giving, and I ain't giving on my end. You made it possible for me to have, so I wanna share with you."

"Damn baby," he said shaking his head. "I guess my own words gonna bite me in the ass here huh?"

"Damn right they are," she said smiling.

"Nigga go on and get that money," Chell said. "The bitch gonna make plenty more for you from what I saw."

"Y'all gonna double team me now? He asked laughing.

"I wish," Chell said laughing.

"Alright bitch," Becky said playfully. "This all mine for now and I ain't ready to share yet, but I may get generous sometime in the future. So daddy, you gonna get this money or what?"

"I ain't got any choice looks like," he said laughing.

Becky broke their embrace, reached in her bra and pulled out a fat roll of bills and gave it to him.

"I still got a couple of grand put up for me so don't sweat that daddy," Becky said smiling up at him. "So what's on the agenda baby?"

"I got a few things to handle since I didn't make it home last night," he said.

"You got a little time for me before you dip?" she asked.

"I'll make time for you sweetheart," he said. "What you wanna do?"

"You got to ask?" She said reaching down and squeezing his crotch.

"Let's go to your room, before you rape me in the street," he said smiling.

"Chell roll with us," Becky said. "You can't get any of this but you can get us some money while we handle our business. For every three rocks you sell you get one, and don't be trying to get slick either. Serve them like you get them and don't turn down any money. Eight is the less a dime go for, seventeen for 20's. Break them down if they got a nickel, is that cool?"

"Hell yeah that's cool," Chell answered.

They got in Kane's car and drove to the rooming house. Becky gave Chell 40 rocks, and she and Kane went into the room.

After they made love and got dressed they walked on the porch, Chell gave Becky $300 and said, "I got a few more but they'll be gone in a minute".

"That's you then," Becky said.

"Listen up little momma," Kane said. "I don't want you on the block at night unless you rolling with Tee. You and Chell can serve from here long as you want to, but I don't want you trying to grind all night, get you some rest alright?"

"Okay baby," she said. "You gonna swing thru tomorrow?"

"Yeah I'll be thru about 5:00 or 6:00," he said.

She moved into his arms and held on tight. She tiptoed and kissed his lips softly then slipped her tongue in his mouth.

"Y'all need to cut that shit out," Chell said. "It's bad enough y'all left me out here knowing what was going down in there, and now y'all gonna come out here and torture me? My pussy burning up as it is and I ain't got no nigga to take care of it. Hell, I might have to buy me some dick."

Becky and Kane laughed. He went in his pocket and counted off 100 and said, "If you can find it, it's on me," and gave Chell the money.

"Shit you can keep that if you wanna serve it," Chell said.

"Bitch you just ain't gonna give up is you?" Becky asked laughing.

"I'm the one told you how good the dick was, or have you forgot?" Chell said. "I done gave him money before. All I want is for the nigga to put out this fire. We girls, and if the shoe was on the other foot and you ain't have nobody I'd do it for you. Hell you and Sherrie the only bitches I'd do that for."

"Damn girl you serious about this ain't you?" Becky asked.

"Hell yeah," Chell said. "I know the nigga got it like that. I'd rather get your permission than be all conniving and shit. Hell you been sharing with me all day plus you ain't gonna miss the little dick he give me. I don't want no head or none of that, just beat this pussy for 15 or 20 minutes and I'm straight. You can watch if you want to."

"Y'all gonna talk about me like I ain't even here?" he asked amazed. "What about my business. How y'all know I'm down in the first place?"

"Daddy this is the second thing I want you to have today," Becky said seriously. "I need to know if I can deal with it anyway. Do this for me, 15 or 20 minutes. I'll sit out here and serve till you're thru. Please!"

"Are you sure?" He asked her.

"Yeah I'm sure," she said. "Chell been down for whatever and I believe she'd do it for me."

"Alright then," he said. "Come on Chell I got shit to do."

Chell and Kane walked into the house and Becky sat in the chair thinking, "He had her before he was ever with me but he chose me. Ain't no need for me to sweat it? Everything he said been straight so far and it got to be more than a fuck thing cause the nigga been really breaking bread, and asked for nothing in return." A baser walked up and broke her train of thought.

Becky served for close to 20 minutes and felt no guilt or jealousy over Kane being in her room with Chell.

"Hey shorty is you doing something?" A dude she knew as popcorn asked her.

Becky knew popcorn was a gorilla. If he thought he could get away with it he'd rough off your dope. He sometimes robbed, but he couldn't keep a pistol. He always ended up selling it for rock.

"Yeah I got a little something," Becky said. "What you need?"

"Can you serve 50?" He asked walking up on the porch.

"Yeah I can serve that," she said. "Show me the color of your money. You know I know you, so don't be with the stupid shit Popcorn."

"Bitch you got a few stones now and you acting like you Jackie O or some shit!" Popcorn said. "I should just take the shit and keep my motherfuckin' money!"

"Do that and you'll be making one of the biggest mistakes you ever made in your life," Becky said.

"So you threaten me now?" Popcorn said walking toward where she stood by the rail. "You just fucked up Bitch!"

"Naw you the one that fucked up," a voice said from behind him.

He turned and Kane stepped out of the door with the big .38 pointed at his face.

"Aw shit Kane. I was just playing with her man," Popcorn pleaded. "I was just joking dog!"

"I heard the whole conversation from the time you first walked up," Kane said. "I saw you coming nigga and I know how you play so I wanted see if you were up to your old tricks. I guess you ain't know Becky was my woman?"

"Naw man," I swear I didn't," Popcorn said pleading. "I'm gone dog. Just let me dip."

Chell stepped out the door and said, "That nigga wasn't playing Kane. He was dead ass serious!"

"You can dip on one condition," Kane said. "If you pull out $50 and let them serve it."

By this time a small crowd of people had gathered to watch. Kane looked out at the crowd and said, "For those of y'all that don't know. Becky is my woman. If you fuck with her, you fuckin' with me and I'm deadly serious bout mine. The only thing saving this piece of shit is y'all or I would smoke his ass. As it is he's gonna serve as a lesson to anyone who steps on my toes. If you try me it's on, so be ready to go all out."

He turned back to Popcorn and asked, "You got that playa?"

"I'm sorry dog," Popcorn said. "If I knew she was down with you I wouldn't have stepped like that dog. I swear I wouldn't have."

Kane struck with the speed of a rattlesnake and hit Popcorn on the left side of his head with the big pistol. The barrel split his head nearly to the skull and he dropped down to one knee stunned by the blow. Kane clubbed him mercilessly with the big pistol until he was just a mass of quivering, bloodied flesh. He was unrecognizable as his head and face were covered with blood. The crowd was stunned by both the speed and ferocity of his attack.

"Daddy! Daddy! That's enough!" Becky shouted. "Too many people are watching baby. You gonna kill him!"

Her voice penetrated the thick fog of his anger, and he froze breathing hard. He looked into the crowd and they recoiled at the rage they saw blazing in his eyes.

"If this goes down again I'm killing!" He shouted. "And I ain't leaving any witnesses! So mind your fuckin' business!"

The crowd hurried and dispersed. Chell just stood there in complete shock. The same man that had just make love to her hard, then soft, had nearly beat a man to death minutes later.

"Go on home baby," Becky said. "I'll be in pocket at about 10:30, so you can call me alright? He needs some help baby."

Kane looked at the bloody pistol he had in his hand and his blood splattered clothes and nodded. He didn't trust himself to speak. He kissed her lightly on the lips then slowly walked away.

"Chell call 911 while I try to revive this piece of shit," Becky said.

Chell rushed from the porch as Becky raced in the house. By the time the ambulance arrived Popcorn was awake. Becky had given him 10 fat rocks to keep his mouth shut. That plus the knowledge that Kane would kill him if he told sealed his lips when the police arrived. After Popcorn was carted off to the hospital, Becky and Chell sat on the porch.

"I told you girl," Chell said. "That nigga something serious, whatever you do don't bring that out in him."

"He would never hurt me," Becky said confidently.

"I've know that nigga most of my life and you just met him," Chell said. "I know what I'm talking about!"

"You were seeing him all your life," Becky said. "But you don't know him. I know that nigga like I was raised by his side. He'd never bring physical harm to me. He'd never beat me. He said he wouldn't and I won't ever give him cause to. It won't be out of fear that I'll do that, but because I love him. I ain't never met a nigga like Kane and doubt I ever will!"

"I hope you're right," Chell said softly. In her mind she felt some of the same things.

CHAPTER 5

When Kane got home the kids were at the park. He pulled up in the driveway and blew the horn. Leslie came to the door and looked out. He had gone to his grandmother's house and cleaned up, cleaned his pistol and dressed. He opened the glove compartment and pressed the button that released the trunk. He got out, went to the trunk and got the tool box and big tote bag and walked into the garage.

He opened the tool box then went in the tote bag and got a thick gold chain, a diamond ring, and a diamond and gold tennis bracelet and set them in the tool box on the top tray. He locked the tool box, set it on the top shelf grabbed the tote bag and went in the house.

Leslie was fiddling with the stereo system when he walked thru the door. He came up behind her and wrapped his arms around her waist and kissed the nape of her neck.

"You never did make it home last night," she said.

"I know," he replied. "I got tied up."

He released her and walked to their bedroom. He sat the tote on the bed and opened it. She had followed him to the room.

"You going out tonight?" She asked.

"Not unless something important comes up," he answered. "Other than that I'm gonna chill. Shouldn't those kids be getting on home by now it's almost 6:30?"

"They'll be her shortly," she said. "I'm glad you're staying in tonight."

He reached in the tote and pulled all of the jewelry out.

"Baby I don't need no more jewelry," she said. "I hardly wear all the stuff you already got me."

"I know," he said. "Get what you want out of it, and then get some for our moms and for my sisters. We'll go to the store and buy some boxes to put it in and give it to them."

"Alright," she said. "But they already got so much jewelry from you that they are walking around looking like Mr. T."

He burst out laughing. "Girl your crazy."

Leslie started picking over the jewelry getting the pieces that she wanted and setting the other stuff aside in four piles. When she finished she went and got four sandwich bags and put the jewelry in them.

"Here baby," he said and gave her the money.

"How much is this?" She asked.

"I don't know," he said. "Roughly 19 or 20 grand I'd guess."

He had put the money Becky gave him with it so it was $22,000.

"What you want me to do with this?" She asked.

"Put it with the rest of the money you hide when I give it to you," he said laughing.

"How much money do you have on you?" She asked

"I got a bill or so, so you might need to give me one or two hundred for my pocket," he said.

She counted out $200 and gave it to him. "I done ran your bath for you if you wanna go ahead and clean up."

"Yeah I do," he said heading for the bathroom.

She brought him his robe and said, "Put that on. Those kids could be home any minute and they don't need to see your dick flopping around."

He grabbed the robe with one hand and her with the other. He pulled her to him and kissed her.

"Baby don't start up," she said. "You know them children nosy enough as it is. If we're in here doing something they gonna be bammin' on the door for nothing, just to try and see what we're doing. So save it for tonight when they go to bed."

"You sure you don't wanna take a bath with me?" He asked.

"Go on with your freaky ass," she said smiling.

He let her go and got in the tub. While he was bathing he heard the children ask, "Momma where's daddy?" Her response was, "He taken a bath so y'all go on and wash up."

They lived in a nice 4 bedroom, 2 bath house that they had been buying since 1987 right before Kane took a fall for armed robbery.

"Y'all go and clean up," Leslie said. "I don't want y'all messing with me because I got to get dinner ready."

Kane heard all of the conversation and screamed from the bathroom, "Leslie! Leslie!"

She came in the bathroom. "What's up baby?" She said as she lifted her dress, pulled down her panties and sat on the stool to pee.

"You don't have to cook tonight," he said. "We're going out to eat. Remember we're going to the store to get something to put the jewelry in, so we might as well make a night of it. You got any money?"

"You know I got some money," she said. "You just gave me a whole bunch. Plus I got the money I been putting aside for emergency purposes and what we got in the bank. Shoot, I ain't touched that since 90. So yeah I got some money. Why you wanna know?"

"Cause you know if we take them children to the store they gonna want something," he said.

They don't have to get something every time we go to the store," she said firmly. "That's your shit. You know I don't put up with all that whining and showing out in public. I'll whip their ass right there and they know it. They just pull that mess when you're there because they know you're weak for them and will buy them something. You need to cut that shit out because you spoiling the hell out of them as it is."

"Damn baby all I asked was if you had some money, he said. "If they want something and I can afford it, you damn right I'm gonna buy it for them. I was raised that way and I'm gonna raise them that way. When they were old enough to take martial arts and wanted to do it because B.K. was doing it, I paid for it for the whole year and have been paying for it since. You wanted Nika to take valet and piano lessons. I paid for that too. Since the boys weren't into it, she showed her ass about it. All the talking and ass whipping didn't make her change her mind. They all still took the lessons and it's good for them physically and mentally. Even you can see they're much easier to discipline, besides it ain't like we gonna spend all of the money on them. I just didn't want to spend the little change I got. But if you don't wanna go in your stash I'll spend this little shit up, and I ain't trying to argue bout this!"

"I got a couple of hundred in my purse so money ain't no problem. What I'm talking bout is you letting them monsters have their way. You need to be sterner with them in certain areas, that is all I'm saying. You know they'll try to play us against each other if we let them."

"As long as they keep getting good grades in school, do their chores around the house, and don't give you much hell we should reward them. Show them we appreciate the efforts they're putting forth," he said. "As long as we're consistent in our parenting and communicate on all of the issues, they won't be able to play us against each other. I keep that job I got for y'all. I drop the whole check in your lap and I don't keep a dime. I work hard to pay for this house and make sure y'all can have some of the finer things this life has to offer. Shit your car is newer than mine not to mention better, but that's the way it should be. I'm glad you're responsible and make sure our bank account and bills are straight. That's why the money I get outside of the job is icing on the cake. I love you and the children and wish I was super rich cause then you could have anything you want. One day I just might be! But for now all I got is you, the kids, and a measly few thousand dollars. If it cost me all of that money wise to see you smile I'd go broke and it's the same for the children. Regardless to how they act, one thing remains true, and that's that they're ours. Good or bad, they're ours!"

He finished bathing, dressed then told the kids they were going out to eat.

"Where y'all wanna go?"

"Pizza Hut!" They yelled in unison.

He rounded up his family and they piled in Leslie's Volvo wagon. It was a new model, 92". He had gotten a .380 and an extra clip and put them in a leather pouch he carried. When he came back to the car from the garage Leslie asked,

"Baby do you have to take that with you everywhere?"

"I'd rather be caught with it than without it," he said firmly.

She shook her head and they headed to the mall. They brought the kids some tennis shoes and Leslie saw a dress she just had to have. He brought a pair of Texas steer boots, which were his favorite brand. They were just as good as Timberlands but $50 cheaper. Afterwards they found some boxes for the jewelry and he convinced Leslie to buy some extras so they'd have them if they needed them.

They left the mall and headed to Leslie's mother's house.

       *   *   *   *

When they pulled up to Leslie's mother Doreen's house Leslie blew the horn. Doreen came to the door, saw who it was and smiled. Doreen was a plump and jovial woman. Her face always seemed to be covered with a smile, and she loved Kane as if he were her own son. She was filled with advice on how to raise the kids which she spoiled, and how to make sure your house stayed straight. She was divorced from Leslie's father Fred who lived in Florida somewhere. They hadn't heard from him in at least 7 years. He had run off with a woman half his age.

Kane listened closely to her advice because it was always solid. He followed it as closely as his personal standards would allow. Doreen was a beautiful woman, her skin had a red tint, and her daughters bore a strong resemblance to her. The same slanted eyes high cheek bones, full lips, and dimpled-smile. Their body types were similar. All 3 were thick women with big breast, wide hips, big arms, big legs, big pretty thighs, and fat round asses. Lucinda was the smallest at 5'2, and 185 pounds. Leslie was the biggest at 5'5, 215 pounds, and Doreen was in the middle.

Kane and his family hung out at Doreen's for about 30 minutes and got ready to go. He pulled her to the side, pulled out his money and gave her $50. Leslie had already given her the jewelry.

"Boy I don't need any money," Doreen said.

"I know that momma," he said laughing. "Go buy yourself a nice dress or something. You never can tell when one of them young boys gonna want to take you out."

"Boy you better go on with that mess," Doreen said laughing and playfully slapping him on his arm.

58

He pulled her in his arms and gave her a kiss. "We gonna swing over to Anna's for a few you wanna ride?"

"Naw I'm cool," she said. "We see enough of each other on the job as it is."

"Alright baby," he said. "Call me if you need anything." He kissed her again, gathered his wife and kids and left.

*   *   *   *

When they pulled up to Anna's house the sun was setting and she was outside in her garden. Leslie pulled up, and Kane got out and opened the gate. B.K. jumped out too, and Kane said, "Close the gate," as Leslie drove thru. B.K. closed the gate then ran past Kane to Anna. He knew he was her favorite because he was her oldest grandchild.

Anna hugged him and said, "Boy you gonna knock me down with all that running."

B.K. at 15 was much taller than Anna who only stood 5'0 and wore 125 pounds. Anna resembled Nancy Wilson but her figure was not as thin. She had nice breast, her waist was slim for a woman of 47. She had gently flaring hips, slightly bowed legs and a nice butt. Her skin was cocoa brown complexioned the same as Kane's and she had long, thick black hair that she wore in a ponytail. Kane favored his mother in face, but had his father's eyes, nose, and head shape.

The kids got out of the car and mobbed her. They were crowded around her like chicks around a mother hen, all of them trying to talk at the same time. She was just smiling, the gold teeth in her mouth sparkling in the setting sun.

Leslie made her way to Anna and said, "Hey momma, I got something for you," and handed her the boxes.

Anna looked in the boxes. "Now y'all know I don't need any more jewelry. Tony came by here this morning and gave me some."

She looked at Kane and said, "Boy you ain't got Tony out there with that foolishness have you? I don't need that kind of stress. I still wake up at night thinking about the phone call I got when Alvin died. If something should happen to you or Tony I don't know if I could go on."

"Momma!" Kane said in a stern voice. "The kids are looking in your mouth so don't start that. You know I wouldn't put Tony at risk like that. He works, I work and you know we do a little gambling, we won the jewelry last night and a nice piece of money."

"That's what he told me," Anna said looking at him skeptical.

"He gave me $1000 too!"

"I guess that means you don't need the little $50 I was gonna give you," he said and started laughing.

Anna went to a lamp stand, opened a drawer, took out some incense, lit them and spread them out around the room. She got a bag of weed and tossed it to Kane and said, "Tony gave me that too." She tossed him some papers and said, "Roll us up a few joints."

"Dang momma, Tony just a regular Santa Claus ain't he?" Kane said laughing.

"It's about time," Anna said. "Much as he comes around here borrowing money and never paying it back."

"Yeah momma," Kane said laughing. "He does the same thing to me."

He rolled 3 fat joints, put 2 in his pocket and gave Anna one. He rolled another one lit it then said, "Les, get us some beer."

She left the room and went into the kitchen. She came back with 3 buds and passed them to Anna and Kane and kept one for herself.

Kane and Anna smoked the joints as they sat and talked. Kane asked about his sisters Jeanette the oldest at 29 and Regina the baby at 28. Leslie went into her purse, pulled out more of the jewelry boxes and gave them to Anna.

"Give these to them from us because you might see them before we do. They haven't been by in 3 or 4 days nor have they called."

"I ain't seen them heifers in a week or so myself," Anna said.

Jeanette was married to a man named Charles McBride. He was a medium level dope dealer and they had two children. Charles Jr., who was 13 years old and called C.J. And Sienna, who was 12.

Regina was following in her footsteps living with Charles' partner Stephen Davis and they had two children. Stephen Jr. called Stevie who was 12, and Lashay who was 11.

Tony and Lucinda had two children, Tony Jr. or T.J who was 13 and Tricia who was 12.

Kane didn't particularly care for either of his brother in laws but he had never really sat down and talked with them. They were good to his sisters and took good care of them and the kids. Kane tolerated them and they were both a little leery of him because they like most everyone else thought he was a bit crazy, because he was a gunslinger of the first order. They were tight with Tony though, so Kane figured they were pretty cool.

"Momma, are you alright? Do you need anything?" He asked after they smoked a joint.

"No, not really," she said. "But I do want you and the boys to come over here this weekend and cut my yard."

"Momma, why don't you get a good yard man to keep your yard up? I'll pay for it."

"I don't want a stranger walking all around my house," she said. "Besides Sampson ain't gonna go for it either and this is his home too. I ain't gonna be chaining him up. What surprises me is that he ain't bit one of y'all children. I can't believe it because he don't let Tony, Jen, Gina or their children play with him. That's the only time I chain him up."

"Sampson knows if he bites me or one of mine I'll kill him," Kane said seriously. "We got that kind of understanding."

"Boy you crazy," Anna said laughing. "By the way, have you heard from your daddy lately?"

"Yeah he writes and calls," Kane said. "Les, talks to him more than I do but I try to talk to him at least once a week. Sometime I miss him when I'm not there."

"Well he calls me all the time," Anna said. "I asked him why he doesn't call his wife Teresa. He told me he's trying to find her to serve her divorce papers, but he can't get in touch with her."

Kane and the others didn't know that Anna visited his father at least once a month without fail. Anna and Kane's father Bishop were divorced in 1983. A year before Bishop was arrested for conspiracy, continuing criminal enterprise, and several murders. They hit him with the Rico Act for running a drug ring. The government took businesses that had been in the Kane family for nearly 60 years. Businesses that were started by Bishops grandfather Raven Kane and passed on to his father Baron, then down to Bishop. The Kane's had been major players in the underworld in Jacksonville since the 1920's, from bootlegging to drugs.

Bishop was sentenced to 40 years and the Kane Empire was destroyed and left in shambles. Kane was in prison when the fall came. Tony was swept up in the net and sent to federal prison but had gotten out in 89 after serving 5 years. Bishop was still there.

Kane knew that regardless to how Anna acted. She still loved Bishop. They had been together since they were teens and had married when he was 18 and she was 16. Kane was born a year later. Kane was their oldest child and something of a momma's boy though people in the street didn't know it. He got his sensitive side from his mother and his ruthlessness was a Kane family trait. His great grandfather Raven had given birth to the town of Ogilvey in South Florida and burned it to the ground after his parents were killed in a land grab scheme. His father and grandfather were in the mold of Raven and death and destruction had followed them doggedly throughout the years. Bishop had a hell of an influence on Kane and Kane had felt he could never live up to Bishop Standards. They were often at odds when Kane grew up, but he loved his father deeply and Bishop loved him too. It's just that they never knew how to show the love so they maintained a strong, masculine, yet strained bond.

"Momma we going to Pizza Hut, you wanna go?" He asked.

"You know I don't eat that mess," Anna said. "If you would've said Red Lobster I would've beat all of y'all getting in the car. Y'all go on and have a good time."

Leslie called the kids and they came running.

"I want y'all to go wash your hand and faces," Kane said.

They raced to the bathroom as Leslie, Kane, and Anna walked outside. They talked until the children came back. They all hugged and kissed their grandmother then piled into the car. Leslie hugged and kissed Anna then got behind the wheel. Kane held Anna in his arms and she said, "Don't forget to come do the yard for me this weekend. I told Tony too, so one of y'all should show up."

"I'll come Sunday morning and bring Leslie and the kids. I'll call everybody else, bring Doreen too and after we finish we can have a cook out. If you hear from my daddy before I do tell him everybody gonna be here Sunday and to call then."

"Alright baby," Anna said. "Y'all have a good time."

Kane kissed her then opened the gate. Leslie backed out. He closed the gate, waved and got in the car.

*   *   *   *

After they had left Pizza Hut where Leslie and Kane had drank a pitcher of beer, they made it home about 10:30. They sent the kids to get a bath and get ready for bed. She laid out their sleeping clothes and then they sat on the porch drinking beer.

"You ought to be feeling pretty good all of that beer you drank," he said smiling.

"Yeah I'm tight," she said smiling.

He pulled a joint from his pocket, lit it and took a couple of deep drags and passed it to her. "It's been a while since we smoked a joint together."

"Yeah it has," she said. "But you smoke this shit every day. I'll be a weed head fucking with you."

They laughed as she took a couple of tokes, coughed and said, "This is some pretty good shit. Do you remember when we were in school and used to smoke weed and drink all the time?"

"Yeah!" He said remembering. "Those were the good old days. We used to have some fun back then. It seemed like everything was fresh and new."

"I didn't really like weed back then," she said smiling. "I use to smoke it just to be down with you. I had never smoked until we started kicking it."

"Bullshit," he said.

"I'm serious," she said in reply. I pretended I had been smoking but I was square as fuck back then. I learned how to be hip from watching you."

She started laughing and passed the joint back to him. They smoked the joint and watched the moon and stars.

"Les you know I really love you don't you?" He asked.

"Yeah baby I know that," she said smiling.

"I realize I haven't been the perfect husband or father," he said sadly. "But I do the best I can."

"I know that honey," she said soothingly. "I often wish that certain things would change or were a bit different. Like I said, I wish you would stay out the street and be more of a homebody, but I also know that would make you feel trapped. It would probably hurt us more than it would help us. You're a free spirit; you're kind of wild, unpredictable and spontaneous. All of that shit is what attracted me to you in the first place. You liked to have fun and you seemed so carefree. I was from a strict household, stuck up and green to the ways of the world. You changed that; helped open my eyes to situations and circumstances I never would've considered. I know I wasn't the prettiest girl, the finest, or flyest girl in school back then but you made me feel like I was. You changed the way I dressed by buying me outfits and things you wanted to see me in, and it wasn't that slutty shit either. It was tasteful, quality, expensive shit that my parents couldn't afford. Then I was the flyest bitch in school."

They both burst out laughing.

"Momma and daddy swore we were fuckin and put me on birth control before you even busted my cherry."

"You were tight with the pussy," he said laughing. "It took me months to get it!"

She laughed and said, "You right about that but I knew you were fucking Wanda, Tracy, Michelle, and 2 or 3 other ho's. I didn't care because they weren't getting any money or being picked up and dropped off to school. I was ignorant about sex back then. I knew what it was and had my episodes of kissing and feeling and shit but I didn't let anybody fuck me until you came along. What I'm trying to say is this. Regardless to if you're the perfect husband or rather I love you with all of my heart. Even though I wish some things would change I wouldn't change you for the world!"

He reached over, grabbed her hand, brought it to his mouth and kissed it gently.

"Come on let's go check on the kids," she said taking his hand and rising from her seat.

They went inside and he locked the front door. The kids had all bathed and were in bed asleep. B.K. and Anika had rooms of their own, Jamal and Damon shared a room. He walked through the house and made sure it was secure. Then he walked in the room where Leslie was undressing, and she was standing there in matching panties and bra. As he undressed she got their robes, handed him his, slipped hers on and picked up their dirty clothes and headed to the bathroom. She cleaned up the children's mess, went to the other bathroom and cleaned up there too then returned to their bathroom.

He walked in as she was removing her robe. He unhooked her bra and helped her pull it off. She removed her panties and threw them in the hamper. He removed his robe and watched her as she bent in the tub and turned on the taps, adjusted the water to her liking then looked behind her. He saw her ass spread when she bent over and it seemed her cunt poked out from between her thighs, fat, puffy, and inviting. He felt himself getting erect and he walked up behind her. His hard penis slid between her thighs, not penetrating but sliding over her cunt and lightly grazing her clit. He gripped her ass cheeks, squeezed and caressed them. He pumped his hips and his penis slid back and forth between her legs. She reached down and pressed his penis to her cunt tighter and swung her ass back to him. They did this for a few minutes then she pulled away from him. She rose up and turned to him. He took her into his arms and kissed her, their tongues swirled and probed, her breast pressed tightly against his chest, his stiff cock pressed against her stomach and pubic area. She broke the embrace, turned and got in the tub. He followed and from long practice and familiarity of each other likes, gave each other an erotic bath. Cleaning, stroking, caressing, and massaging they slowly stroked the flame of their passion. Teasing each other with promises of later delights and priming for the climax. They left the tub, dried each other, put on their robes and holding hands walked into the bedroom.

They had made love passionately and patiently, and then lay there basking in the afterglow. He got up, went to the bathroom and returned with a small basin filled with soapy water and a washcloth. He came to where she lay, spread her legs and gently cleaned her vagina, anus, and inner thighs. He then wiped her body tenderly as if she were a baby.

She watched him the entire time thinking, "He's so thoughtless, he doesn't even realize those days and nights like these when I can see to the heart of him are what makes the not so good days seem worth it."

He took the basin to the bathroom, cleaned himself and got in bed, covered and pulled her into his arms. "I love you baby," he said sincerely.

"I love you too!" she said and snuggled deeper into his arms and fell asleep.

He lay there awake staring at the ceiling thinking, "What the fuck am I doing taking all of these crazy chances when I got all of this at home?" With that thought in mind he drifted off to sleep.

*　　　　*　　　　*　　　　*

He got up the next morning at 6:00 a.m. and dressed as if he was going to work. By 6:45 he was out of the house. He drove to the Jiffy Mart a couple of blocks away from his house and called in sick, then called Emma.

She picked up on the first ring, "Hello".

"Good morning love," he said. "Did you sleep well?"

"Hell no!" She said with laughter in her voice. "I lay in bed playing with my coochie and I couldn't seem to put the fire out. I hope you can do something with it."

He laughed and said, "I'm on my way but you got to give me the directions."

"You'll catch hell trying to find my house so I'll meet you at the Shell Station on Phillips and Emerson. How long will it take you to get there?"

"No more than 15 minutes," he said. "I can see 95 South from here so I'll be there with bells on."

"Come on baby," she said impatiently. "See you then."

He got to the Shell Station and saw Emma's red Cadillac at the phone bank. She blew her horn when she saw him pull in, then pulled off. He followed her down Phillips Highway until she made a left then a number of twist and turns until she pulled up in the driveway of a nice small home. She got out and he saw she was dressed in her house coat and slippers. She went inside as he parked. As soon as he walked thru the door and closed it she was in his arms. She kissed him passionately then led him to the bedroom. Quickly she removed her housecoat and he saw she was naked underneath it. She got in the bed, spread her legs and started fingering her cunt as he undressed.

They lay in the bed on their sides his penis still buried deep in her. "Baby I ain't gonna lie," she said. "I ain't ever had it like this. I'm 50 years old and been fuckin for 34 years, and have never been made love to this good before. I know you got limits on your time but I sure hope you got room for me on your schedule. I was already crazy bout your young ass but now you really got me fucked up. I have never had any children and I'm my parent's only child. All of them are long dead now and I regret I didn't meet you sooner. You are the one nigga I done met that I would have a child from but we're too late for that now. I've got extended family members, cousins and shit like that. We straight but I ain't really got nobody in my life that I can say honestly and truly loves me for me. I'm used to being alone but after yesterday I don't think I can go on living that way or at least living without you!"

"Baby check this out," he said seriously. "When you answered my question yesterday I dismissed all of my preconceived notions and opened my heart to you right then. I love you for you right now and I'm gonna make time for us to share, I'm not just gonna come to fuck. We're gonna do things and go places too. I told you plenty of men would love to sport you on their arm but now they won't get the chance because you're on my team."

"Does that mean we're a couple?" She asked.

"Yeah, a couple of freaks." he said.

She laughed and asked, "Do you have a problem with public displays of affection?"

"Of course not as long as it's not contrived," he said. "If I had a problem with it do you think I would've kissed you in the parking lot yesterday?"

"Yeah but wasn't nobody around," she said. "So you don't mind if when we're on the job I give you little kisses or hug you in the break room and shit like that?"

"Baby if the mood strikes you to kiss me hug me, or even if you wanna make love in the break room in front of everybody I'm alright with it," he said. "But you ain't got to stake no claim or mark your territory. Everybody gonna know what time it is watch and see. They probably assume we're doing just what we're doing now. Wait until tomorrow and see what happens."

"Alright, I'll do that," she said. "I can still feel you hard in me."

"It's a long way from over baby," he said.

"My goodness! Can you do it like this all the time?" She asked.

"You be the judge and ask yourself that question next week," he said.

"Regardless to how I look and act I'm still 50 years old."

"What do you mean by that?" He asked puzzled.

"You're still hard and I've cum at least four times," she said. "You got to let me catch my breath. I haven't eaten breakfast or anything."

"Why did you miss breakfast?" He asked. "You knew I was coming over."

"I was so excited I couldn't eat," she said smiling. "But after that work out you just put on me, I could eat a horse."

"Tell you what. You go hook up a little something to eat cause you're gonna need your strength," he said laughing. "I'll eat with you since all I had was an egg sandwich and some orange juice. I got to run out to my car for a minute I'll be right back. You don't need to put on any clothes I wanna see you naked all day."

She giggled like a school girl and said, "I hate to get up and take it out because it feels so good in me."

"You don't have to," he said and started pumping into her deep and slow.

She wiggled her ass back to him and moaned, "Baby... no please... not yet..."

He pulled her to him tighter and continued to thrust deeply into her and said, "I'm just getting her ready."

"Damn that feels good..." she moaned. "Please don't..." She swung her ass back to him, he stopped but she continued to throw her ass back to him.

"Look at you," he said. "I thought you wanted to stop!"

"I...do... I do... she moaned. "Baby I'm so greedy... It feels too good... to stop..."

He pulled out and she moaned, "No... no..." her ass still swinging back. He slapped a stinging open hand blow to her ass cheek and she yelled, "Oww!"

"Go on and cook," he said firmly. "The faster you get through and we eat the faster we can get back in the bed."

She got up and went to the bathroom as he grabbed his keys put on her housecoat and slippers then went to his car. He opened the trunk went in the tool box and got the boxes with the jewelry he had for her. When he walked into the kitchen wearing her housecoat and slippers she burst out laughing and said, "Peach is definitely not your color. We've got to do something about that. If you want, during one of our breaks we can drive down to the mall and get you a few things. If you're gonna be here regular you'll need hygiene items, a robe, and other things. You'll need a key and let me know the foods you like and I'll stock up on them for you."

"Good idea," he said. "But first I wanna give something to my favorite old lady."

"Who you calling old?" She asked and they both laughed.
He went in the pocket of the housecoat, pulled out the 3 boxes and gave them to her.

"What are those?" She asked surprised.

"Look and see."

She opened the smallest box and inside was a gold and diamond ring. She looked at him and he smiled. She opened the next box and a thick gold necklace was inside. She opened the last one and a matching thick gold bracelet came into view. Tears rolled down her cheeks as she said, "But we just hooked up, you didn't have to go and buy me expensive gifts. I don't have anything to give you!"

"You've already given me the most valuable gift you have," he said sincerely.

"What some pussy?" She asked.

"No, the key to your heart!" he said firmly with conviction.

She rushed into his arms and said, "I ain't never gonna take these off!"

"Let me put them on you," he said.

She gave him the jewelry and he put them on her and said, "Don't burn up my breakfast!"

She finished cooking and they ate in the nude. He put her on the table and ate her cunt until she came. They made love on the living room floor, then in the shower. They got dressed and drove to the mall and she got him all the things he would need and wouldn't let him pay for it. She drug him into a jewelry store and bought him a gold, diamond, and onyx pinky ring for $800. He balked at it but she made him swear he'd never take it off as she slid it on his left pinky. He swore, and then they went and got him a key made. When they got home she wrote a list of the foods he liked and they made love off and on until about 8:00 p.m. then he left.

*   *   *   *

At work things went just as he told her they would, everyone knew they were together and she couldn't stop gloating and showing off her jewelry. They ate lunch together every day and made out in the car, in the park, and at the job. After work he would stay with her from 3:30 until 9:30. They had 6 blissful days together and it seemed as if she had grown 20 years younger before her very eyes.

She told him on that fateful night that she was going to the 24 hours Albertson's to get a few things for him that she was in love with him. He told her they could go the next day together but she insisted. He went to check on Becky, took her home and made love to her then went home his self. When he got there Leslie was waiting up for him. She passed him a phone number and said, "Baby that's Jacksonville Memorial Hospital. A Dr. Sorenson said for you to call him immediately. He wouldn't tell me what it was about."

He took the number and made the call. Leslie stood beside him as he talked and saw the tears as they fell from his eyes. She put her hand on his shoulder and heard him say, "I'll be there in 30 minutes." He hung up the phone and she pulled him into her arms and said, "I'll go with you."

"It's alright honey," he said drying his tears. "I think I'd better do this alone."

"Alright, but if you need me just call."

"I will," he said and headed out the door. He got in the car, wiped his face and steeled himself for the task ahead. Emma had just been killed by a drunk driver who crashed into the driver's side of her car. He got to the hospital and asked for Dr. Sorenson and a tall grey headed black man came in.

"I'm Dr. Sorenson are you Mr. Kane?"

Kane nodded his head and said, "Yes sir."

Dr. Sorenson could see that he was torn apart by grief and struggling to maintain his composure. "Please come with me." He led Kane to a small room and said, "It's better if you sit." He held Kane's arm then sat beside him. "Mr. Kane I did all I could to save her but the internal damage was much too severe I'm truly sorry. I really am. She wanted you to know you made her the happiest woman in the world. Her last words were telling Kane I love him. The police went through her purse that's how we got your number. She made you beneficiary on her insurance policy. You can get her purse and other personal effects.

"Where is her jewelry?" Kane asked.

Dr. Sorenson looked shocked and said in a stern voice, "She still has it on Mr. Kane."

Kane was unaware of the Doctor's tone or shift in attitude. "Doc tell them not to take it off," he said fingering the ring she had bought him. "Leave it on her and I'll clean it if I have to, but she never wanted to take it off after I put it on her. I need for it to stay where it is!"

Dr. Sorenson looked at the young man as tears rolled down his cheeks. When Kane had asked about the jewelry the doctor's first thought was that he wanted it for personal gain but now he saw that the young man had integrity.

"I wanna see her," he said. "I wanna know who has the best funeral parlor in town. I don't care what it cost and you can send me the bill for your services. I'll make sure they get paid."

"I'm pretty sure you will," the doctor said looking at him.

"Can I see her Doc?" Kane asked.

"Sure," Dr. Sorenson said. "Come this way," and he led him to the morgue.

She lay on a table with a sheet pulled over her. The doctor led him over and gently lifted the sheet.

Kane looked at her, bent and tenderly kissed her cold lips and said, "We could've gone together tomorrow baby." The tears flowed freely from his eyes. "I love you baby and I won't ever forget you. I promise!" He kissed her again, looked at her and saw that she looked just like she did when she was asleep. There were no marks on her face. "What happened to the driver of the other car?"

"He's in critical condition," the doctor said. "More than likely he'll survive."

"Not tonight he won't," Kane thought to himself. "Can I see the reports? If there are any papers to sign I'll sign them."

The doctor got all of the necessary forms and Kane took them. He signed all of the papers looked at the reports and got the drivers name. He got her personal effects, shook the doctor's hand and left. He sat in the parking lot for an hour and watched the hospital. He knew the man's name and room number. He went in his trunk and got a new needle then opened the hood of his car. He opened his battery and filled the needle with acid. He went back into the hospital and crept in the man's room. He checked the charts, found his man and injected the acid into his I.V. and hurried from the room. As he got on the elevator he heard ringing at the nurse's station and saw the nurse jump up and run to the man's room calling for help.

*   *   *   *

Emma was laid to rest beautifully. No thick makeup, her hair done to perfection. She lay in a beautiful peach casket with beige silk lining. She wore a beautiful peach silk dress and the jewelry he had given her. All of the workers at the plant attended her funeral. He was the only family represented because her blood relatives never showed up. They were angry that she had made him her sole beneficiary and had left him all of her worldly goods. She had $43,000 in the bank, her home which was valued at $75,000, a $100,000 insurance policy, and $25,000 from her credit union account.

He used $50,000 of her insurance policy to have her funeral, pay off all of her bills and to have a big headstone with her picture in it placed at the head of her grave.

He put the money in his and Leslie's account. Leslie saw how much was in there and asked about it. He told her that his friend that died didn't have any family so she made him her beneficiary.

Leslie told him they needed $25,000 to pay off their house and he told her to go ahead and pay the house off.

*   *   *   *

A week after Emma's funeral and nearly 3 weeks after they had pulled the caper on Jermaine's dope house Kane and Becky were in the hole serving dope. They had been at it for a week. He would get off work go home take a bath then hit the hood.

Tony and Becky had been hanging out getting high and cooking up some of the powder Tony had but they were serving too. Tony had been keeping money lately and Becky had been staying out of the street and getting a little money also. She was giving him 4 or 5 hundred dollars every day and had moved in with his grandmother. She still paid the rent for the room but Kane kind of liked the arrangement because Becky was showing she was down for the cause. She was holding the drugs and serving but she gave him the money. She was enjoying being a little queen pen but she treated all of the baser with respect and if they were short she still served them. A lot of dudes that served in the area caught beef but they didn't get out of line because they knew Kane wasn't to be fucked with. She was good to the basers so when she was on the set they would all come to her and spend their money. She got high and knew what she would spend her money on, so she kept the rocks big.

Kane had told her not to go in the hole without him or Tony that way they could watch her back. Kane saw a bulge in her pocket but didn't think much of it. As it grew late Tony came through and hung with them. Becky hadn't been smoking that day but Tony had made 5 cigarettes with crack in them before he came out. He had them in a Marlboro box.

"You want a brew bro?" Tony asked Kane.

"Hell yeah I want one if you buying," Kane said laughing

Tony laughed, "That's cold bro." He walked across the street to the bootlegger's house and bought a 12 pack of bud and gave Kane and Becky one.

"Bet that up dog," Becky said giving Tony some dap.

Tony sat the other beers on the curb. Kane watched how they interacted and the thought flashed in his mind, "I wonder if they're fucking." He quickly dismissed it because he didn't believe they'd do it like that. He had been sort of out of it since Emma's death, suffering from brief bouts of insecurity and doubt.

Becky caught the look in his eyes and knew that he hadn't been himself lately. She punched him in the arm and said, "Nigga don't trip."

"What's up?" Tony asked.

"It ain't nothing," Becky said not wanting to bring the matter into the open.

"Big bro I got some joints in the ride, blunts to be exact," Tony said. "You want some?"

"Hell yeah Santa Claus," Kane said laughing as Tony stepped to the car to get the blunts.

"I know what you were thinking about me and Tony," she said. "But it ain't even like that. He's the only one of your family members besides Granny that I get to be like family with. Believe it or not nigga I love you. When we first hooked up I told you I might see somebody I wanted to fuck and didn't need that jealousy shit. But since we hooked up I don't need another nigga you're way more than I thought you were. You satisfy me completely, and haven't you noticed that I don't go out in the street no more? I haven't had to since we been together. You keep me straight you give me money, dope, and plenty of good loving. So what I need to go out and sell pussy for if we're not hurting?"

"I see your point baby," he said. "But it wasn't jealousy that I felt. If you wanna know the truth, I don't know what it was. It did cross my mind that y'all were fuckin'. No big deal and no need to make a big issue out of it alright?"

"I think I'm cool with that," she said. "Now come here and give me a kiss!"

He pulled her into his arms and kissed her as Tony walked up.

"Hell naw!" Tony screamed. "Ain't none of that love shit going down on this corner tonight?" He laughed as they broke their embrace and passed Kane 3 fat blunts.

"Ain't none of that shit in these is it?" He asked Tony.

"Nigga don't try me," Tony said playfully. "You know damn well I wouldn't try to sneak you crack because I might have to whoop your ass."

"I'm sure you'd try," Kane said seriously. "But we ain't fought since we were kids and I use to whoop your ass then."

"Yeah you did that," Tony admitted. "But I ain't the same little Tony, nigga I'm 6'3 and 220 pounds. You a lightweight at best to me, what 185 or 190 pounds, if it had to go down I'd drag you dog."

"You just might," Kane said. "But Anna would bury your big ass before long!"

"Damn bro, I was just kicking it with your serious ass," Tony said hurt by Kane's words.

"Yeah I was too," Kane said.

"Yeah right," Tony said and laughed nervously. "They laced with soft, I wouldn't try you bro."

"That's cool," Kane said and lit one up.

Tony pulled out the Marlboro pack and pulled out 2 of the crack laced cigarettes and gave Becky one. She took it and fired it up. She was standing there sort of shocked by the exchange between the brothers. She knew Tony was joking but just like Tony she knew Kane was dead serious when he told Tony in so many words that he would kill him. "Damn that nigga is cold," she thought to herself. Tony fired up and they stood there smoking in silence

"Tee, pass me another brew," Kane said.

Tony grabbed a beer and handed it to him. When he got close to Kane, Kane grabbed the beer with one hand and Tony's wrist with the other. He pulled Tony into his arms and kissed him lightly on the lips. "I love you Tee don't ever forget that bro. I love you." He released Tony and the tension that was in the air evaporated.

Tony sniffed and wiped at his eyes. "Damn! Smoke done got in my eyes."

Becky was looking at Kane with tears rolling down her face. She asked herself, "Damn how many sides does this nigga have? That was the tenderness, most emotional act I've ever seen between two men?"

"You got smoke in your eyes too?" Kane asked her then started laughing. She punched him and he asked, "What's up with the spousal abuse?" She punched him again and laughed.

He pulled her into his arms and felt the bulge in her pocket. "What's that in your pocket?" He had felt and saw it earlier but got caught up and forgot it momentarily.

"What're you talking about?" She asked puzzled.

He pulled her to him and patted her pocket and asked, "What's that?" Of course he knew what it was because he had touched it.

"Oh that!" She said and pulled it out.

He looked at Tony who said quickly, "She asked for it dog so I gave it to her."

Kane grabbed it, looked at it and saw that it was the .25 automatic from the robbery. "Did you teach her how to use it Tee?"

"Naw I didn't," Tony said honestly. "I didn't think too."

Kane pulled Becky close and said, "Watch this." He used his thumb to eject the clip and saw that it was loaded. He gave her the clip and said, "Hold this." She took it and watched him intensely as he pulled the slide back. A shell jumped out and Tony caught it. He held his hand out for the shell and Tony gave it to him. He asked Becky for the clip. "Tee did you load this?"

"Naw bro it's just like it was when I got it," Tony said.

Kane wiped the clip down and held it with his tee shirt. He wiped the shell then put it back in the clip and put the clip back in the gun. "See the small lever here?" He asked Becky and showed her.

"Yeah I see it," she answered.

"That's the safety," Kane said. "When it's up like it is now the safety is on. The gun won't shoot, watch." He tried to pull the trigger. He gave her the gun and said, "Go ahead try to shoot it."

She tried to pull the trigger.

"Now use your thumb and push it down."

She pushed the safety down.

"Go ahead, pull the trigger."

She tried to pull the trigger and there was a click as the hammer snapped down but there was not an explosion since a round wasn't chambered.

"Put the safety on."

She thumbed the safety up.

"Take the clip out."

She thumbed the button and the clip came free.

"Rack the slide."

She racked the slide and a shell jumped out. He caught it and gave it to her. She grabbed the bottom of his tee shirt, wiped the shell and slid it back into the gun, racked the slide, checked the safety, pushed it back up then put the gun back in her pocket.

"Why did you do that?" Kane asked.

"I figured if I do all that, the next time I take the safety off and pull the trigger the gun will shoot," she answered.

"Yes it will," he said. "So be careful with it."

"Oh I will," she said smiling proudly.

"If you gonna give her a gun at least show her how the shit works. What if she had to use it? It ain't any good if you can't shoot it bro."

"You right," Tony said. "But I just thought everybody knew about guns and shit. Hell Beck from the streets bro."

"I can dig it," Kane said. "But from here on-in, assume that everyone doesn't alright?"

"Alright bro.," Tony said. "You ain't mad because I gave it to her are you?"

"Naw I ain't mad," Kane said. "Why should I be? I would've given her one but I never thought about it like that. I looked at it like I'm her pistol and she don't need another one. I was wrong so good looking out!"

They stood on the corner serving and getting high. Kane noticed a car load of men drive by slowly. "Tee, is you strapped?"

"Yeah, what's up?" Tony said.

"Listen up!" Kane said. "Here are my keys, go in the trunk and get the sawed off pump out of the tool box and get a 9mm too while you're at it. Hurry up!"

Tony ran to Kane's car popped the trunk, grabbed the shot gun and the 9mm then ran to his car and got his 9mm. He ran back to where Kane and Becky stood.

"What's up baby?" She asked. "You think them niggas gonna try us?"

"Yeah I do," he said and noticed she had the little pistol out with the safety off. "Put that little shit up," he said smiling.

"I got your back baby," she said sincerely.

"I know you do," he said and reached to his waist and pulled the 9mm out that he had there, and gave it to her. "This one works just like the other one you got. All you got to do is take the safety off and it's ready to shoot. Don't try to aim it, do just like you would with your finger, point it at what you wanna shoot and pull the trigger. Keep both eyes open got me?"

"I got it," She said and pushed the safety down.

Tony gave Kane the shotgun and he thumbed the safety off and held it down tight beside his right leg.

"Beck go get in the car!" Tony said.

"Hell naw!" She said firmly. "I'm staying right here!"

"Make her get in the car Kane!" Tony said forcefully.

"She's cool," Kane said calmly. "I gave her my nine. But listen; I kind of felt like something fishy was going on cause all them niggas that are usually out her serving this time of night are gone. It's just 12:00 and we're the only ones with dope? Come on y'all, I believe them pussy niggas done set us up! Ain't no need in running, and if Beck goes to the car they might back off and try to catch us again. Next time we might be slipping, but we up on it tonight so let's get it over with. See that car?" He motioned with his head so they would pay attention. "Don't stare, don't stare!"

The car drove slowly down the block.

"They can't creep us," Kane said. "Ain't but one way they can come at us and that's straight up this street. This is what we're gonna do. See they gonna pass by us again slow and try to lull us into thinking they ain't up to nothing. Then they gonna come back again expecting us to think they're gonna just cruise by. When they're 25 or 30 feet away they're gonna punch the gas and try to catch us off guard and jump out on us. As soon as y'all hear them punch the gas wait until they slam on brakes and throw open their doors. That's when we got their asses. We gonna open fire soon as the doors open so y'all be ready!"

"How do you know they're gonna do it like that baby?" She asked.

"I know that's how they're gonna do it cause if they wanted to shoot us they would've did that the first time and jetted. So I know they gonna try to rob us," he said. "Y'all just be ready! Put the gun behind your leg like this." He showed her how and she did it.

Tony crossed his arms over his chest and hid the two pistols under his arms. Kane held the shotgun to his leg, put a blunt in his mouth then lit it. He took a couple of deep tokes and held it to Tony's lips. Tony took a couple of hits and Kane pulled it down and passed it to Becky who hit it a few times then passed it back.

The car cruised by slowly on the opposite side of the street.

"Y'all get ready," Kane said. "I think it's about to go down!" He looked at Becky and asked, "You alright little momma?"

"I'm ready baby," she said confidently.

"You alright Tee?" He asked Tony.

"It's on bro." Tony said.

The car disappeared and then Kane saw headlights approaching slowly as the car got closer.

"Here they come!" Kane said excited.

They heard the driver punch the gas and the car swerved towards the curb. Kane, Tony, and Becky just stood their ground. When the car was eight or nine feet away the driver slammed on brakes and the car slid to a halt right in front of them. They could smell the burning rubber of the tires as the car doors were flung open in what seemed like slow motion. The men started to jump out as Kane brought the shot gun up to his waist. Becky swung the nine up and pointed at the man jumping from the backseat, and Tony brought his two pistols into play. They all started firing at the same time.

The man who jumped from the front passenger seat caught a point blank blast of double ought buck shots from Kane's shotgun. The force of the blast lifted him from his feet and threw him on the roof of the car, his chest shredded by the buckshot. Blood, bits of cloth, and pulverized flesh sprayed into the dark night like mist.

Becky's first shot caught the man jumping from the back passenger seat in the chest and punched him back into the car. He slumped forward and her second round hit him in the right eye and exited behind his ear blowing pinkish grey brain matter all over the upholstery. Her third shot ripped thru the side of his face and knocked him on his back inside the car. She kept firing inside the car and one of her round caught the man on the other side of the car in the stomach. He had placed his gun on the roof of the car to try and get off a shot when her bullet hit him.

Tony fired both guns at the same man Kane had shot. His aim was true but he was shooting a dead man. He turned his pistol on the driver who was frantically trying to throw the car in gear. Tony fired the pistols rapidly as one shot hit the man in the side of the head and his brains splattered onto the window. Then his head crashed into the window and it shattered hurling bloody glass in the street. Tony's next shot hit him in the neck and severed his artery and blood gushed forward from the wound. One round crashed into his shoulder and he finally found the gear he was looking for, but it was too little too late and his dead foot punched gas. The car burned rubber and slewed off to the left.

Kane had raised his shotgun and fired at the man leaning on the roof of the car. He was unaware that Becky had already hit the man when his shotgun blast blew the man's face apart. Bone splinters, brain, and blood showered the air when the man's face exploded. The car swerved away and crashed into a building on the other side of the street. Kane had stopped firing, Becky's pistol was empty and so was Tony's.

"Let's go," Kane said urgently. "Tee gave me those guns!" Tony gave him the pistols. "Tee meet me a Gina's house," Kane said. "Go straight there, don't go anywhere else. Don't go home! Go straight to Gina's house and keep your mouth shut alright?"

"Alright," Tony said and ran to his car.

Kane and Becky got in his car and fled the scene. He drove sedately down Riverside Ave. until he came to Friendship Park. He parked as close as he could get to the river and threw the pistols into the river as far as he could. He got in the car and drove to the Amoco Gas Station on Stockton, and they got out and went inside. He bought two packs of cigarettes and walked to the drink box. She was right behind him. "Listen to me baby," he said to her. "I'm gonna ask to use the bathroom, and when I come out you go in and wash your hands all the way to the elbows be sure to wash your gun hand good. While your hands are soapy use your nails and scratch the web of your hands good alright?" He showed her what he was talking about and she nodded her head. They got two sodas and walked back to the counter. He asked the clerk if he could use the restroom and the clerk passed him the key. He washed his hands good, dried them and walked out. Becky went in the restroom and did as he instructed her then came out. They walked outside, got in the car and drove off.

*   *   *   *

Detectives John Samuels and Evan Drummond pulled up to the crime scene, got out their car and walked over to the patrol sergeant. "What you got for us Serge?" Samuels asked.

It appears that you guys got a quadruple homicide on your hand," the sergeant said. "Believe me it's not pretty. One of the Vic's is damn near missing his whole head plus the skin from most of his back, legs, and ass from where he was drug by the car. Another one has a softball size hole in his chest and various other gunshot wounds. I could go on telling you about the driver and the one in the backseat but you've got to see this for yourself."

"You got a read on this?" Samuels asked.

"The way I see it is like this," the Sergeant said. "The four Vic's were all armed, and you can see from the skid marks in the street that they were attempting to either whack or rob the perpetrators, and the perps were prepared. The hunters became the hunted. Instead of finding victims they became the victims and I don't think they even got a shot off. The sidewalk over there is littered with shell casings, 9mm and 12 gauge shells." He pointed to an area. "From the way the casings are dispersed I'd say there were three or four men firing, and they caught those guys well."

"Any witnesses?" Drummond asked.

"Not a one!" The sergeant said morosely. "You know this area. Somebody probably saw something, but whether they'll come forward or not that I can't answer."

"Thanks Serge," Samuels said. He and Drummond walked to where the car was and looked at the bodies. Then walked back to the sidewalk where the shell casings were and look around. There was all kind of trash in the area and they knew they'd have to bag it all, and hope the shell casings had prints.

"What do you think?" Drummond asked Samuels.

"I think Serge got it right," Samuels said. "They were looking for sheep and fucked around and got wolves instead!" I got a gut feeling that this is gonna be a tough one. I can feel it in my bones!"

"I got the same feeling about this," Drummond said. "Let's just hope that there are no retaliatory strikes or we'll have bodies all over the city!"

"You got that right," Samuels said. "Let's do the footwork.

*　　　　*　　　　*　　　　*

Tony's car was parked in Gina's driveway when Kane got there. Him and Becky got out of the car and walked to the door, and he rang the doorbell. Steve came to the door, saw Kane and Becky and asked, "What's up y'all having a family reunion?"

Stephen Davis, called Steve, was a light skinned man with hazel colored eyes. He and Kane were about the same size in height and weight. Kane and Becky came inside and he introduced her to Steve. "Steve this is Becky, Becky this is Steve my brother in law."

"What's up girl?" Steve said. "I already know her name dog."

"Yeah I know him vaguely," Becky said. "I didn't know he was your brother in law. I know his partner Charles too!"

Tony was sitting on the sofa watching the news and Gina was curled up in the love seat smoking a joint.

Regina Kane stood about 5'1 and wore 125 pounds. When you saw Anna you knew what Regina would look like in 20 years. She had the same cocoa brown skin complexion and same build. Her waist was slimmer and she was an inch taller, but that's it. She was called Gina. "What's up big bro?" She asked.

"I'm cool," Kane replied. "Let me hit that joint." She passed it to him and he introduced her to Becky, "Gina this is my baby Becky, Becky is my baby sister Gina."

"Hey girl!" Gina said smiling.

"I like your crib," Becky said as Kane sat next to Tony on the sofa. She sat next to Kane as he said to Tony, "Tee go in the bathroom and wash your hands."

He gave Tony the same instructions he gave Becky about washing his hands. Tony got up and went to the bathroom.

Gina watched all of this from the corner of her eye. She knew her brothers well and she knew something was up. "Big bro what's the deal? What's going on?"

"Girl what are you talking bout?" Kane asked innocently.

"Nigga I know you," she said. "And I can tell when something's up. It's damn near 2:00 in the morning and I just know this ain't a social visit, so what is it?"

"You don't even wanna know," he said. "Believe me when I say that. I wanna talk to Steve but you need to go in the bedroom or somewhere, because you don't need to hear what I'm bout to say."

Steve looked at Kane and asked, "What the fuck is this about?"

Tony coming from the bathroom said, "Chill out Steve It's cool. This ain't about you."

"Oh alright," Steve said relieved. "I thought I had done something wrong."

"Naw dog it ain't like that," Kane said. "I wouldn't disrespect your house and unless it was something real serious I wouldn't have any beef. I'm your kids' uncle so there's blood between us and to me that's important. If you get in a tight and need me to have your back, gunplay or whatever just call me and I'm there!"

"Damn dog," Steve said. "I thought you didn't like me."

"I don't have a reason to dislike you," Kane said honestly. "Gina loves you and that counts for a whole lot in my book. We're brothers whether we like it or not. Cool?"

"I'm cool with that," Steve said smiling.

"Step off for a minute please and take Beck with you," Kane said to Gina.

Gina got up and said, "Come on girl let's let these men talk," and they left the room.

"Kane turned to Steve and asked, "Have you heard anything about them niggas in Brooklyn trying to set me up for a jack?"

"Naw dog," Steve said shaking his head. "If I would've heard some shit like that I would've told you. I heard Tony was making a little noise over there and had this little broad with him. I didn't know it was Becky but I haven't heard nothing bout a jack. The word was out that y'all were serving and I knew if Tony was doing something your hands were in it. Other than that I ain't heard anything. Tell you what, let's call Charles and get him over here and see what he's heard."

"That's a bet," Kane said.

Tony called Gina and her and Becky came back into the room. Steve made the call, then came and told Kane that in 30 minutes Charles would be there, but Jen was coming with him.

"In the meantime would y'all like a drink?" Steve asked.

"Yeah," Kane said. "I'll take a brew."

"Becky you wanna drink some wine with me?" Gina asked.

"That's cool," Becky answered with a smile.

"Get me a brew dog," Tony said as Gina and Steve went to the wet bar that sat in the corner of the living room.

Gina pulled out her stash of weed and passed it to Kane. "Roll us up a few."

Tony pulled out his cigarette pack and shook out one of the laced cigarettes.

"Nigga don't smoke that shit in here," Kane said.

"Damn man!" Tony said, "This ain't your house."

"Think about it Tee," Kane said. "You got time so step outside if you wanna burn, but don't do it in here alright?"

"You right bro," Tony said. "Beck, you coming outside with me?"

She looked at Kane to see what he'd say.

"Be you," Kane said. "Remember what I told you. If you're ashamed of what you do, don't do it!"

She and Tony walked outside.

"Bro, what's up with that little girl?" Gina asked. "Is she fucked up on that shit? I know Tony get high but is Becky a crack head?"

"You need to ask Becky not me," Kane said. "One thing I know for sure is that she's down for Kane! That young girl there got my back and that's gunplay or whatever. She done proved whose team she's on! So trust me when I say that, because if you knew how deep she was you'd be surprised. Shit, she surprised me. You know I'm not one who's quick to place his trust in anyone, but baby done stood up and I got mad love and respect for her."

"Damn big bro.," Gina said. "You act like she done saved your life or something."

"Yeah, or something," he said and lit a joint and passed two to Steve. Steve and Gina lit up just as Becky and Tony walked back in. Becky sat next to Kane and they smoked weed and drank.

The doorbell rang and Kane went to the door and peeped out. He saw Charles and Jen standing there and opened the door.

"What's up dog?" Charles asked, a question in his eyes.

"We gonna talk," Kane said taking Jen in his arms.

"What's up big bro?" Jen asked. "It's got to be something important."

"It's cool," Kane replied as they walked inside.

"Y'all having a set and just now called me?" Charles asked jokingly. "Hey little momma long time no see," he said to Becky.

"That's Kane girl, Becky," Gina said to Jen. "Becky that's our sister Jen and you know her no good ass husband Charles."

Charles Mcbride was a jet black man who had his head shaved bald. He wore 230 pounds and stood 6'3".

Jeanette Kane Mcbride had the same facial features as her mother and sister. She had the same body type except she was 5'5" and wore 135 pounds. She had nice full breast, a small trim waist, nice flaring hips, bows legs, and a fat round ass.

"What's up y'all?" Becky said.

"We're cool," They said.

"Give me a brew and a stick of that weed and I'll really be cool," Charles said laughing.

Kane gave him a joint and Steve passed him a beer.

"Fellows let's step outside for a minute," Kane said. "We got some business to discuss."

They stepped outside and Kane asked Charles, "Did you hear thru the vine that them niggas in Brooklyn were gonna set me up for a jack?"

"Naw dog," Charles said puzzled. "I ain't heard no shit like that. I heard Tony was serving with a young chick and that they were balling. But I done gave Tony enough to get on and he ain't done nothing but fuck it up. I figured if he was serving and making money you had something to do with it. Shit it don't take no rocket scientist to figure that out. I ain't heard nothing bout no jack though, because I would've put you up on it because we're family. What's the deal anyway? Do you need some help or what?"

"Naw I don't need no help like that," Kane said surprised at Charles' willingness to go to bat with him. "But I need you and Steve to keep your ears to the street for me. Me, Tee, and Becky got some business to take care of and we gonna be gone for bout a week. I'll call you every day to see what's up. If you hear any news say momma wanna know where she can reach you and I'll give you the number where we are. You go to a phone booth and call me. Got that?"

"We got you bro," Charles and Steve said.

"Alright," Kane said giving them dap. "Let's go back inside before them nosy ass women start peeping out the windows and shit."

They all laughed and went back inside. They sat drank and smoked, then a special bulletin flashed on the news.

Anchorman Flint Morris appeared. "There was a grisly quadruple homicide in the riverside area earlier tonight. The murders happened in an area known for drug activities. No suspects have been apprehended and the police suspect this is the beginning of a turf war between rival drug gangs. The four victims were brutally murdered. They were all young black males; the names are being withheld until families are notified. The victims were all armed but apparently were gunned down without firing a shot. This is Flint Morris reporting for Channel 4 eyewitness news."

The two couples looked at Kane, Becky, and Tony.

"Don't even ask!" Kane said with authority. "This is what I need you two to do for me," he said pointing at Jen and Gina. "Go to Granny's house and go in my room, look in the closet on the top shelf and get the grey metal box. There's a big black tote bag in the closet on the floor, you can't miss it, bring them both back here for me."

The two women nodded as Kane passed them his keys. "I'd appreciate if y'all would look in the middle drawer of the dresser with the big mirror on it and bring me my life savings," Becky said. "They're in my panty drawer rolled up in a thick pair of sweat socks."

"Alright girl," Jen said. "We got it." They got up and left the others sitting in the front room silent.

"Kane I don't even know how to ask you this," Charles said.

Kane cut him off, "Don't ask bro, trust me. The less you know the better for all of us, let's just chill until they get back. I need to gather my thoughts."

"I can respect that dog," Charles said.

They sat thinking, each contemplating what the next day would bring. 45 minutes later Gina and Jen returned, "Man what you got in this tote bag this shit heavy?" Jen said setting it down at Kane's feet.

"The tools of my trade," Kane said smiling as Gina gave him the metal lock box and his keys. "Tee go get the tool box out of my car," he said tossing Tony the keys.

"Here you go girl," Jen said giving Becky the rolled up socks.

"How much money you got in there?" Kane asked her.

"9,576," she said. "I had four grand before we hooked up that I had been saving for a minute. I'm a lot of things but stupid I'm not. I was saving it to get an apartment but I wanted to make sure when I did I could afford to furnish it like I wanted to. But, it seems like we might need it now. Here you go baby." She gave Kane the money.

He gave it to Jen and said, "Keep that for her." He opened the lock box as Tony walked in with the tool box and a shoe box under his arm. He had 1,000 rocks, 400 bags of powder cocaine, 150 bags of heroin the half key of cocaine and the package of loose heroin. "Y'all give me 6 grand for these 1,000 rocks, he said to Charles and Steve. "Give me 4 grand for these 400 sacks of girl. I don't know if y'all work boy or not but I got 150 sacks. I'm giving y'all 75 on the house and I'm gonna keep the other 75. This other stuff I want y'all to hold it for me. If you need to work it go on and work it. We'll settle up when I get back. Can y'all swing the 10 gees?"

"Yeah I can," Charles said. "Jen I need you to run to the house and get me 5 grand."

"Naw dog," Steve said. "I got it. You just pay me back tomorrow cool?"

"That's straight dog," Charles said.

Tony opened his shoe box and he had nearly 5 ounces of powder and 500 rocks, 200 sacks of powder cocaine and about 50 bags of heroin plus the loose heroin he had got.

"Give me that Tee," Kane said. He got 200 rocks, half of the powder and gave the rest to Charles. "Work that for him we'll square it all up when we get back."

Steve had left the room and came back with the $10,000. He gave it to Kane and said, "You know we're gonna triple our money off the shit you gave us?"

"Yeah," Kane said. "I meant for you too, y'all family so it ain't no sweat." He gave Tony $1,000, Becky $1,000, and counted out another $1,000 for himself. He had kept the shoebox and half of the loose powder cocaine. He put the rocks, heroin, powder and the $7,000 in the shoebox. "Get me a small brown bag," he said to Gina who got up and walked to the kitchen.

She came back with the small bag and he took the money out of the shoebox, put it in the bag and passed it to Becky. "You're our official treasurer." He unzipped the tote bag, unlocked the tool box and started pulling out guns. He gave Tony a 9mm and an extra clip. He got a 9mm and an extra clip. He took out two .380's and two extra clips and gave one to Becky. He took all of his other guns from the tote bag and locked them in the big tool box.

"Baby I still got this," Becky said showing him the .25 automatic. "Give it to Tee," he said smiling. "Steve hold this down for me," he said handing him the tool box. Charles take my car and park it in your garage. I need to borrow your ride cool?"

"Yeah bro," Charles said, "It's straight I'll get a rental till you get back."

"I'll pay for it," Kane said, "so keep your receipts."

"Don't sweat that man," Charles said. "It's all gravy."

"Gina I need you to call Les and Lucinda in the morning and tell them Tee and I got into a little something and we got to lay low for a minute. Be sure to let them know we're not hurt or nothing. Tell her I'll call Doreen in a couple of days, and get her to three way her so we can talk. Can you handle that?"

"Yeah," she said, "But what about momma?"

"Tell her the same thing," he said.

"Y'all gonna be alright bro? She asked concerned. "I know y'all had something to do with them killings."

"He looked in her eyes and said, "We're alright now Gina. We're not the one's dead.

CHAPTER 6

Kane, Tony, and Becky left in Charles' car. He looked over at Becky and asked, "Wanna go get Chell and take her with us to keep Tee company?"

"Yeah we can do that," she answered.

Tony in the back seat cut in, "Naw don't do that," he said. "How bout we go get Sherrie, you think she'll be down?"

"I haven't seen her in longer than a month," Becky said. "I know she with it that's my dog, but I can't find her and her folks don't even know where she is."

"Where does she hang out at?" Kane asked.

"Usually the same spots I use to," Becky said. "Let's ride over on Park and Forrest."

As soon as they got there the first person they spotted was Sherrie standing on the corner talking to a guy. Kane blew the horn. Becky let down her window, stuck her head out and called her, "Sherrie! Sherrie! Come here girl! Hurry up!"

Sherrie looked over, saw Becky in Charles' car and thought to herself, "What's up with this? Charles and Kane are brother in laws and I heard she done hooked up with Kane. One thing I do know is I ain't about to get caught up in no bullshit." But being nosey she walked to the car. The windows had a light tint so she couldn't see inside.

Sherrie Thomas was a redbone, short, bowlegged about 5'3" and 135 pounds. She resembled Vanessa Williams, grey eyes and all. She had big, firm breast, a trim waist, wide hips, and a big, round ass. She was stripper fine and knew it. She had on a pair of white and red Nike running shoes, red daisy dukes with her ass cheeks hanging out of the back and a tight red and white top. Her hair was done in fat dookey braids that hung almost to the center of her back. She leaned in the window to talk to Becky and saw that it was Kane behind the wheel. She saw his brother in the back seat. "What's up dirty bitch?" She said to Becky smiling. "Hey Kane, Tee." She looked at Becky and said, "Break bread bitch. I heard you been rolling."

"Ho where you been?" Becky asked. "I been looking for your ass a month and half and ain't nobody know where you were."

"Bitch I was in jail," Sherrie said. "I caught a bullshit trespassing charge and the motherfuckers gave me 60 days. I got out 12:01 last night."

"No wonder a bitch couldn't find you," Becky said. "You could've left word with somebody ho!"

"I didn't wanna hear my momma shit so I lay down and wore it girl." Sherrie said.

"I just hope y'all ain't planning on talking till the sun come up," Kane said.

"Sherrie we going on a vacation you wanna ride and keep Tee company?" Becky asked. "We gonna be gone for a week or so."

"Hell yeah I wanna go," Sherrie said excited. "Just take me to pack some clothes and it's on!"

"You ain't got to pack nothing," Kane said. "Just jump in. We gonna buy you all new shit!"

"Bet that up," Sherrie said and got in the back seat with Tony.

Kane pulled off and hit 95 North and Becky asked, "Where we going daddy?"

"New York City," he said smiling.

"I ain't ever been to New York," Sherrie said. "Are we gonna take pictures and shit?"

"If that's what you wanna do Red, we can take some pictures and shit," Tony said smiling.

Sherrie smoked rocks too but like Tony she only smoked it in weed or cigarettes. That made her feel like she wasn't a baser. She was a part time whore as well. She didn't have any children and she still lived at home with her mother. She was only 22 years old but wise in the ways of the world. She was a product of the street and a stone cold survivor.

Tony was in the back seat making some cigarettes. She was helping and had seen the dope in the shoebox. Her first thought was, "These niggas running dope to New York. I better pull this nigga Tony because I just might've hit lotto in this spot. I know he digs me because he done tried to get with me a few times. We done smoked out together but he was on that romance shit and I was fucked up financially so that was the last thing on my mind. I always thought the nigga was handsome and fine. Him and Kane both, but I wasn't looking for a man and if I had to choose between him and Kane I damn sure would've chose Kane, because that nigga a stone thug. My girl got him so I ain't gonna push up on him. Besides Becky a crazy little bitch and I ain't looking for any trouble." All of that went through her mind as she helped Tony fix the cigarettes.

"Y'all missed out on all the action," Sherrie said from the back seat. "The rollers been out in force tonight. Some niggas got smoked in the hole. I don't know the whole story but a car load of niggas rolled up to rob somebody and whoever it was, was waiting on they ass. I went round that way cause word on the street was Becky was on that end serving. When I got round there it was so many police I thought they was having a convention. You know a bunch of nosey ass niggas was piled up round there, but wasn't no talking going on. I thought that was strange because niggas got an opinion bout everything. I dipped and ran into Chell who threw me a little something then I hit the block. I ain't made a dime since I got out of jail shit so hot."

Kane had told Becky and Tony not to discuss the murders with anyone else and never if anyone was present, so they just rode and made small talk. Kane had taken Gina's weed which was about an ounce and a half and put it in the shoebox.

"Sherrie you know how to roll joints?" Kane asked.

"Yeah," She replied.

"Get that weed out the box and roll me about five," Kane said. "Lace them for me. Not too heavy so they keep on going out, and not with rock use the powder."

"I got you," Sherrie said reaching for the shoebox that sat on the seat between her and Tony.

"Daddy I would've rolled them shits for you," Becky said.

"Naw hell you wouldn't," he said laughing. "You can't roll worth shit, and Tee won't take his time and roll it right. That's why I didn't ask you or him to roll them. Sherrie when you roll the first one pass it to me. If you don't roll it right you can hold up on the other four and I'll roll them myself."

"Boy I got you," Sherrie said. "Don't worry here's the first one. Tell me how you like it."

Becky grabbed it, put it in his mouth and pressed in the car lighter. She got it and held it to the joint. He hit it and it pulled easy, not too tight. "You got a job red, Kane said. "You're my personal roller for this trip."

Sherrie laughed and rolled the rest of them and gave them to Becky. Becky put them in the ash tray.

Tony passed Becky a crack laced cigarette and she turned it down. "I'm gonna smoke with Kane," she said as he passed her the joint. "Red, look in the cooler and pass me two brews."

Sherrie reached in the cooler and took out four beers. She gave Tony one and passed two to Becky. Tony passed her a cigarette and lit it for her then fired up his. They snuggled up in the Cadillac's plush upholstery and Tony started rapping to her.

"So you done finally came to your senses and see how beneficial it can be to be on the same team with the Kane brothers, huh?" Tony said laughing.

"Tee me and you been alright," Sherrie said. "But I knew you were a dedicated family man even though you be in the streets. I didn't even wanna get romantically involved with a man that already got a family. I ain't into settling down and shit because I'm still young, and you know how I kick my game. I don't need no nigga beating on me and telling me how to live. I like to have fun and I like the finer things in life. When you hook up with most cats it's usually a bunch of emotional bullshit and I just ain't ready for that. Don't get me wrong I'm not saying you like them other niggas, but I was going through some shit and I had to get my head screwed on straight. So it wasn't like I dissed you."

"Naw you didn't do that," he said. "You did give me the time and conversation. You weren't acting all uppity and shit. We got together and I didn't pressure you on the sex tip cause I know what you're about and I damn sure didn't wanna come off like a trick. I believe I could've stepped to you with some bread and bought some of the pussy but I wasn't about to play myself like that."

"If you would've stepped with some cash you probably could've got some," she said. "But I wouldn't have looked at you the same if you had. I would've seen you as a Vic from that point on."

"Yeah I know," he said. "That's why I didn't step like that."

"So what we gonna do, hook up?" She asked. "I see that Beck done hooked up with Kane and word is she ain't been on the stroll, but she stay fresh, keep her some bread and get high," she said. "They tell me she been coming up. So tell me Tee, what bitch in my position wouldn't want a set up like that?"

"I feel you girl," he said smiling. "But you know I'm just small time. I don't roll like Kane but he put me on. I'm not all that tight with managing my bread and Kane keep his shit tight!"

"Nigga if you do me like Kane does Becky I'll manage your bread for you. I'll keep your house tight and me and you tight. I'll stand on the set and serve or whatever cause if we gonna be down, then I'm gonna be down for us. I'm telling you off the top that you can't be half stepping cause I'm a high, I mean high maintenance bitch. I like pretty clothes, painted toes, to smell like a rose, and you know how the rest goes."

He burst out laughing and said, "You a rapper too!"

She laughed and said, "Nigga please."

They had been riding for several hours and the sun was rising. They were all tired and the coke was all that kept them up. They were deep into Georgia so Kane pulled off at the exit for Savannah and looked for a hotel. He saw a sign for Motel 6 and pulled in. He turned and looked at Sherrie, "You got I.D.?" He asked.

She nodded. "Yeah I got some."

He gave her $100 and said, "Get us two rooms, try to make sure there adjoining."

"Alright," she said, as she grabbed her purse and went in. She came back with two keys. "The rooms were $40 each and I had to leave

$10 security deposit for the keys. Checkout time is 12:00 noon tomorrow."
She gave him the change. They drove to the rooms and got out. Kane and
Becky went to one, Tony and Sherrie to the other. Tony had the shoebox
tucked under his arm. Kane unlatched the door that joined the rooms, Tony
unlatched the other.

"You want something out the box?" Tony asked Kane. "Naw I'm
straight," Kane said. "Don't be up all day smoking, get you some rest so we
can find a mall or something and go get us and the girls some gear."

"Alright bro," Tony said and closed the door.

Kane closed the door and looked at Becky sitting on the bed.
"Damn little momma. You look tired as fuck," he said.

"I am" she said. "It's been a long ass night and I just wanna lie
down and sleep for 10 days."

"I can dig that," he said walking over to her. "But let's shower
first alright?"

"Okay daddy," She said as he reached down and picked her up.
They undressed and she put their under wear in the sink and started washing
them. He jumped in the shower as she bent over in the sink washing their
things. He watched her ass jiggle and started getting erect.

"I ain't too tired to break off a piece of that," he said to himself and
started laughing.

She looked over her shoulder and asked, "What's so funny
daddy?" Then she saw his hard penis and said, "Hell naw! Nigga what you
doing looking at my ass, and jacking off?"

"I wouldn't waste this hard-on for that when I got the real deal," he
said laughing.

She laughed, rinsed their underwear, then hung them to dry and got
in the shower. He bathed her, and then they got in bed and made slow love.
Afterwards Kane called the desk and asked for a 3:00 wake up.

      *   *   *   *

When Tony closed the door he turned to Sherrie who was lying
across the foot of the bed. "Baby let's clean up because we got a long day
ahead of us."

They got in the shower and she washed their underwear and hung
them to dry. They got in the bed and she curled up in his arms and asked,
"So this is how it ends?"

"Naw Red," he said caressing her shoulder, "This is how it
begins." And kissed her lightly. "We got plenty of time for that other shit
so let's get some rest and see what Kane has in mind for us later."

"Alright," she said. "But let me ask you something. Your last name is Kane too but why don't they use your brother's name like they use yours; everybody calls him Kane. I've known y'all damn near all my life and I don't even know what his first name is."

"My momma calls him Boy, and my sisters call him big bro. I call him Kane like everybody else, always have. At times I call him boy, big bro or bro but mostly just Kane. I don't know why everybody uses his last name, never really cared. Most people don't know his first name unless they went to school with him, but his name is Berean. Believe this though, Kane is who he is! I mean that in the biblical sense. If you know the story of Cain and Abel, he's that cold. The nigga would kill me if I gave him reason to but he'll also kill about me. Now that you're on his team he'll kill for you, about you, and because of you. So remember that when you're dealing with him. He can be fun and easy going but there's a dark side to the nigga that scares me. He's intensely loyal and expects you to be the same way. When you got in the car tonight you became family and he's serious as fuck about family!"

*   *   *   *

The wakeup call came at 3:00 p.m. as expected and Kane woke up refreshed. He nudged Becky, "Wake up honey." She rolled over wiped her eyes, looked at Kane then stretched like a cat and smiled. They got in the shower then dressed.

"Here, take these $50 find a store and buy us all some toothbrushes and deodorant." He said.

She took the money and headed out the door. Kane opened the door that joined the rooms and stepped into Tony's room. There were two beds in the room but Tony and Sherrie were asleep in one. He walked over and saw that the lovers were down. He could see Sherrie's breast, luscious and large. The strawberry colored areola and nipples as large as the erasers on elementary school pencils; they were hard and thick. He shook Tony, "Wake up nigga."

Tony rolled over and looked up at his brother. "Nigga what time is it?"

Kane said, "3:25".

Sherrie hearing their voices woke up and made no attempt to cover her breast. Instead she stretched out arching them forward and they seemed to swell. She threw the covers off and got up, then said, "I got to pee."

When she rose Kane saw the fat mound of her vagina, the long lips peeking out between the gap in her legs. Her cunt was covered in nappy, bushy,

90

reddish brown hair. She walked to the bathroom twisting because she knew they were watching.

"Damn that bitch is fine." Kane said to himself.

"Sherrie finer than a motherfucker ain't she?" Tee asked him.

"Hell yeah!" Kane exclaimed.

They laughed and Tony got out of bed and headed to the bathroom. Kane heard the shower start and headed back to his room. He turned on the T.V. and watched the news. He heard a key in the door and Becky stepped in with a plastic bag in one hand and a big bag from McDonald's in the other.

"I went to a convenience store and a McDonald's was across the street so I bought us something to eat." She said. "I just know you got to be hungry!"

"What did you buy?" He asked taking the plastic bag from her.

"I bought some bacon cheese burgers, some fish sandwiches, some orange juice, and apple pies," she said smiling.

Tony and Sherry walked in the room. "Bro give me the keys so I can run to the store and get us some toothbrushes and shit," Tony said.

"Lazy ass nigga you a day late and a dollar short," Kane said laughing. "Beck done already took care of it and bought us something to eat," so y'all sit down and let's grub!"

Becky started passing out the food. "Tee do you eat Bacon?"

"Hell naw!" Tony said. "I'm a Kane and we don't eat no swine. Y'all bitches need to stop eating it too!"

"Nigga fuck you!" Beck said laughing. "I was raised on that shit and ain't but two problems with it. One, it doesn't get big as an elephant and two, they ain't figured out how to package the oink!"

Kane, Tony, and Sherrie burst out laughing.

"You a crazy bitch Beck," Tony said holding his side laughing.

"Your brother loves it!" Becky said. "So fuck that." They all laughed again.

After they finished eating Kane said, "Let's see if we can find a mall in this hick ass town!"

They drove around until they found a mall and shopped for several hours. They bought 3 outfits a piece, shoes, underwear, and cosmetics.

"Since we ain't got to check out until 12:00 tomorrow we might as well get our money's worth," Kane said. "I'm sure they got a club in town. We can hit it tonight, but in the meantime let's figure out where the brothers hang out and see what's up."

They found the black section and also where the club was. They parked the car and walked around. Kane saw who all of the big ballers were and a plan formed in his mind. He would run it by Tee and Becky later and

91

see if they were down. This was also a good opportunity to test Sherrie's heart and loyalty. They hung out for the rest of the day and had dinner in a soul food restaurant. They copped a sack of weed and a bag of powder just to test the waters. Kane talked to a few people and found out who the dudes getting the real money were and two men's name kept coming up, Silas and Fat Stan. They were supposed to be strong in the game and they would be in the club later. Kane started thinking of a way to whip one or both of them, and devised a plan. They went back to the motel to shower and dress then they gathered in Kane's room.

"Check this out," Kane said seriously. "We going to the club tonight to have fun but I want y'all to keep your eyes open cause I think we can handle some business in this town before we step."

Becky broke in, "What you mean Daddy?"

"Chill out little momma," he said. "Finish hearing me out then pop your questions okay?" She nodded and he continued. "If you noticed today when we were strolling through the hood I was talking to folks trying to get a feel for the spot. I found out who was balling and two niggas names came up in all the conversations, Silas and Fat Stan. They gonna be at the club tonight and I'm gonna holla at them and see if I can reel them in. The play ain't gonna be for tonight but for tomorrow in the morning if the shit works out. So y'all be on your toes and we might be able to blow this spot with some additional bread. Y'all down?"

"I'm in it to win it Daddy!" Becky said.

"You call it bro, and I'm down for it," Tony said.

"I'm game," Sherrie said. "What you want me to do? Slide under one of them niggas and pull him?"

Kane laughed and said, "Red, you rolling with us. If I need you to pull a Vic by using your female charms I'll send you out solo and shadow you so they wouldn't know we're together. We gonna play it like we got some ounces of dope to sell, hard and soft, and see which one bites. The one that wants to spend the most is the one we gonna get, cool?"

They all nodded. "Becky you and red run to the convenience store and buy a box of sandwich bags. Hurry back." He tossed Sherrie the keys. Kane looked at Tony and asked, "You up for this little bro?"

Tony nodded and Kane asked, "You ain't suffering from the shit that went down are you?"

"Naw bro I'm cool," Tony said. "It was us or them. How is Beck holding up?"

"Man that little girl cold as ice," Kane said. "When I put it to her like I did to you, she said when we find the niggas that sent them at us let her have them for a few minutes first!"

Tony started laughing then said, "You got a winner there."

"Sherrie seems like she down with the lick," Kane said. "So she got heart but we need to find out how she operates under pressure. Hopefully we can pull this off without gun play because we ain't got but two extra pieces, the .380 and the .25, and we don't need another murder on our hands."

"You're right about that," Tony said. "Being honest bro, that killing shit was a little too easy and I don't even wanna get used to it."

Kane lit a joint, took a few tokes and passed it. Tony grabbed it, hit it a few times and passed it back. By the time the women had got back they had smoked it.

Sherrie strutted thru the door with a 12 pack of bud clutched in her hand and said, "Y'all niggas done started without us? I ought to take my beer and drink it by myself."

She laughed and Becky said, "Bitch you crazy if you think my baby not gonna get one of those beers. So what you spent $10 and some change, I told you I'd pay for it."

Bitch please!" Sherrie said. "Y'all niggas better close your eyes because it's about to be a cat fight up in here!"

They all laughed and Kane tossed Sherrie a joint. She walked over and gave him a beer. "I believe baby gonna work out just fine," he said to himself.

"Daddy here are the bags you wanted," Becky said passing them to him.

"Tee go get the dope," Kane said.

Tony went and got the dope and brought it back to Kane. Kane got 2 sandwich bags, took the powder cocaine, Sherrie's I.D, and scooped about half an ounce and put it in one of the sandwich bags. He spread the powder out good then rolled the bag up. He got the rocks, took 40 out, got a knife from Becky who always kept one in her purse and cut each one of the fat rocks twice until he had 120 smaller rocks. He put them in the other sandwich bag and rolled it up too. He gave Becky the dope and she put it in her purse. They got in the car and drove to the club.

When they got to the club Kane said, "Red take these $10 go in the club and see if they're searching for weapons. Just pay, go in, turn right back around and let me know."

She got out of the car walked in the club and came right back. She leaned in the driver's side window and said, "They ain't searching at all." They went in the club found a table and ordered some drinks. The club was jumping and as they danced and drank they saw other people smoking so they fired up. Kane was busy surveying the scene. After they were there for a couple of hours he noticed a big commotion at the door. He looked over and saw a huge fat man come in the club with two other men and a group of women. He could see that the man was trying to lord it over the crowd. He had a lot of gold on his neck and rings on every finger including his thumbs. So Kane figured he had to be Fat Stan. It seemed everyone was trying to get his attention as he and his group moved to two tables in the corner.

A few minutes later another commotion started at the door. Kane looked up and a dapper dressed, medium sized man draped in jewelry stepped in with a woman on each arm. He walked over to where the fat man sat and yelled over the loud music, "What up Stan?" Then gave him some dap.

Stan yelled to the waitress that was hovering in the area, "Give Silas and his girls a drink. Put it on my tab!"

This confirmed that the men were who Kane assumed they were. Silas sat at a table close to Kane. Becky asked Kane to dance so they went to the dance floor. Tony and Sherrie were already dancing and most of the men in the club watched as she danced seductively.

When the song ended they sat down and Kane ordered more drinks. He pulled out a fat roll of bills and paid the waitress, plus he gave her a generous tip. He had been doing that all night. He fired up a joint and they smoked it. He had noticed Silas watching him so he played it cool, because everyone knew that they were new in town. He sent Silas and Stan a round of drinks. They looked over and he raised his glass to them.

Silas was the first to take the bait he walked over to the table and gave Kane some dap then said, "Thanks for the drinks." He pulled up a chair next to Kane. "What's up partner? Y'all ain't from round here."

"No we're from Florida," Kane said. "My name is Jeff. This is my brother John, his wife Sue, and my wife Dee Dee."

"I'm Silas, what brings y'all to these parts?"

"Well Silas to be honest I'm the front man for a group that is interested in engaging in business in your area," Kane said. "We're looking for parties interested in purchasing our product, which is all top quality if I might say. We're also trying to find potential partners who would like to join us in a joint venture, or who are prospective buyers of quantity."

"And just what product are you offering if I may ask?" Silas asked him.

"That depends on whether the market is soft or hard," Kane said.

"Oh I see," Silas said smiling. "Would you happen to have a sample of your product for both markets?"

"But of course," Kane said. "I also have an introductory sample for qualified buyers."

Silas raised his brows and said, "Perhaps we can step to the men's room and discuss this further?"

"Why sure," Kane said.

Silas got up, went to his table and said a few words to the women then walked to the restroom.

"Watch my back Tee," Kane said. "Beck give me the packages." She passed him the dope and he said. "Safety off little momma, watch fat boy and his crew," then he walked to the restroom.

When Kane walked thru the door Silas moved in front of it and leaned against it so no one else could enter. Kane pulled out the 2 packages, opened the powder and held it out to Silas. Silas wore an old school coke spoon on one of the many gold chains he had on his neck. He dipped it into the bag then brought it to his nose and snorted. He dipped it again and snorted then pinched his nostrils together and said, "Damn Jeff that seems like top quality you got?"

"I know y'all pay anywhere from 13 to 15 for an oz. but I got 5 of each for a grand a piece. Since you getting in on the ground floor you can be our representative on this end. You will deal with me or John, no one else; and if needed we can supply the muscle and arms for you to lock the spot down!"

"You're serious ain't you?" Silas asked.

"As cancer."

"I'm kind of tight on cash right now, but I can come up with it first thing in the morning."

"That's cool we can work something for that, but dig this. Meet me at the mall at 1:00 alright?" Silas nodded and Kane pulled out a $20 bill then asked Silas for a card or something and Silas gave him his license. Kane used it to scoop up a good pile of coke which he put in the $20 bill. He gave Silas his license back, folded the bill and passed it to him. "Does your dog the fat man get down?" Kane asked him.

Silas nodded and Kane pulled out a $1 bill and dumped some coke in it and folded it. It wasn't nearly as much as what he gave Silas. "Give this to him," Kane passed him the folded bill. "Dig this," Kane pulled out the bag of rocks and gave Silas 10. "Get somebody to test these for me and holla at me before you leave alright?"

"That's cool," Silas said smiling and giving Kane some dap.

"By the way," Kane said halting him. "When you come to the mall come solo or with one of your girls. I'll be with Sue because she stands out more than Dee Dee."

"You're right about that man," Silas said laughing and shaking his head. Silas stepped out of the restroom with Kane right on his heels. Silas walked over to the fat man and gave him the coke and nodded his head at Kane's table. Kane saw the exchange. Fat Stan raised his drink to Kane who nodded. Silas talked to several more people and Kane knew he was passing out the rocks because every time he left whoever he talked to they stepped out of the club. Silas waved at Kane then sat back with his ladies.

Kane looked around the table and said, "It's on for 1:00 at the mall. We got to find a spot close to the mall to hit the lick. We can't do it where he might scream and we need to silence him. He's expecting to see me and Red so Beck you and Tee gonna have to lay low in the backseat. I'm gonna cover y'all with a sheet or something. Red gonna give y'all the signal when to rise up with the pistols and throw down on the nigga."

Sherrie said, "Give me a gun since I'm gonna be right there with you. I can have mine out before Tee and Beck, and that will give them time to pull their shit."

Tony and Becky looked at Kane who said, "Red you're right, I got a piece for you in the car. Tee gonna teach you how to use it."

Silas came to the table and said, "Jeff let me holla at you a minute."

"It's cool, you can talk in front of them."

Silas pulled up a chair. "They like them stones and wanna buy some more, how much you got on you?"

"About 100," Kane said.

"Them 20's right?"

"Yeah, but I tell you what I'll do since we gonna be working together. Let's say I give you what I got both hard and soft. Give me a grand now and if you make some bread bring me 10 in the morning?"

"That's straight dog," Silas said grinning and mentally counting his money. 100 rocks at $20 a piece was 2 grand easy and he knew he could easily make a grand off of the powder just selling blow in the club, and still have damn near half of it left. He had about $600 in his pocket but he would sell the fat man some of the rocks and make up the difference. He smiled to himself as Kane passed him the dope under the table. "Give me a minute and I'll bring your bread back." He stepped to Fat Stan and said something in his ear. Stan pulled out a fat roll and gave him some cash. Silas walked off and pulled out his money and put Stan's with it then returned to Kane's table and gave him the money. And said, "Count that."

"For what? I trust you dog." Kane called the waitress over, "Here you go sweetheart," he said giving her $250. "Take this and give everyone in the place a drink on me. If there's change you keep it!"

"Damn," Silas said to himself, "these motherfuckers are real high rollers. Nigga done gave me enough dope to make at least 3 or 4 grand profit. I'm gonna be rolling in a minute." He smiled, gave Kane some dap and walked off.

Kane, Tee, Becky and Sherrie partied until the club closed at 2:30 went and got a bite to eat, and then got back to the motel at about 3:15.

"Listen up y'all," Kane said. "We got to be up and out of here by 9:00 a.m. so we can find a spot to sting this Vic. Let's get some rest and be ready because we're hitting the road out of here as soon as we hit the lick. We can get a room in the next state and get some real rest alright?"

They all nodded then Tony and Sherrie went to their room.

*   *   *   *

At 9:00 the next morning they were on their way out. "I got to make some calls," Kane said. "Becky, you and Sherrie go on to the ride and we'll be out in a few." Kane called Charles and everything was fine. He called Doreen and had her 3 way Leslie who 3 way Lucinda. He and Tony talked to them and assured them that they were fine and would be home in a few days. They told them to call their jobs and say they had a death in the family and had to leave town immediately. They said their I love you's then hung up. When they walked out of the motel, Becky in the passenger seat opened the glove compartment and popped the trunk. Kane threw the rest of their stuff in the trunk then he and Tony got in the backseat, and Sherrie pulled off.

"Did you get a chance to show Red how to use the piece?" He asked Tee.

"No," Tony said. "You told us to get some rest."

"I showed her Daddy,' Becky said. "While y'all were handling business."

"Pull over Red," Kane said and she pulled over and put the car in park. "Show me what Lil momma showed you."

Sherrie pulled the pistol from her purse dropped the clip, racked the slide and a shell jumped out. Becky caught the shell and passed it back. Sherrie wiped the shell put it back in the clip, wiped the clip put it back in the gun and racked the slide then pushed the safety up and put the gun back in her purse.

"That was good work Red," Kane said complimenting her. "Good looking out Lil momma you did a jam up job."

"Beck told me if I have to shoot do just like I would if I was pointing my finger. Just point at what I wanna shoot and pull the trigger."

"That's true," Kane said. "But remember this Red. I'll tell you when to shoot unless the situation calls for you to use your judgment. Got it?"

They rode around in the immediate vicinity of the mall looking for a spot to hit the lick. They found a spot that was perfect in a wooded area. Kane made sure Sherrie could drive there with no problem. They made the trip to and from the mall several times. It was a 10 minute drive, 30 minutes by foot. It was 11:45 and they drove to the mall and ate a quick lunch then Tony and Becky went to the car. They had parked in the back section of the mall. Kane and Sherrie stood in front of the mall and waited.

"You gonna be able to handle this baby girl?" Kane asked.

"I'm straight," She said. "Why didn't you ever try to get with me?"

"Red let me tell you something," he said seriously. "You too goddamn fine for me, plus you're smart; I can see that by the way you carry yourself. I've known you since you were a little girl and I knew you were gonna be a stunner. When you were old enough to freak I wanted to freak you but I felt like it would cause me too many problems. The difference between you and Beck is this. Beck don't have a whole lot of family down here and even though she's independent, smart, cute, and fine as fuck; I can control her better because she has few ties. It's different with you having all your folks here. I could more than likely whip you into my corner and I don't mean by beating you cause that ain't my style, but by romancing you. Besides, I'm not a joke between the sheets. It's like I said at first, you're just too goddamn fine for me. I wouldn't do shit but freak you, and once I put this dick, tongue, and fingers on you that's all you'd wanna do. You and I would go broke so trust me on that Red. Dig this; our conversation is between us because I don 't need Beck knowing I think you're finer than her."

They both laughed as a white Benz pulled up and Silas stuck his head out the window and said, "What's up dog?"

"I'm good," Kane said and Sherrie started walking to the back of the parking lot. That was the signal for Tony and Becky to duck down.

Kane got in the car with Silas who slowly drove behind Sherrie his eyes glued to her seductively swaying ass. "Dog your brother is a lucky motherfucker; He gets to sleep with that every night."

"Yeah he sure is," Kane said thinking the same thing.

Sherrie got behind the wheel and crunk up the car. "We can't conduct business right here," Kane said. "I got a spot that's perfect for us. There's privacy so we ain't got to worry about the law rolling up on us."

Silas wasn't worried about the cross because Kane had trusted him first with the powder. He had made nearly $2,000 off of that alone selling snorts in the club not to mention the $1,500 he made off of the rocks, and he still had some left over. He had only brought $8,000 with him and was hoping he could still get the 10 ounces. He had plans to run the whole town with the help of his new friend Jeff.

Kane reached over and blew Silas' horn and Sherrie pulled out as Silas followed. She drove straight to the spot and parked. Silas parked about 8 feet behind her and reached in his glove compartment and pulled out a fat roll of bills and said, "I couldn't come up with nothing but 8 grand this time of day. I'm working that package and got money owed to me. I could have the rest for you later today."

"It's cool dog," Kane said knowing Silas was trying to be slick. "Don't sweat it dog." Kane got out the car and Silas did too. "Red, safety off!" Kane called out and Sherrie got out of the car with the gun shielded beside her leg. As soon as she walked past the tail of the car she swung the pistol up pointing it at Silas' face.

"Oh shit," Silas said. "What the fuck is this?"

The back doors opened and Becky and Tony stepped out, their guns pointed at Silas. Kane never pulled his gun.

"Greed got you dog," Kane said. "Take this lesson to heart. It didn't cost you but 8 grand and it could've cost your life! The way I see it that's cheap; now take off the jewelry cause that's part of the price you pay also. Empty your pockets while you're at it because I just know you were trying to cheat me".

"Fuck you nigga," Silas said. "I ain't giving you shit else."

Kane looked at Sherrie and said, "This chump ass nigga was sweating you last night and today, but he don't want you to have his jewelry. Don't kill him but shoot his stupid ass!"

Without hesitation she pointed at his leg and pulled the trigger. The bullet struck him in the thigh and knocked him against the grill of his car. Blood was flowing from his leg as he crumbled to the ground screaming, "I'm shot... oh God I'm shot...!"

"Shut up silly ass nigga," Kane said. "You should be a dead man, now get that shit off your neck, wrist, and fingers like I asked you!"

"Alright man," Silas said and hurriedly removed his jewelry and handed it to Kane. He emptied his pockets and gave Kane the 2 grand he had held back.

Kane walked over to check his leg and saw that no bones were broken, no artery was hit and the bullet had went straight thru so they wouldn't have to ditch the gun. Kane ripped Silas' shirt and used it to wipe his prints out of the Benz then removed Silas' belt and tied it over the wound. He pushed the piece of shirt under the belt and pulled it tight then tied it off. "I'm gonna drop your keys a couple of blocks down the road. Remember what you learned here today. Should've paid attention to what your mother told you years ago, never take candy from a stranger!"

Kane and the others got in their car and drove off and hit 95 North with Tony behind the wheel.

CHAPTER 7

Tony drove on up I-95 until they came to a little scenic town called Beaufort in South Carolina. There, he pulled off the interstate and found a Best Western. Sherrie went in and got adjoining rooms and paid for 2 days. Once inside they opened the doors and gathered in Kane's room. Kane pulled out the $10,000 they had jacked Silas for and gave everybody $2,000 apiece. He took the remaining $2,000 and said, "This is for our traveling expenses; gas, hotels, meals, partying or whatever. Beck, you and Tee should have a grand over that. I want all of y'all to keep a grand on you at all times. That's in case of an emergency and we should get separated. If that should happen I want all of you to catch a bus and head back home. Beck, you and Tee go to granny's house and lay low, if red is with you take her too. But stay off the streets till we know what's up on that other thing. So far it's cool but what I said is only in case of an emergency."

"What are y'all running from?" Sherrie asked looking from one of them to the other. "I know it's something, but what I don't know. What's the deal?"

Tony and Becky looked at Kane who said, "Check this out Red. It ain't like we trying to keep you in the blind, but it's better that you don't know. All you need to know is that the shit is super serious and could mean life or death for us three. You ain't in it, so you don't need to know alright?"

"I can understand that dog," Sherrie said. "I just thought I could help."

"Red you done passed every test I put in front of you with flying colors," Kane said. "I know you're on the team and you got our trust. Believe me you're gonna have to stick your neck out for the cause sooner or later so be cool."

"Alright," she said smiling proudly at his complimenting and the knowledge that she had his trust. "But tell me this. Who the fuck are we supposed to be, Bonnie and Clyde or some shit?" She burst out laughing and they laughed with her.

Kane said, "Let's celebrate! It's still early so let's see if we can find a bar or something and have some fun."

They rode all over Beaufort but all they saw were places that catered to red necks. They stopped at a liquor store and bought 2 bottles of Hennessy and the mixers, a case of beer and some snacks. They stopped at a Wal-Mart and Becky bought a camera and 10 rolls of film. She looked at the others and said, "This supposed to be a vacation. We done put in some work, we got bread, so let's do it grand!"

"Tell them niggas again girl," Sherrie said laughing.

They picked up quite a few items. Sherrie bought an instamatic camera and 10 packs of film and said to Becky, "You can wait to get them pictures developed, and when you do order doubles so I can have some. But me, I'm a microwave bitch I want my shit right now. Damn all that waiting."

They all laughed and Becky said, "Bitch you crazy but I feel you." They went back to the hotel and stopped in the lounge and had a few drinks. Listened to the bullshit music and tripped for a few then took their purchases and headed for the rooms.

Kane had bought four big overnight bags. He gave Sherrie two and said, "Those for you and Tee's clothes. I see all of y'all were intent on buying bullshit and keeping your clothes in bags."

Tony looked at him with a sheepish grin on his face because he knew Kane was right. Kane has always been practical so he spent his money on sensible things. He would splurge on occasion but not all the time.

Tony had brought a boom box and some tapes. He plugged it in, put in a tape and said, "Now that's music," and started dancing around the room.

Becky went to the ice machine and came back with a bucket of ice. Sherrie and Kane were sitting on the bed rolling weed. She was lacing hers with rock and he laced his with powder. Becky started mixing drinks then passed them around. Tony was just dancing. He grabbed Becky around the waist and said, "Come on little momma let's dance."

They each held a drink in their hands as they danced. Kane had rolled a few joints and lit one and watched Tony and Becky dance. Sherrie had started loading cigarettes with rocks. She took a sip of her drink and glanced at Tony and Becky. Kane held the joint to her mouth and she took a deep toke blew it out then hit the joint again. Kane was looking at her because he didn't wanna burn her. Before he moved the joint from her mouth she flashed out her tongue and licked his fingers looking at Becky and Tony the entire time. After she pulled her tongue away she looked in his eyes and licked her luscious lips.

He said to her softly, "Cut it out freaky red bitch, you done forgot what I told you today?"

"Naw I ain't forgot," she said. "What do you think it does to a bitch like me when a nigga say he can tame her with his tongue, dick, and finger? Shit, my panties been wet all day thinking about it. I want you to know this one thing. I'm gonna do what you say, follow you to the ends of the earth if I have to. And no matter what happens between me and Tee, even though me and Beck tight. I'm gonna make you prove that shit you said if I have to do it at gun point, trust me on that baby!"

He looked in her eyes and knew that she was serious and he'd have to fuck her. He said, "You wouldn't need a gun Red but when the time comes Beck got to know because we keep it real like that. Who knows, she might even want to sit in on it."

Becky looked at them on the bed talking. She couldn't hear what they were saying, but from the looks on their faces she knew it was serious.

"What y'all over there whispering about?" She asked light heartedly.

"None of your business," Kane replied with a smile.

Becky and Tony kept dancing as Sherrie got her camera and put some film in it. She took a picture of Becky and Tony dancing, and one of Kane drinking Hennessy with a joint in his hand. Then she gave Kane the camera and said, "Take a picture of me but hold up a minute." She called Tony and Becky then said, "Y'all let me hold y'all guns."

Tony pulled his from his waist and gave it to her. Becky got hers from her purse and gave it to her. Sherrie had on a red blouse by Guess in blue and white, and matching daisy duke shorts with white and blue trim. She had on red and white Nike Air Max's. She pulled her blouse over her head and revealed her sheer bra, it was fire engine red and her fat nipples seemed to tent the thin material. "Let me hold your gun Kane," she said. He gave it to her. She put the two .380's in her waist and held a 9mm in each hand and said. "Beck light a joint and put it in my mouth." Becky did it and Sherrie spread her legs and squatted down on her haunches. She arched here hips forward, turned her feet outward and raised the 9's. She looked in Kane's eyes and said, "Take the picture now, take 2."

He looked in the camera, saw Sherrie squatted there and framed her then paused. "Damn look at how them shorts biting into her cunt, she might as well be naked," he thought, then took the pictures. She stood and the shorts were still riding in her cunt. She put the 9's on the dresser, pulled the .380's and put them in her waist at the back of her shorts. Picked up the 9's, turned her back to Kane, spread her legs, arched her back until her ass stuck out then held the 9's away from her body.

She looked over her shoulder and said, "Take 2 more."

When he framed her he saw her ass cheeks hanging from the bottom of her shorts. He took the first shot, and when he took the second she released a huge cloud of weed smoke that seemed to halo her head as she glanced over her shoulder. She turned and set down the 9's, pulled the .380's and put them on the dresser. Then picked up the 9's threw one of her feet on the dresser and pointed the pistols at Kane who took 2 more pictures. She sat on the bed bouncing and shaking the pictures in the hope that they would develop faster. She looked at the picture and smiled, then passed it to Kane.

"Damn this bitch looks good. These pictures are erotic as hell," he thought to himself as he looked at the rest of the pictures. He passed them to Tony who looked at them, then passed them to Becky who exclaimed.

"Damn Bitch! You look sexy as hell in these pictures. Daddy, take some of me."

Kane picked up the camera and Becky got the pistols and started posing as Kane flicked away. Becky said, "Red come take some pictures with me." Sherrie got 2 guns and joined her. Becky was wearing a sky blue outfit just like Sherries and when her blouse came off, she had on a sheer white, silk bra. Kane saw her nipples were rock hard and thought, "Little mamma getting turned on taking these pictures with Red." Sherries nipples were rock hard too as they posed for Kane and Tony. The photos took on a more erotic tone as the women put the guns down and lay in one of the beds, wrapped in each other's arms. Kane continued to take pictures as Sherrie scooted down and laid her head on Becky's stomach. She put her tongue in Becky's naval then slid down further and put her face in Becky's crotch. She moved into a 69 position and Kane kept taking pictures.

"Don't move," Kane said and moved to the other end of the bed and took a picture of Sherries ass poised above Becky's face. Becky placed her arms on Sherrie's ass cheeks and spread them. Kane took a picture then said, "Switch places, but stay in that position." They did and Sherrie spread Becky's ass cheeks wide and he took a picture. "Stay just like that," He said and moved to the other end of the bed. Tony sat on the other bed watching, so he couldn't get a good view. Becky's thighs hid Sherrie's head and when Kane got there to take the picture, Sherrie looked in his eyes, stuck out her tongue, and pressed it against Becky's clothed cunt. He saw Becky's ass cheeks tense up. Sherrie's tongue moved and he took the picture. He moved to the other end where Sherrie held her legs spread wide open and he swore he saw a wet spot where her cunt was. He took a few more pictures of them and watched them develop. "Damn these some fine chicks!" He thought to himself and passed the pictures around.

"Red, take some pictures of me and Kane," Becky said while taking off his shirt. Sherrie got the camera as Becky kneeled between his legs, unbuttoned his shorts, and reached in his pants. She didn't pull his penis out; she stood it up, then bent her head and put it in his lap. She released his prick, turned her head to the side and stuck her tongue into the waistband of his boxers. He was rock hard as the photo session had turned him on also.

"Damn that nigga got a big old fat dick," Sherrie said to herself as she looked at the big bulge in his shorts and took the photo. They posed in several erotic poses and Sherrie took more pictures. Sherrie and Tony took some and Tony took pictures of Kane with both of the women. After all the picture taking, they sat listening to the music and got high. They talked for a while, and Tony and Sherrie went to their room. Tony took the boom box and closed the adjoining door.

"Come on Daddy, let's take a quick shower," Becky said grabbing his hand, "I got a surprise for you!"

They showered and came back into the room. She grabbed a bag off the floor and went into the bathroom. She stayed there about 10 minutes then shouted, "Close your eyes and don't peek!"

"Alright," he shouted and closed his eyes tight.

She came into the room and stopped about 3 feet from where he sat on the foot of the bed. "You can open your eyes now," she said.

When he opened his eyes, she stood there as a vision of loveliness in a pearl white satin Teddy with matching G-string panties. "Damn little momma!" he exclaimed. "That looks so good on you, baby don't move, stay right there!" He got her camera and started taking pictures of her. "Pose for me baby," he said.

She assumed all types of erotic poses and he said, "Take it off baby, take it off slow."

She did, and he photographed every position. When she was naked he had her pose in positions he had seen in porno magazines; had her finger her cunt as he photographed her. She had him pose for her then she threw the camera down and got in the bed with him and they made passionate love.

*   *   *   *

When Tony and Sherrie got in the room she said, "Come on baby let's take a shower together cause it's bout time for you to get this pussy; I been waiting. I thought you was gonna get it the first night we slept naked together. I could feel your hard dick pressed against me and again last night you did the same thing. I know you think I'm sexy and fine and I hope you're not intimidated by me."

It was like she read his mind and he felt a little out of his league with her. There was a quality about her that let him know he could never control her and the one man he felt could, was his brother. He had seen the look I her eyes when she shot Silas and knew that underneath her beautiful exterior was a cruel ruthless streak that only a man with the same could control. But he answered her like he knew she expected him to. "Naw Red it ain't like that. I've wanted you for a long time and you know that. I just didn't wanna rush you and make you feel like you had to have sex with me to be down with us. See I wanted shit to be just right when I got the chance to make love to you and now I guess is the perfect time."

"I wouldn't give you any pussy out of obligation Tee," she said. "I'll give it to you because I want you to have it, and I'm use to fuckin almost every day. I been in jail for 45 days and all I did was play with it. You think you can handle this?"

"Yeah Red," he said smiling. "I can handle it."

"I know you don't eat any pork," she said. "But do you eat pussy?"

"That's my favorite meal," he said laughing.

"You ain't got no hang ups I need to know about do you?" She asked.

"Not that I know of." he said.

"That's good," she replied. "Let's do this." She took his hand and led him to the bathroom.

After an acrobatic bout of love making he rolled off of her and they lay there both of them breathing hard. "Damn baby you did a good job," she said. "Is it gonna be that good every time?"

"I damn sure hope so Red," he said but thinking to himself, "I believe I done met the one woman that's too much for me." He held her in his arms and drifted off to sleep.

She lay there staring at the ceiling thinking, "What have I gotten myself into, Tony is an excellent lover? I know I can train him and make him even better. He already done told me I can handle the finances so that base is covered. I won't have to wait on him to parcel out the bread to me. What is gonna happen when Kane finds out that me and Becky been getting our freak on? There are so many angles to this shit and to add insult to injury I got the hots for Kane too. He's a smart ass nigga and a natural leader too, so if this shit gonna work out in my favor it's gonna be because of him. I'd do anything for that nigga right now. If he told me to kill I'd step to the plate because I know he'd have my back. Tony's sweet, considerate, and kind; he's like Kane but softer and not as great a thinker but he has a truck load of potential. All I can do is ride this shit out, and see what happens.

Damn it's gonna be a trip but I can deal with it. I ain't no slow bitch but I know for sure that Kane ain't the type of nigga to scheme against because he always thinking. From what I observed the last few days he stays a few steps ahead. I can see that from the way he planned that jack in Georgia. The nigga swift and don't mind taking advice if you see another angle. Another thing to think about is what are they running from? Ain't none of them scary. Even Becky is dangerous, so it can't be that someone on the streets is looking for them. I believe in my heart that if that was the case Kane would take the fight to them and Tee and Beck would follow that nigga to hell and back if it came to that; shit I would too. They got to be dodging the law that's the only thing that makes sense from my point of view. Boy this shit deep as fuck." She lay there thinking and looked over at Tony. He was breathing evenly so she knew he was asleep. He looked so handsome and at peace. She got up went to the dresser got her purse and pulled out a pack of Newports and lit one. She sat on the dresser smoking, and looked at the adjoining door and saw light seeping thru around the edges. She looked to the bed where Tony slept then put the cigarette out and padded softly to the door. She eased their door open then pushed the other one open a little. She peeped around it and saw Kane standing there naked.

The lights in the room were out except for the lamps beside the beds. He held one hand in front of him and he was rocking back and forth in a slow steady motion, she couldn't quite see what he was doing so she opened the door wider and saw Becky sitting on the bed sucking his big penis. She was sucking and stroking it at the same time. "Damn," she said to herself. "He got a big, fat, long cock." She squatted on her heels and spread her legs. She watched Becky nibble at the head then open her mouth and suck it in. Her hand wandered down to her cunt and slowly she stroked her clitoris. She watched Becky's head bob back and forth as she was fingering her cunt with her free hand. Sherrie couldn't see it but she saw the motion and knew what Becky was doing. She pushed her finger deeper in her cunt and closed her eyes and imagined she was giving him head. She licked her lips and opened her eyes and saw that he was looking right at her.

He looked in her eyes and grabbed Becky's head with both hands and slid his cock deeper in her mouth. He pumped his hips back and forth and Becky released his cock and her hands went to his ass, and she pushed him forward trying to get more of him in her mouth. Sherrie stroked her cunt faster and noticed that he continued to watch her. She wanted to run in the room and snatch his prick from Becky's mouth and plunge it in her cunt. She saw him push Becky's head away and she saw the full length of rod, long and shiny with Becky's saliva.

Becky caught movement out of the corner of her eye and looked over and saw Sherrie squatting playing with her cunt. She didn't let on that she knew Sherrie was there but she said to herself, "I've noticed the attention Red been showing Kane. Did she tell him we were lovers?" She knew Sherrie wouldn't try to steal him but she would fuck him on the sly even though they were friends. She didn't think Kane would do it because he was loyal as fuck. "I've got to prevent any creeping because that destroys trust and I believe in Kane. I know he's strong but I also know he's a man, and Red is a motherfucker; I should know I'm freaking her. I think I got just the thing that will let Kane know me and her been fucking and give her the chance to fuck him so there won't be any static between the three of us. Yes I've got just the thing, but it will have to wait until this vacation is over." She smiled to herself and kneeled on the bed to give Sherrie a good view of him fucking her doggy style.

Sherrie watched Becky position herself on the bed and said to herself, "If I didn't know any better I'd swear she did that so I'd have a better view of the action." She continued to stroke her cunt as he dropped to his knees and buried his face between Becky's ass cheeks. Sherrie didn't know exactly what he was doing but it was working as Becky moaned, "Umm…. Umm Hmm…"

He stood and spread one of Becky's cheeks and Sherrie saw her vagina glistening and pink. He drove two fingers deep in Becky and slowly fingered her juicy hole. Sherrie watched as he increased his speed and she matched his pace drilling her fingers in her cunt. She shifted her position until she was sitting on the floor with her legs jacked up spread open wide. She bit her bottom lip to keep from moaning out loud as she heard Becky moan, "Yes… Oh yes baby…"

He pulled his fingers from Becky's dripping whole and gripped his rock hard penis. He rubbed it thru her slit then with one powerful thrust drove it in deep, looking in Sherrie's eyes the whole while. He drilled his prick into her with deep powerful thrust and Becky moaned, "Ohhh…Oh baby…Oh yes…UmmHmm…" Sherrie saw him wet his middle finger then plunge it in Becky's anus, and she slid a finger in hers. "Fuck me …Fuck me…" Becky moaned as he pistoned in and out of her swiftly. Sherrie plunged her fingers in her holes rapidly as Becky moaned out, "Faster baby… fuck me faster…" She saw him increase his speed and Becky moaned, "Oh yes…. oh baby…. harder…." Sherrie was amazed when he sped up even more and was slamming his penis in Becky at a blistering pace. His finger flying in and out of her anus as he drilled her cunt with machine like precision. Sherrie was close to the edge when she heard Becky scream, "Kane…! Oh baby… I'm cumin now…. Ohhhhh…I'm cumin….!"

He looked in Sherrie's eyes and said, "Cum for me baby."

Sherrie lost it and bit her lip to keep from screaming out because she knew he was talking to her.

He moaned, "I'm cumin…!" And exploded in Becky's tight cunt. He slowed his thrust and Becky moaned, "No more… Please stop… Daddy please stop… I can't take it… Please…!"

Sherrie lay there trembling and watched as he pulled his penis from Becky slowly. Amazingly she saw that it was still rock hard covered in their combined juices. "Goddamn that nigga has amazing stamina," she thought as he bent and kissed Becky's ass which was poking in the air. She watched as his penis began to drop. He looked at her and blew her a kiss as Becky turned and blew her one too. She didn't think Kane knew Becky knew she was there, and she didn't think Becky knew Kane knew she was there. She blew a kiss back and rose on shaky legs and eased their door closed, and then closed the one to their room. She went to the bathroom washed her face and hands and said to herself, "That nigga's a stallion. He needs more than one bitch cause he gonna fuck poor Becky to death. I know they didn't just start so that means they been at it for hours. Now I believe what he told me is true. I think I just saw the one nigga that could tame me and I can't wait to get that dick in me." She didn't feel any guilt as she got in bed with Tony, snuggled up in his arms and went to sleep.

Chapter 8

After spending a leisurely 2 days in Beaufort they hit I-95 North. Sherrie drove and they stopped along the way to take pictures. They had bought additional clothes but were saving most of the money to buy clothes in New York. The further north they went the colder it got. By this time the trip had taken on a festive air and everyone was more relaxed and easy going. They were no longer covered by a cloud of fear, because from the calls Kane made daily it seemed they weren't suspects in the murders. He made sure that he and Tony talked to their wives every day to ease their fears. He almost cut the trip short because he missed his wife and kids.

He didn't want to disappoint his new family because he knew that they depended on his leadership. Sherrie was proving to be very formidable as far as thinking was concerned and she continued to surprise Kane with her intellect. She was smart and caught on quick, and he found himself developing and affection for her that bordered on love. Even though he desired her sexually, if they never had sex he knew he'd love her.

Becky was really something special. She was still independent as ever but it seemed she looked more and more to Kane to make decisions for her, from what to wear to what to eat. She had even stopped eating pork to please him and she went out of her way to make him happy. Tony was Tony and that was the only way he could describe his brother. He knew Tony looked up to him but Tony was a hell of a dude in his own rights, he just wasn't as into the gunplay. He would if he felt it was necessary and Kane didn't want to get him involved in any more killing if he could help it. He knew Tony was down for the cause but he didn't want any of his people to get hurt. He knew there was more death in the future because until he found out who was responsible for setting them up he wouldn't feel safe. He wanted to be able to make sure his wife and kids were straight. He wanted Tony and his family to be straight and Becky and Sherrie too. He knew he'd have to make some major moves to get them some bread. He'd have to contact Tracy and Sonny and see if they had anything for him when they got home.

Sherrie was in the backseat with him and saw how he sat there lost in thought. "Why the serious look?" She asked nudging him with her elbows and breaking his train of thought. "You look like you're 100 miles from here."

"It's cool red," he said and flashed her a smile. "I was just thinking, no big deal."

"If you were thinking, it was a big deal," she said seriously. "I've been around you these last few days and I've seen a side of you that I never would've seen if I hadn't hooked up with y'all. One thing I know for sure is that if you're thinking it's about your family and when I say family I'm including us. I know you're concerned about our welfare and are plotting our next move. I want you to know that whatever you decide I'm down, no matter what. I never thought the day would come when I would want to dedicate myself to a nigga because, I done saw some dog ass niggas in my short life time. It helped me to a degree but by the same token it had an impact on how I thought of men. I placed them in four categories: squares, suckers, dogs, and chumps and you and Tony don't fit any of those categories. I guess some women would call y'all dogs because y'all fuck around on your wives but one thing I know about you is that no single woman will ever be enough for you. And if a bitch is lucky enough to have just a part of you she's fortunate; like me. I dig Tony a lot and I'm gonna be with him, but if I had the chance to be with you I'd drop him. I have to contain myself to keep my hands off of you. After seeing you and Becky the other night it's gotten worse but I'll control it. And even if you never make love to me I'm gonna love you anyway!"

"Red you must be reading my heart," he said. "Cause I'm developing a love for you too, but I wouldn't drop beck unless she made that choice. See I'm a nigga that likes to have his cake and eat it too!" Becky was driving, but every so often she would look into the rear view mirror. She couldn't hear them but again it looked serious. She caught his eyes in the mirror and he winked at her and blew her a kiss. Her face crinkled into a smile and she said to herself, "That's my nigga right there and Sherrie my girl. I don't have anything to worry about in that spot. What surprises me is that Tee can't see what's going on or maybe he doesn't care."

Tony was aware of the attraction and affection that had developed between Kane and Sherrie and was pleased. He knew she wasn't for him and it would make his releasing her easier. He wanted to see how Kane would handle the situation when it arose.

They hung out and took pictures. Kane and Tony took pictures together and separately so they could show them to their wives. Kane vowed that as soon as he got a little cushion he would take his wife and kids to Disney Land or somewhere.

They went to a motel then had dinner and chilled. They got back on I-95 North and rode to Richmond, Virginia where they stayed for a day.

They drove to Washington D.C. and kicked it in Chocolate City for two days. They shopped there because D.C. had some fly shit. Kane called home every day and they grew more comfortable as the days went by. They drove on and stopped in Newark, New Jersey and hung out for a day then went on to New York. Kane had bought a separate overnighter and it was gradually filling up cause when they stopped in Virginia he had started buying gifts for his wife and kids. Tony following his lead did the same thing.

They stayed in New York for three days and nights buying clothes and hitting the clubs then it was time to go back.

"Dig this," Kane said. "We done splurged and partied now it's time to get home, so what we're gonna do is drive straight thru. We gonna take turns driving so when you're not driving you better get some rest. It should take us 26 to 28 hours to get back home driving in shifts, so let's get some rest before we go."

They left New York at 9:00 in the morning and drove straight thru stopping only to eat and use the bath room.

"When we get back to town we're not letting people on the street know we're back," Kane said. "Tee we got to let our wives know but I got a plan for that figured out. Red we got to rent a car so you can go check the streets for us since don't nobody know you're rolling with us. You got to always check your back to make sure you're not being followed back to where we're crashing. If need be you're gonna be our scout, our eyes and ears in the street. Everything we need done you've have to do understand. Red, you got to use your judgment, we're depending on you."

When they got to Jacksonville city limits they drove on until they came to I-295 where they pulled off and drove to 103rd St. They pulled off and went to the Hospitality Inn. Sherrie rented the customary adjoining rooms and they went in and slept until the next day.

Kane called Charles and told him to rent him a low key 4 door sedan in black or navy blue and told him where to bring it. He told him it was cool to let Steve and is sisters know where they were, but no one else because they had company. He told him to get his stuff from Steve and bring it with him. Charles assured him he'd have it all in a couple of hours. They ate breakfast in the room then chilled for a few.

"Daddy we need to hit a Laundromat so I can clean our clothes," Becky said.

"Take the car and go ahead," Kane said. "Me and Tee gonna wait on Charles."

The women left and the men sat and talked about everything except what Tony really wanted to talk about which was Sherrie. He didn't know how to bring it to Kane so he just left it alone.

"Tee you know it's gonna be some bloodshed," Kane said. "Some bodies gonna hit the street and I really don't want you in it, Becky, or Sherrie either for that matter. If you wanna sit it out it's all good. I won't see you any different and I won't view it as a coward move. You know I know how you feel about gunplay and I want you to be safe. I wish there was another way we could do this but unless I end this threat we ain't never gone be safe. The shit could eventually bleed over and touch momma and the rest of the family so I go to stop it. You understand don't you?"

"Bro you one of the smartest dudes that I know and not just on plotting jacks but in almost every way," Tony said seriously. "And if you feel like the only way this shit is gonna end is for us to leave bodies in the streets; then I believe you and I'm in for the whole trip. Whatever goes down, whatever you do I'm gonna be by your side bro do or die. I'm all in!"

"I respect that Tee," Kane said touched with emotion. "I ain't gonna try to make you change your mind cause you're a Kane and I know from experience how stubborn y'all are."

He and Tony burst out laughing and there was a knock at the door. The brothers both grabbed their guns and silently approached the door. Kane peeped out and saw it was Charles and Steve and Kane let them in. They hugged him and Tony. Charles had a large tote bag slung over his shoulder and he set it down as Kane closed the door. He unzipped it and folded it back and Kane looked inside and saw it was loaded for war. Charles pulled out a sawed off pump shotgun and laughed. He laid it on the floor and pulled out an automatic shotgun that was also sawed off. He also removed an AK 47 with a folding stock, and a 32 round clip. He pulled out two .45 automatics looked at Kane and smiled, then pulled out two Glocks. He set them down and started pulling out boxes of shells for the guns.

"Damn Nigga!" Kane said. "You're ready to start a war?"

"They started it!" Charles said. "We're gonna finish it!"

Since the murders Kane had gained a lot of respect for Charles and Steve. He had never really given them a chance and here they were coming thru like brothers.

Kane looked at the men and said, "What have you heard since I've been gone?"

"Hold up a minute bro." Steve said. "I worked the stuff you left with me because we ran out. I made 18 grand but spent 3 on the guns plus there's more at the spot. We started to buy them with our bread but we knew you'd only pay us back, so we used your bread. Here is the other 15." Steve passed Kane a fat roll of money he pulled from his jacket. "We got ours off the top so we're straight! I been checking on shit and Charles been checking on shit, but all we got is talk we picked up from basers so it's not like the information is reliable. But, the root of the shit is supposed to be Big Moe. You know that nigga all them cat's from zone three works for, plus Ted was said to have his hand in it as well. You know him and Moe tight. They supposedly told all their workers and the basers not to be on the set from 12:00 til 1:00 that night those dudes got killed. If that's true then you know they got a big ass clique. It's gonna be hard to touch Ted and Moe but it can be done. It's on you Bro, don't be too proud cause if they're behind it you're gonna need our help. We rented a crib in Pickettville in the woods; 4 bedrooms, and 2 baths. We got a place on Riverside Ave. near Avondale but it's only 2 bedrooms and a bath, but it has a basement. The houses are both stocked up with food and drinks, sheets, and beds but not much in the way of furniture. It'll serve the purpose."

"Good Work!" Kane said proud of his brother in laws. "Y'all were dead right about the money but that's a done deal. When the girls get back I'll tell you what we're gonna do, that way I don't have to repeat myself."

"Bro you got anything in this motherfucker to drink?" Charles asked, and tossed Kane a fat bag of weed and some papers. "I paid for that, it's a welcome home present."

They all laughed and Steve said, "Cee, give me the keys so I can go to the bar and get something to drink."

Charles tossed him the keys and he headed to the door. "I'm gonna roll with you dog," Tony said and got up and followed Steve.

Kane rolled a joint, lit it and took a few hits then passed it to Charles.

Charles looked at him and said, "Dig this bro. I know you don't particularly like me and Steve, but like it or not we're family. You don't have to tell me if you had something to do with them four niggas getting killed, but I know you did. Don't get mad because I don't want the specifics; I know you're a killer Kane. In my heart I believe you're one of the most dangerous men I've ever met, but I do like you because I know where your heart is at. You probably feel like you do about me and Steve because you don't think there's a nigga born that is good enough for your sisters. You're being protective and waiting on us to fuck up so you can come to the rescue. You done categorized us as the typical niggas but it's cool because I feel the same way about my sister. But just like you have love for your wife, I love mine. Do I fuck around on Jen? Hell yeah I do, but it doesn't prevent me from taking care of business, home, and family first. All that other shit can wait. As for Steve, I know how that nigga feels about Gina. If I thought he'd pull some stupid shit I'd beat his ass and run him off myself. Trust me when I say you couldn't have a better nigga at your side; that's my dog. We straight bro, and we got your back. We ain't cowards by a long shot, we believe in live and let live. If you don't fuck with mine I won't fuck with yours and that's how I live. Now you in a position where you gonna need some help and I know you would have to tie

Tee down to keep him from going out with you. Steve and I done talked about this trying to see it from all angles. We don't exactly know what the deal is but we decided a few days after you left that we're going down with you. I love Anna like she my own momma and I'll be damned if I'm gonna see her bury another one of hers if I can help it. And bro, if you don't have more help than Tony and Lil momma, one or maybe all of y'all ain't gonna walk away from this. Even with our help the odds are in their favor but we got the element of surprise as our ally, at least for as long as it lasts. We just may be able to even the odds a bit before shit hits the fan!"

Kane looked at him with even greater respect. "Cee what you said rings true and the possibility exist that I used a brother's love for his sisters as a measuring stick in judging you and Steve. Believe me I never had a reason to dislike you so it's not like that. I just don't trust very easy and we never really got down together. Of course I've heard shit about you in the street. You've always dealt fairly with people and don't take any shit. You done been with Jen 13 or 14 years and she's never said anything bad about you. Steve done been with Gina damn near as long, and I got the same reports on him but I don't judge character on rumors be they fact or fiction and by me being me, I judged y'all too harshly. I talked to Steve that first night, did he tell you what I said?"

"Yeah he told me," Charles said.

"That's good," Kane replied. "That means I don't have to go over it again. Cee we gonna beat the odds cause we gonna plan this shit out first then we gonna make some lightning quick strikes against these niggas if they really the ones. If they're not then we gonna find out who is, but dig this Cee; we got a secret weapon against whoever they are!"

"Oh yeah?" Charles asked excited. "What is it?"

Kane looked in his eyes and said, "Sherrie."

Puzzled Charles looked at him and asked, "Fine ass redbone Sherrie?"

"The one and only," Kane said laughing.

"Where is she?" Charles said.

"Her and Beck went to the washing mat," Kane answered. "They should be back shortly; she went with us out of town." Kane told him about the jack in Georgia.

"No shit?" Charles exclaimed. "She blasted the nigga with no hesitation?"

"Hell Yeah," Kane replied. "Baby got big brass balls."

"Damn dog you sure know how to pick'em," Charles said smiling.

"Tee chose her," Kane said. "I don't think he knew she was down like that, but it worked out fine. Check this out." Kane reached into an

114

overnighter and pulled out Becky's photo album. The first pictures were the ones Sherrie took solo.

Charles looked at them and whistled. "Damn dog that red bitch fine as fuck." Then he flipped the page and came to the pictures of them together. "Oh my god!" He slammed the album shut without finishing and said, "Bro I started having unsure thoughts looking at them pictures," and laughed. "You know red is too much for Tee don't you?"

"Do I?" Kane asked puzzled, even though those were his same thoughts.

"Nigga if anybody, you know." Charles said. "I bet Tee done figured it out too."

They smoked another joint and Becky and Sherrie walked thru the door laughing.

"What's so damn funny?" He asked them.

"None of your business, nosey ass nigga!" Becky said and they burst out laughing again.

Kane sat there smiling shaking his head while Charles rolled on the bed clutching his side.

*   *   *   *

When Becky and Sherrie left for the laundry Becky said to herself, "Now is the time for me to talk to Red about Kane." They hadn't really had the chance to be alone in the last week so Becky decided she would take this time to address the issue. "Baby we need to talk," She said looking at Sherrie.

"Yeah I guess we do and I know what this is all about," Sherrie said.

"We been down since I got here," Becky said. "We each do our thing but we been there for each other and had each other's back. We've been friends as well as lovers, and because we both freaks it has served us well at times. But now we're coming to a critical point in and out of our relationship. This situation gonna make our relationship stronger or rip it apart. See, Kane is a nigga worth fighting for and you know me, I will fight but I don't want there to be a conflict between us for any reason. I'm already sharing him with his wife and I'll be damn if it doesn't seem like he more than enough for both of us. So what I'm saying is this. I don't wanna compete with you for him but I will if it comes to it. Sherrie I love that nigga and I never thought I could feel the way I do about him for any man, and this shit is new to me. But because you're my girl and I love you, I'll share him with you to keep you from going behind my back and doing some sneaky shit."

"Beck I feel you," Sherrie said. "But there wasn't gonna be no sneaky shit because Kane wouldn't go for it. He straight out told me that he wouldn't be with me behind your back. He told me that if we did it, it would be with your knowledge and approval because he wouldn't cross you. You right though, I was gonna try to fuck him on the sly but he chalked that. I'm gonna be honest with you, I want him and it's more than just a fuck thing. Being around the nigga and seeing all the different sides of him, seeing how much he cares about us and how he went out of his way to make sure we were alright. The way he accepted me and made me a part of his family made me feel comfortable; and the loyalty and trust he showed you when I damn near threw myself at him. A bunch of niggas would have been game to creep, but not Kane and that shit touched me. Then there's something animalistic about him, something wild and untamed that attracts me sexually. Just being around him gets me hot and after that episode that night; damn girl that fucked me up! You know he saw me there don't you?"

"No I didn't," Becky said. "He didn't mention it."

"He saw me before you did," Sherrie said. "I don't think he knows you saw me. Anyway, I love the nigga too. Even though I got a love for Tee it's different when it comes to Kane. It's not all sexual, it's deeper than that and I'd fight for the nigga too but I wouldn't fight you! See Beck I love you and I would've fucked him behind your back, but by the same token I'd step and not interfere in y'all relationship. Because I'd rather have a small part of him than none at all. I don't wanna lose your love and friendship. Of course I wanna share him with you and you with him. I'd have the best of both worlds."

Becky pulled up to the Laundromat, parked the car and pulled Sherrie into her arms and kissed her softly then said, "I got a plan."

*   *   *   *

When Tony and Steve returned they were all assembled in the room. Becky and Sherrie served everyone drinks then sat down and Kane began to lay out the plan.

He looked around the room and made eye contact with each of them then said, "What we're about to get into is gonna be bloody and lives are gonna be lost. If we follow the plan to the letter hopefully it'll be them not us. If you're ever faced with indecision, shoot first we'll worry about the consequences later. We've got to be ruthless and we can't give any mercy to our foes. When we strike keep this in mind, the more of them we take out the less we'll have to deal with later. They don't have an unlimited source of manpower and neither do we so we've got to protect each other at all costs! Beck, you and Red will take Charles' car and go to Cassatt Ave. to the uniform shop that's across from Wendy's. Go buy four extra-large black Dickie jumpers, four large ones, and four small ones. If they have skull caps buy 20 black ones. Stop somewhere and get a good pair of scissors and some clothes line. Get at least 50 yards of clothes line and a roll of duct tape, the biggest one you can find. They have a hardware store right over there where you're going, so you should be able to get all of the items in one trip."

Beck and Sherrie rose to leave and he said, "Hold up because I don't want to have to go over all of this again, so everybody wait until I finish then go handle your business. Steve, you and Charles go to the K-Mart right down the street on Blanding. I want y'all to get 12 pairs of the phony Hi-Tech boots. Two pair for each one of us. I wear a 101/2, but get me an 11. Tee what size do you wear?'

"I wear a 111/2 but get me a 12," Tony said.

"Beck what size do you wear?" Kane asked her.

"I wear a 6, but in men shoes a 4 so get me a 5," Becky said. "Red and I wear the same size."

"Go to the sporting goods area and buy 12 pairs of batting gloves," Kane said. "Get large ones for you and Tee, medium for me and Steve and see if they have them small enough for Beck and Red." He pulled out his money and gave Steve $500. "That should cover it," he gave Beck $300 and asked her, "How are you set for cash?"

"I got about $400 left after the shopping spree in New York."

He turned to Sherrie who said, "I'm at about the same spot give or take a dollar or two."

"That's cool cause we gonna fatten our pockets in a minute," he said. "We got about $18,000 I'm gonna use for our war chest. It should hold us until we get more. Steve, Cee, if the money I gave you doesn't cover the cost come out of your pockets for the rest. This is how we're going to do this. Bobo is a lieutenant for Big Moe and is running shit in Mixon town, so if they had anything to do with setting us up he should know. What we're gonna do is snatch the nigga and take him to the house on Riverside and find out what the deal is. Find out where he keeps his cash and dope as well as what he knows about Moe's overall operation. We'll gag him, tie him, and leave him in the basement then hit his stash house and a few of his base houses. He has to die because he'll know who we are."

Sherrie cut in, "That nigga been trying to fuck me so I can set his pussy ass up!"

"Damn girl," Kane said. "What you doing reading my mind? Anyway we're gonna use Red to pull this nigga. Red you gonna rent a room at the Heart of Jacksonville Hotel. They got an indoor garage so get the nigga to meet you there at midnight tomorrow night then get him in the room and get him naked. Also, leave the door unlocked. You don't have to fuck him cause we're gonna be right on the scene. If he wants to leave as soon as you show up go with him we got your back."

"Alright," she said smiling.

"We need a spot closer to town to use as a base of operations. Charles get Jen to rent us a house in 5 points. One that's laid in the cut away from Green and Myra street, we might hit a couple of Moe's spots over there. We're gonna use the house in Pickett for a safe house so if anything goes wrong and we get separated that's where we'll all head. If one of us gets hurt know this; I ain't gonna leave you behind and that's if the police come or whatever. I'll be the last man to leave every time and no arguments about that y'all understand?"

They all nodded and he locked eyes with Steve and said, "Get Gina to rent us another ride and make sure it's a four door in black or dark blue. Get some basers to steal you 4 tags, it don't matter what type of car as long as the stickers are good. In the meantime we'll operate from the house on Riverside until Jen gets the other place. Steve, call Gina and get her on the car, Charles you do the same and if they start questioning you just give me the phone."

Steve called Gina and told her all of the specifics and she didn't question him. Charles called Jen and gave her the specifics about renting a house not an apartment and automatically she started asking all kinds of questions. Charles didn't say a word; he just passed the phone to Kane.

When Kane put the phone to his ear he could still hear Jen asking questions, and he cut in, "Do you know who this is?"

"Big brother?" She asked.

"Yeah this me," he said. "Dig this baby; just do what the man said and quit all that bitching he's doing it for me."

"Oh," she said. "I thought that motherfucker might be trying to set up a love nest for one of them ho's he be fucking with and trying to throw me off by having me get it."

"Girl quit tripping," Kane said laughing. "And handle that."

"Alright," she said, and Kane gave the phone back to Charles shaking his head laughing.

Charles took the phone and talked for a few then hung up.

"Alright we got that settled, y'all ready?" Kane said.

They all nodded and Tony said, "Bro, I'm gonna ride with Steve and Cee if that's cool?"

"It's cool," Kane said.

Steve, Tony, and Charles got up and left.

"I ain't gonna be stuck here by myself," Kane said. "So I'm riding with y'all" and he started loading the guns back into the big tote.

Sherrie had started rolling joints. She rolled 8 and left them on the table for the others, and then she rolled 3 more and put the bag of weed in her purse. She grabbed a bottle of the Henessy that Steve had brought and stood up. She caught Becky's eye and winked, and Becky winked back then stood and headed for the door with Sherrie on her heels. Kane lifted the tote and slung it over his shoulders and headed to the door. He looked over the room closed the door and got in the car. Sherrie pulled out, hit 295 and headed to town. She got off at the Normandy exit and drove to Cassat. They saw an A.C.E. hardware store and pulled in.

They got the scissors, clothes line, and duct tape then drove down the street until they came to the uniform shop. They bought jumpers, black skull caps, and several packs of thick tube socks. Kane got the purchases and they went to the car as Sherrie opened the trunk and he threw the stuff in.

"Since we're this close to town why don't we kill two birds with one stone? Sherrie said. "We can go ahead and rent the room."

"We're not gonna need it till tomorrow," Kane said. "But that's not a bad idea and we can pay for two days. Okay, let's do that and we can make a stop on the way."

Sherrie got behind the wheel and headed to town. She took I-10 to the merge with I-95, drove north and got off on Duval St. She drove to Perk's Place and pulled over as Kane had directed her. He gave her $400 and said, "You and Beck go in there and ask for a nigga they call Dirty Harry. When he comes; tell him to give you $150 worth of heroin, $125 worth of powder, and $125 worth of rocks. Tell him I sent y'all to him."

They got out of the car and he laid low in the backseat. When they walked in the bar it seemed that even the music stopped and stared, and that every eye in the place was on them. "We came to see Dirty Harry," Becky said loudly.

A slim light skinned man with a Valentine mustache got up from a table and approached them. He stopped in front of them looked down and said, "I'm Harry, and just where have I had the pleasure of meeting you two fine ass specimens that embody the very essence of womanhood?"

"Nigga please!" Sherrie said. "You can keep them tired ass lines to yourself. You know you never met us, because if you had you damn sure wouldn't forget us."

He smiled and said, "Damn Red, you sassy as fuck too huh!" And lead them to his table. "Y'all have a seat."

They all sat down and Dirty Harry became all business. "How can I help you ladies?"

"We're Kane's people," Becky said.

Harry sat up straight and said, "Alright, so what's up?"

"We want $150 worth of boy, $125 soft, and $125 hard." Becky said, "Can you swing that?"

"Yeah, hold on a minute," he said and stepped off. He was gone about 15 minutes and as soon as he left he had two drinks sent to them. They toyed with the drinks until he returned. He sat down and caught Sherrie's eye then passed her a thick package under the table. She didn't even look at it she just put it in her purse.

"Ain't you gonna check it red?" Dirty Harry asked her.

"For what, we're Kane's people, if you fuck over us you won't be Dirty Harry no more you'll be dead Harry!" Sherrie said calmly.

"Bitch! You come in my house and threaten me?" Harry said angrily.

Then he felt something hard poke him in his ribs. He looked down and saw that Becky held a compact .380 pressed against him. She leaned over until her mouth was nearly touching his ear and whispered, "We don't make threats baby, we make promises!" She said sweetly then lightly kissed him on the ear and slid the pistol back in her purse.

Sherrie gave him the $400, then they stood and she leaned down and kissed him on the cheek and said, "See you later baby."

"Y'all Kane's people alright," he said and gave them a shaky smile. They waved, he waved back and they left the place smiling.

"You wanna get him today don't you Red?" Becky asked.

"Yeah," Sherrie said. "I do, that's why I winked at you in the room. Shit is about to get real hectic and we don't know how this shit is gonna turn out. Shit, one of us could get killed or Kane could get killed. We don't know what the outcome is gonna be. I believe if we follow his instructions things will come out in our favor, but who knows? We've got today and the time, so why not utilize it to our benefit. Besides girl, don't you think I've done waited long enough? You've been getting the dick, let me get a little." And she and Becky burst out laughing.

"You bout to get your shot," Becky said still laughing. "So don't be greedy." They laughed again and were still laughing when they got in the car.

"What're y'all plotting?" He asked. "I know y'all up to something with all that laughing and shit. What's up?"

"Wouldn't you like to know?" Sherrie asked.

"Damn you a nosey ass nigga," Becky said. "Just chill out for a few."

"Did everything turn out okay?" He asked.

"Yeah it went well," Sherrie said.

"That's good," he said. "Listen they got a drug store right downtown before you get to Main St. and I want to go there first." He gave her the directions and when she got there, he jumped out and ran inside. He was in the store for only 5 or 6 minutes before he came out with a small white bag. He got in the back seat and said, "We set, let's go get the room."

They went to the heart of Jacksonville and got a room in the back that they could access thru the underground garage.

"Let's check the room out and make sure it meets out needs," Sherrie said.

"That's a good idea red," he said. "Come on Beck let's go check it out."

They got out of the car and Sherrie locked the doors. Becky grabbed the bottle of Hennessy and they walked to the room. Kane checked every avenue of their approach and looked to see if anyone would be able to see them coming and going, and it looked good so far. When they came to the door Sherrie opened it and they walked in. Kane looked around and said, "This is gonna work just fine," as Sherrie sat at the desk and pulled out the package.

She set the rocks to the side and said, "Kane you got to come and do this I can't tell them apart."

He walked over and called Becky. She walked over to where he stood next to Sherrie and he opened the packages of powder and said, "Look at them closely." The women looked. "The one with the glossy sheen is coke, the dull white one is boy; now taste them." The women tasted them and he said, "The bitter one is boy and y'all know what coke taste like."

They nodded their heads and he said, "Beck, go buy me a soda, and take this ice bucket and get some ice."

Becky got the ice bucket and left the room as Kane sat on the dresser and watched Sherrie roll a laced joint. She passed it to him and he fired it up, then she rolled 2 and laced them with rock. She rolled him another one and he put it in his cigarette pack.

Becky came thru the door with 2 sodas and a bucket of ice. She gave him one; he opened it and poured the soda in 2 cups. He picked up the heroin and went in the bathroom. He bent the can until it split in-two and threw the half that had the opening in the trash. He turned the other half upside down and bent the side so he could hold it. He pulled the small white bag from his pocket and opened it. Inside was a 10 pack of U-100 syringes, and he tore open the plastic bag and took 2 out. He turned on the faucet uncapped the syringes and placed one under the stream and filled it with 100 cc's of water. He sprinkled a small amount of heroin in the bottom of the can, and then squirted 30 ccs of water on it. He got his lighter and lit it, then held it under the can until the heroin came to a bubble. He set the lighter down and looked at the heroin as it dissolved in the water. It was now a yellowish color, clear with no sediment in it. He took the empty needle and drew up the heroin. He held it up and pushed the heroin to the top. There was a bubble and he thumped the needle until it disappeared. He sat on the toilet and looked for a vein. He didn't have to tie his arm up to make a vein protrude and he could almost hit himself in the dark. He slid the needle in, pulled the plunger back a little and saw a spot of blood appear. He pulled it back further and saw the blood swirl into the needle mixing with the heroin. He pushed the plunger forward and injected the heroin into his vein. Instantly he felt the euphoria that comes when using heroin. "Damn this some good shit," He said to himself. He poured more heroin in the can then got the other needle that held the 70 cc's of water and squirted that onto the heroin. He cooked the heroin then drew up 40 ccs and capped it in the needle. He drew up the remaining 30 ccs and shot it up. He cleaned the needle and put all of the stuff in the small white bag except for the can and walked back into the room.

Becky and Sherrie were sitting at the desk smoking laced cigarettes and dinking. Sherrie handed him a drink and he took a deep swallow and sat on the bed. Becky was sitting on the dresser facing him and Sherrie in the chair with her back to him. She turned the chair so she faced him.

"Daddy there's something I need to tell you," Becky said when she caught his eye. "I don't know how you're gonna take it but I hope you don't get angry."

Kane noticed that Sherrie was watching him intensely as Becky spoke.

"I don't really even know how to say it but it happened before us and hasn't since, even though I wanted it to. There was just never the opportunity."

Before she could go on Sherrie cut her off and said, "Kane baby, what she's trying to tell you is that she and I are lovers!"

He looked at Becky, looked at Sherrie and started laughing. They looked at each other dumb founded.

"Red, remember when you told me you wanted to get with me and I said the only way would be if Beck knew? I also said she might even wanna sit in on it. Remember?"

"Yeah I do," Sherrie replied. "now that you mention it."

"The night we took pictures in Beaufort and you and Beck were posing together, you put your tongue on Beck's pussy. When I went on the other end and looked between your legs I saw a wet spot. I've seen some juicy pussies in my days but none that would soak thru the lining in their panties and a pair of shorts. I suspect that while I was so busy looking in your eyes and up Beck's ass, she was pressing her tongue against your pussy. I knew there was more to it, but I don't like to jump to conclusions; I like solid facts. I'm glad y'all decided you could tell me because I never would've questioned you about it. I can understand y'all being discreet and I'll keep it that way. Tee doesn't need to know because I don't know how he'd react, and he might trip. Me, I'm progressive so I'm cool with it. I'm a man of the 90's so I tend to be more tolerant of what is considered abnormal. My motto is; to each his own as long as it doesn't cause me a problem it's all good. Beck I'm a little disappointed in you, not much, just a little. See I've constantly told you about being honest with me and not keeping secrets yet you held this back from me. I'd like to know why?"

"Daddy I didn't want to lose you," she said. "See most men are intimidated when they find out that their women like other women. They feel they can compete with any man, but how can they compete with a woman? They feel like they can't, so they have crazy reactions. You know that macho I'm a man; I can satisfy any woman mind set. Daddy you're a man's man and macho as fuck so what was I to do? I based my decision not to tell you on that."

"Come here Lil Momma," he said holding his arms spread wide.

She jumped off of the dresser and rushed into his arms crying, "I'm sorry baby, I won't ever keep a secret again I promise!"

Tears rolled down her cheek as he pulled her into his lap and said, "Hush up all that crying I understand baby and you haven't lost my trust. We've only been together for a short time and there are a lot of things we'll learn together. You're not at fault and I'm a man, not superman. You weren't wrong to make your decision based on shit you saw. I'm like this baby; no matter what it is you can tell me anything. And before I react the first thing I'll try to do is understand. I'll try to see it from your point of view without judging you. I'm gonna love you and that's no matter what!" He held her in his arms and stroked her back as he looked over at Sherrie; who was sitting there crying and said, "Bring your slick red ass over here."

She rushed from the chair and came over, pushed Becky's legs and said, "Bitch don't hog up Daddy's whole lap," and sat on one of his legs. They all hugged and the women stopped crying.

"Listen, y'all got to get y'all heavy asses off my legs," he said. Kane got up and walked to the desk, and sat in the chair and said, "Red tighten up my drink."

She fixed up his drink as he pulled out his other joint and fired it up. He gave them one of their joints and they lit up. "I want both of y'all to understand this. I got love for both of y'all and if y'all wanna make love to each other it's cool, and I don't even have to be included. I'm not new to this so it's not like I've never had two women at once. What is new is that

I've never had two women I love at once who also love each other. This should be very special to all of us, understand?" They nodded and he said, "Y'all go ahead then, we might as well get our money's worth out of this room."

Becky and Sherrie finished their joint then turned to each other and kissed softly. They started stroking each other gently never breaking their kiss. He watched the women make love and then he made love to both women. They lay in bed in a tangle of arms and legs. "I don't know what I'm gonna do with y'all," he said. "How regular do y'all expect this?"

"Every time we get a chance," They said.

He laughed and reveled in their soft bodies with one thought on his mind. "What the fuck am I gonna do when Tee finds out?"

Chapter 9

Morris "Big Moe" Jacobs and Theodore "Ted" Burke were the biggest drug dealers in the city. They controlled at least 60 or 70 percent of the drugs that were sold in the city. If people didn't work for them directly they got their drugs from their workers. They had the coke and heroin trade sewed up and was contemplating getting into the weed business. Big Moe was the head man but both he and Ted were greedy, petty, and jealous. They pulled all kinds of stunts like having their workers put the police on competitors, or sending their gunners to jack small independent dealers who they felt were cutting into their profits. They were multi-millionaires and didn't need to do those things, but they felt they could never have too much. When they learned that Kane, Tony, and Becky, were serving, both men were filled with apprehension and a thread of fear. They knew the legends about the Kane family, who had once controlled all of Uptown, Brooklyn, Mixon Town, Riverside, and had branches all throughout the city. They knew they couldn't afford to allow a single Kane to get in power in the underworld, because rumor had it that the Kane's had ties to the mob. Moe and Ted knew this for a fact because they had conspired with the feds to knock off Bishop Kane. Bishop at that time was the head of the Kane's, which was nine years ago. Bishop had ties to Frank Toronelli who was a mob boss. Bishop refused to implicate Frank in his case, and his whole empire came crashing down around him.

Moe's fear was fueled and turned to rage when he learned that the Kane's were dealing, so he set the jack in motion. He had heard about Berean Kane, Bishop's oldest son and knew he had a reputation for being a fighter, but he didn't pay much attention to it. When he helped the feds get Bishop he also helped them take down all of the other major dealers. It was like he was given the key to the city. He almost took over the entire drug trade but there were always small pockets of resistance till this day. He had several legitimate businesses that he used to wash his money and he felt like he was on top of the world. But, there was one thought that kept nagging him, "Kane". He told himself he could handle the young punk. What he couldn't understand was how Kane prevented the jack and killed four of his best gunners. He figured it was a fluke because he knew Kane would kill, but he wasn't about to give him credit for being that good. Since the murders, it seemed like the earth had swallowed Kane up, so he didn't think he'd be seeing him anytime soon.

*   *   *   *

Kane and the girls left the hotel a few hours later and headed back to the other hotel. When they arrived they saw a black four door Taurus parked in front of the room, and next to it Jen's candy apple red Maxima. The other rental, a black four door Buick was on the other side of Jen's car. They walked in and Tony, Charles, Steve, Jen, and Gina all got quiet.

Sherrie walked over to Tony, gave him a kiss, sat in his lap, spoke to Gina and Jen who she knew; then took his drink and sipped from it. Kane and Becky spoke to the women. Then he sat on the bed next to Gina and she leaned over and hugged him. Becky went to the drinks picked up 3 glasses and asked, "Daddy, Red, y'all want a drink?" They both nodded. Jen who was sitting in Charles' lap stared at Kane, who noticing her stare and asked, "What're you looking at me like that for?"

"Nigga you up to something," she said. "And I wanna know what it is."

"Jen don't be a pain in the ass alright?" he said sternly. "What this is about is protecting our family and that's all you need to know, so don't be asking all them questions. Shit! Why can't you just this once trust me?"

"It's not like I don't trust you," she replied. "But you're wild as fuck and I get scared for you. I already done saw my baby brother buried! Damn it, don't you ever see shit from someone else's point of view?"

"Of course I do. And if I do what I've got in mind to do, believe me it won't be me getting buried." he said firmly. "So don't even worry about that. See Jen, no plan is 100 percent sure, but the motherfuckers I'm acting against don't have a plan. They're predictable as fuck, and they got to be here for their shit to work and make money. I don't have to follow a schedule and that's what gives me an edge, so just chill. You got a role in this too but you can't be running and telling Momma, Leslie, and Lucinda what's going on. I want you and Gina to get Beepers, and don't give the numbers to anyone but us in this room. Take your children to Momma's house or to Charles' Momma's house and leave them there for a week or so. Gina you do the same thing. Y'all go home and pack some clothes, and go to Granny's house and stay there. If those beepers go off call the number right back, and find out what you need to do. All y'all gonna do is transport us or our material, so one of y'all got to always be there. Don't drive that red ass car either, get Momma's car or rent one. Gina I ain't got to tell you not to drive that loud ass yellow Saab. Borrow somebody car or rent one, y'all got that?" They both nodded and he asked, "Jen did you rent the place?"

"Yeah," she answered. "It's on Post Street in the cut, up by McDuff."

126

"That's good," he said. "Let's load up and go see the cribs because everybody needs to know where there located. Let's go to Pickett first that's gonna be our safe house, to be used only in an emergency. We gonna use the house on Post St. for our base of operations, and the one on the Riverside if we need to take someone there to get some information . Everybody set on that?"

They all nodded and filed out from the room. They loaded up in the cars and headed out in a convoy.

*   *   *   *

After they went to all of the houses they ended up on Post St. They had all of their things from the hotel, and they took it all in the house. Gina and Jen took off in the Maxima to handle their business. Since it was too late to get the beepers they would get them in the morning. The house on Post St. was furnished with 3 bedrooms, and 2 baths. Jen had thought to bring sheet spreads, first aid kits, linen, ware's, a portable color TV, and a small stereo system.

"Damn that girl thinks of everything," Kane said smiling.

"Bro, I think that's a family trait," Charles said. "But it had to skip one of y'all cause that nigga there," he pointed at Tony. "Can't think worth a damn!"

They burst out laughing and Tony said, "Fuck you, black ass nigga!"

"We gonna set it off starting tomorrow night as soon as it gets dark," Kane said. "This is what we're gonna do. Red you're gonna call a cab from the bar down the street. Take the cab to Mixon and head to Bobo's dope house. Cop a few stones to make it look good. I want you to wear that skin tight red and white polka dot dress you bought in New York. Wear those red roman strap sandals too. Steve, you and Tee gonna drive over there in advance and find a spot to watch the hole. Beck, Charles, and me will follow the cab. Red if he doesn't leave with you right then walk up to Forrest St. and beep the girls. One of them will pick you up from there. Me, Beck, and Charles will keep an eye on the spot until he leaves and follow him to the hotel. Y'all got that?"

They all nodded and Sherrie went in her purse and pulled out the package. She threw the coke on the table and Charles scooped it up then went to get a plate. He came back, poured some coke on the plate then chopped it up. He scooped some up and snorted it.

"Goddamn big nose ass nigga," Steve said. "Leave us some of the shit."

They laughed and Charles said, "Fuck you, shit colored ass nigga," and scooped up some more and snorted it then passed the plate to Steve.

Sherrie crushed some rocks and made a few cigarettes. She gave Becky and Tony one then fired one up.

"Y'all have a ball tonight," Kane said. "Cause tomorrow it's all business." He made eye contact with each of them and said, "Our lives are gonna be on the line tomorrow so ain't no getting high as long as we're working. I mean none at all, no drinking, weed, none of that shit!"

They all nodded and he said, "Red twist me a joint; plain no lace." Then he grabbed the plate of coke, took out a bill and scooped up some. He put the plate back on the table, grabbed his white bag and went in the bathroom. He got his works, fixed up his boy, added the coke and shot a speedball. He cleaned his works then went back up front and got the joint from Sherrie. He sat in a chair and Becky brought him a drink as he smoked and chilled. Tony and Sherrie got up and went to the bedroom.

"Bro, I'm gonna step," Charles said rising from his seat. "I'll be back first thing in the morning. If Jen comes, tell her I went to take care of some business."

He looked in Kane's eyes and Kane smiled. He knew Charles was going to get his freak on. "Don't let your business keep you up all night."

"Cool," Charles said and gave him some dap and smiled.

"I'm rolling with Cee," Steve said. "But we got to make a stop and have somebody get the tags first. You cool with that?"

"Yeah," Kane said. "I'm cool with it, but let me ask you niggas something. Do y'all do everything together?"

"Except fuck your sisters," Steve said and laughed.

Kane burst out laughing and gave him some dap. "Seriously, y'all need to know this. If we're gonna be down I need to know where I can reach y'all at all times."

They looked at each other and said, "Alright."

Steve said, "Hold on a minute." Then ran to Charles' car and got a pen. He wrote a number on a piece of paper and gave it to Kane then said, "We set some little heads up in a crib and that's the number. I'll bring the tags and the rest of the guns with me in the morning."

"Be easy," Kane said. "I'll see y'all in the morning."

When they left Kane and Becky got up and walked to the bedroom. As they passed the door to the room Tony and Sherrie were in they paused. Then they heard Sherrie scream, "Tee... Tee... Eat my ass baby... Oh shit... Eat...My...Ass." They looked at each other and laughed. They went to their room and Becky asked, "You alright baby?"

"I'm cool Lil Momma," he said. "It's gonna work out in time baby."

They made slow love then drifted off to sleep. Early in the morning about 4:00 Becky felt a light touch on her ass cheeks. She rolled out of Kane's arms and there stood Sherrie naked. Becky sat on the edge of the bed and Sherrie spread her legs, and knelt between them. She thrust her head between Becky's legs and tongued her clitoris furiously. Becky almost came instantly. She bit her lip as she felt her orgasm take over. She fanned her legs, gripped Sherrie's head and whispered, "Oh fuck....I'm cumin." After she had cum Sherrie stood, licked her lips and walked to the other side of the bed. Kane lay on his back, legs slightly spread. Gently Sherrie spread his legs wider, grabbed his semi-erect penis and started sucking it. She could taste Becky on him and her hand went between her legs. She stroked herself until she was good and wet and until his rod was stiff. She straddled him lightly and slid his penis inside her and rode it swiftly.

Kane, with his eyes closed mumbled, "Damn Beck take your time, you caught me off guard. I'm about to cum so ease up girl." He felt her hands pinch his nipples and he opened his eyes and saw Sherrie bouncing up and down on his stiff cock. "Red....?" He whispered.

"Yes Daddy...." She moaned softly. "I'm.... stealing.... some....dick..." she rode him faster and moaned, "I'm almost there.... Here I go....I'm cumin baby...."

He grabbed her waist and thrust up into her rapidly and moaned softly, "Here it is Red.... I'm cumin...." and he erupted in her.

After she came she got off of him, grabbed his still stiff cock and sucked her juices off then said, "Beck take over I got to go." She gave them a quick kiss then left the room as Becky straddled him. She stopped in the bathroom and cleaned herself up then eased back in the room. Tony lay there eyes cracked watching her as she crept back to the bed. He had woken up when he felt her rise from the bed and he knew what she was up to by the way she stealthily left the room; she was going to Kane. He smiled as she eased in bed and snuggled into his arms. There was no anger in his heart because he knew she was too much for him. His brother was the man for her and it would be that much easier when he broke the news to her.

*   *   *   *

They woke up about 10:30 to the smell of breakfast. They showered, put on their robes and went to the kitchen. There stood Sherrie in a big tee shirt knotted at the side, and a blue scarf on her head; her jean shorts with her ass cheeks hanging out, and white sandals cooking breakfast. She had set 4 plates at the table.

"Red I didn't know you could cook," Kane said. "I thought you were a microwave bitch, at least that's what you said."

"Nigga I like almost everything fast," she said. "I'm also southern born and bred, and I can cook my ass off. You gonna find out!"

"Girl I can't cook worth a fuck!" Becky said.

"I'm gonna teach you when we get the time if you want me to," Sherrie said.

Charles and Steve came at about noon. Steve carried a big tote bag and Charles a small sack.

"Bro we would've got here sooner," said Charles. "But we stopped at the other places and dropped off some refreshment." He laughed and opened the sack. He took out a fat bag of weed, an ounce of coke, a spoon of heroin, and a bag of rocks. "I know you said no getting high when we work but we ain't gonna be working all the time, so I dropped a bomb at each place."

"That's cool," Kane said. "Cause we gone have some down time and that will help us to relax."

Steve had put the tote bag on the floor and opened it. He pulled out four sawed off pump shot guns, four 9mms, four .45 automatics, and shells for all of the guns and said, "This is it as far as our arsenal is concerned, but I'll stay on the lookout for more."

"Put the word out because I think we will need more," Kane said. "I don't want us riding with guns that got bodies on them."

Steve pulled four tags out of the tote and asked, "Do you know Junky Slim?"

"Yeah," Kane said. "I know him, we go way back. Nigga used to be tight until crack hit the scene. They used to call him Pretty Slim."

"Well we paid the nigga to get the tags," Steve said. "I gave him $50 dollars and 10 rocks. Charles sent him to the airport to the long term parking area, and gave him a general description of the kind of cars we wanted the tags off and he came thru. The tags won't be hot for a minute."

"That's a good deal," Kane said. "All we have to do now is wait until tonight. Red you can keep your .380 in your purse for the job tonight. Beck I want you to get two 9's, one for you and one for Red. Y'all can choose your own weapons as far as pistols go, but us four." He pointed at the other 3 men. "We're gonna use the shot guns as our primary weapons and the pistols are for back up. Beck and Red, y'all gonna be the drivers. No speeding and follow the traffic laws. We're gonna always have 2 or 3 ways to leave the scene and we don't want tires squealing to draw attention to us; got that?"

Both women nodded and he went on, "Red, go get the gloves out of that bag over there." He pointed to the bag.

130

She went and got the gloves and gave them to him. He got a pair and laid the others out so everyone could get a pair. "Beck, go get two towels." She went to get them as he got the scissors. They had bought two pair and two rolls of duct tape. He got the clothesline and gave it and the scissors to Becky and said, "You and Red cut these in 2 foot lengths." They took them and started cutting.

He called Charles and Steve and threw them the towels and said, "Wipe down all of the guns. Wipe the clips, unload them and wipe the shells then reload them. From this point on no one touches the guns without gloves!"

They put on their gloves and went to work as he motioned Tony over. "Get the keys from Charles and go in his trunk and get some screwdrivers."

Tony got the keys as Kane put on his gloves, wiped the tags and headed out the door. When they came back inside he had the women to cut holes in the skull caps to make face masks. Afterwards, they all tried on their gear.

Gina and Jen swung by and Charles and Steve retired to the rooms with them. They had given them their beeper numbers.

"Beck, Tee, I want y'all to go to the mall and find some full body stockings, buy twelve, two for each of us." Tony and Becky walked from the house, and then Kane and Sherrie left.

They went to a Home Depot and bought 30 square yards of thick plastic, 5 square yards of foam padding, and a sturdy pine chair. They dropped the stuff off at the house on Riverside. They made love on the Kitchen counter then went back to the house on Post St. Gina and Jen were gone when they got back. Tony and Becky drove up about 10 minutes later and came in loaded with bags.

Tony set his bags down and said, "I decided to get 24 body suits instead of 12, because we caught hell finding them."

He pulled one out and showed it to Kane who nodded and said, "Good work. Y'all go on and get some rest we gonna be busy tonight."

They all found places to get comfortable and took a nap. As night approached Kane stood in the front room and said, "Let's get ready. Red go get ready it's gonna take you the longest." She left the room and went to get dressed. He looked around at the others and said, "It's on, so if you have any questions now's the time to ask them." They all shook their heads.

"Put the body stockings on first but don't put on the mask until we get ready to strike. Becky, get your gear and get dressed. Steve, Tee, and

Cee, we gonna cut up the towels and wipe the rentals down. I don't want us to leave any prints in case we have to jump out."

They cut the towels and wiped down the rentals then went back inside. Standing there dressed in all black was Becky, looking sexy as hell. The jumper was tight and it hugged all of her curves, and was pulled up tight in her cunt.

"Goddamn!" They said in unison, then Sherrie stepped in the room and they all whistled. The red and white polka dot dress clung to her like a second skin and the roman strap sandals emphasized her beautiful curves.

"Damn Red," Charles said. "You could lead me to the slaughter!" Steve said, "Me too!"

"Y'all niggas better check yourselves," Tony said laughing. "I got that."

They all laughed and Kane said, "Come on fellas let's get dressed."

They all went and put on their gear and grabbed their weapons. It was dark as they went to the cars and got in. "Tee, you and Steve head over there and find a good spot to check the scene out, and keep your eyes out for Red. When she shows up you'll know we're close by."

"Alright," Tony said. "We're out!" They got in their car and pulled out.

Kane and the others loaded into the rental and drove to the bar. Sherrie went to the phone and called a cab. She came back to the car and stood by the passenger side and waited. When the cab came she leaned down and kissed Kane deeply. She leaned in the back and gave Charles a peck on the cheek, then walked to the driver's side and gave Becky a deep kiss. She rushed to the cab and got in, as the cab pulled off Becky followed. She knew where they were going so she tailed them loosely.

Charles sitting in the backseat was lost in thought, "Damn the way Red kissed Kane they got to be fucking, and damn if she didn't do the same to Beck. Kane fucking both of them and they're comfortable with it. I wonder if Tee suspects it. I knew Red was too fast for Tee, but Kane, that's a horse of a different color." He smiled and shook his head.

The cab dropped her on Copeland St. and she walked to Way Dr. The men on the corner were trying to rap with her but she just ignored them and kept strutting.

Tony and Steve had parked on Forrest St. They got out of the car, ran thru an alley and lay under an abandoned house. With the masks covering their faces they looked down Way Drive. Where they lay at they had a clear view of three houses that served BoBo's drugs. The one across

132

the street from the first one is where BoBo sat and kept his eyes on things. He didn't serve from his house ever.

Kane and the others had parked across the street from the Pepsi Cola plant on Edison Ave. They sat and watched Sherrie as she strutted down the street. She went to the house across from where BoBo sat and walked up on the porch. BoBo's house had a screened in porch, but he saw Sherrie and stood up.

"Damn there's that bad red bitch I been trying to catch," he said to himself. "I don't know why she won't break for me." He watched as she walked up on the porch. He opened the screen door and yelled, "Don't serve her!" And then he came down the steps.

Sherrie heard him yell and knew he was talking about her. She pulled out a wad of cash and said to the man on the porch, "Serve this $100," then she started peeling off bills. The man just stood there, not reaching for the money.

BoBo stepped on the porch and asked, "What's up Red?" She said, "Ain't nothing Bo, what's up with you?"

"I'm just chilling," he said. "But dig this baby; you ain't got to spend no money. You can get all you want for free if you step over to my crib with me."

"Bo you done shot that same line at me time and time again," she said. "And I keep batting it down, so haven't you learned anything about me yet?"

"I know you get down," he said. "I know you're in the game but you act like my money doesn't spend with you."

"Baby it ain't always about the money," she replied. "Sometimes it's about the way you present your game. See I like you, but I ain't gonna let you handle me like I'm one of your lil tricks. If you're real about getting with me I got a spot at the Heart of Jacksonville and we can go kick it over there for a few if you want to."

"Are you serious Red?" He asked looking at her skeptically.

"Bo I don't even play games like that, trust me!" She said seriously.

"I can dig that," he said. "Hold on for a minute and let me get my shit straight." He looked at the man on the porch and said, "Beanie give her what she wants," then he yelled thru the door, "Snookie! Come here! Hurry up!"

Snookie rushed out the door and asked, "What's up boss?"

"Go tell Vin and Trevin to close the other houses, bring all of their shit down here and all of y'all work from this spot." BoBo said. "I'm leaving you in charge. Let beanie handle your end while you sit in my crib and keep an eye on things alright?"

"Alright boss," Snookie said then left to tell the other men the news.

"Come on Red," said BoBo taking her and leading her to his car.

Beanie had just given her 10 big rocks, so she put her money back in her purse. BoBo opened the passenger side door and she got in. He had a box Chevy with a dark blue and black bowling ball paint job, dressed in chrome.

Vin and Tre walked up and BoBo said, "I know Snookie told y'all what I said."

"Yeah he did," Vin responded.

"Do that," said BoBo. "I'll be back in a few hours." He cocked his head in Sherrie's direction as the men smiled.

Tony and Steve saw Sherrie get in the car. They rolled from underneath the house and ran to their car and drove to Orion Street. They parked with the nose of the car headed towards town.

Becky pulled out, went around the block and headed down Orion in the opposite direction of Tony and Steve. She saw BoBo's car pull out and head towards McDuff Avenue. She followed and Tony turned around and followed her. BoBo drove to the Jax liquor store on McDuff and went to the drive-thru and bought something then got on Interstate 10; he drove to the 95 merge and headed north. As he got off on Union Street Tony blew his horn and passed Becky. They stopped at a red light on Jefferson St. and Tony pulled beside BoBo's car on the passenger side. He looked over and caught Sherrie's eye then winked and she smiled. When the light changed Tony raced off and left them. They got to the hotel first and parked in a dimly lit corner of the underground garage and waited. A few minutes later BoBo and Sherrie pulled in. They stepped from the car and headed for the room.

When Tony saw Becky pull in, he got out of the car and motioned to her to park next to him. When Becky parked Steve and Tony walked to the car as the others got out.

"Let's go," Kane said and pulled the .45 automatic he carried. They put on their mask, pulled their pistols and hurried to the room.

*   *   *   *

When BoBo and Sherrie entered the room she said, "Baby I don't need to get high to be with you. I wanna see why all them ho's be sweating you." She reached down grabbed the hem of her dress and pulled it over her head. She didn't wear a bra and he had seen her nipples were hard from the beginning. When he saw her naked breast he saw that they stood proudly with little sag. He looked down and saw the way the red lace panties hugged her fat mound.

"Damn Red," he exclaimed as she turned and folded her dress neatly and placed it on one of the beds. He saw her fat ass and almost instantly he was erect. He kicked off his shoes and hurried to undress.

He stood there naked his cock hard as tempered steel and she said, "Baby go wash that dick off for me. I wanna see what it tastes like."

He rushed to the bathroom and when she heard the shower come on she went and unlocked the door, then sat on the bed and lit a cigarette. The door opened and she placed her finger to her mouth then pointed to the bathroom.

Kane and the others came in the room and spread out. Tony and Charles positioned themselves on either side of bathroom door while Kane and the others got in the closet. They heard the shower stop then BoBo stepped in the room with a hard dick and a smile. As soon as he passed the thresh hold Charles stepped in front of him and got him in a bear hug, trapping his arms. Tony stepped behind him and put him in a choke hold, and he was out in less than a minute. Charles carried him to the bed where Kane checked his breathing then placed a piece of tape over his mouth; then tied him up and covered him with a spread. Becky and Sherrie grabbed his clothes and bundled them up in a sheet.

"Red get his keys and search his car good," Kane instructed. "Take a towel and be sure to wipe it down. Don't leave any of your prints."

"I got you Daddy," she said. "Anything else?"

"Check the trunk good." he said. "Look for hidden compartments but I doubt if you'll find much. He won't have any dope in his car if I read him right."

"Alright baby," she said and headed out the door.

"Beck you brought Red's gear?" Kane asked.

"It's in the trunk baby," she said.

"Alright Lil Momma," Kane said. "Let's just chill until Red gets back then we'll know where to go from here."

Sherrie came back about 20 minutes later. BoBo was still unconscious but breathing evenly. She had a small tool box in her hand. She gave it to Kane who opened it and saw that inside were two 9 mm's and a large sum of money. "That's all there was," she said.

"Okay, listen Red," Kane said. "Get Beck's gloves and go in the trunk of the Taurus and grab that small tote. All of your gear is there but just get the gloves for now. Go to the Buick and take all of the stuff out of the trunk and put it in the Taurus okay?"

"Alright daddy," she said and left the room again to handle business. 15 minutes later she came back. "That's a done deal," she said and gave Becky the gloves.

"Red this is the deal," Kane said. "You leave the room first and make sure the coast is clear. If you see somebody coming say, "Damn I left my shit in the room", drop the tool box and block the way for a second. That should give us enough time to get back in the room before we're seen. Tee, throw that nigga over your shoulder and get ready. Becky, grab that bundle with his shit in it, and Charles help Tee get the nigga up. Steve you follow Red, and Beck you're behind him. Cee, you're behind Tee in case he needs help with the nigga and I'll pull up the rear. Let's roll!"

She stepped from the room tool box in hand, then casually looked to see if anyone was there and walked away. They left in single file with Kane at the drag. Quickly Sherrie walked to the Buick and popped the trunk as the others spread out in defensive positions. Sherrie put the tool box on the floor in the back of the car then climbed behind the wheel. Becky threw the bundle in the back of the Taurus and got behind the wheel, as Tee threw BoBo unceremoniously in the trunk of the Buick. Steve slammed the trunk and the men got in the car. Sherrie pulled off as Kane and Charles got in with Becky who immediately followed Sherrie. They removed their masks and drove to the house Riverside. Sherrie backed down the drive between the big hedges that hid the side view of the house and the outside door to the basement.

Becky pulled in behind her as Steve and Tony jumped from the car and quickly pulled BoBo from the trunk, and drug him into the basement. Kane and Sherrie had set everything up before they left. They had put down 5 square yards of the thick plastic and tacked it down with duct tape. They taped the legs of the chair with the foam padding and sat it in the middle of the plastic.

Steve and Tony sat him in the chair then quickly untied him and retied him to the chair. His hands and arms they tied to the arms of the chair, his legs were tied to the chair legs, his chest and mid-section to the back of the chair. He was well restrained and could barely move. They stood in the basement in front of the bound man and Kane said, "Beck get some water and revive him."

Sherrie went in the back and quickly undressed, slid the body stocking on then the rest of her gear. Becky came back with the water and flung it in his face. Bobo swung his head from side to side trying to clear it. His eyes popped open and he saw the six people standing there dressed in black. He knew them all and also knew he was in deep shit. He said a silent prayer as he looked at the steely eyed men and women, "God if you get me out of this I'll give it all up, I swear. Please God save me in Jesus name I pray."

Kane snatched the tape from his mouth but left it attached to the side of his face.

The first words out of his mouth were, "Kane I didn't have anything to do with that shit man, that was Moe and Ted. I told them niggas not to fuck with y'all man. I swear I didn't have a part in it." His words confirmed it for Kane. He had just signed his, Moe's, and Ted's death warrants. But not before Kane could find out what he wanted to know.

"You get only one chance," Kane said. "Tell the truth and I swear on my family that I won't kill you. Tell me a lie, and I'll kill you so slow you'll beg to die! Got it?"

"Yeah man I got it," BoBo said pleadingly.

Before Kane could ask him a question Sherrie cut in, "Sweety, he told all of his boys to work out of one house until he gets back, so all the shit and cash is right there."

"Is that the truth Bo?" Kane asked.

"Naw," BoBo said. "I got 40 grand in my car in a tool box and another 100 grand in a safe at my crib. There is also 2 birds in the safe. I got all the bread they done made since the night before last, because I let them work 3 days then give them 3 days off."

"Do all of Moe's dealers work that way?" Kane asked.

"Yeah," BoBo answered, "He's the one that came up with that system."

"So how can I catch the fat motherfucker slipping?" Kane asked.

"That's easy," Bobo said filled with hope that he just might survive this after all. "All you got to do is wait until Thursday night and drive out to Sweetwater. Get on Firestone Rd. and drive down to Jack Horner street, take a right and there you'll see a white house with aqua blue trim; you can't miss it. The number is 3488 and it's in big black numbers hanging over the front door. That's his little hideaway and every Thursday night at 8:00 he goes there. It's a love nest he thinks nobody knows about, but everyone does. He's fucking Ted's wife Elvira over there. Ted knows about it, so every Thursday at 8:00 he goes to Turtle Creek and fucks Moe's wife Brenda. When Ted found out Moe was fucking his wife he knew he had to take it, so what he did was got Brenda and showered her. Now their fucking is get back for Moe fucking Elvira."

"Thanks Bo," Kane said. "Once I check this shit out I'll let you know if I'm gonna kill you or not."

"Man you said if I tell you the truth you wouldn't kill me," Bobo alarmed. "You swore on your family man!"

"That I did Bo," Kane said eying him. "I'm a man of my word Bo and you know that."

"Yeah I've heard," Bobo said. "It's all true dog trust me."

Kane left the basement and went and got the heroin that Charles had left. He got a spoon and a needle then came back to the basement. "Bo, where is Moe's closest base house to you?"

"He got one on Crystal St. that Boonie works; and one in Lackawanna right behind the store on the corner. Tip serves for him in Woodstock across from the Frito Lay plant behind the Silver Fox," Bobo said. "Know what I'm talking about?"

"Yeah," Kane replied. "I know them spots."

"He got one in the green apartments behind daylights off Myrtle Ave., bottom apartment on the right; you'll know it by the traffic. Another one is down by 13th St. in the apartments behind Murphy's on Myrtle Ave." Bobo said. "Jermaine serves everything across 20th St. expressway for him so I don't know all those spots, but Pookie, Jermaine's dog would. He serves from the apartment right behind Pearls Place. They got robbed about 2 months ago but they're booming again. Kane I got something more to trade with, some information that you wouldn't believe!"

"Bo I made a vow on my family that I wouldn't kill you," Kane said. "I keep my word. I ain't asking you to trust me. Shit, you a snake you ought to be able to recognize one when you see one. So tell me the shit that could save your life!"

"Nine years ago Moe and Ted set Bishop up!" Bobo said expectantly.

"Those niggas are the ones who took him down so they could get a lock on the city. Remember all the dudes that had been in the game for years started falling back then?" Kane nodded and Bobo started calling off the names of the men Moe and Ted had set up, "Johnny Boy, Pretty Earl, Big Time, Sly Johnson, Big Ricky, and Eddie Bee."

"Alright the deal still stands," Kane said. "I won't kill you if this shit pans out. Beck get me a glass of water."

Becky went and got the glass of water and Kane motioned Sherrie to him. She came and he gave her the spoon and showed her how to hold it. Becky held the water and everyone watched. Kane put the needle in his mouth then poured some of the heroin in the spoon, took the needle from his mouth, dipped it in the water and drew up 50 cc's of water. He squirted it on the dope, took out his lighter, lit it and held it under the spoon until he saw a slight bubbling. He saw that there was no sediment in the spoon so he used the needle to draw up the dope; he walked up to Bobo whose eyes grew wide as saucers.

He pleaded with Kane, "Please man, don't kill me, you said you wouldn't, please God!"

"I ain't gonna kill you" Kane said smiling. "I'm gonna get you high!" He found a vein and tested to make sure he was in, then injected the dope. BoBo, whose face was covered with fear visibly relaxed as the dope hit him.

He smiled and said, "Thanks man".

"It's all good," Kane said. "But dig this. I'm gonna cover your mouth then we gonna step off for a few, we'll be back. By the way how do we get in the safe?"

Bobo head drooping looked up and said, "The combination is 23-32-31. The best way to get in is to come out of the house behind it. I rented that one too. It's the key with the blue paint on it. The one with the yellow paint on it is to the back door of my crib. That's how I creep off and make the workers think I'm still watching. They can't see thru the screen on the porch. I don't allow nobody but girls inside so Snookie gonna be the only one there. He'll be on the front porch watching the workers".

"Alright," Kane said as BoBo nodded off and he pressed the tape back over the man's mouth. "Beck when we pull out stop to the Seven-11 down the street. Go in and buy six of them cheap watches, but make sure they have the same time on them. As soon as you get out of the car take your gloves off okay?"

"I got you baby", she said.

It was Friday night so they knew the scene would be jumping. They stopped to the Seven-11 and got the watches. They each got one and strapped it on, then drove to Mixon. They stopped in Forrest Park and got out of the cars. "This is how we're gonna do it. Red, you Tee and Steve go down to Orion St. turn up Copeland St. and park in the lot there. Wait exactly 10 minutes then Steve, you and Tee get to the alley way between BoBo's spot where they're serving. Wait till you see me and Cee come out of the house across the street and then y'all rush the house. Go up shooting so they know we mean business. Got it?"

They nodded and he said, "Red when your watch hits 15 minutes, drive around to the front of the house. Leave the car running, and if you see anyone standing around watching fire a few rounds to run them off. By that time Beck should be there too. Beck you do the same thing when your watch says we've been gone 15 minutes. You got the front, Red you got the back and don't shoot to hurt bystanders, just to scare them alright?"

They nodded and the men got the shot guns and got in their cars. Becky drove to the house behind Bobo's and parked. Kane and Charles got out of the car with shot guns, Becky with a tote bag over her shoulder and a 9mm in her right hand. They came to Bobo's back door. Kane opened the door as Becky and Charles trained their weapons on the door. The door opened silently and they crept inside. They walked thru the kitchen and came to a closed door. Kane stepped in as Becky and Charles stood guard. He saw the safe, stepped out and motioned to Becky who came over quickly. He pointed and they walked into the room and moved swiftly to the safe.

They dropped to their knees, he opened the safe, and he leaned over until his mouth was nearly on her mask covered ear and whispered, "Fill the tote, don't leave anything. Hurry up and fill it and keep your eye on your watch." She nodded her head.

He rose then left her in the room loading the tote. He and Charles hurried thru the house checking it as they moved to the front. The house was empty and the front door was open. They eased up to it and peeped out. Snookie was leaned back in a chair asleep. Kane rushed silently out of the house and swung the shot gun in a vicious arch. The barrel crashed into Snookie's forehead with a sickening crunch, crushing his skull. He never woke up and when he did it would be in hell. Kane looked at his watch torn between going back to see if Becky was gone, and stepping out the door. He had to trust that she would follow the orders to the letter. He stepped to the screen door, pushed it opened with the shot gun shielded by his legs. As soon as the door was open he saw Steve run from around the side of the house and fire at the men on the porch. He saw Beanie take the blast in the chest and lower part of his face. The shot gun blast lifted him from his feet and threw his body thru the front window. He crashed thru it in a shower of blood and glass with his feet hanging over the sill. Another man on the porch screamed and dived to the floor.

Tony came from the other side of the house concentrating on the front screen door. He saw a shadow approaching and the screen door started swinging outward. He fired his shot gun a second after Steve and whoever it was at the screen door was snatched back as if attached to an invisible cord.

They rushed up onto the porch firing, Steve thru the window, Tony thru the door. Tony snatched the door open, and jumped over the body that lay a foot or so from the door. The man's face was erased by the buckshot. They raced in the house firing and Kane and Charles were seconds behind them.

"Hold your fire!" Kane yelled. "Hold your fire unless there's resistance!" There was none.

Charles grabbed a woman who cowered on the floor in the front room. He knew she was a dealer. "Where is the dope and the re-up money," Charles asked menacingly. "We know y'all ain't got to turn it in until 12:00 tonight."

She pointed at a cabinet.

Steve rushed over, opened it up and there were big tote bags inside. Two filled with cash, one with rocks and powder, and one with weed. Steve scooped it up with one hand as Kane asked her.

"Where's the boy?" She pointed to a drawer in the cabinet. Steve dropped the totes and snatched the drawer open. He saw a Ziploc freezer bag filled with heroin in small bags. He opened one of the totes and put it in, then looked at Kane who nodded towards the front door; just then they heard shots. Kane looked at his watch and smiled under his mask. "Move it!" He said and Steve raced from the room with Tony behind him, Charles released the woman and raced out. Kane looked around and backed out. The women stood in defensive positions panning the area. When the women saw Kane come out they got behind the wheels. They loaded up and pulled off.

Two blocks away they removed their masks, and stopped in the parking lot of the Brown Jug. They could hear sirens screaming as they gathered at the back of the Buick, and Kane said, "We gonna go straight down Edison and turn on Crystal. Becky, do you know where Boonie serves on Crystal?"

"Yeah baby I know," she said.

"This is the play," Kane said. "You pull up and stop right pass his spot. Don't slam on brakes, just pull to the curb and stop. Keep your eyes on the street, and when Red stop behind you we're gonna jump out of the car and rush the house shooting. You and Red do just like you did at the last spot?" They nodded and loaded up.

The hit on Crystal Street went just as planned, only this time they didn't leave bodies. They got two bags of cash, dope, and then hit the house in Lackawanna, and the one in Woodstock on Kings Rd. Then they drove to 13th St. and saw all of the traffic flowing to an apartment on the bottom right-hand side. They saw two men flanking the door with big pistols in their hands. They watched as the basers went to the door, passed in their money, and the dope was passed back thru a hole in the screen door. They drove by at regular speed and Kane had Becky go around the block and pull in at a small park.

They gathered between the two cars and Kane said, "They got two gunners on the door, so we got to play this one a little different. We're gonna circle around the block and come back so we're on their side of the street. When I say hit it, punch the gas. When you get fifteen feet from the spot slam on brakes. Red when you hear Beck punch it, punch it too. When you see her brake lights, slam on brakes too. You got to watch closely Red. When the cars stop, we're gonna jump out shooting and screaming, vice freeze don't move. That should give us the time we need to clear the cars. Cee you got the dude on the right, I got the one on the left. As soon as we get close we're gonna blast them. Tee, Steve, y'all got the door but don't fuck around and shoot us alright?" They nodded. "Beck, Red, y'all know what to do from there so let's do it!"

They drove around the block and as Becky approached the apartment she punched the gas pedal to the floor. A second later Sherrie did the same. Becky swung the big car up on the curb 20 feet from the apartment and slammed on brakes. Tires screeching, the car slid to a halt a few feet from the apartment door. Sherrie had used the same maneuver and her car slid to a halt inches from Becky's bumper. The men jumped out of the cars screaming, "Vice, freeze! Vice! Don't move!"

The basers started running in every direction. The gunners hesitated because they didn't want to fire on the police. Their indecision cost them their lives. Kane and Charles fired at the same time. Kane's shot gun blast caught the gunman in the neck. He took the full brunt of the double ought and it decapitated him. His head hit the back wall and bounded into the air like a volley ball as blood geyser from the stump of his neck. His muscle reflexes caused him to pull the trigger of his pistol and he shot himself in the foot. He never felt it as his body dance in place then tumbled sideways to the ground.

Charles' man ended just as badly, as the blast from his shot gun hit the man in the face. The man's head exploded like a rotten tomato thrown against a wall. Blood, brains, and bone fragments showered the air as he flew against the wall and bounced off. He fell face forward and crashed to the ground with a sickening thud, his body twitching uncontrollably.

Seconds after Kane and Charles fired Tony and Steve fired thru the door. The man who stood inside taking the money and passing out the dope had seen the cars and turned to flee as he heard the blast from the shot guns. His thoughts were, "Them stupid ass niggas shooting at the police." There was no back door but there was a back window. No sooner had he turned to run that he felt a heavy blow slam into his back. It knocked him to his knees as his momentum carried him forward. He tried to break his fall with his hands but couldn't. His chest and face crashed into the floor and he skipped a few feet, stunned, his nose and one wrist broke. Little did he know his quick thinking saved his life. The screen door and his distance away from it nullified some of the force of the twin shot gun blast. He was hit but the wounds weren't life threatening so he survived. Though It would be a while before he slept on his back.

Tony snatched the door open and rushed in with his shot gun raised. He saw a body on the floor. It moved, and he ran to it as Steve behind him quickly searched the front. Tony dropped to one knee and asked the bloody and tattered man, "Where's the dope and money?"

The man moaned, obviously in excruciating pain. Tony knew he'd learn nothing from the man so he joined the others who were quickly yet thoroughly searching the place.

Kane yelled, "I got it all," and came out of a room with 3 big tote bags slung over his back. "Go, go, go!" He shouted and the other men sprinted from the apartment. He knew there was no threat so he was hot on their heels. The women stood behind their car doors panning the street with their pistols. When the men ran out of the house the women got behind the wheels.

They loaded up and pulled out. A block away they removed their mask and got on the expressway. The entire strike only took two and a half hours. They were back at the house on Riverside with all the loot. There was only one bag of weed all sacked up in nickels and dimes. It was nearly four pounds of weed. They counted the rocks and came up with 48,000. They didn't take the time to separate them by size. They had two keys of coke and 36,000 bags of powder cocaine. 14,400 bags of heroin and then they started counting the money.

They knew they had $140,000 from BoBo's tool box and safe. When they tallied up they had $750,000 plus the $140,000 which was a total of $920,000. Kane did a quick calculation and said, "We get $150,000 apiece. We're gonna set $20,000 aside for our operating expenses. And put $150,000 aside for a defense fund so that means you'll all have to put $25,000 a piece in. We get 8,000 rocks a piece, 6,000 bags of powder, and 2,410 bags of heroin. Let's start separating this shit."

They separated the money and drugs into six piles and each person gave Kane $25,000 for the defense fund.

"Put my dope with yours daddy," Becky said.

"I'll put your dope with mine but you keep the money separate," he said. "Give your granny some and ball with the rest alright?"

"Okay if you say so," she replied.

"Bro let me put mine with yours too," Tony said.

"Me too," Sherrie said as they pushed the piles together.

"Kane, me and Steve wanna pool ours with you too," Charles said.

"Damn it!" Kane screamed. "Y'all motherfuckas had me sittin' down here finger fucking all this shit, now y'all tell me y'all wanna put it all together? I expected it from Beck and Red, but the rest of y'all? Hell naw."

"Dig this bro," Charles said. "At least we ain't got to break down the two birds." They burst out laughing, all except Kane. "These other niggas might not say it but you the head of our crew," Charles said looking Kane in the eyes. "They all know it. Beck and Red will admit it but these two macho niggas here," he pointed at Steve and Tony. "They ain't gonna say shit cause they don't wanna feel like followers or chumps. I don't feel

143

that way. Anyone of us has qualities that are lacking in the others. I've been asking myself; am I fit to lead a group as diverse as this? I answer, No! Is Tee? No! Is Steve? No! Is Beck? No! Is Red? Maybe! See I've been studying everybody and I've seen that Kane and Red got the swiftest minds. That's not to say the rest of us are slow or dumb. I'd come to the same conclusion as Kane if given enough time to analyze a situation. Red grasps shit quicker than me though she may not be as quick as Kane. I've seen how in planning she takes the plans Kane tosses out and adds another twist to it. She'll fool a lot of motherfuckas because she's pretty, red, and fine. I saw thru her a long time ago that's why I never approached her and warned Steve to stay away from her. Beck is smart too, but her strong point is in providing support as is Steve's. Two better people you couldn't ask to be on your team. They're low key but tend to think too much and that's a problem at times. Tony is strong and dependable, if he can ease up on that shit like he's been doing. He's an immature version of Kane, apt to act before thinking a situation thru. As for me, I'm philosophical as fuck and can be too much of an analyst which leads to hesitation. In life and death situations that could be too costly. The price is too high for me to take a chance. Do y'all agree with me at least in theory?"

Everyone but Kane said, "Yes".

"Cee, I don't want the responsibility," Kane said adamantly.

"Well now," Charles said staring into his eyes. "That's not a choice you have to make. Your actions dictate that you lead. The decision is out of your hands!"

"Yeah, I guess you're right," Kane said reluctantly. "We have a piece of unfinished business so let's get to it."

They went to the basement where BoBo was, awake. His eyes were hooded showing he was still under the influence of the narcotic. Kane walked over to him and snatched the tape from his mouth.

"Well Bo we put a little dent in your boys business tonight," Kane said.

"So you see I was telling the truth," Bobo said smiling. "Now you can let me go!"

"Bo, I'm afraid I can't do that." Kane said feigning anguish.

"But you said you wouldn't kill me if I told you the truth," Bobo said fearfully. "I told you about your dad and how I feel about the circumstances behind it and all. Don't that count for something?"

"You waited nine years too long for that dog," Kane said regretfully.

"But you swore on your family that you wouldn't kill me!" Bobo screamed.

"And I won't," Kane replied. "Steve, kill that snitching bitch!"

144

Steve stepped forward and pointed his pistol at Bobo's face. Before he could fire Sherrie grabbed his pistol, looked at Kane and said, "Let me do it daddy."

"Go ahead," Kane said.

"Not like that," she said. "It's too messy. Give me the boy and the needle."

Kane came back with the stuff and gave it to her. "I'm going to need a lot more heroin," she said. "Go get a bunch."

BoBo sat there crying, snot running from his nose as he begged, "Please Kane... Please man...Oh God...Save me...Oh Lord...I want my Momma...Jesus save me."

Charles stepped over to him and forcefully slapped the tape back over his mouth and said, "Nigga you knew this was a part of the game. At least die with dignity like a man."

Becky gave Sherrie some more heroin, and she poured nearly the whole package in the spoon. She got a lighter and brought the dope to a bubble and said, "Daddy, did I ever tell you I used to do blood work?"

"No you didn't," Kane replied.

"Yeah I had this dream of being a nurse," Sherrie said. "I took classes, got a job and was on my way but that shit was just too boring for me." She drew up the dope, held the needle up to the light and thumbed it until the bubbles was gone then said, "Wouldn't want that to bust his heart would we?" and laughed.

Tony watched her every move. She was heartless or at least for this moment she was.

"Bobo, you dying because you stupid as fuck," Sherrie said. "I wouldn't fuck you for money so what made you think I'd fuck you for free? Oh that's right, you can't talk right now." She laughed again then knelt in front of him. She grabbed his penis and started stroking it slowly. Gently and tenderly she stroked him until he started responding. When he was rock hard she said, "See what I mean, you're stupid as fuck? You know I'm gonna kill you but I still turn you on." She stroked him all the while she talked and Tony watched as she toyed with the condemned man. She stopped stroking him and found a big vein in his penis and slid the needle in and injected the heroin. Almost instantly he started to organism. "I'll see you in hell." She said and gave him a light kiss, then wiped his cum on his leg as his head slumped to his chest.

They watched her with the same thought in mind, "Red is a ruthless bitch." Tony knew right then that she was surely out of his league. Bobo shuddered and pissed, and as his bowels relaxed he shit. "Nasty ass nigga," Sherrie said and burst out laughing.

They all looked at her and shook their heads. The men cut him loose and rolled him up in the plastic as Becky went thru his clothes. He had $3,000 in his pocket. She tied his clothes in the sheet and threw the bundle on the plastic. The men rolled his body up in the plastic and taped it shut. They put the body in the trunk, drove a good way from the house, and dumped his body in the St. Johns River.

Sherrie and Becky cleaned the chair then freaked each other to orgasm. When the men returned they were smoking a joint and drinking.

"Y'all go call Gina and Jen," Kane said. "Tell them to meet us in Pickett." and they hurried to make the call.

*   *   *   *

Detective Samuels and Drummond stood at the crime scene on thirteen and Myrtle Ave. "Damn I don't know what the fuck is going on here, but I damn sure hope this isn't an instant replay of what happened with Vince Carrol and his crew," Samuels said.

Vince Carrol was a police officer that led a group of rogue cops. In 1986 they were robbing and killing drug dealers and giving the drugs to Vince's brother to sell. Samuels had headed the task force that brought their reign of terror to a screeching halt.

"Yeah we couldn't afford a scandal of that nature with the public's perception of the force right now. Especially with all the police brutality cases and so on," said Drummond.

"I know this much Drum," Samuels said. "The same people hit five spots with lightning speed. The only inconsistencies are in the number of suspects, but we're dealing with six at the least and ten at the most. The witnesses here said they jumped out yelling vice and firing. I hope we can get a lead here, because we couldn't get shit from the other scenes."

"I got a bad feeling about this one Sam," Drummond said. "I don't think this is the end of it. We may have a full scale drug war on our hands!"

"I got the same feeling Drum and I pray we're both wrong. There's not much we can do here so let's call it a night. Hell it's nearly 5:00 a.m., come in by 1:00 p.m. and we'll see where this leads us."

146

Chapter 10

They left the house on Riverside and drove to Post Street. They changed clothes and Kane, Becky, Sherrie, and Tony packed some clothes. They left most of their weapons but each one kept a pistol. They got the drugs and money then drove to Pickett.

When they arrived they saw a dark blue Grand Am parked in the driveway. It was Anna's car and as the door opened, Gina and Jen ran out and embraced Kane.

"Y'all married to that nigga or us?" Charles said sarcastically.

Jen ran to him and hugged him then said, "Black ass nigga, don't start that shit," and laughed.

The women hugged them all after they unloaded the car. It was nearly daylight when they sat on the floor around the living room watching television. Being that Gina and Jen didn't have anything to do after getting settled, they sat around and rolled a few joints. They laid out two plates, one with powder and one with rock. They didn't bother the heroin since Kane was the only one who used it. They had several bottles of wine, beer, and a bottle of Hennessey chilling in the refrigerator. The ladies started making drinks as they watched the late news.

When they were all seated a news flash came on, and there was the handsome face of Flint Morris with a concerned look etched in it. His melodious voice floated from the speakers, "This is Flint Morris reporting. The city is possibly in the midst of a drug war. Sources at the J.P.D report there were six grisly murders earlier tonight. All occurred on the Westside of town and our sources tell us that several innocent people were wounded in the Melee. They suspect it's the result of an escalating war between rival drug gangs. No suspects have been apprehended at this time and we'll be giving further updates as they come in. This is Flint Morris reporting from the newsroom".

They sat and chilled for a few then Kane said, "We're gonna take a couple of days and just chill. Cool out and do the domestic thing. No one knows were here so we should be cool, but stay on your guard." They all nodded.

After fighting over the bathroom they all got dressed and gathered in the living room.

"Are y'all gonna keep this spot when y'all finish with your business?" Gina asked. "Cause this would be a nice chill out spot for the family".

"Yeah under three conditions," Kane said. "No kids! Leslie and Lucinda can't ever know! And no Momma's ever!"

"Why not bro?" Jen asked puzzled.

"Cause Beck and Red have a part in this and if it can't be their home, somewhere they can feel comfortable, then I don't want any part of it."

"We didn't mean it like that bro," Gina said. "Beck and Red family but by the same token we didn't exclude the rest of the family. I understand and I agree 100 percent. Beck, Red, I see y'all as sisters so don't take that the wrong way."

"Gina speaks for the both of us," Jen said. "Y'all are welcome in my home anytime, for as long as y'all wanna stay regardless if y'all still with them niggas or not okay?"

Becky and Sherrie came over and hugged the other women.

"Alright," Kane said. "That's enough of that, can we go find somewhere to eat."

"You ate enough last night didn't you?" Jen asked. The others burst out laughing.

"Alright bitch," Kane said. "Watch your mouth or should I say wash your mouth, because I can smell your dick breath all the way over here." They all laughed again. "Today is Saturday so we gonna chill till Tuesday then it's back to the grind," Kane said. "Cee, you and Steve can't be running home to change clothes every day and I don't want y'all back on the set till this shit is over. You got plenty of money so we gonna ride to Orange Park Mall and shop. Besides, if them hookers there," he pointed at Jen and Gina. "Gonna be here with all that fucking and shit they gonna need some more panties." They laughed and he went on, "Seriously though, we need to get this place furnished nice. We can do that too when we leave. Since this is all of our place we got to get everybody keys to the doors. We ain't gonna disrespect our house so the rules are these. Any of us can come here anytime, no restrictions. But, no other male or female sleeping companions are allowed to cross the threshold. No fights ever and no arguing. This remains a safe house. Once you cross the threshold it's all love. Does everyone agree?"

They all said "Yes."

"That's good then," Kane said. "Let's roll."

They all gave $2,000 towards furnishing the place. They stopped to eat and saw a quality furniture store. They bought furniture for every room of the house to be delivered at 4:00 p.m. then they drove to the mall. The ladies spent 3 or 4 thousand dollars apiece; the fellows only spent a couple grand. They ate lunch then drove back to Safe House.

They got there about 3:30 and sat around smoking and drinking.

When the furniture arrived and was unloaded Kane paid the men to get rid of the stuff that was already there and gave them a generous tip. They sat around getting high and the women started teaching Becky to cook.

After they had eaten, Gina said, "They got a nice little club in Pickett. I think we ought to go and party tonight. What y'all say?"

All of the ladies were for it so the guys went along with it. The ladies rushed to their rooms and started picking through their new clothes for outfits to wear. The women tied the bathrooms up, Gina and Jen in one, Becky and Sherrie in the other.

Kane suspected what Becky and Sherrie were up to and said, "Damn I got to take a shit," and got up and went to the bathroom where Sherrie and Becky were.

He knocked on the door, "Y'all let me in I got to use the bathroom." He heard the lock snap back and went in. They were both standing there naked.

Sherrie rushed into his arms and whispered, "Becky had all of you last night so I want the nut today."

Kane looked at Becky and could tell that Sherrie had been sucking her cunt. Becky just stood there thrusting her finger in and out of her cunt. He dropped his shorts and boxers then said, "Come here Beck."

She walked over never taking her finger from her cunt. He grabbed Sherrie and said, "Sit here," and placed her on the floor in front of the cabinet that was built around the sink fixture. He pushed Becky to the sink so her cunt was in Sherrie's face and bent her over. She placed her hand on the cabinet as Sherrie pulled her hand from her cunt. Sherrie used one hand to push back the folds of Becky's pussy lips and exposed her clit. She trapped Becky's clit between her lips and flicked her tongue against it as Kane squatted, took his penis in his hand, and slid it in her to the hilt. She drew in a deep breath and he started rifling his stiff prick in her hot, wet hole. He thrust into her hard and fast pounding into her deep.

The shower covered her moan as she hummed softly, "ummm... ummmm..." Sherrie's tongue flicked over her clitoris rapidly as her free hand dropped between her own legs and started stroking her clit swiftly. It didn't take Becky 5 minutes to orgasm. She whispered, "I'm cumin Daddy....Oh Daddy...Oh Daddy...Red... Y'all making me cum... It's so good...." And shuddered as her organism hit.

He thrust into her a few more strokes then said, "Trade places with Red."

Becky her legs shaky and wobbly hurriedly sat while Sherrie, her cunt burning with desire moved to replace her. She arched her back, looked over her shoulder and whispered, "Fuck me hard daddy." Becky trapped her clit and flicked her tongue over it rapidly as he slid his cock deep in her and started pounding. He thrust into her with deep swift strokes and she moaned, "Fuck yes... Oh... Fuck me daddy... Yes baby... Get this pussy... Beat it..." He hammered into her hard and fast. Then he put his middle finger in his mouth and got it coated with saliva then roughly shoved it deep in her anus and she moaned softly, "Hell yes... Goddamn... Finger my ass... Oh baby... Just ... A ... Little more... I'm gonna cum...."

The power thrusting was taking its toll on him and he felt his orgasm quickly approaching. He felt the cum rise and blast into Sherrie's hot, tight, cunt. He moaned, "Red... Here it comes... I'm cumin..."

She moaned out, "Give it to me... Oh baby... I'm cumin too... Oh shit..." They shook to completion as he pounded into her a few more strokes. He pulled out and she sat on the toilet reached for him and sucked him deep into her mouth.

Becky stood got a wash cloth, gently pulled him from Sherrie's mouth, bent over and sucked him in. She sucked him for a few then washed him and let his penis go. He had been in the bathroom about 12 minutes. "Y'all hurry up you got other people wanna use the bathroom." He said walking back to the front.

Charles threw him a face towel and said, "Dry off nigga you sweating." Kane took the cloth and sat next to Charles. Tony and Steve were in the kitchen.

"What you gonna do when Tee finds out?" Charles asked eyeing him.

"I don't know Cee," Kane said. "I've been thinking bout it seriously but I don't know."

"I understand Bro." Charles said. "Both Red and Beck love you the same way. They both call you daddy. I ain't the only one gone notice it dog, trust me. She's out of Tee's league and if I had known in advance that he was gonna shoot at her, I would've warned him off. You can control her and believe me there are few men who could. I believe that if she asked Tee to leave his wife he might do it."

Kane cut in, "Naw, he wouldn't do that Cee. We got to give the nigga some credit."

"You got a point bro," Charles said. "But she wouldn't ask him because that would limit her time with you. Don't waste your time feeling guilty, if Tee finds out he'll understand. In the back of his mind he knows Red is too much for him. Then again he may never find out cause a woman like that could blind a man and make him see only what she wants him to see."

"I heard that," Kane said.

The ladies finally freed the bathrooms and the men showered.

Becky wore a skin tight, baby blue, tank style mini-dress by Fendi with matching ankle strap pumps and purse with the gold Fendi emblem. Kane wore a baby blue walking suit by Bill Blass and Powder Blue gators by Mauri. Sherrie wore a Red, skin tight silk and lace dress by Donna Karen with matching Chanel ankle strap pumps and clutch purse. Tony wore a red Bill Blass walking suit and red velvet Bally loafers. Gina wore her favorite color, a canary yellow mini-skirt suit with ankle high yellow boots and matching purse. Steve wore a yellow Bill Blass walking suit and calfskin dress boots by Armani. Jen wore a burgundy mini-skirt and cropped top by Anna Sui and matching pumps and purse. Charles wore a burgundy walking suit by Bill Blass and burgundy ostrich skin loafers by Gucci.

They were all razor sharp and when they walked in the club everyone stopped to stare. They found seats and ordered drinks. They had a ball and at 2:00 a.m. it seemed the night ended to soon. They drove back to the safe house still in party mood, and since there were no close neighbors they boomed the sound system and had a great time. They vowed to hang out at the safe house and party at least once a month. Everyone went to their rooms and The Safe House lived up to its name; it was filled with love and love making. They all would awake late.

They spent Sunday getting the house arranged to their liking. The ladies wanted to go and get pictures for the walls and rooms; the fellows' equipment to keep the yard in order. They all left on their separate missions.

The men had to rent a truck and trailer to bring the equipment back. They bought a riding mower, 2 push mowers, 4 rakes, a weed eater, push broom, edger, hedge trimmers, a leaf blower, and several shovels. They bought a fully equipped tool box, chain saw, hammers, and nails. The women returned with African art, sculptures, and several beautiful painted pictures by up and coming black artist. They took all day Sunday hanging pictures and fixing up Safe House. They went back to the club again that night and they partied hard, came back to Safe House and loved even harder.

Monday Jen arranged for phone and cable services to be hooked up, and they chilled out and enjoyed the day. About midnight as they chilled in the den Kane got up and left the room. When he returned he had a small tote bag and a plastic covered pack of brown paper bags. He also had a black felt tipped marker. He tore open the package of bags, took out 4 and wrote names on them. It was one for Anna, one for Leslie, one for his grandmother, and one for Doreen. He opened the tote and counted out $25,000 and set it to the side. The others watched him puzzled and he said,

"For the defense fund." He put $40,000 in a bag for Leslie, and $20,000 in each of the other 3 bags. He still had close to $20,000 left.

The others seeing him went and got their money and started doing the same. Jen took $10,000 from Charles and tried to give it to Becky, "Your life savings Beck."

"Keep it," Becky said. "Buy something nice for the kids. Kane put this $10,000 in there for your mom, and $10,000 in there for Leslie."

"Beck you don't have to do that," Kane said.

"If you love them they must be special baby, so just take the money. Remember we're in safe house, no arguing!" He got the money and put it in the bags.

"Give them this too daddy," Sherrie said giving him $20,000. He looked in her eyes and she put her finger to her lips. He took the money and put it in the bags.

Leslie's bag had $60,000 in it when Becky said, "Put this $10,000 in for your granny," and gave him the money. No sooner had he reached for it than Sherrie gave him $10,000 for his grandmother too. The others watched how the women acted towards Kane and knew they were looking at love. Inwardly Tony smiled but it never touched his face.

Tony put $40,000 in a bag for Lucinda, $20,000 each in 3 bags for Anna, Doreen and his grandmother. Steve and Charles gave Gina and Jen $40,000 a piece, put $20,000 in 2 bags for Anna and their mothers. Becky put $40,000 in a bag for her mother in Detroit. She wrote the name and address on the bag and asked Jen to get a box and wrap it up, and mail it overnight express. She got a pen and wrote a short letter on one of the bags, tore it off and told Jen to make sure it went with the money. She put $20,000 in a bag for her grandmother and Kane gave her the rest of his money to put with it.

Sherrie only had one bag. She put $40,000 in it for her mom and wrote the address on it. Gave Becky $10,000 for her grandmother then looked at Kane and said, "Daddy you look like you're running short on cash, so I'm gonna loan you 10 gees. I want my money back when you get on your feet." They burst out laughing.

"I'm straight Red," Kane said smiling.

"Fuck that nigga!" She said. "You done forgot where you at?" He took the money reluctantly. She gave Gina $10,000 and said, "Pay the rent for safe house with this."

"Damn girl," Jen said. "We would've chipped in."

"We family." Sherrie said. "No need to chip in. Remember, no arguing this is safe house!"

Gina and Jen got all the money and started packing up to go and Kane said, "Tell Les I'll see her one day this week and tell Lu the same for Tee." They all turned in and called it a night.

Chapter 11

Big Moe was furious. "What the fuck is going on?" He asked Ted. "We had six spots hit in one fucking night!"

"Fuck if I know?" Ted said. "But the word coming from the street is that it could possibly be a group of renegade cops. At least that's what they look like wearing Ninja masks and black jumpsuits. They're hitting the spots with military precision and appear to be well trained. It just doesn't have the feeling of a job by street niggas. It's like some shit you'd pull but I can't see where you'd profit from killing your own people; plus that nigga BoBo just disappeared. We lost more than a million in cash more than likely, and damn near that much in product. I just can't read this one Moe, so what you wanna do?"

"If it's the Rollers ain't shit we can do," Moe said. "Remember back in 86? The same kind of shit went down and it just stopped. Maybe they just laid low until their funds got flakey and their back on the scene. If it's them then our regular channel ain't gonna be worth shit. All we can do is wait to see what happens next. One thing though. I want you to change the schedule for our cash pickups. If BoBo is in on this he knows when we make the pickups. That way we won't take as hard a hit as we did this time. Call all of our people and tell them to bring what they've got Tuesday night at 12:00. You be there to make sure everyone shows. The first nigga that doesn't show up I want to make an example of him. Cool?"

"Alright," Ted said. "But it's Monday and I might not be able to reach them all."

"We need to do something to make these niggas tighten up anyway. If you have any problems call me and I'll be there, alright?"

"That's cool," Ted said and turned to pick up the phone and make his calls.

Ted's wife Elvira was standing in the door of the hall in a short see thru night gown; with no bra and matching bikini panties pulled up tight to her hairy cunt. When Ted turned to make his call she looked Moe in the eyes, flashed out her tongue and slowly licked her lips seductively. He smiled and winked at her.

*   *   *   *

Tuesday as everyone packed their bags and loaded them in the cars the women checked to make sure Safe House was clean.

154

Kane called them together. "Cee, y'all take the truck back I've got to make a run. Y'all go to Post St. and wait till I get there. I'm taking Beck and Red with me. This run is necessary before we go handle the next step of our business alright?"

"I got it bro," Charles said and gave Kane some dap. They got in the Grand Am and the truck and pulled off.

Kane got behind the wheel and drove to Orange Park. He drove down Wells Rd. until he came to a gated community. He told the security guard at the gate that he was there to see Mr. Frank Toronelli and that his name was Berean Kane. The guard picked up the phone and made the call. He spoke for a second then hung up and popped the gate.

Kane drove thru and went to the Toronelli Estate. It was a lush circular driveway, well-manicured lawns, a fountain in the center spewed water skyward; and a beautiful gazebo off to the side surrounded by beautiful flowers in full bloom. The house was palatial with four broad white columns in front, beveled glass windows, and large oak doors with big brass lion head door knockers. A four car garage that was raised and revealed 4 luxury cars sat to one side. A metallic grey Bentley, a candy apple red B.M.W., a big Mercedes Benz, and a long black Cadillac limo filled the area.

Kane parked in front of the big doors and got out. Becky and Sherrie just sat there with their mouths hanging open wondering, "How does Kane know someone who lives in a mansion like this?"

"Come on y'all," Kane said. "Let's go." They got out of the car and followed him as he walked to the door and rang the bell. They could all hear it echoing in the big house.

A moment later the door opened and there stood an elderly black man in a finely tailored dark blue, pinstripe, single breasted suit, crisp white starched shirt, and a regimental striped tie in dark blue, powder blue, and white. He was clean shaven and had close cropped steel grey hair. He smiled and revealed a set of beautiful, pearly white teeth. "So you finally decided to come see us huh?" The man asked. "It's about time; now get your ass in here."

The man's name was Jimmy Lewis. He was a close friend of Kane's father Bishop. Bishop had helped Jimmy avenge his father's murder in the late 50's.

"I've been sort of busy," Kane said sheepishly.

"Yeah I know," Jimmy said.

"Busy bullshitting when you should've been trying to get the family straightened out. You know we're here for you and you should've come to us long ago, it's been six years son. I damn near came and got you myself but Frank forbid it. He said you'd come; how do you think you got three concurrent nine year sentences for armed robbery, armed kidnapping and attempted murder? It wasn't the money we gave Anna and Les believe me. Frank called in some markers for you boy."

Becky and Sherrie stood there in awe as the man kissed Kane. They were used to seeing him in control and didn't believe he would let someone dress him down like the man was doing.

Jimmy closed the door behind them and wrapped his arms around Kane, and kissed him lightly then said, "You Kane's are a stubborn lot. You know we're family son you should've come to us."

"I didn't want the safety net Jimmy," Kane said softly. "I needed to do things my way, on my own."

"I understand kid," Jimmy said smiling. "Come on let's go see Frank. I didn't tell him you were coming."

They walked thru the elegantly furnished house and came to a set of oak paneled French doors. Jimmy walked in with Kane and the women behind him. The study was beautifully decorated, and sitting behind a large desk with a big cigar clenched between his teeth was an olive complicated man with a head full of snow white hair. He looked up and saw Kane and a big smile lit up his face.

He stood and said, "So you finally came to your senses eh?" He walked from behind the desk with his arms open wide. He was a big bear of a man, built like an offensive lineman going to seed.

He was Francisco Luigi Toronelli II, Frankie Knuckles to his peers and Frank to his friends and family. He was a semi-retired mob boss and also a close friend of Kane's father Bishop. The Kane's and Toronelli's had a long history dating back to the 40's. Franks father was like a son to Kane's Great grandfather Raven Kane, so the bond was thick. Frank's uncle Sal had conspired with an upcoming mob boss to kill Frank's father Francisco the first. Jimmy, Frank and Frank's wife Donnatella, fathers were all killed in an ambush. Bishop, Frank, Jimmy, and a group of Kane's exacted the revenge.

"So tell me Berean, what took you so long to come see me?" Frank asked as he held Kane in his arms.

"I've lived in the shadows of my father and his fathers before him. I didn't feel I measured up to the Kane legend so I just wanted to be me. I didn't want to be respected by virtue of being a Kane. I wanted to be respected because of who I am, not who my father is or who his father was. Bishop is a legend, as was Baron before him, and Raven before him. Who am I?"

"You are Kane!" Frank said authoritatively. "Don't ever forget that. You set the standards for the generations of Kane's to come. It is you who will determine what your legacy will be. You are the descendant of

156

great men and it is your family duty to live up to the name. You have no idea what it's like to be fatherless, to have to set the standards for your own. I learned this from your grandfather, from your father. All that I am today I owe in part to the Kane's. Whenever there was a need, a Kane was always at my side. I had hoped it would be the same for my son and his son after him. Don't think for a minute that I haven't been keeping an eye on the family. Your mother and grandmother are the only ones that maintain contact. I talk to your father every week without fail. He's the only true brother I have besides Jimmy. Remember son, our bond is as deep as blood!"

Kane looked into the vivid blue eyes and knew that every word came from Frank's heart.

"So what's going on Berean?" He asked, and then looked to Becky and Sherrie asking silently if they could talk in front of them.

"Frank this is Becky and Sherrie. They're my wives," Kane said. Frank's brows rose as Kane went on, "They're both made and I trust them with my life!" Frank walked from Kane to the women, hugged and kissed them both and looked at Kane with new respect in his eyes. "Have you been watching the news lately?" Kane asked Frank as they all took seats.

Frank nodded and said, "I try to keep my ear to the street. Four murders in Brooklyn a couple of months ago or so; I can't remember exactly. Then six murders a few nights ago scattered all over the west side. Just this morning they fished a body out of the St. Johns, so yes I've seen the news."

"All of those are ours," Kane said and nodded at Becky and Sherrie.

Frank's eyes got wide and he asked, "All eleven of them?"

"Yeah," Kane replied. "Do you know Big Moe?"

"Not personally," Frank said. "But I've heard of him and his questionable business practices."

"Those were all of his people," Kane said. "Moe is responsible for my father being in prison, and all of the others that fell."

"That cocksucker!" Frank exclaimed. "Say no more Berean I'll take care of it."

"I can handle it," Kane said. "But thanks anyway. This is personal Frank and what I need is a special tool, one that doesn't make any noise."

"No problem," Frank said. "Do you need muscle, because if you do I got plenty?"

"I'm good," Kane said. "There are three more of us."

"Alright," Frank said. "But if things get too heavy don't hesitate to call alright?"

"I won't," Kane said.

157

"Jim, go to a phone booth and call Pete at Arnie's pawn shop. Tell him that Berean Kane will be coming by and to give him anything he needs no charge." Jimmy nodded and left.

They sat around and talked for a while until Jimmy came back. "That's done Frank," Jimmy said.

"Thanks Jim," Frank said looking at Kane. "If you don't see this thru, Big Moe won't see the end of this week and you can trust me on that. Call me or go by Arnie's and let Pete know if the job is done and he'll get word to me. Your father could've taken me and Jim with him but he bit the bullet. We grew up together, the three of us, so it's personal for me too son!"

They all stood and Frank threw his arm around Kane's shoulder and said, "Bishop told me to look out for his family and I've done the best I could, but you Kane's are not only stubborn but proud as well. Don't let six years pass again before I see you again, hear me?" Kane nodded and Frank went on, "Come see me more often, I might have some work for you okay?"

"Okay," Kane answered as they walked out the door.

Frank hugged and kissed him then squeezed his face between his big hands and said, "Be careful. If you need me call me. Don't let pride be the reason you don't contact me, alright son?"

"Alright Frank," Kane said. Frank hugged and kissed the women then they got in the car and drove off.

"Who was that Daddy?" Sherrie asked.

"My Godfather," Kane said. "He's family, and you're part of his family now. If something should happen to us he won't stop until he has avenged us!"

"Daddy what did you mean when you told him we were made?" Becky asked.

"That just meant that y'all have killed," Kane said.

"So that's what y'all were running from when we went on vacation," Sherrie said. "Y'all killed those four niggas. Damn I wish I could've been down on that."

"Girl you sound like you drunk," Becky said. "Daddy you said no drinking or getting high before we get ready to work, so we need to do something to get that shit out of this ho's system," she pointed at Sherrie. "I saw a hotel up the road a piece, let's get a room and work that shit out of her."

"Beck we ain't had but one drink," Kane said. "You need to slow your freaky ass down." and laughed.

"But daddy when this shit is over we ain't gonna have you with us all the time like we do now," Sherrie said. "You already done spoiled us. I wish you could get Leslie down with the program. We don't mind sharing you with her but we don't want you to forget us."

"It's obvious to me that y'all done sat down and talked about this," Kane said. "When y'all had the time to I don't know, but dig this. Y'all my girls and y'all heard what I told Frank. I meant that shit. I love you both, no question, and it ain't just about the fucking. I like your company too, so this gonna be the deal when this shit is over. I'm gonna take Leslie on a cruise for a week and y'all can keep each other company till I get back. Y'all gonna be getting money so you got to stay on your P's and Q's. Charles and Steve got your back, because I'm taking Tee with me. I got to get him away from Red for a while before he start acting stupid and wanna leave his wife. We ain't wrecking homes, you got me Red?"

"Daddy you may be under estimating Tee," Sherrie said. "I don't think he'd do that anymore than you would. As it is he seems a little distant; he'll start to say something then stop. When I ask him what's up he just says never mind. So something's up with him and I don't believe it's leaving his wife. He still hits it, but seems like he falls asleep afterwards. And by the way, ain't but one nigga I'd go domestic for and that's you. I dig Tee, but my love for you is different. I love him like a bother but I love you like my man. I wouldn't intentionally hurt Tee for the world Daddy; believe me. Oh yeah, Jen knows what time it is. She caught me coming out of y'all room Sunday morning. She hugged me and said she understands. She said if you weren't her brother she would want you too. She just asked me not to hurt Tee, so I know the others know now too."

"Will you please let me finish, talking woman?" Kane said, "Like I was saying. When I get back from the cruise I'm gonna spend three days with y'all. Red you got to come up with an excuse to disappear for three days. Me and Beck can't go missing, but we'll knock off early and you can just chill in the hotel until we get there. After that I'll do a day with Les and a day with y'all. When one of y'all period is on, the other one gets me all to herself. I just hope all of y'all don't get them at the same time. I might have to find me a substitute." He started laughing as the women punched him playfully.

"Nigga if you cheat on us we gonna put you on pussy rations," Sherrie said and they burst out laughing.

*   *   *   *

Two hours later they pulled out of the motel and headed for town. They drove to Arnie's Pawn Shop got out of the car and went in. The ladies browsed around looking at Jewelry as Kane walked towards the back. He saw a big olive complexioned man standing at the back counter. His shirt

159

was unbuttoned, and his neck was festooned with gold jewelry that rested in a mat of dense black chest hair. He wore a gold Rolex watch and rings on three fingers of each hand. His hair was jet black and slicked back.

"I'm looking for Pete," Kane said to him.

"Who's looking for Pete?" The man asked.

"Berean Kane is looking for Pete," He said.

The man smiled and said, "I'm Pete," then lifted the gate and motioned Kane thru. They walked to a back office and Pete walked to a safe as big as a closet and opened it. He turned to Kane and asked, "What do you need?"

"A silencer," Kane said.

"I'll do you one better," Pete said reaching into the safe and pulling out a small case and handing it to Kane.

Kane took the case and unzipped it. Inside was a 9mm Beretta with a silencer attached to it. He dropped the clip and Pete said, "Sub sonic rounds, so when it's fired it's no louder than a cough. There no serial numbers, and no bodies on it. It's clean."

"Thanks Pete," Kane said appreciatively.

"No thanks necessary," Pete said. "You're family!"

Kane zipped the case close and they walked back to the front of the store where Becky and Sherrie were paying for their purchases. "Give them back their money," Pete yelled to the cashier. "The whole store is theirs if they want It." and the man behind the counter gave them their money back. Pete hugged Kane, waved at the women, then Kane and the women left. When they got in the car Sherrie reached over the seat and gave him 2 jewelry boxes.

"What's this?" He asked.

"Nigga just open the boxes," Becky said. He opened one and there was a gold Rolex Presidential, and the other box held a complex wedding band which had 3 rings in 1.

"What's this for?" He asked.

"We wanted you to have a watch so we were gonna split the cost," Becky said. "Notice the wedding ring has 3 bands? Well, one is for Leslie, one is for me, and one is for Red. We're your wives right?"

He sat behind the wheel and tears welled in his eyes. When the women saw them Sherrie said, "If we did wrong Daddy we're sorry."

"Naw baby," he said. "Y'all did right," then he got out of the car and rushed back into the pawn shop. He came back with 2 wedding bands identical to the one Leslie had and slid them on their fingers and said, "I love you both," then kissed them. "Let's rent a room for a few hours since we don't need to take care of business till later on." They went to the Heart of Jacksonville and rented the same room they first made love in.

Chapter 12

After they left the hotel they drove to the house on Post Street. When they pulled up Tony was sitting on the porch drinking a soda, smoking a cigarette lost in thought. It was about 7:00 p.m. when they walked up the driveway and Kane asked, "What's up Bro.?"

"I'm cool," Tony said. "Listen Bro," he hesitated then said, "Oh never mind."

"What's up Tee? Kane asked looking in his eyes. "You got something on your mind, I can tell."

"Just thinking about Lu and the kids," Tony lied. He was trying to find a way to tell Kane that he could have Sherrie, but he didn't know how to put it.

"You sure everything is alright?" Kane asked genuinely concerned.

"Yeah," Tony said. "I just wanna go home, that's all."

"A few more days' bro," Kane said. "This should be over by Friday so just chill. Don't go soft on me nigga I need you to have my back."

Kane smiled as Tony said, "Who you calling soft?" And grabbed him in a bear hug, kissed him on the mouth and started laughing.

"Where are the others?" Kane asked.

"Them niggas been locked up in the room all day with your freaky ass sisters," Tony said laughing.

They walked in the house and Kane yelled, "Gina! Jen! Y'all better leave them niggas some strength because I need them tonight! Charles! Steve! Get y'all asses out here! And brush your teeth before you come, I don't want y'all blowing no stink pussy breath in my face!"

He started laughing as Charles came out and said, "Nigga you better watch your mouth, because my baby pussy smell sweet and taste like some shit Sarah Lee ought to sell in the grocery store!"

They all laughed as Steve came from a room and went straight to the bathroom and they could hear him brushing his teeth. Charles shouted, "Nigga you must've been eating Gina's ass quick as you ran in the bathroom!"

They all laughed then Gina stuck her head out of the door and said, "From the shit I heard Jen saying thru the wall you ate some ass yourself nigga!"

They all looked at Charles and burst out laughing as he headed for the bathroom. Jen looked out the door and said, "Gina you a nosey ass bitch. If you would've been as busy getting fucked, as you was listening to us you might be too tired to run your damn mouth." And the house echoed with laughter.

When they were all dressed and gathered in the front room Kane said, "Gina, Jen y'all go on and drop off the money then go back to Granny's house and wait for us to beep you." They got up, hugged and kissed everyone then left. "Tonight we're gonna hit one of Jermaine's spots," Kane said. "We'll try to find out where all of his houses are and hit them. I want y'all to be extra careful. Our last job went smooth but I don't want us to get careless alright?" They all nodded and he went on. "We're gonna hit the apartment on West 21st. It's on the bottom floor. It's only one apartment building so it should come off alright. Red, you, Steve, and Tee will drive around to 22nd. Tee you already know where the place is, so go between the houses on 22nd and come up on the spot from the back. Red give them 10 minutes then pull up out front, and you know the drill. Beck, you, me, and Cee going to 20th, and we'll get out there, cut thru the alley and come up on the place from the front. Give us 10 minutes Beck, and then come to the front. We're gonna drive by one time so you'll know where it is. We won't leave until 11:00. It's 7:40 now so y'all go on and get some rest. Tee you alright?"

"I'm cool Bro," Tony said. Sherrie had been watching him. She looked at Kane and said, "I know what he needs," and walked over to Tony and took his hand.

"I'm straight Red," Tony said. "Go on and get you some rest, because I was sleeping off and on all day."

Sherrie stood there holding his hand with a puzzled look on her face. The room was silent. Tony looked up into her face and said, "It's alright Red." She visibly relaxed and the tension that was building evaporated. Everyone expected this to be the time that Tony mentioned the situation with him, Sherrie, and Kane. Instead Tony just smiled.

"Y'all niggas get some rest," Kane said pointing at Charles and Steve. "Come on Lil Momma let's take a nap." He grabbed Becky's hand and they walked to the bedroom. Her hand went to his crotch and he said, "Don't even think about it. We gonna get some rest." Becky just smiled and rubbed her thumb on her new wedding ring.

*   *   *   *

At 10:30 Charles knocked on Kane's door and said, "It's 10:30 Bro time to get started."

Kane came to the door and said, "Did you get some rest?"

"Yeah," Charles said. "I got a couple of hours in."

Kane walked back in the room, shook Becky and said, "Wake up sleepy head; it's time to get busy." She sat up, stretched, and rubbed her eyes. They went and took a shower and 30 minutes later they were all dressed. "Everyone got their watches?" They all nodded. "Okay let's roll," Kane said.

They grabbed the 2 totes with the shot guns in them, Charles one, Steve the other. They got on the interstate and drove down to 20th Street Expressway until they came to Myrtle Ave. They made a right, then drove to 21st Street and made a left. Kane showed the apartment to Charles and Becky, Tony in the other car showed it to Steve and Sherrie. They drove down 2 blocks and parked beside a beauty parlor that sat on the corner. They got out of the car and Kane said, "10 minutes from now Beck, you and Red hit the front. Let's go."

They got in the cars and Becky drove left and Sherrie right. Sherrie made another right, drove up 2 blocks, pulled to the curb, and doused the lights. Steve and Tony silently left the car and ran between the houses until they were at the back of the apartment. They split up and each took one side of the building. Then they eased to the front where they dropped low and waited at the corner of the building.

Becky made another left, drove up 2 blocks, pulled to the curb, and doused her lights as Kane and Charles hurried from the car. The 2 men ran silently thru the alley until they came to the back of the church that was directly across from the apartment building. They kneeled and Kane pulled a lighter from his pocket and flashed it once. An answering flash came from across the street. Before Kane could move he heard the sound of a car approaching so he froze and flashed his lighter twice. Next to the apartment a light flashed twice and they held their position as a dark colored Jag pulled to the curb on Kane's side and stopped. Kane knew Jermaine had a dark blue Jag and he watched as the door opened and a light skinned, slim man got out. The man locked his doors and started adjusting his clothes. "Look at this nigga primping." Kane said to himself and eased quietly from the side of the church. Swiftly yet silently he rushed towards where the man stood with his back to him. Tony and Steve rushed from the side of the apartment towards the man who froze in his tracks when he saw the 2 shadows detach themselves from the building and rush him. Tony and Steve provided a perfect distraction and he never heard the soft footfalls that approached him rapidly from the rear.

Kane raced around the front end of the car, raised the shot gun, and swung it in a vicious arch. Jermaine caught movement from the corner of his eye but he was too late in reacting as Kane's shot gun crashed into the right side of his head behind his ear. He crumpled to the ground in an untidy heap. Kane knelt beside him and quickly searched his pockets. He

163

pulled his keys from his pocket and tossed them to Charles who was crouched in a defensive posture.

Tony and Steve rushed over, turned and trained their shot guns on the apartment. Charles opened the door of the Jag and looked to Kane who motioned towards the back door. Charles opened the door and Kane tossed his shot gun on the backseat and he grabbed Jermaine under his arms. Then he drug Jermaine to the car and roughly shoved him onto the floor. He motioned to Charles who got behind the wheel of the Jag. Sherrie pulled around the corner and Kane motioned Tony to get in the car. Just then Becky pulled up and he motioned to Steve to get in her car and he got in the back seat of the Jag as Charles pulled off.

Charles and Kane were the first ones to arrive at the house on Riverside. They drug Jermaine from the car into the basement and tied him to the chair. Kane checked his head. There was no blood just an egg sized lump. His head was slumped forward on his chest and he breathed evenly. The others arrived and Kane tossed them the keys to the Jag and said, "Beck, Red, search the car good, I don't think you'll find drugs but there might be cash. Steve, go get me some ice and a rag and be sure to wet the rag." Steve hurried from the room as the women went to search the car. Kane and the others just stood there watching the unconscious man. Becky and Sherrie came back with a large tote bag. They dropped it on the floor, bent and unzipped it. The others walked over and looked into it and it was filled with cash. The men whistled. They knew it was just as much as they hit from the other night.

Steve came back and looked in the bag and said, "Damn!"

Kane took the towel and ice from Steve. He laid the towel flat on the floor, poured ice in it and walked over to the sink in the basement. Then he ran water over the towel and ice, and then let it drip for a minute. He walked to Jermaine and pushed it in his face. Jermaine shook his head and Kane said, "Tee get that bucket over there," and pointed to a bucket that sat in the corner. Tony got the bucket and brought it over. "Cee get a glass of water." Kane said pressing the cold towel to Jermaine's face. He shook his head and his eyes flew open. He was disoriented and Kane could see that his eyes were still glazed. Slowly he regained consciousness. He looked around at the people surrounding him. Kane could tell he was about to vomit so he said, "Tee hold the bucket in front of his face." Tony pushed the bucket forward just as his head leaned forward and vomit spewed from his mouth. He threw up until he heaved. "Give him the water Cee," Kane said. Charles held the water to his mouth and he drank it thirstily then vomited again.

He looked around and asked in an unsteady tone, "What the fuck is this?"

"We gonna be asking the questions," Kane said. "All you do is answered them. I got to warn you the first time I think you're lying, you die. No questions we just smoke your ass. To prove we're serious do you remember the hits Friday night?" Jermaine nodded. "That was us," Kane said. "The police don't have a clue so if you don't wanna end up like them; you need to know the severity of your situation."

Jermaine looked at the stone faces of the men and women then asked, "What do you want?"

"We wanna know the locations of all your dope houses," Kane said. "We're gonna hit them tonight!"

"I'll make a deal with you," Jermaine said.

"You're not in a position to deal," Kane said. "Your life is on the line. If you tell me what I wanna know I won't kill you. If you don't I will."

"Why should I trust you?" Jermaine asked.

"You really don't have a choice," Kane said.

"Alright," Jermaine said. "But listen. I went to all of the places I run and picked up the money. By now they've made a few bucks but it won't be much so you'd waste your time. You'd get some dope but that's not gonna be much either. See me and all of the others that run the areas got a call from Ted last night. He told us to bring the cash we had on hand to the spot we drop off at by midnight tonight. That's where I was going when y'all got me. I had one more pick up then I was gonna take the money you got over there in that tote bag."

"And just where is this drop off spot?" Kane asked.

"I'll show you if you don't kill me, "Jermaine said.

"Alright," Kane said. "You got a deal. I won't kill you but if you try to be slick or pull any stunts believe me, you'll be dead before God gets the news. Am I making myself clear?" Jermaine nodded. Red dumped the money and filled the bag with something to make it look good. Steve cut this nigga loose," Kane said and looked at his watch. "It's 12:15 so our boy here is already late. Jermaine is the house guarded by gunmen or electronics?"

"Neither," Jermaine said. "Moe doesn't believe any of his lieutenants would cross him. Besides, only Ted, him, and the accountant knows where the spot is. It's laid back off the main street in Alderman Park over in Arlington. The closest neighbor is 7 or 8 houses away. It has a big privacy fence around it plus there's no attention drawn to it."

"Is there a back way in?" Kane asked.

"There's probably a back gate but I really don't know. I've never been there in the day time," Jermaine said.

Sherrie came back with the bag and Kane said, "The same way we came we leave. Jermaine, put your hands behind your back." he did as Kane ordered. "Beck duct tape his hands and put a strip across his eyes." He looked at Jermaine as Becky taped his hands behind his back and said, "The strip over your eyes is so you can't see where we live. I'd hate to think I'm making a mistake by not killing you." Becky pulled a piece of tape over his eyes and Charles got the key to the Jag from Sherrie. "Steve ride with Beck, Tee with Red," Kane said. "We've wasted enough time. Let's go!"

They went to the cars and Kane pushed Jermaine to the floor and they left. They drove to Arlington, got off on the Service Road, made a left at the Gulf Station, and drove under the arch that leads into Alderman Park then headed around the curve.

Kane reached down and pulled Jermaine up then removed the tape from his eyes. He held the shot gun against his ribs and asked, "Which way?"

"Go on around the curve," Jermaine said. "When the road straightens out go 4 blocks and you'll see some woods on the right. The first street you come to take a right. You'll see a group of houses close together. Then down a little farther you'll see a group of houses close together. Then down a little farther you'll see a house set back from the road with a big privacy fence around it. That's the place."

*   *   *   *

Ted looked at his watch and said to himself, "Damn its 12:35 and Jermaine hasn't showed up yet. Fuck! Where is that nigga?" Ted sat in the house where the cash was dropped off in Alderman Park. "I've got to go on and call Moe," Ted said to himself. "I like that nigga Jermaine but it's better his ass than mine." He picked up the phone and beeped Moe, hung up and waited. 5 minutes later the phone rang. He picked it up and said, "Moe?"

"Yeah this me," Moe said on the other end sounding out of breath. "What's up?"

"Jermaine is the only one that didn't show," Ted said. "Everyone else had and we've got what they've made in the last few days. The accountant estimates we've got about 4 miles here so you need to contact the banker so we can drop it off in the morning."

Moe breathing more ragged said, "I'll be there in an hour and a half." Then looked up at Elvira who was riding his cock rapidly and moaning, "ummm....ummm....ummm...."

"Nigga what's that I hear in the background?" Ted asked.

166

"Just....A....Little....Head....I....Picked....Up...." Moe moaned
and exploded in Ted's wife's hot, wet cunt then hung up laughing. Moe
knew Ted would be tied up so he went to Ted's house and fucked his wife
in his bed.

*   *   *   *

Charles followed Jermaine's instructions and drove past the house.
They came to a turn in the road that lead to a wooded area and there they
parked. They got out of the cars and crowded near the jag. "This is how
it's gonna go down," Kane said. "Beck, you and Red give us 15 minutes
from the time we leave here then drive to the house. Tee, you, Charles, and
Steve will ride in the Jag with us. When we get to the gate, bail out. Steve
since you're probably the fastest, run around to the back and see if there's a
way to get in. If not, jump the fence and cover the back of the house. Tee
you go to the left side and jump the fence. Cee you do the same on the right
and I want you to cover the front of the house. If this nigga," he pointed at
Jermaine. "Tries some stupid shit either me or you can blow his ass up.
Got it?"

"I got it Bro," Charles said.

"Steve cut him loose so he can drive," Kane said and pointed at
Jermaine. The women got in their cars as the men piled into the Jag.
"Don't try any stupid shit," Kane said to Jermaine pressing the shot gun to
the back of his head. "Just drive up to the gate and stop. When they get out
wait a minute then open the gate and drive in. Keep in mind I'm gonna be
watching you the whole way."

"I got you man," Jermaine said. "I ain't gonna pull no junkie stunt.
I don't wanna die."

"That's good," Kane said. "Now go on and let's get this shit over
with."

Jermaine pulled out and drove back to the house. When he got to
the gate he stopped as he was told, and the 3 men exited the car and raced to
their positions. When Kane figured they had cleared the fence he motioned
Jermaine to get out and open the gate. Jermaine followed his instructions
and swung the gate wide. The lights from the Jag bathed the house and two
cars with the harsh light. Kane had ducked low peering around the head
rest to see if he could spot Charles or Tony, but all he saw were shadows.
Jermaine came back to the car, drove thru the gate, got out, and closed the
gate behind him. Then he parked next to the Lexus that was in the
driveway.

Ted saw light flash thru the crack in the curtain, got up, and went
to the window. He pulled the curtain aside slightly and looked out. He saw

Jermaine as he got back in the car and drove thru the big gate. "Good the nigga finally arrives an hour late," he said to himself. "He doesn't know it but that hour just cost him his life. I guess I'll put my cousin Lil John in his spot." He moved from the window, sat down and looked at the accountant who was stuffing money into a large duffle bag. Five bags were filled and he had damn near filled the last.

"What's the tally so far?" Ted asked.

"3.6 mill not counting what the last guy should bring; which should give us 4 mill or better," the accountant answered.

The car came to a stop and Jermaine got out with the big tote bag. Kane left the back seat and eased the door shut. He motioned for Tony to join him and a shadow rose from the ground and swiftly approached. Kane pointed to the left side of the door as he moved to the right. They flattened themselves to the side of the door aiming their shot guns at Jermaine. Jermaine rang the doorbell and a voice yelled out, "Yeah."

"It's Jay," Jermaine said.

Ted looked out the peep hole then said, "Nigga stand back." Jermaine stepped back from the door. Ted looked out, it looked cool so he said, "Come on," and unlocked the door. He pulled it open as Jermaine approached. When Jermaine's lead foot crossed the threshold Tony spun from the left side of the door raised his leg and delivered a vicious kick to the small of Jermaine's back. The kick caught him off guard and launched him into the half open door. His momentum caused the door to crash into Ted who was thrown backward to the floor. Jermaine tripped over him and landed hard on his shoulder. The side of his head crashed into the floor with concussive force and he lost consciousness.

After Tony kicked Jermaine he leaped into the room over the bodies and quickly scanned the room. Kane behind him always scanned the room as Charles rushed in. Kane motioned to Charles to search the house as Tony had his shot gun trained on the accountant. He sat there with his mouth open in shock.

Kane and Charles quickly searched the house. It was empty and they came back to the front room as Ted was trying to regain his feet. "Nigga stay where you are!" Kane shouted. "Don't move a fucking muscle. Cee get Steve." Charles hurried from the house and moments later he and Steve returned. They heard cars and Kane said, "Go check that out." Steve and Charles rushed from the house and peered thru the gate. It was Becky and Sherrie. They opened the gate and the women drove in. They closed the gate and returned to the house with the women. "I want y'all to search this house quick but thorough," Kane said to the women who nodded and went to work.

Kane had Ted get up and drag Jermaine to the sofa. "Cee get the tape from the Taurus and look under the front passenger seat and bring me that black case." Charles hurried from the house.

Ted was on the sofa with Steve guarding him. He was looking at them thinking, "Who the fuck are they? I don't know but if I survive this they're dead." He noticed that the man who appeared to be their leader didn't wear a mask, neither did the women so he committed their faces to memory. The other 3 wore mask so it was obvious they didn't wanna be recognized which to him seemed to be a good sign.

Becky and Sherrie came back. "Not a thing daddy," Becky said. "Except in those," She pointed at the duffle bags.

Charles came back with the black case and the duct tape. Kane pointed at Ted and Charles taped his wrist together. Then he taped Jermaine's wrist and ankles, then the accountants.

"Tee, Steve, Cee, load those duffels in our cars and hurry." They dropped their shot guns on the table and each grabbed a duffle. Becky, Sherrie, and Kane stood guard over the prisoners. "Hey dude, what's your name?" Kane said looking at Ted.

"I'm Ted and I wanna know just what the fuck do you think you're doing? Man do you know who we are? You're fucking around in the big leagues here kid."

"Yeah I know," Kane said. "But it's cool, so where's the dope?"

"Moe and his bodyguards are the only ones that can answer that and if y'all asses ain't gone in bout 30 minutes this shit's gonna hit the fan; because Moe, Big Jim, and Cecil are on the way. Trust me, you don't wanna be fucked up with them."

"Is that right?" Kane asked.

"Hell yeah," Ted said.

"Does Moe carry heat himself?" Kane asked.

"What for?" Ted said. "He's got Big Jim and Cecil, and those niggas is straight scary to look at. If it wasn't for them I'd have stung Moe a long time ago, but I knew they would hunt me to the ends of the earth just like they gonna do y'all."

The men had finished loading the duffels. "Cee, you and Steve take the cars to the spot we stopped at first," Kane said. "Tee you follow them in the Jag, drop the cars off and y'all come back here. Hurry we don't have much time. Moe could show at any minute and he has 2 gunners with him."

They ran to the cars and raced away. "Nigga are you death struck or what?" Ted asked. "You done got 3.6 million dollars. Take that and run for as long as you can."

169

"Nigga we don't do no running from shit!" Sherrie said menacingly. "We run shit! That's why you in the situation you in now!"

"What is she talking bout?" Ted asked.

"When you and Moe sent the jack boys at us in Brooklyn y'all fucked up," Becky said.

"It didn't help matters any either, that y'all put my daddy behind bars," Kane said calmly.

"Nigga I don't know you or your daddy," Ted said.

"Before the night is over you will," Kane said firmly.

The others came back and parked the Jag next to Ted's Lexus then came in the house. "This is the play," Kane said. "Charles, you, Steve, Beck, and Red will stay in the house with them," he pointed to the prisoners. "Me and Tee are gonna be outside waiting on Moe and his gunners. When they show up me and Tee will handle them. If this nigga makes a sound blow his goddamn head off. Better yet tape his legs and all of their mouths. We won't need them anymore." Charles and Steve got busy and the women walked over to Kane.

"Daddy be careful with them niggas," Becky said.

"Don't give them a break baby," Sherrie said.

"Don't worry I won't," Kane said unzipping the black case and pulling out the silenced Beretta. He made sure it was ready to fire then he and Tony went outside. "Find a good spot over there," Kane said pointing to the left side of the house. "And lay low you're my back up. Don't move until you see me move alright?"

"I got you Bro," Tony said then moved off and melted in the darkness.

Kane moved to the right, looked the area over then knelt next to the Jag. He looked around to see if there was any place better and closer to the door. He didn't see one so he rolled underneath the car, pulled his mask down to better blend into the darkness and waited.

*   *   *   *

Big Moe, with Cecil behind the wheel and Big Jim on the passenger side up front, laid deep in the backseat of the Cadillac limo. He was thinking, "Damn I wish I could've stayed all night with Elvira. That bitch got good pussy, good ass, good head, and she's a scheming bitch on top of that. Shit if me and Brenda didn't have the kids I'd kick her ass out and take Elvira from Ted's punk ass. He thinks I don't know he been skimming money off the top. He done got a bit too greedy. He's just about wore out his welcome and soon his ass is gonna come up missing. Then Elvira is all mine," he smiled to himself. He thought of more serious matters, "Wassup with all these robberies roun' here and where is this shit coming from and who's behind it. Niggas in the street would be dumb as fuck to risk their lives fucking with me. I just can't see average street niggas pulling stunts like that." He had contacted sources within the J.S.O and didn't get anywhere there either. If dirty cops were behind it his source would know or either be in on it. He decided that in the morning he was gonna offer a reward for anyone who could provide information, and see how that worked out.

Cecil drove deeper into Alderman Park until he came to the house. Big Jim jumped out, looked around then swung the gate open wide. Cecil drove thru and Jim closed the gate. Jim walked behind the car as Cecil parked behind the Jag. He walked to the left rear passenger door and opened it. Big Moe stepped out draped in jewelry wearing a $5000 custom made Armani suit. Cecil got out and the men flanked Big Moe then they walked towards the house.

When Kane heard the car outside the gate he tensed. He wondered if he had chosen the right spot to attack as his feet pointed towards the gate. He wished he had lain with his head that way and had almost decided to change positions when he heard the gate swung open and lights illuminated the driveway. He knew it would mean death to move now so he lay still listening to the car approach. It came to a stop and he heard doors open and close, then footfalls as the men approached the house.

He turned his head so he could see from under the Jag. He waited then saw 3 pairs of legs pass. He rolled from beneath the car, rose to his feet and crouched between the 2 cars then silently crept forward as the 3 men approached the door.

When Moe, Cecil, and Big Jim reached the front of the house Cecil and Big Jim were about 2 feet behind Moe. When Moe reached out Kane ran silently, yet swiftly from between cars with is pistol raised. He aimed at the back of Big Jim's head and when he was two feet away he stroked the trigger. The pistol coughed and the slug smashed into the base of Big Jim's skull and exited from his forehead in a spray of blood, bone, and brain matter that splattered the back and side of Big Moe. As Jim appeared to stumble Kane adjusted his aim and shot Cecil in the lower right side of the head behind his right ear. The bullet angled upward and his head seemed to expand as the bullet blew thru his head and made its exit close to his left eye. Bone, blood, and brain flew as the force of the bullet passing behind his eye made it pop from the socket and fly like a marble erratically thrown by an angry kid. It hit the door, dropped and rolled between Big Moe's feet. Cecil fell like he had been pole axed, loose and boneless.

Tony had raise from where he lay and ran towards the 3 men his shot gun raised but in a matter of seconds it was over.

When Moe felt the blood and brains splash him he raised his hand to wipe his face. He saw the red and pinkish grey stuff on his hand and started to scream like a bitch. He pissed in his pants because he was sure he was next.

Tony slammed the barrel of his shot gun into the back of Moe's head. Moe dropped to one knee his head crashing into the door. He fell back into a sitting position dazed and shaking his big head. The door came open and Becky and Sherrie stood there with their pistols pointed at him. He looked up uncomprehendingly and shook his head to clear it. He couldn't believe what he was seeing, 2 pretty women, one brown skinned the other light skinned pointing pistols at him. He tried to gather his feet beneath him but he couldn't. He was still dazed.

Kane and Tony stood behind him but he never looked back he just stared at the women. After he had somewhat recovered he stood and looked around. He saw 2 men behind him with mask covering their faces. He looked at the women again and saw they were no more than girls and shook his head.

"Go on inside," Kane said to him and he walked in the house. Becky and Sherrie backed up their pistols still trained on the big man. He looked around and saw Ted and the others on the sofa taped up. He saw 2 more masked men armed with shot guns and stopped in the middle of the room. Kane and Tony drug the bodies in and closed the door then Kane motioned Moe to a seat. "Steve take the tape from their mouths," Kane said. Steve stepped to the sofa and snatched the tape from the men's mouth roughly.

"Who are you?" Big Moe asked Kane.

"The death of you if you don't answer my questions," Kane replied. "Now where is the dope?"

Moe looked around the room not answering.

"We're the ones that hit your spots Friday night," Kane said. "The same ones you sent the jack boys at a few months ago!"

Recognition sparked in Moe's eye and one name flashed in his mind as the man removed his mask, "Kane." Moe had never seen Kane to his knowledge that he could recall. But from all the shit he had heard about him he expected a much bigger man for some reason, but he knew this was Kane. The big man next to him removed his mask and that confirmed it because he looked just like Bishop where Kane just resembled him. "Where's BoBo?" Moe asked.

"She killed him," Kane said pointing at Sherrie. "Bo got the hots for her and it proved to be too much for him. If you watch the news you would've learned that they pulled a body from the river. That was Bo. Stupid ass nigga went swimming tied up in a bedspread," Kane said laughing. "Where's the dope Moe?" Moe just looked at him. "Here Steve," Kane said smiling as he tossed him the silenced 9mm. "Choose one of them," he pointed at the 3 bound men. Steve pointed the pistol at Jermaine who was still unconscious and shot him in the face at point blank range. Blood and brains exploded from the back of his head and coated the sofa, his legs shot out and his heels drummed the floor as his muscles twitched. He slumped back, took a deep breath then laid still. The accountant fainted and Ted screamed over and over, "Oh my God....Oh my God...!" Then piss in his pants.

"Where's the dope Moe?" Kane asked again.

"Tell him nigga! Please tell him or he's gonna kill us all!" Ted screamed.

"If I tell him he's gonna kill us anyway," Moe said calmly.

"I just might unless you got something to bargain with," Kane said. "Steve give Red the gun." Steve gave her the pistol and Kane said, "Pick one Red." She turned the pistol to Ted who screamed, "Please don't, please God, Don't kill me, kill Moe!"

"Moe ain't the one that talked shit about us running away, you did," Sherrie spat venomously. "If you had kept your damn mouth shut you just might've come out of this alive. But no! You just had to be a big shot and impress us with your power. Well Ted I hate to say it but it wasn't a pleasure meeting you! See ya!" Then she pulled the trigger and blew his brains out. Quickly she swung the pistol on the unconscious accountant and blew him away, then walked towards Moe and said, "Daddy we got 3.6 mill we don't need no dope."

Then she pointed the pistol at Moe who screamed, "Wait! Wait! I'll tell you! Don't let her kill me man! I'll tell you where the dope is!" Then he started blubbering and crying. As many young women as he had exploited he never ever felt fear. But when he looked at the young red bitch he saw death in her eyes and he had never been more afraid in his life. She scared him more than all the rest of them combined. He thought, "This nigga Kane is much more man than I gave him credit for being. He got to be to control a bitch like that." He looked at Kane and said, "Listen man. If you don't kill me I can give you 5 million in the morning. As soon as the bank opens I can get the money. I'll leave town and you'll never hear from me again; I swear on my children!"

"I swear on my children that if you tell me where the dope is I won't kill you or she won't either," Kane said pointing at Sherrie.

"Alright," Moe said. "Let's go!" And he stood up.

"Where is it that we're going?" Kane asked.

"Out thru the back gate," Moe replied. "About 100 yards in the woods there's what looks like a pump shack. It's really a climate controlled storage. No one knows it's used to store drugs but me and my bodyguards. We would come and get it, take it to the cut house; cut, cook, bag it, and have runners drop it off.

"You got a good head for business," Kane said. "What I wanna know is why you are so petty?"

"I guess I wanted it all," Moe said. "But I'll give you the 5 million then get Elvira and you won't ever hear from us again."

Kane thought to himself, "This nigga slimy to the end. He would run off and leave his wife and kids."

Kane, Big Moe, Tony, and Becky left the house, walked out of the gate then thru the woods until they came to what looked like an old abandoned pump shack. Moe used several keys to unlock the elaborate system then pulled the door open. Inside was state of the art. The room was cool and stacked on a shelf was 15 keys of cocaine and 3 keys of heroin. There were several large tote bags on another shelf. Becky and Tony grabbed the totes and loaded them with the drugs. After they were done they left the shack and went back to the house.

"We got it," Kane said to the others as they came inside.

"Moe sit over there," he pointed to a straight back chair near the coffee table. "We're gonna wait to go get the 5 mil then it's over, but I got to tie you up. We need to get some rest plus we got to do something with these bodies in here."

"So we got a deal?" Moe asked. "You ain't gonna kill me?"

"What the fuck," Kane said. "We got a deal." Moe sat in the chair and Steve taped him too it good.

"Tee you wanna kill this piece of shit?" Kane said.

"Wait a minute man!" Moe screamed. "We got a deal."

"Yeah," Kane said. "You're right we do. Just like the deal you made with the feds to lock my father up. You couldn't get rid of him yourself so you got them to do your dirty work. In this case these are my feds," he pointed at Steve, Becky, Tony and Charles. "We made a deal that me and Red wouldn't kill you. I didn't say anything about the rest of them."

"What about the 5 million?" Moe asked.

"It's only money," Kane said. "And if I'm guessing right we should be able to make that off the dope we got from you because we won't be serving keys or ounces; just nickels, dimes, and quarters and we can get that same 5 million. You're the kind of guy that won't take it sitting down. Your pride won't let you. Of course you would leave to get out of harm's way, but you'd pull the strings from long distance to get some revenge. You might even go so far as using your friends "the feds" and I would never be so foolish as to think I'm up to challenging them. So Moe you're dying tonight. No doubt about that, but I won't be pulling the trigger trust me." Then he laughed.

"Please man," Moe begged. "I got a wife and kids, who gonna look after my babies?"

"You should've thought about that when you were talking about leaving them and running off with Elvira," Kane said.

Tony got the silenced pistol and walked towards Moe. Becky called him, "Tee let me have this one."

"Are you sure?" Tony asked.

"Yeah I'm sure," She answered then walked to the kitchen. She came back with a small transparent trash bag. She picked up the tape and slapped a strip over Moe's mouth then slipped the bag over his head and taped it around his neck. She sat on the coffee table in front of him and watched then said, "My man's daddy has suffered 9 years in prison because of you. I wanna see if you can last 9 minutes with that bag over your head."

Kane came and sat next to her and said, "Moe if you believe in your God no need to pray to him because you'll be meeting him in a few minutes."

They sat and watched Moe breathe slowly thru his nose trying not to use up his sparse air. With each exhalation the bag inflated each time he inhaled it deflated. Soon the bag was filled with carbon dioxide and condensation. His breathing became laborers as his eyes protruded and his chest heaved. They could hear him moaning, "Mmmm....Mmmm...." Then suddenly he took a deep ragged breath, his body shook and shuddered violently almost tearing the tape from the chair as it vibrated and shook. His body arched straining against his bonds then froze. He farted, pissed, then his bowels voided, and his eyes slowly glazed over.

Kane and his people looked around the house one last time then exited. They all got in the limo and drove to the spot where their cars were parked threw the drugs in the trunk and headed back to town.

*   *   *   *

After going to the house on Riverside, picking up the cash they had left there and thoroughly cleaning the house. They bagged the groceries and other odds and ends put them in trash bags and dumped them on the trash pile. They threw the shot guns and shells in the river, dropped the jumpers in the Goodwill box along with the boots, threw the extra tags and gloves in a dumpster then drove to another spot and bagged the masks then dumped them. They stopped and called Gina and Jen, told them to meet them then drove back to the house and waited.

A few minutes later the 2 women arrived and hugged everyone and Jen said, "We dropped off the money and I guess y'all know there were a slew of questions. Leslie wanted to know where you were, were you alright, and when you were coming home."

"Momma was tripping too," Gina said. "She didn't wanna take the money at first. Doreen and Lucinda had a fit too."

"But grandma and Becky's grandma were the calmest about the whole situation," Jen said. "Red's Momma was skeptical. She thought there had to be an angle to it. Charles and Steve's Momma were angels about the whole thing, but y'all need to make some calls when y'all get a chance. They all nodded.

"I know y'all are tired," Kane said. "But let's load the rides and sanitize this place and go to Safe House. We've still got work to do!"

*   *   *   *

The next morning at Safe House they were all awake by 11:00. There had been no sessions of love making since everyone was too tired. They drug themselves to the den and sat around in various positions of comfort, Becky was curled up on Kane's lap. Sherrie had her head on his shoulder and her feet in Tony's lap. Gina was sitting on the floor with Steve's head in her lap. Jen was sitting in a chair with her legs spread wide and Charles sat on the floor between her legs with his head resting between her legs. "Well it's over now and we can get on with our lives," Kane said. "We got plenty of money and drugs but the question is; where do we go from here? I'm open for suggestions."

"Bro I see where you're headed with this," Charles said smiling. "I don't know if what you told that dude last night about nickels, dimes, and quarters was the truth or if you were just running a line, but that's the way I think we should go. When I say we, I mean us collectively as a unit, a team, a crew. You're trying to weasel your way out of the leadership role when we all know that you're the only one fit to head our family at this time. If Bishop were here he could do it. But he's not, so the mantle falls on your shoulders. You don't have to lead but if you walk away from it we got to count all that loose shit again." They all laughed.

"Daddy you know Cee is right," Becky said. "So you might as well take the lead!"

"We're all in this together," Kane said looking around and making eye contact with each of them. "No one of us is greater than the others. If y'all chose to say I'm the leader, then so be it. I guess I don't have a choice in the matter but y'all need to know right now that I'm gonna leave for about a week, and so is Tee. So the rest of y'all got to take care of business until I get back. I ain't leaving until everything is set up like I want it. I've thought it over and we've got a great deal of work to do in the next few days. The first thing we got to do is count the money and divide it. So y'all go get it and bring it in here."

Tony, Steve, and Charles got the money and drug it back into the room. They dumped it in the middle of the floor as Becky went and got the tote bag that held the money they had taken from Jermaine, and she dumped it with the rest. They sat and stared at the big pile of money then they started counting.

They got pens and paper and made stacks of $1,000. They took breaks for food and the bathroom but other than that they kept at it. About 7:00 p.m. they finished and handed Kane the slips of paper so he could double check after they counted the stacks. It was a total of 3.9 million dollars.

"Us six," he pointed at the 5 others who went on the hit. "Will take $600,000 apiece. That's 3.6 million. Gina and Jen will split the $300,000 because they were our support. Does anyone have a problem with that?" Nobody did.

Everyone started putting their money away in big tote bags.

"Daddy I want you to have $200,000 of my money for yourself," Becky said.

"Beck honey," Kane said softly. "Keep your money, you deserve it."

"I want you to have it baby," she said. "There's plenty left over for me $400,000 is plenty. What the fuck am I gonna do with that kind of money?"

"Alright baby," he said. "I understand and I love you more than you could know!"

Sherrie was putting her money away next to them. She leaned over and whispered in his ear, "I wanna be the bitch that makes you a millionaire so here's $200,000 of mine too!"

"Do I have to say it Red?" He asked her softly.

"Nigga you better," She said smiling broadly.

"I love you baby," he said aloud.

Caught up in the moment she leaned over and kissed him deeply. Everybody froze and she said, "Oh shit!"

They all pretended not to have seen what happened and went back to stacking their money and putting it away. Occasionally they stole peeks at Tony and there was a growing cloud of tension filling the air.

After everyone had put their money away Tony said, "I guess that means I get to bring a female companion to Safe House?"

"Yeah Tee," Kane said. "But she has to meet our approval and unless she's tested she can't be all in our business. Cool?"

"That's cool," Tony said smiling. "But let me clear the air here and I'm talking to all of y'all. I saw from the very beginning the way Red looked at you Bro. I was afraid at first that there would be a conflict between Red and Beck but there never was. I listened to what Charles said about her and believe me I did some serious thinking. After Friday night I knew for sure that Red was too much for me. Don't get me wrong. I don't feel inferior or less than any man, even that nigga there," he pointed at Kane. " And I do have affection for Red, I love her but not in that way. I would wake up and notice she was gone. I knew where she was and what she was doing. I never felt anger or jealousy; I was cool with it as a matter of fact. I began to feel guilty when we make love because I love Red like she's my sister. Do you remember when you came up yesterday and I was on the porch?"

"Yeah I remember," Kane answered.

"You asked me was I alright and I lied," Tony said. "I was trying to come up with a way to tell you that I knew what was going on and that I was going to step back, but I didn't want you to take it the wrong way."

"I understand Tee," Kane said sincerely.

"She loves you Bro and I'm sure she loves me in her own way, but I believe you're the only man for her. Trust me on that, plus Red scares me. She is too fucking intense and ruthless for me. I found out quick I was in over my head, Bro. I want you to know that nothing can come between us; not even that sexy red devil there," he smiled then leaned over and kissed Sherrie on the cheek.

She was crying which caused all of the ladies to cry.
She sniffed and said, "Tee I never wanted to hurt you and I do love you. I'd give my life for you and I'd kill for you. I've proved that haven't I?"

"That you have Red," Tony agreed. "I'm not hurt or upset baby girl, I understand."

"Do you really understand?" She asked. "Cause if you don't I'll never make love to Kane again no matter how badly I might want to. I promise you that!"

"I really do understand," he replied. "And I'd never be so vindictive as to keep you from the man you love for selfish, hateful reasons. I can love you like a sister. I'm more comfortable that way with you. I know I can depend on you, if and when I need you so don't sweat it. It's cool." She threw her arms around him and hugged him. The other men were busy comforting the other women.

Kane said to himself, "Well that's one bridge I won't have to cross."

178

"Beck I know the perfect girl for Tee," Sherrie said.

"Who?" Beck asked. "Don't say Chell cause daddy done had her already."

"Lisa," Sherrie said smiling.

"Red Lisa with the fat titties and ghetto booty?" Becky asked.

"Yeah," Sherrie replied. "Tee would love her and she'll work for us too! Tee she ain't no ho, she don't even sell pussy part time. She sells a little dope and ain't got no kids plus got her own place and her own ride. But most important she ain't got a nigga right now. She probably got lil friends or whatever. So once we hook y'all up and you freak her like I know you can, you gonna have her sewed up. Trust me."

They all laughed then Kane said, "It's almost 9:00 and I don't think we'll be thru with this session until maybe 12:00 or 1:00 a.m. so everybody listen close. Gina, you, and Jen are gonna keep track of our money and we'll keep it here. Tomorrow I'll buy a safe and each of us," he pointed at Steve, Becky, Sherrie, Charles, and Tony. "Are gonna put $100,000 in the kitty. That plus the $170,000 we already got for our defense fund and operating expenses will bring that to $770,000. Out of that I want Gina and Jen to get $200,000, then get Charles and Steve's Momma's to open up 2 pool halls, 2 game rooms and a couple of hole in the wall beer and wine joints. I want them in Mixon and Lackawanna. Beck and Red get $100,000 and get our grannies to open a store. Red, get your Momma to open a beer and wine joint in Brooklyn. She can work if she wants to cause I know your fine ass Momma gonna want her hand in the pie!" They all laughed. "Now when we get the spots, we got to find us some houses and apartments close by as well as some workers to serve out of them. I don't want dope being sold from our businesses. This might take you a few days and we're gonna need at least six or eight hoopties for our workers. The $300,000 should cover all of that and we'll still have $470,000 to work with. We want the houses to be open 24 hours a day and we wanna sell beer, alcohol and anything else that's in demand. Find basers in the area and see if we can get them to let our clients get high in their cribs. We don't want any smoking in our spots. Dig?" They all nodded. "The money is to be picked up every night at 12:00. Whatever money is there is to be dropped at one of the stores and Gina and Jen will pick it up and bring it here the next day. The money the businesses earn is not to be taken because we'll be banking it properly. Gina, Jen, make sure y'all beep us before y'all make the pickups so someone will always be watching your backs; got it?" They both nodded. "I want you three," he pointed at Steve, Tony, and Charles. "To start looking for workers, it should be plenty of them looking for work now. I'm gonna get us a supplier for when we get low. I don't want the streets to get dry, so be sure to tell our people to sell our shit just like they get it. We ain't paying a salary, we're paying a percentage. They get 30 cent off of every dollar. There are 6 of us, which mean we get 10 cent of every dollar, the other dime goes towards operating expenses weekly. Let our people know that the more they sell the more money they make. We can use the house on Post St. as our Base until we get things straight, then we'll move our base to the center of the action. Red, where were you living?"

"With my Momma," answered Sherrie.

"You're moving," Kane said firmly. "You can leave all of the shit you got there unless you get something with sentimental value. You got enough money to buy all new shit. Besides, I don't want you two near any of the clothes you had before you hooked up with us. No panties, no bras, no shoe's, nothing. Leave all that shit cause we gonna get you more. Beck did you hear what I said?"

"I already know that applies to me Daddy," Becky said. "I'm gonna throw all of your old shit out too and we gonna buy you a new wardrobe."

"I'm cool with that," he said. "You and Red keep the rental until I can get y'all cars suitable for your new station."

"Bro If you're finished I'd like to go home," Tony said.

"Yeah I'm through," Kane said. "Go ahead and tell Leslie I'll be home in the morning."

"I'll do that," Tony said. Charles threw him the keys to Anna's car and said, "Take it light little bro."

Tony hugged and kissed them all, picked up his money and left.

"Damn! Tee much brighter than I gave him credit for," Gina said. "I knew what was up the first time I saw Red with y'all."

"Yeah me too," Jen said. "When I caught the hoe creeping that morning it just confirmed it for me." They all laughed.

As they headed for their rooms Gina said, "Me and Steve getting married next month on his birthday and I want y'all ho's to be my maids of honor. I don't know how I'm gonna work it but I ain't having it no other way. Y'all ho's my sisters and y'all got to be there."

"Bitch please," Becky said. "We got your back."

"Damn right!" Said Sherrie as she, Kane and Becky walked into the room. When the door closed Sherrie said, "Daddy I'm kind of glad it went down the way it did. Now I ain't got to creep. We can all sleep in the bed together and I ain't got to jump up and leave."

"You right about that Red," Kane said. "But we gonna sleep sometimes too!" They all laughed and started getting undressed.

*   *   *   *

9:00 the next morning they left Safe House. Becky and Sherrie went to Kane's grandmother's house. Steve and Gina dropped them off then went to get their children. Kane picked up his car and went home. When he stepped thru the door Leslie flew into his arms. He dropped the tote bag he carried and held her tight. "I got a lot of stuff in the car for you and the kids. Presents I bought along the way, but this," he released her, picked up the tote and gave it to her. "This is for you."

She grabbed the tote bag, noticed how heavy it was and looked at him. She sat on the sofa, put the big tote in her lap and unzipped it. She saw all the money, looked at him and asked, "How much is this?"

"$900,000." he said. "Tax free!"

"You're shittin me right?" She asked incredulously.

"I'm not joking Les," he said seriously. "That's really $900,000."

"Did you rob a bank?" She asked seriously.

"Yeah you can say that," he answered. "I'm quitting my job if they haven't fired me yet."

"Well baby you don't have to quit because they fired you." They both laughed.

"What are we gonna do with this money?" She asked.

"I thought we'd get Lu, Doreen, and Anna the beauty salon and restaurant y'all wanted plus open me and Tee a detailing shop."

"Hell yes," She shouted. "That's what we'll do."

"I figured it won't take but bout $300,000 to get it done up like you want," he said. "Tony gonna give you $150,000 of that. How much money do we have in the bank?"

"With the money you inherited from the friend we got $160,000 give or take 5 or 6 thousand," she answered.

"This is what I want you to do," He said. "I want you to take $100,000 out of the bank, get a mortgage for $50,000 on the house my friend left me on our house. That way you won't have to be careful with the way you spend the money and we won't have any problem with the I.R.S. Be sure to set aside the money that Tee gives you. You can pay the mortgages off with that and use some of the money because we'll be getting good money. I got a few deals going down that are sure to pay off."

"Baby I've missed you," she said.

"I've missed you too Les," he said sincerely. "But hold up I got a call to make."

He picked up the phone and dialed. After the first ring a voice said, "Arnie's Pawn Shop, Sal speaking. How can I help you?"

"I'd like to speak to Pete please," Kane said.

"May I ask who calling?" Sal asked.

"Tell him it's Kane."

He heard Sal yell, "Pete! Mr. Kane is on the phone!" Then he heard Pete's voice yell back, "I got it!" Kane heard another phone get picked up as the other was put down.

"I see you made it back from your hunting trip," Pete said. "Shoot anything?"

"Yeah I shot a few things," Kane replied. "But I also got in some fishing. I hooked the big one and he didn't get away."

Pete laughed. "I'm sure our friend will be glad to hear that. He asked me to tell you to call him if you came by. He has a business proposition for you."

"Could you tell him it'll have to wait a week," Kane asked. "I've got to take the wife on a cruise. I've neglected her these past few weeks and I don't wanna be in the dog house."

Pete laughed then said, "You better tell him that Bro you got the number?"

"Yeah I've got it," Kane answered. "I'll give him a call when I hang up with you."

"Do that," Pete said. "If you need anything else, just stop by. I got some jewelry in that I think you'll like."

"I just might do that," Kane said and they hung up.

"Are you really gonna take me on a cruise?" Leslie asked.

"Yeah baby we're really going on a cruise," he said. "Let me make this last call."

He dialed Frank's number and Jimmy picked up and said, "The Toronelli's residence."

"This is Berean, Jim and I need to speak with Frank."

"So I take it your trip went well?" Jimmy asked.

"Much better than I expected," Kane replied.

"Let me get Frank for you," Jimmy said then switched the line over.

Kane heard a man then Frank's voice, "Frank! This is Berean," Kane said with laughter in his voice.

"How did the trip go?" Frank asked.

"It went better than I expected," Kane said. "I caught a big fish and got in some shooting. I got 15 turkeys and even managed to bag 3 bucks. On a scale of 1 to 5, I'd say it was a 3.9. It could've been better had I stayed until the next day but I had personal business to tend to."

"You did well," Frank said. "Very good, but if I read you right you won't need my services for a minute."

"That's true," Kane said. "But I do have a proposal for you. It has to wait though because I've got to take the wife on a cruise. I've neglected her these last few weeks. I can get my associates to bring the details if needed. I've drawn it up so all they'll really need is a yea or nay from you to get the ball rolling. I have plans to go into business and I know your services will be required. It'll be mutually beneficial."

"Good. That's good," Frank said. "Tell you what; it's gonna be yea on the proposal but can it wait until your return?"

"Yeah," Kane said. "It's not a pressing matter so it can wait until I get back."

"Let's do it like that then," Frank said. "Enjoy you trip."

"Will do," Kane said and hung up.

"Baby we're really going on a cruise?" Leslie asked again.

"Yes we are," he said sincerely. "No kids. You'll have a couple of days to look for locations we can visit. I'm sure Tee and Lu will wanna go with us. We'll take about $25,000 with us, but first we'll go shopping to buy clothes for the cruise."

She squealed with joy. "Baby this is just great, should I call a travel agency?"

"Yeah," he said. "But we got time. We'll get our Moms to stay over here so the kids won't have to be driven to school. I'll lay out all of the plans for them tonight. You can call the travel agency a lil' later and get us booked for the cruise. Use your credit card to get 4 plane tickets and to book out berths on the ship. We'll give the trip to Tee and Lu as an early anniversary present."

"That's a good idea baby," She said. "This is gonna be so much fun. We can go shopping at about 5:00."

"Yeah and be stuck in the mall until it closes," Kane said. "Anyway I guess that just about covers it."

"Not quite" Leslie said with a smile. "You got some more business to take care of.

He looked at her and noticed she had a mischievous glint in her eyes. Seductively she licked her full, luscious lips and he asked, "Girl what are you talking about?" Even though he knew what was on her mind. He stood in front of her as she sat on the sofa. She still wore her housecoat and night gown. The floral printed housecoat was open showing the pale yellow bra and matching French cut panties she wore under it. She grabbed him by the waist and pulled him to her. His crotch was lined up with her face. She unbuckled his belt, popped the button on his jeans, unzipped them, and slid them from his hips until they were bunched at his ankles. She pulled his boxers down and his penis sprang free.

"For me," she whispered.

After they made passionate love she lay on his chest and he whispered in her ear, "I love you baby."

"I love you too," She said. They lay there and drifted off to sleep.

Chapter 13

Leslie and Kane woke up at about 12:30 p.m. and she fixed them a light meal that they ate in the nude.

"Baby should I call the travel agency?" She asked.

"You might as well before you worry me to death," he said smiling. "Make the arrangements for the day after tomorrow because I got a few things to do tomorrow. Alright?"

"Okay," she said. "I'm calling right now."

He got in the shower while she made all of the arrangements.

She came in the bathroom and said, "Baby it's done. Our plane leaves at 12:05 p.m. and the ship leaves port at 5:00 that evening. I called Lu and told her to bring the kids and her husband over here at 4:30. I called Doreen and Anna on their jobs and told them what you said. They said they'd be here around 2:30 or 3:00. Was that alright?"

"Yeah that was cool baby," he said stepping out of the shower. She got in and he said, "I got a few calls to make." He walked to their room, got his robe and slipped it on, then picked up the phone and called his grandmother's house and she answered the phone, "Hello."

"This me Granny," Kane said.

"Boy, Becky and this other girl name Sherrie in your room sleep. They told me you said for them to give me $50,000. I already got bout that much left from what Gina gave me. What am I gonna do with $100,000 or more? I ain't had that much money in my life at one time. What am I gonna do with it?"

"Keep it baby," Kane said. "Fix up the house or something."

"I could get a few repairs done," she said thoughtfully.

"Do that," he said. "Don't let nobody, I mean nobody know you got that kind of money at the house; you hear me?"

"Boy you think I'm stupid?" She said. "Merlie and those kids of hers wouldn't leave me alone for a minute. As it is they don't come by until they want something. I don't know why she can't be like Anna Mae. You want me to get Becky for you?"

"Yeah Granny," he said.

"Boy be careful of that Sherrie," she said. "I've seen her kind before. Becky better watch her around you too!"

"It's a little late for that," Kane said laughing. "Both of them my girls."

"You got them and Leslie? You some kind of man," she said. "If I had met a man like you 50 years ago wouldn't have been any other girls because I would've put it on you." They laughed. "Let me wake up your women," she said and sat the phone down. She walked to the room, knocked on the door and said, "Becky! Boy's on the phone!"

The door opened and Sherrie stood there in a short nighty. "Mam?" She asked.

"Boy's on the phone," Granny said.

"Beck wake up and grab the phone Daddy want us!" Sherrie yelled. Becky rolled over and picked up the phone as Sherrie followed Granny and picked up the other phone. "Daddy this Red, I love you."

"I love you too," Becky said on the other line.

"Get up off y'all lazy asses and get busy," Kane said. "Now ain't the time to be sleeping. How many cars y'all got?"

"One," They said in unison.

"Look outside and make sure," he said. Sherrie pulled the curtains aside and looked in the driveway. Both of the rentals were parked there and she said, "Charles must have brought the rental by when we were asleep."

"Red, go get your Momma and find a spot," Kane said. "Don't come back home until you do! Beck you take the Grannies and do the same. Look for spots only in Brooklyn. Try to find at least a couple of houses too. I'll swing thru at about 11:00 or 12:00 tonight to spend some time with y'all. I got a few things to do tomorrow and I'll be gone the day after so y'all get yo asses in gear, got it?"

They both said, "Yes".

"I love y'all," Kane said. "Tell Granny I send my love. I'll see y'all later." He hung up the phone then beeped Charles and hung up the phone. He beeped Steve then hung up and waited. A few minutes later the phone rang and he picked it up. "Hello this Kane."

"This Steve. What's up Bro.?"

"Where are you?" Kane asked.

"I'm at a real estate office downtown with Gina and Momma," Steve said. "We've already found an apartment and a house in Lackawanna. We got a store on Dignan St. that we can take over, a pool hall on Lennox a few blocks down from the Magic Market, and The Sandwich Shop across from the park. I called Charles and let him know I had this end on lock. He's at a real estate office in Five Points."

The phone beeped and Kane said, "Hold on a minutes Steve," then clicked the line over. "Yeah this Kane."

"This Cee. Me, my mom, and Jen are doing the paper work right now for 4 spots on Edison Ave. Remember Club Funky Town?"

"Yeah I remember it," Kane answered. "It's closed down isn't it?"

"Yeah," Charles said. "But it's got everything except a sound system. We got that, the pool hall next to it, the B.B.Q joint across the street, and a 2 story house right behind the club. All of it is ours Bro."

"That's good," Kane said. "Everything is falling in place and I'll call you back, I got Steve on the other line. Peace Bro." He clicked back over to Steve.

"Damn nigga," Steve said. "I thought you had forgotten about me."

"Naw I ain't forgot you," Kane said. "That was Charles and he got everything set up in Mixon. All we got to do is get the places cleaned and stocked. Try to get Gina, Jen, and y'all Mommas to get all the licenses and permits we'll need today if there's time. We'll need beer and wine licenses for the pool halls and the stores so get on that right away. Get in touch with Cee and y'all check on a liquor license for the club cause we gonna need one."

"Alright Bro." Steve said.

"I'm going to the mall later," Kane said. "I won't be back until the mall closes then I'm gonna hook up with Beck and Red. I'll be here till 5:00 but call me first thing in the morning. Get the word to Cee."

"I got you Bro." Steve said.

"I'm out," Kane said and hung up. He lay back on the bed thinking, "It's all falling in place. Now I got to come up with a way to wash our money without going through a banker. The less people there are the better security." He felt a hand slide between the flap in his robe and grip his penis. He opened his eyes and Leslie stood there naked.

She looked at the clock and said, "It's 1:15 we got time for another quick one." She stroked him slowly then threw his robe open and crawled in the bed and straddled him. He looked up at her as she rubbed his penis between her moist slit then slipped it in and slowly lowered herself on it. She rode him slowly until they both reached orgasm.

*   *   *   *

Doreen and Anna came by at 2:30, and by that time Kane and Leslie were dressed. He explained what he wanted for them and they both agreed. They would live off the money that Kane and Tony had given them. Kane gave them $50,000 apiece to live on until the businesses picked up. He told them that he and Leslie were taking $100,000 from their bank account and mortgaging the two houses they owned for another $100,000. He made sure he detailed his plans so they would fully understand them.

186

The children came home at about 3:30. They hugged and kissed their grandmothers then went and changed clothes. At about 4:15 Tony, Lucinda and their children arrived.
Tony gave Anna and Doreen $20,000 apiece, and gave Leslie $150,000 for the businesses.

"Momma," Leslie said. And both women answered. "Y'all keep the kids for us until we get back from the mall."

They both nodded and Kane, Leslie, Tony, and Lucinda went to the mall. They shopped from 6:00 until the mall closed. They bought clothes, shoes, cameras, and anything else they thought they'd need. They stopped and had a late dinner then headed back to the house. It was about 11:00 when they got back to Kane's house.

"Les we got some business to take care of," Kane said. "We'll be back in a few hours." They hugged and kissed their wives and mothers then left.

"We gonna leave," Anna said. "We'll be back the day after tomorrow packed and ready to stay.

"Lu I'll help you pack the kids some stuff tomorrow," Doreen said. "We'll all stay over here there's plenty of room. I'm gonna look for you and Tee a place over here. Since y'all got a little money y'all need to start buying a home like Kane and Les and move out of that neighborhood y'all stay in."

"Alright Momma," Lucinda said smiling.

After Anna and Doreen left, Leslie and Lucinda sat in the living room drinking wine. Leslie looked at Lucinda and they burst out laughing.

"Girl we rolling with rush now!" Leslie said.

"Oh yeah!" Lucinda said laughing. "It's on big sis!"

        *   *   *   *

When Kane and Tony pulled up to their Grandmother's house they noticed a money green Box Chevy, chromed out, with Daytons' parked at the curb. The two rentals were parked in the driveway.

"I've seen that car before," Kane said. "Do you know who it is?"

"Naw," Tony said. "I've seen it too but I can't recall who drives it."

They took out their pistols and headed for the house. Kane opened the door quickly and they eased inside. They could hear music playing softly coming from Kane's room. Their Grandmother's door was closed so she probably was asleep.

Tony quietly walked into the kitchen as Kane eased into the guest room. They checked the bathroom then approached Kane's bedroom door.

Kane grabbed the knob and twisted it gently. He looked at Tony then threw the door wide. They rushed into the room with their guns raised. Becky and Sherrie who sat on the bed in daisy duke shorts and tank tops were smoking a joint. When the door was flung wide the two women rolled to opposite sides of the bed. They hit the floor and came back up with 9mm's clutched in their hands pointing at the door.

Kane and Tony had moved to the right and left of the door so they weren't in the women's line of fire. Sitting in a chair to one side was a short Toni Braxton looking woman with big breast. She jumped up and Kane saw she had a small waist and hips, and he just knew she had a fat bubble butt. When she jumped up the green tennis skirt she wore rose in the front and he could see she wore lime green panties that were pulled up snug, over what looked like a fat cunt. He could see the split between the lips and he said to himself, "Damn that girl is fine." She held a joint tight in her hand as she stood there afraid because she didn't know what was going on.

"Daddy what's wrong?" Sherrie asked.

They all lowered their guns. "That was great reaction time you two," Kane said then turned his attention to Becky. "Beck I could understand if Red had done this but I told you never to bring anyone here. I see a strange car, tricked out, what the fuck am I supposed to think?"

"I'm sorry Daddy," Becky said contritely. "We just wanted to surprise Tee. That's Lisa, the girl we told you about. She done heard of y'all but she ain't from over here. She wanted to meet y'all. She's straight baby. Red and her are girls. They went to school together. She was a couple of grades in front of Red but you know Red been a fly bitch so they hung out together."

"We didn't mean to upset you baby," Sherrie said. "You know we wouldn't do that."

"Alright," Kane said. "But don't pull anymore stunts like this. Excuse me Lisa, I'm Kane. This is Tee the nigga they been telling you about." He walked over to her and gave her a hug.

Tony walked over, gave her a hug and asked, "What's up shorty?"

"It's got to be you if all I hear is correct," Lisa said relaxingly.

"It just might be," Tony said. "Cause I'd hate to think that my sisters would drop salt on me."

She laughed and said, "Naw it ain't like that. They gave me your pedigree and I just hope they ain't blowing you up too much." They all laughed.

"So how did it go today?" Kane asked them.

"Me and Momma got the place on the corner of Price and Spruce St. and the one on Pepper Hill. You know the 2 story red brick building?"

"Yeah," he said. "I know the one you're talking about."

"Well Momma's gonna open the one on Price and Spruce," she said. "She got beer and wine license for both places. Susan and her done started cleaning it already. She got the coolers and shit coming tomorrow. All of the vendors are coming too. They deliver the pool tables, and juke box in the morning. She expects the place to be ready to open by the weekend. The building on Pepper Hill needs a little work, not much but it could be ready in two weeks at the most."

"Damn that was fast," Kane said. "What's up Beck?"

"We got the place on Park and Price a block form Red's spot next to National Linen Service," Becky said. "And the shack on Price and Elm a block from Red's spot in the other direction. The Grannies got the place on Park almost ready to go. They wanna make it a sandwich shop because of how close it is to the businesses on Park St. It would probably be a good idea to turn the shack into a pool hall since there isn't one in the area."

"That's what we'll do with it then," Kane said. "We'll do the same with the place on Pepper Hill. I want you to get the second floor remodeled so it can be used as a trick house Red. What about some houses to serve our product from?"

"I got Chell to rent a house across the street from the place on Price and Spruce," Sherrie said. "I also got one down by the park."

"That's good," he said.

"I didn't do anything on the houses," Becky said. "But I'll get on it when you leave. Can I get the spots in Mixon? We got a lot of shit piled up close together in Brooklyn."

"Get with Cee on that," he said. "I want you to do whatever you feel needs to be done to get us established alright?"

"We can keep our packages at The Sandwich Shop and store our cash there," Sherrie said. "I think we should serve from the houses only. We can get workers to work outside of the spots but don't let them deal from the inside."

"That's good thinking Red," he said. "Make sure it's enforced." He told them about Steve and Charles then let them know the club in Mixon would serve as their base. They would store their dope in the house on Post St. He turned to Lisa and said, "You've heard everything that was said; do you understand what that means?"

"Not really," she said looking at Kane. "But I would like to know where I fit into your plans? I get a little money, nothing major. I serve over on State St., but I ain't a baller. I do alright."

"Lisa it's like this," Kane said looking in her eyes. "I said all I did in front of you to let you know what scale we're working on. Nobody except us in this room and 4 more people know this. If it gets out we'll know where it comes from. Can you dig that?"

"I feel you on that," she said. "Red can vouch for me. I'm down for whatever and ain't nothing soft bout me but my breast and ass. I did two bids and kept my mouth shut so it ain't that kind of party."

"That's cool then baby girl," Kane said. "That covers that. Red give me that joint and you, Beck, and Tee listen closely. That rock smoking shit stops tonight! No more after today. Smoke powder, snort, but no more Crack after tonight alright?"

They all nodded their heads in agreement.

Tony walked over to the dresser, poured some weed on a magazine then sprinkled it with powder cocaine until it looked like snow on grass. He grabbed some papers looked at Becky and asked, "Y'all ain't got any drinks up in here?"

"Nigga the bar up front is stocked with all kinds of shit," Becky said. "But if you gonna be drinking up Kane shit you better be buying him some more so go get it yourself."

Tony folded the magazine and said, "Come on little Momma," to Lisa. He held out his hand and she took it. He pulled her up and they left the room.

Kane watched Lisa's ass sway as she twisted from the room. Two pillows hit him; one in the back, the other in the back of the head. He spun and looked at the two women. "Nigga I'll scratch your eyes out if you even think about it," Sherrie said.

"You better leave me one," Becky said.

"I just know y'all done seen how nice that girl's ass is," he said and laughed. He started undressing. "You ain't freaked with her Red?"

"Naw Daddy," Sherrie said. "She's strictly dickley." They laughed.

Tony went to the bar and got a bottle of Hennessy and 2 glasses. Then he went to the kitchen, got some ice and a coke, while Lisa was behind him the whole way. They went to the guest room and closed the door. He poured them both a drink, rolled them a fat joint and lit them. He passed her one then sat next to her on the bed.

"Lisa I know you don't know me," he said. "But Red and Beck done told you a few things about me. I'm not much when it comes to rapping. All I know how to do is be straight up. You knew the deal when we showed. You knew you were coming to meet somebody. I don't know how you'll figure out whether you wanna be down or what. But if you and I can't hook up romantically I won't prevent you from getting down with us financially. I'm not that type of nigga."

Before he could go on she put 3 fingers on his lips to stop him then said, "Check this out Tee. I got a few dudes I freak with when I feel the need to get my rocks off. Ain't anything serious, no emotional attachments on my behalf. Red and Beck gave me the whole story about you; the thing with you, Red, Beck, and your brother. They told me how you handled yourself and I thought, "Damn the nigga sounds like he sensitive." After I got over my fear when y'all burst into the room and I found out who you were I said to myself, "The nigga cute and fine too. If your skills in bed are half of what Red said they are then you're tailor made for a bitch like me. See I'm a freak and I heard you are too so that ought to work out for us. Financially I'm alright but it's from one bomb to the next with me. It ain't just about the bread but it has its place. I'm being up front with you on that. I ain't a gold digging ho. I get my own but if a nigga wanna show love I'm with it. I know about your domestic situation and if you pass the test I can deal with it. From what your brother said I can get some tonight and some tomorrow to see where you're at so let's stop wasting time with drinking, and smoking, and talking because you got work to do!"

She stood up and removed her blouse and revealed a lime green bra. She reached back and unhooked it then dropped it on the floor. He saw her big firm breast and watched her as she gently massaged them until her fat nipples got hard. She reached to her side and unclasped her skirt, unzipped it and let it flutter to the floor. She stood there in a pair of lime green bikini panties that hugged her fat cunt so tightly it almost looked like they were painted on. He could see the lips as if they were naked. She stood before him topless with her panties and a pair of green and white tennis shoes. She turned her back to him, spread her legs and bent over to untie her shoes.

"Goddamn," Tony said to himself. "Look at the fat ass on this fine motherfucker. It's so round and firm looking." He leaned forward and reached out to touch it.

She looked at him from between her legs then stood and made her ass cheeks jiggle.

"Damn baby," he said as she turned and hooked her thumbs in her panties then pulled them down. He saw that her fat cunt was covered in silky hair, the lips full and pouting. She stepped out of her panties then lay in the bed, spread her legs with her feet flat on the bad and her knees up. "Come on Poppa. Show Momma what you got," she said sexually.

He hurried and undressed then lay between her legs and stabbed his tongue deep into her cunt. After eating her cunt and fucking her in several positions, until she got multiple orgasms they lay in bed smoking a joint.

"Goddamn baby!" She exclaimed. "You're better than Red said you were."

He got up and grabbed his pants. He pulled out a fat roll of bills and counted off $5,000 and gave it to her. "Buy yourself some new clothes tomorrow and stick with Beck and Red."

She got up and put the money in her purse.

They got back in bed and made love again then lay there and talked until there was a knock on the door.

"Yeah," Tony yelled.

The door opened and Beck and Sherrie walked in the room.

"Daddy's taking a bath," Becky said. "He said to tell you you're next so, get ready to roll."

"Alright," he said and leaned over to kiss Lisa. "Welcome to the family! Y'all heifers gonna step out so I can get up or what?"

"Nigga please," Becky said. "We gonna turn around so get your ass on up!" They turned their backs to them and Tony got up and put on his boxers.

When Tony left the room the two women looked at Lisa, then Sherrie asked, "Well girl, what's the verdict?"

"That nigga is an animal," Lisa said then laughed. "I thought he was gonna eat me alive. And then he put the dick down, oh shit! My pussy ain't never been that satisfied. I just hope it wasn't a one-time thing. I'll find out about that tomorrow."

They all burst out laughing.

There was a knock at the door and Sherrie said, "Come on in." Lisa was under the covers and the other women sat on the bed with their legs curled beneath them as Kane walked into the room and asked, "What's up with all that laughing and shit?"

They looked at him then back to Lisa as he said, "Welcome to the family sis. Y'all introduce her to the others when y'all get a chance, and go get some beepers. Get 2 apiece; one for business and the other one for me. Don't give anyone else the number for the one that's for me. I mean nobody. I'm gonna get one just for y'all. Lisa you and Tee work y'all shit out on your own."

Tony stepped in the room and said, "I'm ready Bro."

"Give Lisa some money Tee," Kane said.

"I already did," Tony replied. "Just a little something for her pocket."

They hugged and kissed the women then left.

$*$ $*$ $*$ $*$

When they got to Kane's house it was about 2:30 a.m. They went in and sat for a minute. "How much money you got on you?" Kane asked.

"I don't know?" Tony answered. "Maybe 3 grand."

"Give it to me," Kane said. "I'm gonna buy us all a safe tomorrow. The 3 grand should cover yours and the ones for the businesses. I'll get Charles and Steve's tomorrow when I see them. Ain't any need for you to wake up them kids and drive home so let's spread them out. Tricia probably in bed with Nika anyway. All we got to do is get B.K. and Lil Tony to go in the room with Jay and Dee since they got 4 bunks in there."

They got the kids situated then went to Kane's room where Leslie and Lucinda were curled up in bed together looking like twins. Tony woke Lucinda and she sat up. Leslie woke up too.

"Come on baby," Tony said.

"It's too late to be waking up them children and driving cross town," Lucinda said sleepily.

"Woman hush up and come on," Tony said. "We're going to sleep in B.K.'s room."

"Oh," she said and got up.

As they were walking from the room Leslie said, "If y'all fuck in my baby's bed take the sheets off soon as y'all get up. He doesn't need to smell no pussy and dick on his sheets because he grown enough as it is!"

They laughed and walked out of the room. Kane undressed and got in the bed with Leslie.

"You ain't too sleepy to let me get a little piece are you?" He asked.

"Nigga I ain't never that sleepy," she said as he laughed and pulled her into his arms.

Chapter 14

9:00 the next morning Kane called Charles. Jen answered the phone and woke Charles. "What the fuck is up?" Charles asked as he got on the phone. "Nigga can't you wait until a decent hour to call?"

"Fuck that, smoke black ass nigga?" Said Kane on the other end. They both laughed then Kane asked, "So how did it go Cee?"

"Everything fell in place Bro." Charles answered. "We got all the spots and the vendors coming today. We hired a cleaning service to get the places in shape. I got the coolers, beer, wine all of that. I met Steve downtown when we were getting the licenses so we called all the places together and set all the shit up. We had to get our moms to empty their retirement funds to chip in and get the liquor license. That shit cost $125,000, but we got the money from Safe House and gave it back to them with a little extra, so we still got about 150 gees in operating expenses left. Jen got a line on 6 decent cars; nice ones and we're getting a bargain at $2,600 apiece. Steve got everything set up too so we should be ready to open up in the next week or two if not sooner. Our moms are gonna operate the B.B.Q joint so that would be a good spot for the cash."

"Good thinking," Kane said, then told him about Sherrie and Becky and told him to pass it on to Steve. "Listen Cee, the club gonna be our base so no dope gets sold there. Cool?"

"I'm following you," Charles said. "By the way, the house has 9 rooms and I was thinking we could rent them to the ho's for $10 for 30 minutes and come up."

"That's sweet," Kane said. "Do that. Now let me speak to Jen." Jen got on the phone and Kane said, "You and Gina got a nice piece of money so this is what I want y'all to do. Go out to the mall and find a nice spot to open up a salon. Don't worry about cost and get a loan on your house and use that to keep it legit. I'll give y'all $100,000 that should be enough to do it in style. You can get workers from the barber college on Park St. and the one in gateway. Rent them space and be sure to get both white and black stylist, male and female, someone to do manicure and pedicures too. Alright?"

"That's a damn good idea Bro," Jen said. "I'll get on it first thing this morning."

"Tell Charles I said to meet me at the club at 5:00 and to bring Steve with him."

"Alright," she said and hung up.

Kane walked back into his bedroom. Leslie was still asleep with a smile on her face. "Damn I'd do anything to keep that smile there," he thought to himself. He walked to the kitchen and started cooking breakfast. The smell of the breakfast woke the kids and Lucinda. Lucinda walked into the kitchen, eased behind Kane and wrapped her arms around his waist. She was wearing one of Leslie's robes and smelled like her so he thought it was Leslie.

"Damn I wanted to serve you breakfast in bed," Kane said.

"Tee would kill us both," Lucinda said and burst out laughing.

"Damn Lu," Kane said. "I thought you were Les."

"I know," she said. They had always been affectionate towards each other, but in a brother and sisterly kind of way. Nothing sexual, they were just close.

"I've noticed a change in Tee," she said releasing him. "It's a good thing. You've always been good about looking out for us, even when you were young. I really appreciate all you've done. Paying the bills when Tee fucked up, checking on me and the kids to make sure we were alright. I could never repay you for all of that."

"You don't owe me for it," he said firmly. "Or anything else I might do in the future. I love y'all, we're family and family should look out for family. If shit was the other way around; I'd expect no less from you. So don't be tripping like I'm a stranger doing good deeds for some poor unfortunate niggas. Family got to stick together and that's the way it should be. We both got folks that we only see when someone dies. That shit ain't cool. I ain't going out my way to try and be alright with them if they act like we don't exist until they need us, but me and you, Leslie, Tony, Gina, Jen, Charles, Steve, Doreen, and Anna. We're gonna stay tight. You think I don't know about the money you send my daddy every month. It's little shit like that, that means something to me. I love you for that and more."

She threw her arms around him and he hugged her and gave her a light kiss. "Sit your fat ass down and let me finish cooking before I burn my shit."

They laughed as she released him and he walked back to the stove. She sat down and watched as he finished cooking.

The children didn't go to school that day and they all came into the kitchen and sat around the table. Tony came in and sat down then asked, "Nigga what you cooking?"

"What it smells like I'm cooking?" Kane said. "It's food nigga so don't act like you don't know what that is."

They both laughed. He finished cooking, looked up at Lucinda and said, "Lu feed your family," then reached up on the top shelf and got a tray with fold out legs. He wiped the tray then sat a plate on it. He filled the plate put it on the tray and walked to his room. He opened the door slowly and peeked in; Leslie was still asleep. He walked into the room, closed the door with his foot then walked to the bed. The covers had slid down exposing her upper body and her big full breasts were in view. He could see the smooth skin of her shoulders and he reached down and gently shook her, "Les, Les, wake up honey."

She rolled over onto her back, stretched, then looked up at him. She saw the tray in his hands and said, "No you didn't?"

"Yes I did," he said smiling as she sat up her breast hanging free. He placed the tray over her legs and sat on the edge of the bed and kissed her cheek.

"Damn baby," she said smiling brightly. "You threw down this morning." She started eating and with her mouth full she asked, "You gonna eat?"

"Later," he said. "Right now I'm gonna watch you." When she finished he moved the tray.

"Want a little piece?"

"Naw," he replied. "I got some shit to do and I need to get on it if I'm gonna make it home tonight."

"Alright," she said. "I'm gonna pack our stuff so we'll be ready to go tomorrow."

"That's cool," he said. "By the way, did you give the kids the stuff I bought for them?"

"Yes I did," she answered. "And they loved them; I love the stuff you got for me too! Thanks baby."

"No need to mention it," he said then kissed her. He showered, dressed and as he walked toward the door he said, "Tee!"

"Yeah," Tony said coming to see what Kane wanted.

"Can you get in touch with Tracy and Sonny?" Kane asked.

"Yeah," Tony said. "I got their beeper number so I can reach them anytime."

"Get in touch with them and have them meet us at the club at 5:00," Kane said.

"Alright," Tony said. "I'll do that. I got a couple of young cats I wanna holla at who might be able to get down with us."

"That's cool," Kane said. "But don't bring them to the club and I don't wanna meet them. Alright?"

"I got you," Tony said as Kane walked out the door.

Kane went and rented a U-Haul with the motorized lift then drove to the safe company on Forsyth and Broad. He parked in the front and walked in, as he looked around a salesman came to assist him.

"Yes sir. How might I help you?" The salesman asked.

"I'm looking for a home safe," Kane said. "Not a wall safe or something I'd have to hire carpenters to install, but a nice sturdy safe that can be easily hidden."

"I've got just the thing for you," the salesman said. "Please come this way." He led Kane across the huge showroom and they came to a section that seemed to be filled with octagonal shaped nightstands. The clerk grabbed a knob on one and swung it open. Inside was a small safe.

"That's nice," Kane said. "How much is it?"

"It retails for $400 but I'll let you get it for $350," the man said smiling.

"Can you open it up so I can look inside of it?" Kane asked.

"Sure," the man said. "It's fire proof and difficult to breach." He kneeled and spun the combination that hung on a price tag. He pulled it open and it had another door inside with a keyhole. There were several small drawers that also had keyholes which the man promptly opened.

"Do any of these come without the drawers?" Kane asked.

"The drawers are removable." The man said. "But we have a slightly larger model with more capacity for storage."

"Can I see it?" Kane asked.

"Why sure," the man said. He rose to his feet moved over several rows and then he stopped. He bent and opened another one. Kane couldn't tell the difference by eye but he didn't think the man would try to swindle a potential customer.

"How much is this one?" Kane asked.

"$500," the man said. "But for you $450."

"If I bought more than one would you cut me a deal?" asked Kane.

"Sure," the man said. "A good deal. Say you bought both of these; I'd cut $50 and give you both for $750.

"I want that one and five of the other one," Kane said. "Could I get the five for $300 apiece?"

The man was smiling openly as he said, "Yes sir."

"Okay," Kane said. "I'm also looking for six for business purposes."

"What size did you have in mind?" The man asked.

"The same as the first one would be just about right," Kane said.

"We have that same model without the stand in three basic colors beige, gray, and black."

"That's alright," Kane said. "I'll just take 11 with the stand. I can get the 11 for $300 apiece right?"

"Yes sir," the man said excitedly.

"With the other one at $400 and 11 at $300 I owe you $3,700 plus tax am I right?" Kane asked.

"Well sir," the man said. "Adding 7 cents to the dollar which is the current sales tax would bring the total to 3,959."

Kane laughed then said, "So it will. Are sales confidential?"

"Yes sir," the man said. "That is unless you spend $10,000 or more."

Kane peeled $3,960 off of his roll and passed it to the clerk. He peeled off an additional $100 and said, "A tip for your excellent service. Can you load them in the U-Haul outside for me? I'll give you a hand."

"Sure," the man said. "No need to strain sir. We've got workers in the back for such tasks. Would you like a cup of coffee or a soft drink while you wait?"

"A soft drink would be nice," Kane said. "Preferably something with flavor; no Coke or Sprite please."

"Fine," the man said. "Give me a minute." He left the room and walked to the back. He returned shortly with 3 men and gave them instructions. He brought Kane a soda and they went outside and sat on a sofa in front of the store and drank sodas as the men loaded the truck.

"Should you have a problem with any of the safes be sure to call me. Here's my card," the man said passing Kane a card with both his office and home phone number. "Feel free to call."

"Thank you," Kane said rising and shaking the man's hand. The other men had finished loading the truck so Kane got in and drove off. He went to the AT&T building on Church St. and was surprised to find Becky, Sherrie, and Lisa there purchasing beepers. He bought 2 and got them activated then he noticed that Becky and Lisa had 4. "What's up with that?" He asked Becky.

"These are for Cee and Steve," she answered. "Gina and Jen already got some."

"These 2 are for Tony," Lisa said. "One for business and the other for pleasure."

"That's good looking out," Kane said. "I want y'all at the club by 5:00 okay?"

They all nodded, he hugged and kissed them then left. Since Charles had Jen's beeper until Becky brought him his, Kane beeped him from a phone booth. A few minutes later the phone rang and Kane picked it up.

"It's me," he said. "How soon can you meet me at The Sandwich Shop in Brooklyn?"

"Give me 30 minutes," Charles said.

"Alright," said Kane. "See you then."

Kane got in the truck and drove back to the Safe Company. When he walked in the salesman hurried to him and asked, "Back again soon, I hope there's not a problem?"

"There is, sort of," Kane replied. "I noticed the dollies y'all used to move the safes are not standard and I just thought I'd need to move my safes. How much are they?"

"They're built to specifications," the man said. "They can be used like regular dollies but they were designed especially to move safes. They cost us $500 to make them and that's on order. It takes about 2 weeks before we get them."

"I'll give you $700 for one right now," Kane said.

"I'm not authorized to sell them," the man said. "But I do believe Mr. Rabinowitz would slit my throat if I turned you down." Both he and Kane laughed. He went and got the dolly. Kane paid him and they shook hands then Kane left.

*   *   *   *

Charles met Kane at The Sandwich Shop. It was filled with vendors making their deliveries. They dropped off a safe then drove to the club. They dropped safes at all of their places of business and at their homes then took the U-Haul back. They stopped to get Charles' car then went to the club.

When they arrived Charles' mother Glenda was taking deliveries. She saw Kane and said, "Kane why haven't you been to see me?"

"I been busy Ms. Glenda," Kane replied.

"I can see that," Glenda said. "Y'all hit lotto!"

Charles didn't know that Glenda had tried to get with Kane. Glenda was dark skinned, a beautiful face, and a fantastic body for a 50 year old woman. She looked like Janet Hubbert Whitten, the first lady to play the mother on the Fresh Prince of Bel-Air. She was Charles' mom and that was the only reason Kane had declined, but still she kept at him.

"Olivia is at the other place holding it down for me," she said.

Olivia was 25 years old and the spitting image of her mother; dark chocolate skin, and a beautiful body. Sammy was Charles 24 year old brother and he looked like Glenda too. Same dark skinned complexion but he only stood about 5'4" and wore about 125 pounds. He was at the pool hall next door so they were all on the ball.

When Glenda left, Charles and Kane sat in the club talking. "What are you gonna do about the grand opening?" Charles asked.

"What do you mean?" Kane asked in response.

"You know Leslie is gonna want to be there," Charles said. "So is Lucinda. Not to mention Anna, Doreen, Glenda, Silvia, Becky, Lisa, Red, and the girls me and Steve kick it with, Naomi and Vanessa. So how we gonna deal with that?"

"No sweat Cee," Kane said. "All we got to do is have the grand opening at all of the places the same day. Everyone will be way to busy. We can let the girls work the club; then bring the wives later if they're not too tired."

"That's a good idea," Charles said. "Silvia got the ball rolling in Lackawanna."

Silvia was Steve's mother, a high yellow woman with hazel color eyes. She was beautiful even if full figure at 48 years old. She and Steve's sister Antoinette were at the store. Antoinette was a beautiful brown skinned girl with the hazel eyes that ran in their family. She had huge breast, a trim waist, a nice little ass and she was 24 years old. Steve's brother Vincent was running the pool hall on Lennox. Vincent and Silvia looked just alike. Vincent was about 5'10" and wore at least 250 pounds. He was beyond chubby.

Kane saw things falling in place nicely and, he and Charles hung out at the club until 5:00 p.m. when the others started arriving. When they were all gathered Kane passed them drinks then sat on the stool behind the bar. He made eye contact with each person then turned back to Sonny and Tracy, "Did Tee tell y'all what time it is?"

"Yeah," Tracy said. "But not in depth."

"Alright," Kane said. "This is the deal. If y'all wanna work with us it's all good; if not that's cool too but I'm gonna lay it down for you. Each of us has a position and every job is important. I want you a Sonny to work with Tee, with Tee is in charge. All of Brooklyn is y'all ball park. Recruit workers for the houses and for each of the businesses. I want y'all to have 2 shifts. On a day then off a day, or 12 hours apiece. Whatever is most comfortable for y'all and the workers. We gonna serve 24 hours; dope, beer, liquor or whatever. If the houses got 4 or 5 rooms tell whoever is running it to rent the rooms to the tricks on a 30 minute basis for $5. If they wanna stay longer they pay longer got it?" They nodded and Kane went on. "Cee, Steve, y'all do the same thing in y'all area. I don't need to know the guys y'all choose and they don't need to know me. I'm gonna be our troubleshooter. If a problem comes up I'll try to fix it, so let your people collect the money and give it to you. Y'all know where to drop it off. Beck, Red, Lisa, y'all gonna be dropping off dope for us," he pointed at the women. "Y'all cut and package the dope. If y'all wanna get down, do it from the pool hall in Brooklyn but I really want y'all to stay away from that end of things. I don't want any of our people to serve in occupied territory. Lisa, start serving our product to the clientele you built up where you were working; when I'm gone take the girls to check it out. Be sure to let them know where they can find our product. I want this shit to operate like a well-oiled machine. No one that works for us will exploit the users, no beating them up for being short or getting them to do fucked up shit for a rock. No breaking down our product to try and make more money. Every day I want you to keep an eye on the quantity of our products. The first time you notice some bullshit put a stop to it right then and there. Get rid of the motherfucker who doing it cause he's got a me, my, and I mentality. We're a team. While I'm gone I expect y'all to put all of your pieces in place and set everything in order. I want you to set it off. Get the ball rolling, keep a close eye on shit and cover each other's back. Trace, Sonny, y'all gonna work with the ladies until Tee gets back. Cee and Steve, when you get time take Lisa and handle that on her end. Y'all can take Red and Beck with you. I've got confidence that if anything comes up y'all can handle it. I don't wanna come home to bodies in the street Red. I'm talking to you especially; got me?"

"I got you daddy," she said. "If it comes to it, am I allowed to use my discretion?"

"Absolutely," Kane said. "Well, that's it for now. Me and Tee are leaving tomorrow and we'll be gone for 7 days which means we'll be back next Friday. Cee we gonna need some fine girls to work the club. If you want to, you can let Naomi and Vanessa work here because I know Beck, Red, and Lisa gonna do it. Y'all ain't getting paid, so I want y'all to know that off the top." They all laughed.

"That's cool," Charles said. "Will they be working on grand opening?"

"Yeah," Kane said. "They can handle it. This is as much theirs as it is mine and I won't deny them that."

"I can dig that bro." Charles said.

"Ladies let's roll," Kane said walking from behind the bar. Becky, Sherrie, and Lisa rose.

Lisa walked to Tony and said, "I did like you asked me to and I bought some things from the mall but I haven't been home yet."

"That's cool baby," Tony said. "But you still can't go home yet, after tonight you can go. By the way, you never told me where you live."

"On Dot St. in an apartment," she said.

"I don't even want to see it," he said. "Cee, Steve one of y'all drop my dogs off for me!"

"Call me at Granny's at 9:00 Cee," Kane said.

"Okay," Charles said.

"Come on," Kane said to Becky and Sherrie. "I wanna spend some time with y'all before I go. Oh yeah! Steve I'm giving you and Gina a cruise as a wedding gift. I know you gonna take that black ass nigga with you so it's gonna be 4 tickets. I'm giving all you motherfuckas cruises and ain't none of y'all thought to give me and my girls shit. That's fucked up," he walked out the door laughing.

Tony and Lisa were just pulling off when he stopped, turned around and stuck his head thru the door and said, "Trace! Check this out." Tracy stepped out the door and Kane said, "Drive this rental and park it for me. Charles will show you where." He turned to his ladies and asked, "Who got the keys?"

Sherrie tossed them to Tracy then they got in Kane's car.

*   *   *   *

When they reached the house Lisa's car was still parked in the same place. Tony and her sat in his car rapping. Becky pulled beside the gate and parked then they got out of the car. It was 7:30 when Kane banged on the hood of Tony's car then they all went inside.

"Red roll me a joint," Kane said. "Lace it for me baby and Beck pour us some drinks."

His grandmother was still at The Sandwich Shop getting things in order so they had the house to themselves. They sat and smoked laced joints and drank Hennessy. Becky played some music and they partied. His grandmother came in at about 9:30 looked around and said, "This ain't a damn club.... Red Girl pour me a drink!"

They all laughed as she sat down and Sherrie made her a drink and brought it to her.

"I'm gonna give Merrie and Christy a job Boy," Granny said. "Unless you already got somebody lined up."

"No I don't have anyone lined up," Kane said. "That place is for y'all and I ain't got anything to do with who you hire and fire. Who Ms. Essie wanna hire?"

"Her granddaughter Chloe," Granny answered. "She a good girl, responsible, doesn't run the street and active in the church."

"That's good," Becky said. "Cause me, Red, and Lisa gonna be floating from spot to spot on a rotating basis. We gonna be real busy."

"That damn Essie," Granny said. "She got me tired as hell. I'm gonna take me a bath and turn in. Y'all young people go on and have fun."

They all bid her a goodnight.

After his grandmother came out of the bathroom Tony and Lisa rushed it.

"Y'all go on and bathe," Kane said. "Don't be in there with that freaky shit, we wanna clean up too."

Tony and Lisa laughed and went on in the bathroom. After everyone had bathed they went to their rooms.

"I'm gonna be gone for 7 days," Kane said. "I expect for y'all to keep shit rolling. Get Lisa's feet wet and keep her with you. When y'all hit the spot she was working if it looks good sit down with Charles and Steve and see what y'all can come up with on that end. If you have any trouble and it can wait till I get back, let it wait. If not, Red you plan it out and sit down with the others. Iron out the wrinkles and handle your business. If it comes to gunplay just let Lisa drive. Be sure to teach her how to use a gun alright?"

Becky wearing a powder blue teddy with matching G-string panties said, "Alright baby."

Sherrie wore a red Teddy with black piping and matching panties and Kane just a pair of boxers. They all sat on the bed.

"Tonight I'm gonna make love to each of you separately," Kane said.

"No joining until I say so. You can watch but no touching got me?"

They both nodded then Sherrie asked, "Who's gonna go first?"

"Flip a coin and call it in the air," Kane said.

Becky got up and went in her purse and pulled out a coin. She thumbed it into the air and said, "Heads." The coin landed on the bed with the tail's side up.

"You're first Red," Kane said and took off his boxers.

* * * *

"Tee I want you to close your eyes," said Lisa. "Don't peek."

"Come on girl," Tony pleaded. "Let me see what you got for me."

"No, no, no," she said. "I want this night to be special."

"Baby it's already special," he said. "You're here with me."

"Damn it I'm serious," she said taking off the big Tee shirt she wore. Tony was struck again by how fine she was. She rolled the tee shirt up, put it over his eyes and tied it to his head.

"Don't take it off until I tell you too alright?" She said.

"Okay," he said nodding.

She walked over to where her bags were and reached in a bag and pulled out an outfit she had bought from Victoria's Secret. She hurried and put it on then walked in front of him and said, "Okay, you can take it off now."

He took the tee shirt off of his head and what he saw took his breath away. She stood there in a short, sheer, money green, house coat. It barely reached her thighs. It was shot thru with gold threads that glistened as they caught the light. A matching bra with the space at the nipples cut out, matching crotch less panties, thigh high money green stockings that squeezed her succulent flesh, and money green ankle strap stacks.

"Damn!" He exclaimed. "You look so sexy in that outfit! Whatever you do don't take it off." He got up from the bed and slowly approached her. He pulled her into his arms and kissed her, sliding his tongue into her mouth while his erect penis pressed against her stomach. She reached down and grabbed it then stroked it slowly as they kissed. He stepped back and looked at her again and saw that her nipples were rock hard and poking thru the open space of her bra. He bent, and took one into his mouth and sucked it in. The silk of her bra rubbed his lips as he gently bit, licked, and sucked her nipple. He switched to the other one and did the same. She moaned, "Ummm....ummmhmm.... that feels nice baby.....yes...."

*   *   *   *

At 8:30 the next morning Charles gave Kane a wakeup call. Kane picked up the phone and Charles said, "Boss, I thought I'd give you 30 minutes to get yourself together. You know a little leeway?"

"Good thinking Cee," Kane said. "I know I can count on you while I'm gone but I want you to coordinate all your activities with Red. Between the two of y'all I think you'll be able to cover all of the bases. How do you feel about that?"

"Next to you she's the best thinker in the crew so I don't have a problem with that," he said.

"Alright," Kane said pleased with his response. "When y'all go to the spot with Lisa if it looks like we can work it over there go on and set up shop. Always get a legit front and even though you and Red are coordinating you're in charge. Red is a little too blood thirsty for me to leave in complete control so your work is final and I won't tolerate any bullshit from her alright?"

"I got you boss," said Charles.

"When you get the phone at the club be sure to leave the number with Anna or Doreen." Kane said. "They're staying at my house until I get back. I'll be calling everyday around 7:00 p.m. I don't wanna cut this trip short Cee."

"Don't worry about a thing bro." said Charles. "We got it. See you when you get back."

"Alright," Kane said and hung up the phone.

Sherrie was awake and she had heard the entire conversation. When he noticed her she said, "So you think I'm blood thirsty huh?"

"Yes I do," he said. "I also think you're ruthless as fuck, fine as a motherfucka, beautiful, lovable, loyal, and one of my favorite fucks."

She smiled and said, "I won't let you down baby, I promise. You trust me with the responsibility to co-head our crew. Though I have to admit I don't like that "Charles has the last word" shit. I trust your judgment and I'll follow your orders. Now give me some more of that dick before you go."

She spread her legs and pulled him to her. She stroked him until he was fully erect then guided him in. They made love hard and fast, and the rocking bed woke Becky. She stretched and looked over at Kane and Sherrie making love and said to Sherrie, "Sneaky bitch. You think you gonna hog up all that dick? Baby save some for me since she didn't wake me up."

He laughed as he thrust rapidly into Sherrie and moaned, "Don't....Worry. There'll be enough....Left for you...."

*   *   *   *

It was 9:45 when Kane and Tony got to his house. They saw Anna and Doreen's cars in the driveway. Leslie, Lucinda, Anna, and Doreen all stood on the porch with suitcases ready to be loaded. Leslie and Lucinda had camera cases around their necks along with their purses.

"Y'all didn't even get a chance to tell the kids bye," Leslie said angrily.

"Les don't start," Kane said. "We were busy baby."

Leslie pulled her camera and gave it to Anna and showed her how to work it while Lucinda did the same with Doreen. The two women snapped several pictures of the couples then Kane and Tony loaded the suitcase into the cars. They drove to Jax International Airport, and arrived by 11:00 a.m. They checked their bags in and Doreen and Anna left. They went to the lounge and had a few drinks as they waited on their flight. At 11:50 their flight was announced and they boarded at gate #5. Their flight left promptly at12:05 and at 1:00 they touched down in Miami. They flagged a cab then went to a hotel room and left their bags, then went sight-seeing. At 3:40 they went back to the hotel and collected their bags and headed to the port.

They had two berths side by side on the Caribbean cruise line ship, The Ocean Princess. As they approached the ship they noticed how huge the ship was. Kane and Tony carried two big suitcases while Leslie and Lucinda carried a small carrying case each.

"Baby set the suitcases down," Leslie said. "I want a picture of you in front of the ship."

He sat the suitcases down and smiled as Leslie took his picture. Lucinda took a picture of him and Tony, then Leslie and Kane. Leslie took pictures of Tony and Lucinda and Kane and Lucinda. They got a couple passing to take a picture of the four of them then they boarded the ship. They went to their berths and unpacked their bags then returned to the rail as the ship pulled away from port.

Kane had brought $20,000 even though it was an all-expense paid cruise because there was a casino on board, and he planned to buy gifts for everyone. Leslie brought $5,000 for the same purpose not knowing Kane bought so much. Tony brought $10,000 and Lucinda $5,000.

After the ship was at sea they strolled over the ship, checked out the casino, the pool area, the club, lounge, and restaurants. By the time they had checked out all of the things the ship had to offer several hours had passed. They went to their rooms showered and changed then had dinner. After dinner they hit the club and drank and danced until midnight then went to the casino. Kane brought $1,000 worth of chips and gave Leslie half and they went to the crap table. Kane dropped $50 on the 6 and Leslie $10 on the 8. The dice were rolled and Kane lost. Leslie won and acted like she hit for a million dollars. She let her money ride and Kane dropped $50 more on the 6 and lost again, and again Leslie won. She placed her winnings on the 6 and Kane put $50 on the 8. The dice were rolled again and landed on 6.

"Damn Les done won again," Kane said to himself.

The dice had come around to Leslie and she placed her money on the 7. Kane put his on the 6 and Leslie rolled the dice. They stopped on 7. She rolled 5 straight 7's in a row before she changed her number to 11 and rolled 3 of those. Her piles of chips were getting bigger. Looking at the stack Kane estimated she was playing close to $4,000 as she switched back to the 7 and rolled the dice. Again they stopped on 7.

Kane had been steadily losing. Leslie passed him the $490 in chips she had left from what he had given her. He took them as Leslie put all of the money on the 5. She had close to $8,000. Kane wanted to say no but instead he put the $490 on the 5.

"You're my lucky charm," she said and gave Kane a kiss. "Blow on these for me baby."

He blew on the dice as the crowd that had gathered around the table grew quiet. Leslie rubbed the dice and said, "Momma needs a new diamond ring," then she rolled the dice.

You could hear them as they tumbled across the felt of the crap table and a soft double clap as they hit the wall and did a rebound spin. One dice stopped on the 1 as the other spinning like a top finally came to a stop on the 4. The crowd roared as Leslie jumped up and down pumping her fist in the air, her big breast juggling. She turned to Kane and hugged him.

She pulled her winnings to her and said, "Baby let's go to the jewelry shop."

Tony and Lucinda were playing blackjack. They weren't winning but they weren't losing either. Kane and Leslie walked over and Leslie said, "Come on y'all we going to cash in these chips and hit the gift shop." They got up and followed Leslie and Kane to cash in their chips and hit the gift shop. Leslie paid the taxes on her winnings and still walked away with $13,500.

When they got to the gift shop Leslie couldn't find anything special to buy all 4 of them, so Kane and Tony bought gifts for the kids. It was about 4:00 in the morning so they retired to their rooms and went to sleep.

11:00 the next day they all put on bathing suits. Leslie and Lucinda wore 2 piece bikinis with sarongs and big straw hats. Kane and Tony wore Nautica swimwear trunks and tank tops. They all wore sunglasses and lay in beach chairs sipping fruity tropical drinks. They took pictures, frolicked in the pool for a while then ate a light meal. They retired to their rooms, made slow love then dozed off for a few.

The shops bell woke them announcing that they would soon be pulling into port at Nassau, Bahamas where there would be a 6 hour layover. They showered and dressed, ready to hit the island.

When the ship docked Leslie said, "I wanna go to a jewelry shop before we do anything else alright?"

They all agreed and set off to find one, which wasn't hard as all of the businesses were concentrated in the port area. They walked in one and looked around. Leslie spotted a gold pendant shaped just like their ship. It was an inch high and 2 inches long and beautifully detailed.

Leslie called a clerk and asked, "How much for the ship?"

"$400 Madame," the clerk answered smiling.

"Do you have 4 of them in stock?" She asked.

"Yes as a matter of fact we do," the clerk said. "They're not as big a selling item as we had hoped they'd be."

"Do you do diamond settings?" Leslie asked hopefully.

"Yes we do," the clerk said anticipating a big sale. "We even sell loose stones."

"I'd like to see some of your loose stones," Leslie said. "And I'd like 4 of these ship pendants

207

"Follow me please," the clerk said leading them to a back counter. He got 4 of the pendants and several black velvet bags. He pulled the draw string on one of the bags and poured some beautiful small stones on a tray he had sat on the counter. Leslie shook her head and he scooped them up and put them back in the bag and opened the next one. Again she shook her head and he went to the next one.

After he had gone thru several of the bags he poured out some clear blue diamonds and she said, "Those are the ones I want, how much are they?"

"$300 a piece Madame," he replied.

"Alright," she said smiling. "Give me 16 of those and please let me hold one of the pendants, and I'll show you how I want them set."

The clerk got the 16 diamonds and gave her one of the pendants. She sat the pendant down and laid 4 diamonds across it spaced out in a straight line.

"I want them just like that on all 4 of the pendants," she said. "Can you do it in 4 hours?"

"Yes Madame, most certainly," he said and rushed to the back. She could hear him in back talking loudly to someone else. He came from the back smiling and said, "It is done. Can I help you with anything else?"

"Yes you can," she said. "I'd like to see your very best solid gold chains. I don't want hollow chains. I want solid ones."

He led them to another counter and pulled out a tray of thick gold chains, ropes, and various types of links. She chose a Gucci link and asked, "How much for 4 of these?"

"Madame you will have spent a great deal of money before we complete our transaction," the clerk said. "These chains normally sell for $1,500 but for you $1,200 okay?"

"Why thank you," she said gracing him with her beautiful smile. "Can you give me a total please?" She asked.

"Just a moment please," he said and they walked to a cash register. He rang up her purchases and said, "That will be $11,984.00"

She opened her purse, pulled out a huge wad of bills and counted out the money.

"Thank you Madame," the clerk said graciously. "Your pendants will be ready in," he looked at his watch, "two and a half hours."

"Thank you," She said and they left.

They walked all over the island taking pictures, stopped at an outdoor café ate lunch and had a few drinks. They bought gifts for everyone at home then Kane looked at his watch and saw that it was time to go back and get the jewelry.

"Baby I've been meaning to ask you about that watch and the beautiful wedding band but it keeps slipping my mind," Leslie said.

"They mine and that's that," Kane said with finality.

"I was just asking because I wanted to get you something nice so it could be special," she said.

"You already special believe me," he said. "Now let's go get the stuff you did buy."

They went and got the jewelry and it was done just like Leslie wanted. They boarded the ship and a half hour later they were back at sea. They all wore the new necklaces and the fat diamonds glittered as they caught the waning sunlight. They went to their rooms and took a nap until around 9:00. They ate a late supper and stayed in the club until midnight.

Tony looked at Lucinda and said, "Baby let's go for a late night swim."

"Okay baby," she said smiling broadly.

Kane and Leslie went to the casino as Tony and Lucinda went to their room and changed into their bathing suits. Lucida wore a white 2 piece bikini and a white sheer sarong and white backless sandals. Tony wore his Nautica trunks and tank top with Nike flip flops. He took off his shirt, kicked off his flip flops and dived in the pool. She took off her sarong, kicked off her sandals and dived in behind him. She swam over to him and he grabbed her in his arms. They sank beneath the surface and kissed then kicked back to the surface. They swam to the shallow end and embraced noticing they were the only ones in the pool area. They kissed deeply and she held on to him tightly and said, "This is wonderful baby. We should do something for Kane; he's been so good to us."

"Yes he has," Tony said agreeing with her. "Even before we got the money he made sure we were straight and when I was fucking up he always had my back. I think we should buy him something nice and surprise him. He loves that Buick but we ought to buy him something nice and surprise him. We can't pay for it all at once but we can get money orders or cashier's check and pay for it like that. I wanna get him a nice Benz for 25 or 30 grand. If we drop that kind of cash at once the I.R.S is sure to come so we'll drop 9 grand as a down payment and from there pay two months at a time. That's gonna be your job to keep up the payments and I'll set the money aside."

"That's good," she said. "We can do that as soon as we get home."

They kissed again and she reached down and squeezed his penis. He palmed her ass cheeks then ducked under the water and pulled her bikini bottoms to the side and sucked her clitoris until he ran out of breath. He pushed his finger in her and plunged it back and forth as his free hand unleashed her breast. He ducked under water and sucked at her nipples as he fingered her.

She unzipped his trunks and pulled his penis out then broke loose from his embrace and dropped below the surface and took his penis into her mouth and sucked greedily at it for as long as she could, then came up for air. She slowly stroked him and looked in his eyes and said, "Make love to me right here!" She threw her arms around his neck then jumped up and wrapped her legs around his waist. He held her ass in one hand and his penis in the other and she rose up so he could guide it in. As he slid deep in her she moaned, "Oh Tony...Oh baby...."

He held her ass as she bounced up and down on his swollen manhood and moaned, "It feels so good...sooo good...."

Kane and Leslie left the casino and hand in hand they walked the deck. It was late, a full moon overhead, the stars glittering in the inky black sky like millions of tiny diamonds. They stood at the rail watching the sky and the luminescent foam left from the wake of the ship.

"Thanks baby," Leslie said. "This is one of the best things you've ever done for me."

"Sweetheart you deserve even more," he said with sincerity. "If it was in my power to do, I'd build a net that would capture all of the stars and present them to you as your due. I'd crown you with the moon, make your bed and pillows the clouds. I'd clothe you with the summer winds and make you queen of all that exist, but baby those things are beyond my reach and this was the least I could do."

"Baby you've never really understood that it's not the material things that matter most to me," she said. "If I had to choose between riches and your love, I'd choose your love every time. The money and all it can buy are nice, but when we were broke and struggling I loved you then."

He took her face and held it gently and kissed her as she wrapped her arms around him.

She wore a beautiful sky blue sundress with white orchids hand painted on it by Anne Klein and sky blue sandals by Chanel. He wore a pair of white linen pants, a white linen shirt both by Yves St. Laurent, and white gator sandals by Mauri. His shirt was open almost to the waist, the feeble moonlight flashing from the diamonds on the gold ship that hung from his neck.

He guided her to some deck chairs that sat back from the rail, sat down and pulled her into his lap. She rested her head on his shoulder and said, "Baby this is beautiful," then kissed him deeply. She got up, hiked up her dress and straddled his legs. She sat down on his lap, looked in his eyes and said, "I love you baby!"

"I love you too," he said as she reached down unzipped his pants and fished his penis out. She stroked him until he was hard, looking in his eyes the whole while. She rose and with her free hand pulled her panties aside then guided him in. Slowly she lowered herself on his stiff cock and then she grabbed the arm rest of the deck chair and slowly rode his cock. His hands moved to her waist as she leaned forward and kissed him passionately.

She moaned into his mouth, "Umm…umm…" as they too made love under the stars.

Chapter 15

Kane and Tony had been gone 4 days. Charles and the others had made big steps in getting their operation up and running. Charles had gotten two dudes he use to give a little work to and told them what he was doing, and both men wanted to be a part of it. Their names were Pookie and Ced.

Steve had recruited two small time dealers that he knew to hook up with them. Their names were T-Bo and Hammer Head.

Charles had hired a man named Shorty Fat to run the pool hall on Edison, and an ex-whore named Eileen and her man, Slim Dixon to run the house behind the club.

Steve had a man named Bowlegs running the dope house in Lackawanna, and all of the spots were jumping.

Sherrie and Becky got Chell to run the dope house in Brooklyn and Sherrie's mom Sarah had her place open by Saturday. Sherrie's sister Susan was dropping off the drugs in Brooklyn and things were booming all over.

*   *   *   *

Charles, Steve, Sherrie, Beck, and Lisa sat in the club.

"Well it looks like things are going pretty good," Charles said. "Were making money already so I think it's time we expand over there where Lisa used to serve and see what time it is. Lisa is there anybody over there we might have a problem with?"

"I can't really say Cee," Lisa answered. "I was just small time and you know how niggas are about ho's, so I can't really call that. The lick might read different if y'all show up. Big Moe and Ted had something going on the other end of Kings Rd., but they're out the picture now. A nigga named Chico who thinks he's a big shot got a little something rolling on State and Tyler. I use to be down on that end but I didn't stay stationary. It's some Dreads serving too but they mostly deal weed."

"Well ain't but one way to find out," Charles said. "So we gonna roll over there. Kane said if it looks good then we can set up shop. Lisa since you know the niggas over there you should know who we can work with. I don't wanna take niggas from over here to set up shop over there."

"I see your point," Lisa said. "It would be better having a nigga that already knows the clientele."

"Y'all strapped?" Charles asked looking around.

"Nigga you got to ask?" Steve replied.

"We strapped all day, every day," Sherrie said.

"What you holdin?" Charles asked her.

"We done moved up," Becky said. "We toten 9's, and Lisa got a .380 and knows how to use it."

"We shouldn't need anything heavier," Charles said. "I done copped some new shit with the company funds but I'm keeping track."

"I have too," Steve said.

"Me and Beck done bought some shit too," Sherrie added. "You know how daddy like them pumps. We have to keep track of what we spend and wait till Kane gets back before we get paid. We all been paying the workers, we know what they get and we done made a nice piece of money already."

"We ain't really got to worry about our pay right now," Charles said. "We should all be straight money wise for a minute, Lisa you alright on cash?"

"I'm straight," Lisa answered. "Tee gave me 5 gees to buy clothes and 5 more before he left. I moved in with his granny and all of us are cribbin together," she pointed at Becky and Sherrie.

"That's cool," Charles said. "Let's roll!"

Becky and Charles got in a black 4 door Chevy that Jen had bought, Steve and Sherrie got in a 4 door navy blue Taurus that Jen bought, and Lisa drove her own car. They drove down to Stockton and took a right and rode until they came to Beaver St. They took a right on Beaver and drove down to Tyler St. and took a left. When they got to State St. they made a right and drove a half a block and parked.

Lisa got out of her car and they all walked over to her. "This is the spot here," she said. "All we got to do is chill and the customers will come." Lisa wore a green, jean jumper that hugged every curve of her body, her hair freshly braided with money green extensions strategically placed. A money green bandana tied gangster style, and money green and white Nike running shoes.

Sherrie wore red stretch jeans, a Red and white tank top, a red Kangol cap turned backwards, and red Timberland construction style boots.

Beck wore a pair of electric blue capri pants with a matching blouse, an Orlando magic baseball cap cocked to the left, and a pair of white on white Nike Air Max's. Her hair was freshly braided to the back. All of the women had bags that matched their outfits.

Steve and Charles wore baggy jeans, baseball caps, and big tee shirts with college logos and Reebok Classics.

A group of men sitting on the porch of an abandoned house across the street from where they were looked at them closely; they recognized

Lisa and her ride. She only wore green, never any other solid color always a shade of green.

A man named Wimp jumped off the porch and walked over. William "Wimp" Patterson was a short man. He was 5'4" and wore 145 pounds. He was perfectly proportioned and nicely built. He was a small time dealer who basically lived from package to package. He looked at Charles and Steve then asked, "What's up?"

"Ain't nothing," Charles replied warily. He could look at Wimp and see he wasn't a baser, he was too healthy.

Wimp walked over to Lisa, looked at Becky and Sherrie then whistled. "Damn! If I ain't know no better I would've thought Luke was fixing to shoot a video round here. Y'all some fine ass honeys, what's your name little one?" He asked Becky.

"Poison!" She replied. "Believe me when I say I could kill you!"

"Damn baby, I didn't mean any harm," he said laughing. "What's your name Red?" He asked Sherrie.

"I'm Poison Two," Sherrie said seductively. "And you don't even wanna be fucked up with me."

He laughed then turned to Lisa and said, "Lisa talk to your girls and let them know I'm straight. I was just trying to give them a compliment that's all." He looked over his shoulder at Charles and Steve and said, "I ain't mean any disrespect to y'all ladies dogs."

"Nigga them ain't our ladies," Charles said. "Didn't you hear them say they were poison? Bro if we fuck with either of them, Lisa included they'd be the death of us." Charles, Steve, and the women burst out laughing and Wimp catching on laughed too.

"Y'all working?" Wimp asked.

"Yeah we working," Lisa answered. "What's up dog?"

Wimp said. "Them niggas over there work for Chico and they wanna know what y'all doing. Now I ain't no errand boy, so I ain't come over here for them. Far as I'm concerned fuck them pussy ass niggas. They won't serve me and they boss won't either. They don't want anybody else serving on this end so they have been trying to act semi tough. They have done beat down a few niggas these last few days. Ever since they found Big Moe and Ted dead, them niggas been halfway tripping so y'all be careful alright?"

We cool," Lisa said. "You still stay on Grunthal?"

"Yeah me and my lady still there," Wimp replied. "But shit a little tight right now because I can't get any work. I got $500 I been trying to spend all week."

"Come here baby," Becky said.

214

He walked over to her and she opened the back door of Lisa's car and sat down. She reached under the front seat and pulled out a small black case and opened it. It had 3 compartments, each filled with drugs. "Give me the 5 bills," Becky said.

He pulled out his money and counted off $500 and gave it to her. She opened up one of the compartments on the side and pulled out a medium sized Ziploc bag and gave it to him then said, "Hold that open sweety."

He held the bag open and she put 70 big rocks in it. He knew he could make 3 fat dimes out of each rock, so he said. "I'll give you your other $200 as soon as I work some of this."

"You don't owe me anything," Becky said smiling. "Those 20 were for you, your lady, and your kids, so handle your business. Just make sure when you spend your money you spend it with us."

"Bet that," he said. "Where y'all gonna be when I need to cop?"

"We gonna be right here bro." Charles said.

"Listen man," Wimp said. "Y'all seem like good people so don't put yourself out there man. These niggas round here is stupid dog, trust me on that."

Sherrie looked at Charles and said, "I don't know about you Cee but I don't particularly like the idea of these niggas capitalizing off our work!"

"Me either," Charles said. "So what do you think we should do?"

She looked at Becky and Steve and said, "Safeties off?"

"Hell yeah," they both replied.

Sherrie eased up to Wimp and in a sweet, sexy voice asked, "Bout what time does Chico come around here?"

"Every night from about 8:00 till 11:00 or12:00," Wimp answered. "He sits out here with his boys and hold court."

"They the only ones been tripping like that on this end?" She asked.

"Yeah," he answered. "They already done ran the dreads off."

"Dig this baby," she said. "It's gonna get hot around here for a minute so don't come around here tonight. Lisa give him your beeper number so he can contact you. Give her your number little ass nigga so she can call you when shit gets straight. Alright?"

"That's cool Red," he said. "Y'all got a pen?"

Lisa opened her purse and got a pen and some paper, wrote her beeper number on it then passed it to him. He wrote his number down, tore it off and passed it to her.

As he passed her the number, three men walked off the porch and headed in their direction. All three men had guns in their hands.

"Heads up y'all," Steve said softly. "We got company and they all strapped.

They had been watching the men on the porch all the while. "Be cool," Charles said. "They probably gonna try to boo us up and not get too stupid this time. Beck hurry up and close up that bag."

"I'm ahead of you on that Cee," Becky said.

The three men walked up and one asked, "Wimp, what's up nigga?"

"What you want to be up Wop?" Wimp asked.

"Nigga don't let that fly mouth get your ass tore up," Wop said menacingly. "Lisa you done been off the set for a couple of days and the game done changed. I don't know why you brought them niggas and they bitches round here, but ain't no serving so pack up your shit and haul ass. That goes for you too," he pointed at Wimp.

"Nigga who you supposed to be the new sheriff or some shit?" Lisa said sarcastically. "These ain't your streets. I was serving when your broke ass was snatching chains and riding a whip!"

Wop's hand flashed up and smashed into Lisa's face with an open hand slap that sounded almost like a pistol shot. Her head whipped around and she stumbled back and crashed into her car. She reached out and caught her balance as the blow had momentarily stunned her. She leaned against her car and gathered her wits. When she had fully recovered, her eyes blazed with anger. She turned her head and spit. Blood flecked, and her saliva splattered in the street. She spun her purse and Sherrie grabbed her and whispered, "Be cool baby. Just be cool."

"Nigga you done fucked up," Lisa said venomously.

"Bitch don't let your smart ass mouth get your ass stomped," said Wop.

"Dig this bro." Charles said calmly his eyes filled with fury. "You didn't have to do that."

"Nigga that was fucked up," Wimp said angrily. "You been knowing Lisa, she always been sassy!"

"Nigga I done told you!" Wop said angrily and clubbed Wimp in the head with his pistol knocking him to the ground. "What you got from that bitch?" Wop asked him pointing at Becky.

Wimp looked up defiantly and said, "Man don't do me like this!"

"Nigga give it up!" Wop said pointing his pistol at Wimp's face. Wimp pulled the package out and tossed it on the ground. Wop walked over and picked it up then viciously kicked wimp in the stomach and said, "Nigga I always wanted a reason to do that." He turned back to Lisa and said, "Bitch tell your little friend in the car to give me the dope!"

Becky stepped from the car her eyes blazing with anger and handed him about 100 rocks and said softly, "This a robbery?"

"Call it what you want," Wop said. "Now get y'all asses from roun' here and don't come back!"

"Come on y'all," Becky said angrily. "Fuck this shit!" She opened the driver's side door of Lisa's car and got behind the wheel. Lisa looked at Wop one last time then walked around the car and got in. Steve and Sherrie got in their car and Charles helped Wimp to his feet and into the Chevy.

"Let me give you a lift dog," Charles said.

"Alright bro," said Wimp.

Becky pulled off and they all followed. She drove down to Myrtle Ave. and turned left. She drove up a little and made another left on Kings Rd. then pulled in the parking lot of Daylights Grocery Store.

They all got out of the car and Wimp said, "I guess I'll step."

"Hold up a minute dog," Charles said. "Beck break him off."

Beck went to Lisa's car, bagged 100 rocks and gave them to Wimp and said, "That's you baby."

Wimp turned to leave and Charles called out, "Yo!" He looked at Charles and Charles tossed him the keys to the Chevy and said, "It ain't hot. Know the club and pool hall on Edison?"

"Yeah," Wimp said. "I know where they at, but hey closed now ain't they?"

"Not anymore," Charles said. "Meet me there in the morning at 11:00 alright? Stay off that set around there tonight, cool?"

"I'll be missing," Wimp said. "See ya," He got in the Chevy and left.

"Is there any doubt about what needs to be done?" Sherrie asked.

"I ain't waiting till Kane gets back on this one," Charles said. "Those niggas put their hands on one of ours. I don't think Kane would want us to wait."

"Let's hit the plaza in Paxon," Steve said. "They should have everything we need."

Sherrie, Becky, and Lisa got in Lisa's car and Steve and Charles got in the Taurus and they drove to Paxon. They stopped at Payless and bought 5 pairs of phony Hi-Tec boots. Went to Eagle Army and Navy Store and bought 5 black combat fatigues. They went to the Dollar General and bought 5 black skull caps then stopped at Pic-N-Save and bought 5 pairs of batting gloves then drove back to the club.

It was about 3:30 p.m. when Charles went to the store room and came back with a large tote bag. He sat it on the counter and unzipped it. He pulled out 2 sawed off pump shot guns and a box of shells. He gave

Steve one and set the other aside for himself. He pulled out 3 slim Beretta; blue steel 9mm's and handed them to the ladies. They checked the clips then chambered a round.

"Get y'all gloves on and let's wipe these weapons down before we do anything else," Sherrie said. "No mistakes, no prints!"

They all reloaded the weapons and wiped them down.

"Get the rentals," Steve said. "We gonna use them one more time then we taking them back."

Lisa, Becky, and Sherrie left as Charles walked to the house behind the club and knocked on the door.

Eileen looked out and saw him then asked, "What's up Cee?"

"I need two tags and I need them before dark," Charles said. "Make sure they got good stickers and don't get them from close by here. When you get them, bag them and bring them to me."

"I got you baby," she said.

"Is everything alright?" Charles asked.

"The house next door is vacant and I was thinking about opening it up as a base house," She said. "That way the smokers won't have so far to go but I didn't know how you'd feel about me doin that. The girls that bring their tricks here be smoking in the rooms and I didn't know how I could stop that, so I just let them do it."

"I see your point," he said. "It doesn't matter what the girls do with their dates as long as every 30 minutes they kick out 5 more bucks. Don't be soft on them and you can open the base house. That's yours you ain't got to give us nothing out of it unless you move our product out of it. And make sure don't nobody try to sneak in and serve. We ain't gonna put up with that."

"Okay baby," she said. "I'm gonna let my basin ass sister Fee-Fee work it. It might keep her ass out the streets."

"Alright baby," he said. "I'm out," and walked back to the club. When he got back to the club he saw the rentals parked on the side. The ladies were sitting at the bar talking to Steve.

"How we gonna do this Red?" Charles asked as he walked towards where the women sat.

"I been thinking about that," she said. "And I've got an idea I'd like to run by you. Remember the vice play we used last time?"

"Yeah," Charles said. "It went down smooth."

"Let's take it a step further," she said. "We go to Pic-N-Save on McDuff and buy 5 black vests and some bullshit badges from the toy department. Go to the paint store on Park St. and try to find some yellow fluorescent paint and a stencil, and spray paint "police" on the vest. Pin the badges on and scam it that way."

"That's good," Charles said. "But we gonna need somebody on the ground to prevent our targets from running and we got to time it just right."

"That's true," Sherrie said. "We still got the A.K with the folding stock?"

"Yeah," Steve said. "We ain't used it. It's in the trunk of the Ford."

"I'll use that," she said. "Steve and I will come thru the alley on both sides of the house. Lisa can drive one car, Beck the other with you on the driver's side in the back screaming police."

"Alright," Charles said. "We got that settled let's go get the rest of the shit we'll need."

Lisa sat there listening at the plan and didn't know exactly what was going on except the fact that they were going to strike back at Chico's crew.

Steve and Sherrie went to the paint store while the others went to Pic-N-Save. They got the stuff they'd need and met back at the club. They lay all the vest out on the counter. Becky got the paint and stencil and painted police on each vest in fluorescent yellow block letters. They turned the big fan on the vest to dry them.

Charles pulled out some boxes that held plastic guns and wallets. Inside each wallet was a tin badge. The box said official F.B.I sized badges inside. They took the 5 badges and pinned them to the left side of the vest. They would pass inspection in the dark. Lisa cut out the skull caps into mask and they waited.

At about 7:00 Slim Dixon came in with a folded paper sack under his arm. He nodded his head at them in greeting then walked to Charles and handed him the bag. He never said a word as he turned and walked out.

"That's my kind of nigga there," Steve said and burst out laughing. The others did too.

"We pulling out at 8:30," Charles said. "So we got an hour and a half. Does everyone understand the plan and their part?"

"Yeah," Becky said. "But we forgot one thing Cee?"

"What's that?" He asked.

"We ain't got any watches," Becky said.

"Damn!" He exclaimed. "Beck, go get some from the Starving Marvin on Stockton."

When Becky left to get the watches Sherrie turned to Lisa and said, "Listen up baby; this gonna be some serious shit so if you think you can't handle it that's cool. We can come up with another plan and set if off another day."

"Red I went to prison for a nigga putting his hands on me," Lisa said. "That's some shit I ain't having. If you hadn't stopped me I would've killed that nigga or he would've killed me right then. This shit is personal!"

"I can dig that," Sherrie said.

Becky came back with the watches and passed them out. They each called out the time to make sure they all had the same time. The ladies grabbed their jumpers and went to the store room. Charles locked the front door then he and Steve changed into their fatigues. After they were all dressed the men changed the tags and they all got rags and wiped down the cars and the weapons. They put their mask in the strap over the shoulder of their shirts and each one got a vest. They went over the plan again and fine-tuned it. Everyone would get out of the car once the hit was on. Charles, Steve, and Sherrie got back up weapons. Then Steve got the semi-automatic A.K 47 and gave it the Sherrie. The A.K had a 32 round banana clip in it. They checked their watches and it was 8:45 so they got in the cars and pulled out.

When they got to the corner of State and Tyler they drove to the next street over and packed by some abandoned houses which were right behind the target house.

They put on their vest and mask then Charles said, "Red, you and Steve got 10 minutes to get in place. When our watches show 8 minutes have passed we're gonna go around the corner and drive up. Beck you know when to gun it and slam on brakes. Lisa you just listen for the sound of Beck punching the gas and you do the same. When you see her break lights come on then you slam on brakes and jump out. Make sure the safety is off of your gun."

"Alright Cee," Lisa said calmly. "I got you."

"Don't cover your faces yet," Charles said to Lisa. "Drive roun' there and see if they're all there. Just drive by regular, don't slow down. You know Chico and what he drives, so look to see if he's there."

Lisa jumped in the car and drove around the block. She came back and said, "He's there with about 8 of his crew. They're drinking, smoking, and bullshitting around on the porch."

"Let's do this," Charles said. "Beck I'm in your backseat and me, you, and Lisa gonna be shouting Vice. Don't move. Got it?

They both nodded as he turned to Steve and Sherrie, "Be careful and don't take any chances, got me?"

They both nodded then they all pulled their mask down and put on their vest. Steve and Sherrie ran down the alley on both sides of the house bent low, merging with the shadows. Steve couldn't see Sherrie on the other side of the house as he stopped and cocked his head to the side listening. He heard a splashing sound in the dark ahead of him. He squint his eyes and saw a man leaning against the target house pissing. He crept forward and smashed the barrel of his shot gun against the side of the man's head. He fractured the man's skull and the man dropped soundlessly to the ground. He kneeled and smashed the butt of his shot gun into the man's face twice viciously, crushing his face in. He froze and listened then silently moved forward his shot gun aimed straight ahead.

On the other side of the house Sherrie in the shadows bent low crept silently forward. Her A.K was pointed forward, and at about 5 feet from the front of the house she stopped and kneeled down.

Becky turned the corner, and almost as soon as she hit State St. she punched the gas, swung up on the curb, and slammed on brakes. The big car slid in front of the house its back door level with the steps. Lisa had swung her car up on the curb too and slid to a halt right behind Becky as her car almost kissed Becky's car's ass. Lisa, Becky, and Charles were all shouting, "Vice! Don't move!"

Chico and his men saw the cars come hurtling towards them and heard the voices shouting, "Vice! Don't move!" And they froze.

Sherrie stood and rushed to the side of the porch. One of the men that was with Wop when he slapped Lisa placed one hand on the porch rail readying himself to jump and hit the alley; he held a pistol in his other hand. When he put his foot on the rail he looked down and saw Sherrie. He swung his gun toward her but she had the A.K aimed and her finger was on the trigger. As soon as she saw the man she squeezed the trigger and fired. Her first round hit him in the stomach, blasted thru and shattered his spine. The second hit him in the chest and smashed his breast bone, mangled his heart and collapsed his lung. Her third round hit under his chin and severed his tongue; blasted thru the roof of his mouth, made jelly of his brain and exited in a shower of crimson from the top of his head. The shots were so close together when they struck him it looked almost like he was pop-locking before he crashed backwards to the floor.

Another man had jumped to the ground and turned to flee towards Steve who fired a round that caught the man at almost point blank range in the upper left side of his chest, right in the joint of his shoulder. The blast didn't have time to spread and it ripped his left arm from the socket and knocked him backwards. Blood geyser from the gaping wound where his arm once was. He fell to his back and fainted from blood loss.

Charles, Becky, and Lisa jumped from their cars and Charles yelled, "Freeze!" They heard the gunshots from both sides of the house then suddenly there was silence. Chico and the other 7 men raised their hands over their heads and Charles screamed, "Down on the ground! Hands on your head!"

The men hit the ground and put their hands on their heads. Steve and Sherrie rushed from the sides of the house aiming their guns at the men on the ground.

Lisa walked over to Chico and pointed her gun at him. Charles moved over to him and kneeled down and asked, "Where's the dope?"

Chico was deadly afraid as he answered, "Under the porch next to the steps."

Becky rushed over, bent down and reached under the porch and pulled out a big brown bag then rushed to the car and threw it in. When she came back Lisa and her hurriedly frisked the men on the ground. They removed money, dope, jewelry, and guns from their pockets, socks, and crotches.

Lisa knelt down next to Wop, leaned in close to his ear and whispered, "Nigga I told you when you slapped me you fucked up."

He took his hands from his head, looked up into her eyes and said, "Li," before he finished saying her name she shot him in the face. His body jumped up as blood, brain, and bone chips sprayed the man next to him. She stood and walked down the line of men until she came to the other man that was with Wop when he slapped her and shot him in the head thru his hands. His legs drummed the ground reflexively.

"Y'all ain't the police!" Chico shouted.

"Boy you're smart," Charles said. "We ain't the police, we're your executioners," then placed the shot gun to his head and pulled the trigger. The shot gun blast removed the back section of his head all the way to the back of his neck. Blood and brains sprayed over his body like dew and floated in the air like mist.

Lisa threw her gun down and backed to the car. The four other men that lay on the ground were crying and pleading for their lives. Steve moved to the car besides Lisa and pulled his pistol then slid the shot gun under the car.

Charles moved to the car as Becky got behind the wheel. He pulled his pistol and slid his shot gun under the car.

Sherrie standing to the side of the men opened fire on them. She hosed down both the living and dead. Their bodies jerked and spasm as the big A.K rounds smashed into them. Blood ran in rivulets as she tossed the empty A.K on their writhing bodies then calmly walked to the car and got in.

They sedately drove from the scene and went back to the club where they changed the tags and called Gina and Jen to take the cars back. Lisa and Becky followed them.

When they returned they all sat in the club drinking and smoking weed for a few hours.

*   *   *   *

Detectives Samuel and Drummond arrived at the murder scene on State St. and were mildly shocked at the body count. They had seen some atrocities of late but this one took the cake, with 9 victims and 7 dead. If the statements from the Vic's are true then it could be 1986 all over again.

In 1986 there were a group of rogue cops terrorizing drug dealers, and damn if it didn't seem like it was starting again. This time there was a twist. The murder weapons were left at the scene.

"Drum how are you reading this?" Samuels asked his partner.

"It seems like an 86" to me Sam," Drummond said. "They're using the same tactics."

"That they are," Samuels said. "I don't understand why they'd leave the murder weapons behind. That's what got me puzzled."

"Maybe they don't wanna get caught with a weapon that has a body on it," Drummond said.

"That does make sense," Samuels said. "I want forensics on all of the weapons and shells. Let's do the footwork."

*   *   *   *

Kane, Leslie, Tony, and Lucinda were enjoying their cruise. They stopped for a night on the beautiful island of Antigua; from there they crisscrossed the Caribbean and stopped at St. Croix, St. Kitts, Barbados, and on their final destination, Montego Bay in Jamaica.

Once there Kane hired a cab and asked the driver to take them to see the real Jamaica, not the tourist spots. The cabbie smiled when Kane gave him $500 to be their guide. He took them all over. They went to parties, smoked the best weed and took hundreds of pictures, but all too soon it ended and they were headed home the next day.

Leslie and Kane lay in bed. They had just made love and her head lay on his chest.

"I've had a wonderful time," she said.

"Baby we'll be doing this at least once a year," he said. "And when school's out we'll take the kids to Disney World or Busch Gardens. That's a couple of months away."

"Yeah that would be nice," she said.

"I'd like all of us to go," he said. "Me, you, and the kids, Tony, Charles, Steve, and their families could all rent a nice bus and go to all of the theme parks for a week or so."

"Could we really do that?" She asked.

"We'll have to see how the businesses are doing first," he answered. "It's also contingent upon who we can leave to run them. If we've got reliable as well as dependable people it's possible. If not we'll go two at a time for a few days. I talked to Charles, and he has some of the projects off the ground already and they're making money. Gina and Jen are ready to open plus they got workers for their place and yours. Doreen and Anna are ready to open the restaurant. Everybody is just waiting on me. The detailing shop is on McDuff, but me and Tee got to finish that up ourselves, and shit should fall in place soon. By your place being in Gateway you and Lucinda should do great."

"Baby I love you so much," she said snuggling up tighter to him. "Things are really falling in place for us."

He pulled her on top of him and kissed her then said, "I'm gonna be real busy for a few days. Nothing that will bring you stress so don't sweat it. I'm gonna need Tee with me cause we got a lot of loose ends to tie up. The work won't take me out of town and I'll call, plus you'll have my beeper number. All you got to do is dial in 911 and whatever number you are at and I'll know it's you, but don't beep me unless it's an emergency okay?"

"Alright baby," she said and reached down between them and squeezed his penis. "What if I wanted some of this; can I beep you then?"

"You heard what I said. Don't play. When I get everything taken care of you gonna have enough time to take care of that." They both laughed.

She slid down his body still holding his penis tight. She stroked it then ducked her head and gently sucked his balls into her mouth. She released them then pulled his penis to her mouth and sucked in as much as she could. She tenderly rolled his balls as her head bobbed slowly up and down on his cock. She released his balls and got on her hands and knees. Still sucking his penis she turned and straddled his head and lowered her vagina to his mouth. He sucked her clitoris and she moaned around his erection, "umm...umm..."

*   *   *   *

When they got back in town they rented a Mini-Van at the airport and drove home. They unloaded the van and separated the gifts. Kane had bought Becky and Sherrie beautiful Donna Karen dresses with matching purses but he bought Gina and Jen some too, to throw Leslie off. He also bought them solid gold necklaces with big, diamond encrusted "K" pendants. He bought 4 and hid 2 of them in his shaving kit. He had bought gifts for everyone.

Tony following his lead had done the same. Kane and Tony put their gifts in the trunk of Kane's car and headed to the club. When they got there it was 1:00 pm and their crew was there waiting. They got hugs and kisses then Kane gave Charles his keys and said, "Go get that stuff out of my trunk, take Steve with you cause you gonna need some help. Becky and Sherrie were all over him. "Calm down, he said. "Y'all acting like a nigga been gone for 10 years."

Lisa was draped all over Tony as Steve and Charles came back with their arms loaded with bags. They sat them down and went back to the car for the rest. After they had unloaded the car everybody crowded around the tables and Kane and Tony started passing out gifts. He had got something for Charles and Steve's mothers too, so there were gifts all around. Becky, Sherrie, Lisa, Gina, and Jen all loved the dresses they had bought them. When Kane gave them the necklaces with the diamond encrusted K's the women jumped up and down with joy. Kane didn't know Tony had bought Lisa one until he gave it to her.

"Put it on me now Tee," Lisa said smiling brightly.

"Too many people in here for me to put it on you girl," Tony said laughing.

They all burst out laughing.

"Nigga I'm talking about the necklace," Lisa said smiling.

He put the necklace on her and it fell right above her beautiful breast. Kane put Becky, Sherrie, Gina, and Jen's on and they all kissed him and thanked him.

After all the gifts were passed out there was still a small jewelry box sitting on the table. They all looked at it and Sherrie asked, "What's that?"

Kane opened the box and showed it to them. It was a big embroidered gold ring with a black onyx stone that had a T in diamonds in the middle of the stone.

"Who's that for?" Charles asked.

"A special friend who I'll introduce some of you to Sunday," Kane said.

Charles said, "We got something for you since you made that comment last week. Come on let's go."

They left the club and drove down Edison Ave. until they got to Stockton St. and made a left. Then they drove until they got to Riverside. Ave. where they had just built some condominiums on the water front facing the river. They pulled in to two marked parking spaces and everybody got out. They rode the elevator to the third floor and walked to 3A.

Jen opened the door and they walked in. The living room was beautifully and tastefully furnished in white leather, glass and chrome tables, and lamp stands. A beautiful white and chrome big screen T V a chrome entertainment center with a silver Sony stereo system. African sculptures in mahogany and marble were generously scattered throughout the living room. African masks and weapons dotted the walls in various patterns, and there was a thick beige carpet under their feet. The windows were draped with white and beige curtains threaded with silver, and silver ropes to tie the curtains. Next to each end of the sofa sat Chrome wine stands with ice and champagne bottles leaning as if placed there carelessly.

"This place is beautiful!" Sherrie said.

"Hell yeah!" Becky added.

They walked down the hall and went thru two French doors and entered a combination den and study.

The room was paneled in varnished cedar. The entertainment center, sofa, love seat, and wing back chair were all cedar. One corner was dominated by a cedar desk varnished to a high gloss.

They left the den and walked into a room done in various shades of red. A bathroom done in black marble with gold veins and brass fixtures shined until they gleamed like gold. It had a huge sunken tub that doubled as a Jacuzzi. It could hold at least 10 people comfortably. They walked thru another door and came to another room done in various shades of blue. Then they moved across the hall and went into a room done in shades of green. The green room had its own full bath in white marble and gold.

They toured the entire place then came back to the living room where Jen passed out 9 champagne flutes. Everyone took a seat except Charles who got a bottle of champagne, popped it and filled everyone's glass.

No one had said a word as they toured the condo. Charles looked at Jen who opened her purse and took out 5 envelopes. She gave one to Kane, Becky, Sherrie, Lisa, and Tony then said, "These envelopes hold the deeds to this condo and you are all equal owners. It cost $150,000. Me and Gina got a loan for $75,000 a piece on our homes. Charles and Steve gave us $50,000 and we used that to furnish this place. We've got the money set aside to finish paying for it and it's our gift to you!"

Kane and the others had tears running down their faces. The red room was for Sherrie, the blue room was for Becky, and the green room for Lisa.

"Let's celebrate!" Charles said and pulled out a fat bag of weed and another of powder. They turned on the music and partied until about 7:00 then headed back to the club.

When they arrived Charles gave Kane a rundown on the action that took place on State St.

"Have you got somebody to manage the club?" Kane asked.

"Yeah," Charles answered. "I got Big Chilly Simmons and Smoove B to D J. You know them don't you?"

"Yeah," Kane said. "I know chilly but I don't know the D J."

"He's good," Charles said. "I'm gonna use Pookie and Ced as bouncers. I got two girls, Naomi and Vanessa as waitresses. Beck, Red, and Lisa gonna work on the weekends."

"That's good Cee," Kane said. "We're gonna have the grand opening for all the places on Saturday."

Gina and Jen sensing where the conversation was going got up said their goodbyes and left.

"Now about the trouble we had," Charles said. He got up and went to the office and came back with a newspaper and gave it to Kane.

Kane read it then passed it to Tony who read it and whistled. Kane looked hard at Sherrie and she dropped her head. The paper reported that 7 men were killed and 2 critically injured in what was obviously an ongoing drug war.

"I told you and Red no bodies if it was possible," Kane said.

Lisa jumped up and told Kane the story. He looked at Becky and Steve for confirmation and they nodded their heads.

"She left some of it out though daddy," Becky said. "She didn't mention that she killed the nigga that slapped her and one of the niggas that was with him. She just blew their fucking brains out. You should have seen her baby. Charles took Chico out. I'm the only one didn't see no action. Red sprayed them other fuckers while they were on the ground."

"Red, next time make sure you kill all of them," Kane said.

"If somebody touches any of our people we gonna smoke they ass so y'all did right. By waiting they might've solidified their position which would've made it harder for us to hit them. That was good work; Cee what kind of money we made?"

"We got $300,000 in the safe here. $100,000 across the street, $200,000 in the safe at The Sandwich Shop, and Steve got $250,000 in the safe at the store. That's $850,000 total. We paid out about $250,000 to the workers and the only ones that haven't got paid are us."

"How much have we got at Safe House?" Kane asked.

"About $200,000 not counting our defense fund," Charles said. "We all used company funds but it never amounted to more than 5 or 6 gees."

"Did you have to use any more product?" Kane asked.

"Yeah," Charles said. "We had to break down 5 of the bricks to make stones and powder. We didn't know how to cut the boy and we're close to dry on that. We may be out by now so you need to get on it."

"Alright," Kane said. "I'll take Tee and the girls and get right on that. Here's the play. We're gonna need at least 4 full sized pickups in the names of our businesses for when we have to go to the warehouses or whatever. Our pay is $75,000 a piece a week as long as we clear $800,000. The more we make, the more we take. From a mill to a mill and a half we get $100,000 and Gina and Jen get $50,000. Subtracting our pay from the week earnings leaves us with $225,000 plus the $200,000 at safe house gives us $425,000 for the kitty. Every 2 weeks we'll put $25,000 a piece in the defense fund. Go on and pay Lisa, Beck, and Red from what you got here. Steve pay yourself and Gina. Cee pay yourself and Jen from the money you get when you collect the defense fund from those three," he pointed at the women. "I'll pay me and Tony and leave our money for the defense fund and the remainder in the safe. Have Gina and Jen pick up all the cash we have in the morning and drop it at safe house. Be sure to keep the defense fund separated from our operating expenses. Get somebody on the trucks tomorrow."

"Got you boss," Charles said.

"By the way what happened to the dude Wimp?" Kane asked.

"He been coming thru," Lisa said smiling. "And I have been working with him. Charles let him use one of the cars the day that shit went down, but hell in 2 days the nigga had copped a Caddie and dressed it. I had him to open us a house over there and he was talking about getting him a pool room in between State and Kings Rd. He been doing well, and he got two of his dogs rolling with him. He done brought us about $75,000 in the few days he been working."

"Good work Lisa," Kane said. "Y'all listen. You can invite all of your lieutenants and their ladies to the grand opening. Cee will reserve seats for them on the V.I.P tip, but I don't wanna meet them. I'll be going to all the spots but this gonna be my last stop. Tee, Lisa, Beck, Red let's roll, we got work to do. All you need is boy, Cee?"

"Yeah," Charles said. "We should be straight everywhere else. We need a weed hook up cause people asking' and I see bread in it bro."

"Alright," Kane said. "We can address that Sunday when I see my friend. We should be back in about 2 hours."

*   *   *   *

After cutting, bagging, and dropping the heroin off, Kane took $100,000 from the safe at The Sandwich Shop and gave Tony half then they went back to the club.

Kane called Frank's house and Jimmy answered the phone. He made the exchange and Frank came on the phone.

"This is Berean I just got back, how are you?"

"I'm fine," Frank answered. "I'm glad you called. Did you hear about the incident that transpired out north? Their C.E.O had some Spanish name but I can't remember it. I understand that the business was growing and I can't see why their services were cut short. You might wanna look into it; it would be a great area to operate your franchise."

"I'm familiar with the company and its former owner," Kane said. "The reason the company ended badly was merely a dispute. Some of my employees filed a legal complaint. They saw no other way to resolve the issue so they took the necessary actions, successfully I must admit. I'm testing the water with one of the local sales representatives and it appears to be an open as well as lucrative market. It worked out for the best, though I had expressed to my associates before leaving that I would like them to stay in line with company policy. They used their discretion and after disclosing all of the facts I can see only one thing I would've done differently. I would've filed suit against the entire company and disposed of the whole issue."

"Don't you think that's a bit extreme?" Frank asked.

"When it comes to the safety and care of employees who I must say are like family, no measure is too extreme!" Kane said. "I believe in providing comfort and excellent health care insurance."

"You have a point there," Frank said admiringly. "So what's up?" How can I be of service?"

"I was thinking of bringing the family out to your place Sunday," Kane said. "I've got some people I want you to meet."

"That'll be good," Frank said. "I'll set up a big bash for you so make it around noon. Oh yeah, will Anna be coming?"

"No," Kane said. "She's opening a new restaurant across from the Regency Mall called Mama's Kitchen on Saturday. It's grand opening and if you're there by 6:00 p.m. I can bring you the gift I bought you then."

"Wild horses couldn't drag me away," Frank said. "Even if I see you then are we still okay for Sunday?"

"No doubt," Kane replied. "That's a must. I'll see you later."

After Kane hung up the phone Becky, Lisa, and Sherrie came back. The women were all smiling and Sherrie asked, "Daddy can we have you all day tomorrow?"

He looked at Charles and said, "I'll drop us off another package tomorrow night so we should be straight in all the spots. Lisa if Wimp comes thru I'll have Pookie serve him so you can stay with that nigga there," he pointed at Tony, "at least until tomorrow night."

The women smiled and they all left Steve and Charles in the club.

*   *   *   *

When they got to the condo they sat in the living room smoking, drinking, and listening to music. They chilled until nearly 1:00 a.m. then they went to their rooms.

Becky and Sherrie argued about which bed they would take and Kane cut them off. "Red you got it first both times before I left so stop being selfish. We gonna sleep in Beck's room tonight."

"Alright baby," she said pouting.

They went into Becky's room and undressed. Kane walked to the closet and opened the door. There were three beautiful velvet, navy blue robes, trimmed in sky blue, hanging in the closet. On the floor were three pairs of velvet, navy blue slippers with monogrammed K's in sky blue. He turned the lapel of one of the robes outward and saw that it too was monogrammed with his initials "B.K." in sky blue. He looked at the robes and gave the women theirs. Their robes were monogrammed too.

He walked naked thru the bathroom and into Sherrie's room and he opened the closet. Inside were scarlet color, velvet robes that were monogrammed and velvet slippers to match.

"This is Jen's work," Kane said smiling and shaking his head. He turned to leave and almost knocked over Becky and Sherrie who had put on their blue robes.

Sherrie took his robe and held it open as he slipped his arms in it. Becky dropped to her knees and slid his slippers on. Becky had filled the big tub so they turned on the jets and got in. The tub was huge so there was plenty of room. Sherrie got out and wrapped one of the black towels around her and hurried out. She came back about five minutes later with a bottle of champagne and three glasses. She gave the bottle to Kane who opened it and poured their drinks. They lay in the tub and chilled.

They heard a knock on the door. "Yeah!" Kane yelled.

"It's us can we come in?" Lisa asked.

Kane looked at the women and shrugged his shoulders. "Come on in."

Lisa and Tony had come thru the blue room's door. They wore money green velvet robes with gold piping and matching monogrammed slippers.

"We just wanted to know if we could join y'all in the tub?" Lisa asked boldly.

Kane looked at Tony who shrugged. "Come on," Kane said. "But y'all need to get some more smoke and drink, and your own glasses."

"I'll be right back," Tony said and left. He was gone for 5 or 6 minutes then he came back with weed and two more bottles of champagne. Tony threw off his robe and with the champagne and glasses clutched in one hand, and an ashtray with 5 blunts in it along with a lighter in the other.

Lisa just stood there; then slowly she untied the robe and flicked it open then quickly closed it. They all got a quick glimpse of her front.

She was proud of her body and knew how to show it off to its best advantage. She turned her back and shrugged the robe from here shoulders to the small of her back then slowly she revealed more of her ass. She spread her legs and released the robe. There was an intake of breath as she made her ass cheeks jump. She bent over and her fat cunt popped from between her legs, then she stood, turned, and strutted to the tub.

Kane, Becky, and Sherrie started clapping and shouting, "Bravo!" as Lisa stepped into the tub.

"Girl have you ever stripped for a living?" Kane asked her.

"Hell naw," she said. "I ain't with that exploitation shit!" She burst out laughing. "Yeah I use to work at the Doll House."

"You're good," Kane said sincerely.

They lay around in the tub and smoked and drank for an hour or so then got out.

Tony was staring at Becky, checking her out and shaking his head. Kane watched him and smiled then said to himself, "He has never seen Beck naked so he didn't really know how fine she was, and how pretty her brown skin was all over. She was very evenly proportioned and he was drinking her in."

Tony felt Kane watching him as he looked at Kane and shook his head then said, "Damn!" Out loud and laughed.

Kane looked at Lisa, caught Tony's eye and said, "Damn!" And they both laughed.

They hugged and kissed then went to their rooms. Kane and the women lay in the bed and he said, "That Lisa is a fine motherfucker. I bet both of y'all want some of that," and he burst out laughing.

"You want some too," Sherrie said. "So cut that shit out. Me and Beck don't fuck with other women, just each other. Besides we ain't trying to cut in on our brother."

"I feel you baby," Kane said.

*　　　　*　　　　*　　　　*

Lisa and Tony got back in the green room and sat on the bed.

"Damn baby you sure put on a show," he said. "I thought there was gonna be an orgy the way you came off."

"Naw baby," she said. "That ain't my cup of tea but I would like to see Kane fuck both of them. I bet that's a sight to see."

"Yeah," he said. "I bet it is."

"I saw you looking at Becky," she said. "She is fine ain't she?"

"Hell yeah," he replied. "I knew she was fine, but when I saw her naked I saw how fine she really was."

"She does have a nice body," Lisa said.

"That she does," he agreed. "But neither one of them is as fine as you!"

She smiled then stood up and took off her robe. She mad a production of it as she dance seductively. She bent over and spread her ass with her hands on the floor. He moved from the bed and got on his knees.

*   *   *   *

8:00 the next morning they got up bathed and got dressed. The ladies got in Lisa's car and went to Granny's house to pack their clothes.

"So y'all gonna move?" Granny said. "I want y'all to know if you ever need a place to stay; it's your home also. Hear me? This y'all home. Y'all my granddaughters and I'm gonna miss y'all being here. Make sure y'all stop by. Don't be strangers alright?"

"Granny we gonna see you every day," Becky said. "And we still gonna come over and spend time with you. We ain't taking all our stuff and we leaving some of Kane and Tony's stuff too. It ain't like you won't see us."

"Yeah you right about that," Granny said smiling.

Kane and Tony had to get a U-Haul. They came to Granny's house and loaded up their stuff. Kane and Tony wrestled the safe on the truck then they drove to the condo.

Sherrie had called several photographers and had finally found one that would take the type of photo's she wanted. By 10:30 they had unloaded all of their stuff. Becky made lunch, which was decent since the other women had been teaching her to cook.

"Alright," Kane said. "It's 11:30 let's go to the car lot. Red, you and Beck need cars."

They all jumped in Lisa's Chevy and headed to the south side.

"I don't want y'all to buy expensive cars," Kane said. "Y'all gonna be getting checks from The Sandwich Shop and the club, so that will be your place of employment. That way you can show you have legitimate income. $300 a week from both places should cover you. That goes for you too Lisa."

"Let's get Toyota's Beck," Sherrie said.

"That's cool," Becky said.

They pulled into a Toyota dealership in Regency and started looking at cars.

Sherrie saw a Camry that she wanted, 2 doors, fully equipped and she said, "I want that one."

A salesman appeared as if by magic and asked, "How can I help you?"

"I want that car right there," Sherrie said pointing at the Red Camry. The sticker price was $19,000.

"Would you like to test drive it?" The salesman asked.

"No," she replied. "I wanna drive it home."

"Alright," said the salesman rubbing his hands together and smiling. "Let's do the paper work."

"Not yet!" Becky said. "Cause I want one too, but I want a navy blue one."

"We don't have it in navy blue," the salesman said sadly. "But we do have a dark blue one."

"Is it exactly like that one?" Becky asked.

"Yes it is," the salesman answered. "That is except for the color."

"That's good," she said. "I'll take it."

The salesman rubbed his hands together quicker anticipating the commission he'd get from the sales.

"I want one too baby," Lisa said imploringly to Tony.

Tony looked at the salesman whose eyes gleamed with greed, pointed at the Chevy and asked, "Do you have one in that color?"

"I can come close sir," the salesman said. "That's a custom paint job."

"We'll take it," Tony said.

They walked to his office and did the paper work. They opened their purses to pay and Kane stopped Becky and Sherrie. Tony stopped Lisa.

Kane pulled out a thick envelope and gave the salesman $19,998, and said. "Do these sales have to be reported to the I.R.S?"

"One dollar more on each sale and I would've had to," the salesman said.

Kane peeled off an extra $1,000 and gave it to him then said, "For your excellent service."

The salesman looked quickly around and slid the money into his pocket and said, "The monthly payments will be $150. Is that too much?"

"No," Kane said. "That'll be fine."

Tony gave him $9,999 and $500 for his pocket, and then they got temporary tags and put them on their cars.

Kane and Tony got in the Chevy and followed as the women pulled out with Sherrie leading. Sherrie pulled into a Ford dealership a block away and jumped out. Lisa and Becky followed her lead.

"What's up?" Kane asked looking at Tony.

"Fuck if I know," Tony said shrugging his shoulders.

They got out of the car and followed the women to the showroom where they had a salesman cornered. They walked in mass toward a black Ford Bronco. The sticker price was $25,000.

By the time Kane and Tony caught up with them they were headed back outside. Lisa said something to the salesman and they walked to the Chevy. Tony had left the keys in the ignition.

The salesman looked the car over inside and out, then got in and cranked it up. He drove it around the lot a couple of times and parked. He looked at Lisa and said, "$5,000."

"$6,000," she said.

"$5,500," the salesman said.

"$6,000," Lisa said again.

"$5,800 is as high as I can go," the man said. "It's a deal," Lisa said and they shook hands.

The whole group walked to his office and he left to get more chairs. He seated them all and then started doing paper work.

"Daddy give me your license," Becky said to Kane. He took it from his wallet and handed it to her. She took it and gave it to the salesman.

"Baby give me your license," Lisa said to Tony. He passed it to her and she passed it to the salesman.

"Beck, Red, what's going on here?" Kane asked finally speaking.

"We buying a Bronco today," Sherrie said.

"I already got a car," he said.

"Give it away or something," Becky said. "Today you getting a Bronco."

He just shook his head and listened as Lisa said, "I'm getting you one too Tee. I just sold the Chevy for $5,800 on the trade in tip."

After they finished the paperwork the women paid and gave the salesman $500 for his service and they got the temporary tags.

They drove down the street to a place called Jax Automotive and stopped. Jax Automotive did custom paint jobs, tints, rims, air brushing, and sound systems.

When they walked inside a man jumped up from behind a desk and walked up to Lisa with his hand extended and said, "Ms. James, it's been a while since last I saw you. What can I do for you?"

"I just got a new ride and I want you to hook it up for me," Lisa answered.

"Alright," he said. "Let's go see what you got."

They walked outside and stopped beside her car and she said, "I want it painted money green with silver flakes, chromed out, a good sounding stereo system, a light tint, some Daytons, and I want L.J.K. airbrushed right here," she pointed at the rear driver's side of the car.

"I can do that for 6 gees," he said.

"Do I get a discount if I get them to get theirs done?" Lisa asked him.

"If they get the same hook up, I'll do all 3 for 5 apiece."

"That's a bet," Lisa said smiling.

"I want mine candy apple red, high gloss with silver flakes," Sherrie said. "I want the works and S.T.K airbrushed on mine in the same place."

"I want mine painted robin's egg blue, high gloss, silver flakes and the works," Becky said. "And B.S.K airbrushed on it."

"I got you," the man said. "You can come pick them up Tuesday."

"Listen," Kane said. "I want a light tint, stereo system and a big K with a crown on it airbrushed on both sides at the rear. How long do you think that would take?"

"4 or 5 hours at the most," the man said. "It's what?" He looked at his watch. "It's 1:15 so say by 5:15 or 5:20, is that alright?"

"That fine," Kane replied.

"Can I get the same done to mine in the same time frame?" asked Tony.

"Sure," the man said. "We could have them both done in that time."

They walked back to the office and the women paid.

"What kind of price are we talking?" Kane asked.

"2 grand will cover it," the man said.

Kane and Tony paid him and he said, "I've got a mini-van you can use until your trucks are done."

"Thanks," Kane said. "I believe we've got a few errands to run," then he looked at his ladies.

Sherrie got the keys and drove them to the mall. She went straight to Dillard's and headed for the men's department. She went to the Men's suit department and picked Kane a white linen suit by Yves St. Laurent for $700; a beige silk shirt by Calvin Klein, and beige suede belt and loafers by Gucci. She picked Tony a beige linen suit by Hugo Boss, a white silk shirt by Dior, and a white belt and loafers by 51 East.

She bought Kane a crimson silk shirt and one in sky blue by Lagerfield. She got Tony a money green silk shirt and white duck pants, both by Armani. She bought Kane a crimson red silk robe, and a sky blue silk robe. She got Tony a money green silk robe then they headed to the women's department. She selected a snow white silk mini-dress for Becky and a beige one just like it for her. She picked Lisa a soft green mini-dress with beige piping, and she bought them all shoe's to match their outfits. She bought Becky a crimson car suit and a crimson mini-dress for herself. She got Lisa a money green mini-skirt suit then bought a sky blue cat suit for herself and a sky blue mini-dress for Becky.

They went to Victoria's Secret and she bought crimson panty and bra sets in different styles for her and Becky, with short silk housecoats in the same color. She bought red garters and fishnet stockings, and red ankle strap stacks for them. Then she bought them sky blue outfits with all of the accessories. She picked money green panties and bra for Lisa along with accessories.

They loaded the van and Sherrie drove to the plaza on the other side of the street and parked in front of Alfredo's photo gallery.

"Get the bags and come on," Sherrie said. They got all of the bags and trooped into Alfredo's.

"I'm Ms. Kane and I have an appointment," Sherrie said to the receptionist.

The woman smiled, looked in her book and said, "Please have a seat for a moment," then picked up the phone.

They sat down and a few minutes later a beautiful olive complexioned man in a velvet suit with ruffles flounced into the room. He was very flamboyant, and they instantly knew that he was gay.

Sherrie rose from her seat and he rushed over and took her hands, "Ms. Kane it's a pleasure to meet you, I'm Alfredo. If you will, please follow me," he led them to the back where several props were set up.

There was a group of people there, hair dressers and makeup artist. They had several screens set up and you could change them if you choose to.

"Everybody put on the first outfits I picked for you," Sherrie said. They all got their things and went to the changing rooms to dress. When they were finished Alfredo sat each at a makeup booth and the makeup artist went to work.

Kane didn't like the idea of make up being used on him but for his girls he'd do it.

It took only a moment; then Alfredo led them to a white outdoor prop set. There was a marble bench, a white trellis with flowers of all colors, and artificial turf on the floor. Alfredo arranged the women on the bench in various positions until he was satisfied then arranged the men. He rushed to his camera and took the picture.

He took photos of them in every combination in different positions. He took about 50 photos and gave the negatives to his assistant who rushed off with them.

Sherrie told Alfredo what else she wanted and he raised one of his beautifully arched brows, smiled a crooked smile and shrugged his shoulders then said, "Of course we do erotic photos, but nothing vulgar mind you. We're not into pornography here."

"I want it tasteful, artistic, but nude," she said.

"But of course," he said.

"The photos we just took," she said. "I want the first group shot poster sized and the others 8x10's and 5x7's"

He called one of his assistant and gave him the instructions.

"Daddy go put on the red silk robe," Sherrie said. "Don't wear anything under it. Lisa put on the Victoria's Secret, Tony you heard me. Come on Beck."

They all went to get dressed then returned. Lisa, Becky, and Sherrie wore the outfits they bought. Kane and Tony had on the robes.

Alfredo hit a switch and the white background turned to a red softly lit scene.

"Go lay on the bed baby," Sherrie said to Kane.

Kane lay on the bed and Sherrie grabbed Alfredo and got him to arrange Kane in a seductive pose with his robe open. The diamond filled ship, Rolex watch, and his two rings glittered in the dim light.

Becky looked at him then stepped over and stroked his penis until it was half erect then stepped back.

"My God! Alfredo exclaimed and rushed to his camera to take the shot.

Kane found it somewhat exciting and his penis grew even more.

"Alright Tee it's your turn," Sherrie said after Alfredo had taken several photos of Kane in different positions.

Tony lay on the day bed whose background was turned green by a flip of the switch. He was already semi-erect from looking at the 3 women in their provocative outfits.

Alfredo arranged him in a seductive pose and hurried to take the picture.

He took several pictures of Tony alone then Lisa joined him and Alfredo took pictures of them in several erotic yet tasteful poses. He took some of Lisa alone then Becky, Sherrie, and Kane. He took pictures of them in red and blue, Kane and Sherrie, Becky and Kane, Sherrie and

Becky and every combination of the three. After that they took pictures in their other outfits then looked at the proofs.

Sherrie picked which pictures they wanted poster sized and the others that would be 8x10's and 5x7's. Lisa chose her and Tony's. They bought frames from Alfredo, collected their pictures and left. They spent $5,000 on the photo session. It was almost 6:00 and they went back to pick up Kane and Tony's Broncos.

When they got to Jax Automotive the Broncos were parked out front. Kane looked at the crowned K's and smiled. They gave the keys to the mini-van back then got in the Broncos and left.

They got to the condo and hung the pictures throughout the house then chilled for the rest of the day.

Chapter 16

On the day of the grand opening everyone was busy. Kane had gone and bought big banners with grand opening on them and he and the men hung them.

The salons opened at 11:00 that day and would stay open until 11:00 that night. The restaurant and B.B.Q joint would stay open until 12:00 and Leslie, Lucinda, Gina and Jen would go to The Sandwich Shop until it closed. None would go to the club as Kane had forbid it. Gina and Jen were only allowed there in the day time. Kane's excuse was that the area was like Dodge City at night which was true. Kane and Tony floated from place to place. They arrived at the restaurant at 6:30.

When they walked thru the door Kane saw Frank seated with several others in an area with a red velvet rope surrounding it.

They stopped and kissed Anna and Doreen who had hired both white and black wait staff. The manager was a big, gay, African American named Antonio Williams. He bustled thru the restaurant like a mother hen, making sure the customers were satisfied with their services.

Kane and Tony walked to Frank's table and Frank stood, grabbed Kane and kissed him then repeated the process with Tony.

"Little Tony," Frank said smiling. "You're the spitting image of your father. Sit down."

Kane moved around the table to a small Italian woman and leaned over and kissed her cheeks. "Mrs. Toronelli."

Donnatella Toronelli was a Sophia Loren look alike in face and body except she was smaller. What drew people to her was her hair. It was jet black except for the front part that framed her face, it was snow white.

Tony came over and kissed her and she said, "We're family so there's no need to be formal. Enough with the Mrs. Toronelli just call me Donnatella!"

Kane grabbed a young man who was the spitting image of Frank and kissed him on the forehead. "Frankie! Where've you been bro?"

"The question is where have you been?" Frankie said. "I've been in Miami running the old man's import and export business. The old man pretty much lets me run the whole operation so I won't be in town long. This is my wife Shelia," he reached out his hand to a beautiful olive skinned woman who had lovely doe like eyes, and jet black hair. She resembled Salma Hyack, except when she stood Kane and Tony saw she had ass like a black woman.

Kane pulled her into his arms and kissed her cheeks, "I'm Berean."

"I've heard so much about you," she replied coyly. "It's a pleasure to finally meet you."

Tony came forward and kissed her then introduced himself. He punched Frankie in the shoulder and said, "You sly dog! You been hiding her from us"

"Shelia these are my brothers," Frankie said. "Though you wouldn't know it by the way they act. I haven't seen you guys in at least 5 or 6 years. What gives?"

"I won't make any excuses Frankie," Kane said. "I would offer you an explanation, but since my father got knocked off shit has been kind of hectic. My head wasn't in the right place and relationships suffered for it. Trust me; you'll see more of me than you'll want to from now on. Besides, Frank and Jimmy already chewed me a new asshole so don't add insult to injury please."

Frankie laughed as Jimmy walked over and said, "How are you boys?"

Kane and Tony hugged him and he went back to the table where another big man sat.

They all sat down and Kane went into his inside jacket pocket and pulled out the small black jewelry box and passed it to Frank. "A little something I thought you'd like."

Frank took the box an opened it then said, "Will you look at that!" and presented the case for everyone to see.

"It's beautiful," Donnatella said.

"Yes it is," Shelia said nodding her head in agreement.

Frank pulled the big ring from the box and slid it on his pinky. The diamonds that formed the T sparkled in the fluorescent light.

"Thank you Berean," Frank said and kissed Kane again. "The food here is excellent. Eat something."

"Later," Kane said. "I just wanted to give you the gift. I've got to run; I've got a lot of business I still need to take care of. Besides, I'll see you tomorrow." He looked at Frankie, "Boy it's been years since we hung out. Why don't you and Sheila ride with me? You can give Frank the run down after you see my operation."

"I couldn't Bee," Frankie said sadly. "I've barely spent time with Momma and Poppa."

"Go on Frankie," Donnatella said. "Me and Poppa won't let you and Shelia go until we're ready, and by that time you'll wish you had gone with Berean."

They laughed and Frankie looked at Frank who nodded his head.

"What about Lou?" Frankie asked.

"Lou can come too," Kane said looking Frankie in his eyes. "But only unofficial. He can let his hair down when you're with me! Ask Poppa."

Frankie again looked at Frank who nodded.

They got up to leave and Kane said a few words to Doreen and Anna; then they drove to Gina and Jen's salon.

As soon as they walked thru the door Gina and Jen spotted Frankie and ran over and hugged him.

"Boy we haven't seen you in years," Jen said.

Frankie told them what he had been up to then introduced Shelia and Lou who they hugged and kissed. They grabbed Shelia and took her to a chair then came back over to Kane and the others.

They told Kane how business was going and admired his and Tony's outfits. Kane told them Sherrie had picked them.

They moved to a plush reception area where they were served refreshments. They sat and talked over old times with Frankie. Then Jen got up and left. She came back 15 minutes later with Shelia who had been given the full treatment, manicure, pedicure, hair styled, and face professionally made up.

Kane, Frankie, Lou, and Tony whistled and Shelia blushed.

Kane looked her over and said to himself, "Damn she's sister fine, breast, hips, and a fat ass. She's also wearing the shit out of that mini-dress."

It had taken about an hour and a half for Sheila to get the works so they only stayed for a few more minutes then left.

Gina had slipped Kane 5 blunts laced with powder. Kane, Sheila, and Frankie sat up front in Kane's Bronco with Sheila in the middle. Tony and Lou sat in the back.

Kane and Tony were always strapped and so was Lou. Frankie never carried heat.

"You still smoking pot?" Kane asked Frankie.

"Yeah," Frankie answered. "Me and Sheila are probably the last ones in the group we chill with that do. Most people are heavy into the coke scene now. We get our noses dirty every so often."

"That's cool," Kane said and passed Sheila a blunt.

She thought it was a cigar and passed it to Frankie who thought the same thing. He pulled out a gold Dunhill lighter and fired up the blunt. As soon as he took a deep hit he started coughing.

"Damn!" He said tears rolling from his eyes. "At least you could've warned me," he hit the blunt a few more times then passed it to Sheila.

Kane gave Tony one and he fired it up and took a few hits then passed it to Lou.

"Frankie?" Lou said questioningly.

"You're off tonight Lou," Frankie said.

Lou smiled, took the blunt and hit it.

They rode out to Gateway and stopped at Leslie and Lucinda's salon and Frankie was mobbed again.

Frankie, Kane, Lucinda, Leslie, and Tony all went to school together. He introduced his wife to them and the women fawned over her.

"Girl who did your hair?" Leslie asked. "You're beautiful."

"I just got it done at Jen and Gina's," Shelia answered.

Frank introduced Lou to them and they hugged him.

They told Kane how the business was going and sat and talked for an hour, then they drove to The Sandwich Shop. By then they all had the munchies so they sat at a booth and the grannies served them personally. Business was booming and they told Kane that they wouldn't close until 2:00. It was 10:45 then and Kane nodded his head. Frankie was introduced to Essie, Becky's grandmother as he already knew Ester, Kane's grandmother. He introduced Shelia and Lou and they talked for a while as they finished their meal.

At about 11:30 they left and drove to the club. Kane had named the club Kings Crown and the "K" in kings wore the same crown that graced the rear ends of Kane's and Tony's Broncos.

Kane parked next to Tony's Bronco and they walked inside. Kane in the front, Shelia and Frankie behind him, and Tony and Lou brought up the rear.

As they walked in the young lady on the door said, "That'll be $5 sir," then she looked up and saw who it was. "I'm sorry Mr. Kane."

"It's just Kane," he said, "never Mr., alright Janet?"

She nodded her head and he said, "These people are with me. I want you to memorize their faces. For them there's never a cover charge, Cool?"

"That's cool Kane," she said smiling as Kane showed Frankie, Shelia, and Lou thru the door and into the club proper.

Frankie, Shelia, and Lou were the only whites in the club. Becky, Lisa, and Sherrie were behind the counter. There were two bartenders so they really weren't needed. Naomi worked the cash register and Vanessa worked as hostess.

Vanessa came up to Kane and said, "This way sir."

She was very professional and led Kane and his party to a special V.I.P section where there was one huge booth raised and positioned so you could view the whole club. She unhooked the red velvet rope and held it while Kane and his party entered. The big booth could comfortably seat 12 people. It had a large leather horseshoe shaped sofa and the table was custom made to fit. Kane sat and surveyed his surroundings. He saw that Tony had gone to the bar. Becky, Sherrie, and Lisa walked from behind the counter and headed towards the table.

It seemed like every eye in the place was on them. They wore the first outfits that Sherrie had picked for their photos. They glided to the table with Lisa in the lead; she kissed Kane softly on the lips then sat next to Lou who was on the left end.

Becky was next and Sherrie last. Kane stood as Becky stepped up into the booth. She raised her head and moved in close as Kane grabbed her waist and kissed her deep. Shielded by her body no one saw her reach down and squeeze his penis as he kissed her. She sat next to Frankie and Sherrie floated up and threw her arms around him and gripped his ass and kissed him.

He sat in between Becky and Sherrie as Tony came to the table with two Magnums of Dom P. A waitress followed with a tray filled with champagne glasses.

Tony sat the champagne down then kissed Lisa, Becky, and Sherrie and took his seat next to Lisa on the end. Kane's caught Frankie's eye, then Lou's and looked at the three women and said, "They're all made!"

"You're kidding me right?" Frankie asked.

"Frankie, in all my years I've never seen a group as accomplished," Kane said. "Talk to your Pappa."

"Mr. Kane are you serious?" Lou asked incredulous.

"Lou always be informal when you deal with me," Kane said. "Call me Kane, Berean, Bee, I know you won't disrespect me. We're family and I'm deadly serious about them. I'd trust them with Big Frank's life because they'd die before they betray you or let you down. Don't let their looks fool you Lou, believe me, I wouldn't lie."

Charles and Steve who were in the back saw them and went to the table. Kane made the introductions and Tony poured them a drink.

"They're made too," Kane said.

Frankie shook his head and thought, "Me and Shelia are sitting with a group of killers and she doesn't even suspect it."

They sat and talked for a while then Kane asked Lou, "Do you like black women?"

"I don't have anything against any women," Lou said smiling. "Color doesn't matter to me. It's more of what's in the heart."

Kane leaned over so he could whisper in Charles' ear, "Get Lou a companion for tonight. Pay her well and let her know it's for all night and some of the morning. If she's extra good there's a bonus in it cool? Oh yeah make sure she's good looking, fine, and well dressed. Don't ruin your reputation Cee."

"Nigga please," Charles said smiling as he got up from the table and walked over to where Eileen and slim Dixon sat.

"Baby I need a favor," Charles said to Eileen. "I need a fine, good looking, nice dressing young lady for all night and some of the morning. Can you swing that?"

"Do bears shit in the woods?" She asked. "I know a young lady that fits the bill and she's in here now. She sells pussy on the DL to pay her rent, car note, and to buy clothes. She smokes weed and does a little powder but she ain't a rock head. She mostly fucks with young dope niggas, she bout a dollar and her shit tight. That's why I like her. That's her over there in the corner with them other part time ho's," she pointed to the area where 6 young ladies sat. "All of them would fit the bill but personally I like the little bitch style. She the one in the yellow dress and heels, with her hair did up with the pearls."

Charles looked and saw she was talking about a young lady he sweated when she first came in. She was cute with a single gold cap on her right canine. She had nice sized breast, a slim waist, a nice round ass, and fat thighs. In short she was fine. "She'll work," Charles said.

"Hold on a minute baby," Eileen said. "I'm gonna go holla at her." She got up and walked to the table where the woman sat and leaned over and said a few words in her ear and pointed at Charles then walked back to where she was previously standing.

"She coming in a minute," Eileen said smiling. "Her name is Teecy."

A few minutes later Teecy strutted over, hips swinging and asked Charles, "What's up black?"

"Hey baby," he said greeting her. "My name is Charles and I'm part owner of the club. I'm not trying to be disrespectful and I surely don't mean to offend you but Eileen told me how you kick your game. She said you're about getting a dollar so I'd like to make you a proposition."

"I'm straight," she said. "Go on."

"I wanna give you a grand to stay all night with a special friend of mine who's gonna be in town for a few days." Charles said. "The grand is for all the night and some of the morning and he's sitting right over there," he pointed at Lou.

Lou was 6'2" and muscular. He was handsome, had a nice build, blue eyes, long black hair tied in a ponytail, and a swarthy skin complexion.

He wore a dark blue Hugo Boss 2 piece suit, a light blue button collar shirt open at the neck revealing a thick gold Gucci link chain with an ivory and gold horn, and a pair of glossy black Johnston and Murphy cap toed shoes.

She looked at Lou and said, "Alright, I can do that."

"Come on," Charles said and lead her to the office. He had her sit as he went into the safe and got the $1,000 and gave it to her. "Treat him right and stop by here tomorrow night and I'll have a bonus for you."

"That's cool," she said smiling as they left the office and went to the table where Charles introduced her to everyone. She sat next to Lou and said, "So you're Lou. I've heard some fine things about you."

They bent their heads closer and got lost in conversation.

"Let's dance," Kane said to Sheila and extended his hand. They got up and hit the dance floor and Kane saw that she was a pretty good dancer.

Soon the others were on the floor. Sherrie and Becky sandwiched Frankie and they all had a good time.

They crowded in the office and smoked blunts, snorted coke and washed it down with champagne. Then they partied the night away.

At 3:00 they all got ready to leave. Kane pulled Charles to the side and said, "Make sure you and Steve are at the condo by 12:00"

"I got you boss," Charles said then hugged and kissed everyone. Steve came and did the same thing and they left the club.

"Tee dig this," Kane said and Tony came over to him. "You and Lisa go to Granny's tonight. I'm taking our guest to the condo cause there's no need for them to spend money on hotels this late at night."

"That's cool bro," Tony said then he and Lisa hugged and kissed everyone and got in his Bronco and left.

Kane gave Sherrie his keys and she got behind the wheel. Kane sat in the middle with Becky on the end. The others got in the back and Sherrie drove to the condo.

Once they got inside Shelia and Teecy complimented them on the décor. They all walked to the poster sized portrait that hung over the faux fireplace.

"Who took this picture?" Frankie asked.

Sherrie said, "Alfredo. He's very good!"

"Give me the address and number," Frankie said. "I've got to take Momma and Poppa to get some family photos from this guy. You say he's Italiano?"

Sherrie nodded and then they took them on a tour of the condo.

"Frankie," Kane said. "You and Shelia can choose either the red room or the blue room to sleep in. Lou you get the green room. There are robes in each room for you and the ladies."

Sherrie went and started the Jacuzzi and Becky went and got a magnum of champagne.

Frankie and Shelia went to the blue room undressed and put on the robes.

Kane and his ladies went into the red room undressed put on their robes and took the champagne, glasses, and a blunt to the bathroom. They got in the big tub and smoked a blunt. While relaxing, Kane poured them all drinks, and they kicked back chilling.

There was a knock at the door. "Come on in!" Kane yelled.

Frankie and Shelia stepped thru the door and he asked, "Is there room enough for us?"

"There's plenty of room," Kane said. "Come on."

Frankie took off his robe then Shelia took hers off. "Damn!" Kane said to himself. "Frankie got a dime piece," as he looked Shelia over. Her breasts were full, olive tinted with raspberry colored areola and pert nipples. Her hips flared beautifully, a trim waist, and plump mound with neatly trimmed black hair. He could see her cunt lips, full and long hanging between her legs. "She been sunbathing nude because she doesn't have any tan lines," he said to himself.

They got in the big tub and were drinking from the 3 glasses smoking a blunt and laughing loudly when there was another knock at the door.

"Come on in," Kane said, and Lou and Teecy stepped thru the door.

"I thought I heard fun," Lou said. "So I decided to investigate."

"Lou go in the kitchen and get another bottle and some glasses and join us," Kane said. "Teecy go look in any nightstand and you'll find crystal cases with powder in one and blunts in the other, get them and bring them back."

She walked in the blue room and came back with the crystal cases and Lou came back with the Magnum and 4 more glasses. They took off their robes and got in the tub.

Teecy was stripper fine and knew it. Her breast were nice sized and firm with no sag, as they stood up proudly. Her waist was slim, her hips were spread beautifully, and thick lush hair surrounded her fat cunt. She had fantastic thighs and looked good.

They sat in the tub drank, smoked, and had a great time. When they got out of the tub to dry off Sheila and Teecy looked at Kane and had the same thought, "Damn! He's got a big dick," and a little thrill went through them.

246

Frankie and Lou had one thought too but it wasn't about Kane's dick. It was about Becky and Sherrie, "Damn! He's got 2 fine ass women falling all over him. He's got it made."
And they retired to their rooms.

*   *   *   *

"Baby I had a wonderful time tonight," Sheila said looking at Frankie. "Do you think we could go out with them again tomorrow night?"
"Sure," he said. "Bee is my brother; you're his sister so that won't be a problem. He'll take care of you and protect you with his life."
She reached down and grabbed his penis and said, "He's hung like a fucking horse. Damn he's gonna kill those poor girls, but what a way to die," and slowly stroked his rapidly rising penis.
"It turned you on didn't it?" He asked.
"Yes it did," she answered and bent over and took his penis into her mouth. Slowly she sucked him down deep. She bobbed her head and sucked at him with hunger and passion.
He looked at the nude photos adorning the walls. Becky and Sherrie together, separate, and with Kane and he could see the way they moved in his mind's eye. Their breast bouncing, asses jiggling as they dried off and he said to himself, "Bee you're a lucky bastard," and smiled as Sheila sucked him greedily.
She stopped then straddled his body and slid his hardness in her and said, "I just want you to fuck me," then she started bouncing on his penis rapidly her hands flat on his chest.
She rode him hard and fast all the while looking at the nude picture of Kane with a semi-erect penis that hung poster sized over the bed.
"Oh Yes...." She moaned as she stared into the eyes on the photo. "God yes!"

*   *   *   *

Teecy lay on her back, legs spread wide as Lou expertly licked her cunt. She was a part time whore but she sold hers because she couldn't stand to give it away for free. She never pretended to enjoy a fuck so if she didn't like it she made it known, and she genuinely liked to fuck.
"Shit!" She thought to herself. "Good as Lou is eating my pussy I'd pay him," then the sensations took over and she moaned, "Ummmhmm....Yes....Oh baby....Rub my clit harder....Oh yes....Just like that....Just like that....Damn baby....I'm cumin!"

She grabbed his head and pulled him to her tighter. She spasm and started to shake uncontrollably.

Lou was an accomplished lover but he had never had a black woman and never a woman as vocal as she was when receiving pleasure. He'd had whores before but he knew this was no act. She was really getting off.

As she finished her orgasm he lapped up her juices then slid up her body and drove his stiff penis in her. He thrust in deep slow strokes and she moaned, "Ummm yes... Damn baby... Oh yes..."

* * * *

Becky rode Kane's penis swiftly while Sherrie rode his face. They faced each other and were kissing and pinching each other's nipples. They broke the kiss and Becky leaned back. Sherrie leaned forward and Becky fed her, her breast. Sherrie sucked and bit at her nipples and Becky moaned, "Harder Red... Bite them harder..." Sherrie chewed her nipples and Becky screamed, "Yes...Oh yes...." and bounced faster on his stiff prick. "Daddy...Fuck me...," she moaned as she increased her speed.

His tongue plowed into Sherrie's cunt. He moved to her clit and trapped it in his mouth, then drove his fingers in her wet slot and thrust them in and out rapidly as she moaned around the breast in her mouth. "Umph...Umph...Ummm...." Then she bit down on Becky's nipple harder than she meant to and Becky screamed, "Oww...Oww...That hurts so good... Oh shit...."

Becky's nipple slipped from Sherrie's mouth and she moaned, "Kane... Oh baby...Eat my pussy..." And she ground her cunt in his face faster.

"Oh....Ohh....Oh...." Becky moaned. "I'm cumin now!" And she bounced on him faster, pummeling his thighs with her soft ass.

"Daddy....Daddyyy...I'm cumin toooo!" Sherrie moaned and he exploded in Becky's spasming cunt.

* * * *

The next morning at 9:30 Becky and Sherrie were dressed in the kitchen cooking breakfast and they had the whole place smelling good. Kane came in fresh from the shower in the scarlet robe and slippers. He sat to the table and Becky brought him a glass of orange juice and he asked, "What y'all cooking?"

"Pancakes, eggs, bacon, sausage, and grits," Sherrie said. "You got to make your own toast if you want some. And you also got to wait until everyone is seated before you can eat."

248

Becky had put 2 pieces of bread in the toaster. When they popped up she buttered them, put eggs and bacon on them and looked at Sherrie and said, "Go easy on him Red, he put in some hard work last night."

"Okay," Sherrie said. "But just that sandwich, we don't wanna spoil him. He might get lazy and stop treating our pussy's good."

They laughed as Becky gave him the sandwich.

He wolfed it down and Frankie and Sheila walked in smiling.

"Good morning. Red did the same guy do the photos in the bedrooms?" Frankie asked.

"Yes he did," she said. "Not vulgar and pornographic but tasteful and arousing."

"I agree whole heartedly sweetheart," Frankie said.

*   *   *   *

Teecy woke Lou up with his penis in her mouth. She sucked him until he was fully hard then climbed on him and rode him. She was bent over on his chest as his hands spread her ass cheeks. His stiff rod drove up into her rapidly and she moaned softly, "Oh yes Lou…Yes…." She swung her ass downward to get as much of him as she could as he thrust upward with swift strokes. Her hands were on his chest, and her fingers pinching at his nipples. They were thrusting fast and hard against each other when she moaned, "Oh shit Lou…..Oh baby….. I'm cumin for you….." she bounced her ass faster and he erupted in her.

The door opened just as they were having an organism. Becky stood there and watched the last few strokes then said, "We're waiting on y'all before we eat so hurry up."

They were so caught up in their sexing they never heard the door open and didn't know she was there until she spoke. Lou still held Teecy's ass cheeks spread wide. When they heard her Teecy's head spun around and Lou rose up. They looked at her and she smiled and walked from the room closing the door behind her.

Lou massaged her ass and said, "Listen Teecy, I've been married but I'm divorced now and don't know if I'll ever get married again. But, I want you to think about coming down to Miami and living with me for a while. I know this is sudden and I would understand if you didn't want to, having just met me and all. But let's say you try a month of weekends with me. I'll get you a nice place or you can stay at my place. I make good money and I can keep you living in style. All you'd have to do is be there for me and don't see anyone else sexually. Would you like to give it a shot?"

"Of course I would," She said. "You're sweet, kind, and considerate. You're an excellent lover and it's been a while since a man satisfied me as fully as you did."

She didn't feel the need to try and game Lou, so she was honest with him, and they got up and hit the shower.

*   *   *   *

"Did you wake them up Becky?" Frankie asked as she walked back into the kitchen.

"Shit they were already woke," she said. "I thought I was at a rodeo show the way Teecy was riding Lou's dick when I walked in." They all burst out laughing.

About 15 minutes later Lou and Teecy walked into the kitchen and they started laughing. Lou blushed and Teecy just stood there and smiled. They sat down and ate then everybody went and got dressed. They sat around drinking beer and smoking weed when Lisa and Tony showed up.

Charles and Steve arrived no later and Charles said, "Goddamn! Y'all motherfuckas have been partying all night?"

"It damn sure looks like it," Steve said. "The least y'all can do is pass the joint to a hard working man."

Frankie passed him the one he had just lit.

"Why thanks don't mind of I do," Steve said taking the joint as they all laughed.

Charles pulled Teecy to the side and said, "I can see that things went well, so see me tonight and I got something for you."

"It's alright," she said. "I'm straight. It worked out well and I had a great time. Lou gave me 3 gees and asked me to move to Miami with him and I just might do that."

"That's good baby girl," Charles said. "I'm happy for you but dig this. I got a spot for you at the club if you wanna quit your little sideline job. It pays $350 a week for 5 days work."

"I can swing that," she said. "Lou wants me to do a trial run where I come down on the weekends for a month. That would give me time to make up my mind."

"Alright," Charles said. "You start Monday night."

When they were all heading to the door Shelia stopped Kane and said, "Bee I had a great time last night, could we do it again?"

"Of course we can," he said. "When do you want to?"

"Tonight," she said and blessed him with her smile.

"Baby can do it every night until y'all leave if you want to," he said and pulled her into his arms.

She smiled and they left.

In the parking lot Kane said, "Teecy take the keys to that car," he pointed at the Buick. "Leave it at the club and meet us back here at 7:00."

"Alright Kane," she said and hugged him and the others. She kissed Lou deeply then in got in the Buick and left.

They loaded up in the Broncos and headed to Orange Park.

*   *   *   *

They arrived at the Toronelli mansion and the front door came open before they stopped. Frank had been watching and waiting for them. He came out and stood there as they got out of the Broncos. He hugged and kissed them all.

"Poppa we had a great time," Frankie said. "It's not often that Shelia gets to hang out in the hood. She wants to go back tonight, is that alright?"

"For my daughter?" Frank said. "Of course it's alright!" He turned to Sherrie, "Red you're looking as lovely as ever."

She wore red capri pants, a red and white polka dot tank top, red sandals that laced up to her calves, a red bandana tied with the knot to the side, and red framed Guess sunglasses.

"Becky what on Earth do you do to make your beautiful skin glow?" Frank asked then added, "By the way you're looking lovely too!"

She wore faded Gloria Vanderbilt jeans and matching vest with no shirt, blue high top boots by Candies, a blue and white Dallas Cowboys baseball cap cocked to the left, and blue framed Guess sunglasses.

Frank turned to Lisa who wore green overalls made of denim by Exhaust Jeans, a green tub top, green high top canvas Converse, a green bandana with the knot tied in the front, and green framed Guess sunglasses.

"And who is this lovely creature?"

"This is my wife Lisa," Tony said proudly.

Kane introduced him to Charles and Steve who noticed the big ring on his finger and thought, "So this is our special friend."

Frankie, Shelia, and Lou had gone to change. Frank led them to the gazebo and they all had a seat.

"So this is your family?" Frank asked waving his hands to encompass the whole group.

"Yes sir," Kane replied. "All made and all totally loyal. We didn't have an elaborate ceremony but they were all tried by fire. Each one proved his or her worth. I think I could get 6 more good men if I need them, but if there's to be wet work I choose these 5. Thus far they've proved to be enough. Those 5," he pointed at Becky, Sherrie, Lisa, Steve, and Charles.

"Took care of that business last week. They planned it and executed it without a hitch so they've proved themselves to me."

"That they have," Frank agreed.

They looked up and Frankie and Lou were approaching. They were both surprised to see Frank discussing business with the women present, that wasn't the Italian way.

As they stepped into the gazebos Frank said, "Frankie you can speak freely in front of them," he indicated Kane and the others. "They're family, just the darker branch!"

They all laughed then Frank continued. "Son we're in a treacherous business, cut throat, and deadly. Keeping secrets is essential, even from other family members; always remember that! Berean and his family are an extension of our family. It has been that way for more than 50 years. The Kane's and Toronelli's have a long history. Only in the last few years has that changed. Bishop's fall created a rift because Berean was going thru a stage where he wanted to emerge from the shadow of his father and be judged by his own merits. I'm sure that now he has come to the conclusion that he is the keeper of the flame. He is the very embodiment of the Kane's and he has taken his place as the head, as it should be, as it always has been! The Toronelli's and Kane's have always stood together, they are our secret weapon or better yet our dark horse," he smiled but no one laughed because he was dead serious. "How much do you trust Lou?" Frank asked Frankie while making eye contact with Lou.

"With my life obviously," Frankie answered.

"That's good," Frank replied, "because he is to be your mediator with Berean and his family. No one else! I mean no one from the family on your end is to even know they exist, just Lou. Pete and Jimmy are the only ones that know on this end and they are my hands. No one else needs to know Berean is in business, and he'll use our services. One hand washes the other. If we need him to terminate business ties with other family members or extended family members he can do it without sanctions and that's anywhere in the country. If he needs us to do the same for him the same rules apply. We can provide him and his people with a much more superior grade of tools as well as bullet resistant vests and little things that go boom. All at a minimal cost of course. That will keep a constant flow of cash funneled to each side of the family."

"I like the way you're thinking Frank," said Kane. "Do we have to do anything to cement this?"

"It has always been this way between us son," Frank said. "I know from this day forth it will continue to be that way. I know you are a proud man. I see your father in you and I know you're loyal, dependable, and reliable. I believe in my heart that I could trust you with my life and the lives of my family, and it may come to that. You are my second son and I'll protect you as you would me. Agreed?"

"I agree," Kane answered in reply.

"Frank if I might, can I say something?" Charles asked respectfully. "It's concerning business."

"Go on Charles," Frank said. "Speak freely."

"We need a large quantity of top grade weed," Charles said. "At least 100 or 200 pounds. The more the better and money is no object."

Frank looked to Frankie who said, "I can do 200 for $100,000."

"Done," Charles said. "Will you deliver?"

"Sure," Frankie said. "And you don't pay until I deliver. Lou will run with the shipment and guide it in. Give him the money."

"That's cool," Charles said. "Can we get 20 keys of snow for 10 apiece?"

"You're family," Frankie said. "I'll get you the 20 for another 100."

"How soon can you deliver?" Charles asked.

"I'll fly down tomorrow so Wednesday or Thursday at the latest."

"We'll probably need a couple of blocks of boy soon, can you swing four?"

"I can do that but the price is gonna be steep," Frankie said. "50 apiece is the less I could swing them for."

"Put that with the order," Charles said. "I'll have 400 gees waiting for Lou when he gets in."

"Frank I want permission for any of my people to contact you in case of an emergency, or to keep business going." Kane said.

"That didn't need to be said Berean," Frank said.

They left the gazebo and joined Donnatella and Shelia for the meal Donnatella had personally prepared. After they ate they sat around drinking wine and talking.

When they were leaving Frankie stepped to Frank and said. "Me, Sheila, and Lou are gonna stay with Bee tonight. I've got me and Lou booked on a flight at 12:05 Monday afternoon. The ladies will bring Sheila home sometime Monday. I'll be back later that night or Tuesday morning after I set everything up. Lou will stay and make sure the shipment gets here then we'll stay with you and mamma for the rest of the week and go home next Sunday."

"Alright son," Frank said.

Sheila had an overnight bag with a change of clothes for all 3 of them. She kissed Frank and said, "See you tomorrow Papa."

They all hugged and kissed then got in the Broncos and left.

When they got back to the condo a cherry red Toyota Tercel with chrome Daytons was in the Buicks space. They parked and Teecy got out of the Tercel. She had on a pair of gold daisy dukes made of denim, a matching vest opened, and a gold and white tube top; and white on white Nike running shoes.

As she strutted towards them Charles thought, "Damn that bitch fine. If she decides not to go to Miami I got to get some of that."

Teecy had a Nike gym bag thrown over her shoulder. She fell in step with them and hooked her arm around Lou's waist, and they went up to the condo.

They started the party early and Charles and Steve left to make sure the club was ready.

At 10:00 the ladies piled in the blue room then got in the tub together. The men could hear a great deal of laughing and squealing. They took turns showering in the green room then they got dressed and sat in the den smoking weed and drinking Hen.

At 11:30 the ladies filed in. Becky, Sherrie, and Lisa wore Donna Karen jumpsuits. They hugged their every curve and were rather snug at the crotch, their mounds prominent.

Shelia wore a black Chanel mini-skirt and jacket embroidered with gold interlocking C's. Black ankle boots by Chanel with their emblem on the side in gold and a matching Chanel purse.

Teecy wore a skin tight, purple, silk mini-dress by Fendi, purple ankle strap, open toed pumps by Fendi with the purse to match. The ladies looked stunning.

Kane wore a crème 2 piece Armani suit, a light brown shirt by Dior, and light brown crocodile sandal shoes by Mauri.

Tony wore a hunter green silk suit that Lisa bought him by Tom Ford for Gucci, an olive green silk shirt by Alexander Jalian, and green gators by Mauri.

Frankie wore an excellently cut suit by John Varvotos in black silk, a gold Versace silk shirt, and black suede boots by Brioni.

Lou wore a tastefully cut 2 piece beige linen suit by Hugo Boss, a tan silk shirt by Ralph Lauren, and calfskin tasseled kilties by Hanover.

Everyone was looking good as they headed for the club. They partied the night away then went back to the condo. Kane refused to put Tony and Lisa out of their bed for another night so he and his ladies made a pallet on the floor in the den.

*   *   *   *

The delivery was made that Wednesday. Lou got the money, and the driver of the van told Charles to get the van to Pete then they left. Steve and Charles took the van to the stash house and unloaded it then drove back to the club. Steve followed Charles to Arnie's Pawn Shop where they left the van with Pete.

They called Kane who had got the detailing shop up and running but didn't have anyone to manage it. He had found 3 workers plus he and Tony worked there too. For the last 2 days he and Tony had worked like they were the last 2 slaves in America. All he could tell Charles was to handle it.

"Car washing ass nigga," Charles said. "You supposed to be the boss and you making us look bad. I got Big Chilly's brother Artess on the way over there. You can depend on him so let him run that shit."

"Fuck you black ass nigga," Kane said. "How long that nigga been gone?"

"Damn nigga!" Charles said. "You in a hurry to leave that rinky dink ass job. He should be there any minute."

A blue Chevy pulled in as Kane hung up the phone. A big man got out and walked towards the office. He stepped in and said in a voice that sounded like it came from the bottom of a well, "I'm looking for Kane."

Kane could see the family resemblance in him and Big Chilly but still he asked, "Who are you?"

"I'm Artess Simmons, Chilly's brother."

Kane extended his hand and said, "Man I'm glad to see you." They shook hands and he had Artess sit behind the big desk, and they filled out some paperwork.

"I'm gonna let you run this," Kane said. "Your pay depends on your profits. If you have any ideas on how to generate more capital run it by me. You're in the yellow pages and the white pages and you got flyers all over town. If you need money for anything you've got your check book. Just keep me abreast of what's going on."

He picked up a pen and pad and wrote all of his numbers. "Beep me first," Kane said. "If I don't call right back, give me 10 minutes. If I haven't called by then and it's something you can't handle, track me down. Do us a good job. When I say us, I'm talking you and me. You can only go up bro."

Artess nodded and Kane went on, "If you don't wanna get your hands wet you got to hire another worker. Come on and let me introduce you to the workers. They went and met the men and Kane said, "Don't pay this nigga here no mind," pointing at Tony. "He's my brother and part owner. He's going with me when I leave."

After Kane gave Artess the run down him and Tony left and went to the club. When they got to the club Kane brought in a briefcase and sat it on the bar.

Charles, Steve, Vanessa, and Naomi were sitting behind the counter. "You niggas look like y'all could use a cold drink," Charles said and passed them 2 long neck buds.

They took the beers and drank a big swallow then both of them said, "Ahhhh!"

"Nigga we got business to take care of," Kane said to Charles and Steve. "Let's go to your office." He looked at the 2 women and said, "Y'all heifers live in here? Cause it damn sure seems like it."

They all laughed then the 4 men went into the office and closed the door.

"Have all of the pickups been going smooth?" Kane asked. Charles and Steve nodded. "What kind of money have we made since we checked last Thursday Steve?" Kane asked.

"We cleared $900,000 after all the workers got paid," Steve said. "But we've got to subtract that $400,000 from that, so we sent $500,000 to safe house."

"That's good," Kane said as he opened the briefcase and pulled out a sheaf of papers. "These papers will consolidate our businesses into one company. "Crown Incorporated". I'm C.E.O, Cee, you're C.O.O, Steve, you're C.F.O, and Tee you're president. We'll receive $400 a week from each business but we won't take the money from the businesses. What we'll do is put $400 in each business to cover our checks. Steve that's your job to make sure the money gets there. Every month we'll increase our income. When we get a million at safe house and enough to purchase more products we'll start flushing the money thru the businesses. These other papers will consolidate the B.B.Q joint, The Sandwich Shop, The Store, and Sarah's; so Beck, Red, Lisa, the grannies, and your moms can get $400 apiece from them a week. Beck, Red, and Lisa will pay their way like we do. Glenda is C.E.O, Sylvia will be C.F.O, and my grandmother C.O.O, Essie will be president, and Beck, Red, and Lisa vice presidents. The company is "7 Ladies Incorporated." All we have to do is sign the papers, get them to sign and it's a done deal as soon as the lawyers file the papers. Steve how are the wedding plans coming along?"

"Just fine," Steve answered. "Jen done straight took over and were only doing business with African Americans."

"Was the 100 grand enough?" Kane asked.

"We didn't need it bro." Steve said. "I got plenty of money I could've paid for the wedding."

Kane punched Steve in the shoulder and said, "Nigga I know you got bread, but it's traditional for the bride's family to pay!"

"Man you gave us $100,000, Tee $50,000, Lisa, Beck, and Red gave $10,000 apiece. Frankie sent $50,000 for their branch of the family. Shit even old stingy ass Cee gave us $50,000," Steve said exasperated. "There's no fucking way we're gonna be able to spend $280,000. We turned down money from Anna, Doreen, the grannies, my mom, and Glenda. All of them were pissed off. We're buying the outfits for everybody. That's where we won't take no for an answer so don't even think about arguing, cause I ain't with it!"

Kane looked at his face and saw how serious he was.

"The wedding is in 2 weeks," Steve said. "And we all, that's you, me, Charles, and Tee got an appointment with the tailor tomorrow at noon. Jen has designed our suits and they'll be custom made, as will the gowns for the ladies. By the way, Frank, Frankie, and Lou will be at the Tailor's tomorrow too. Kane since you're standing in for Bishop, Tee and Cee are gonna be my best men. All of the women will be bridesmaids and shit is gonna be hectic but it's worth it. Me and Charles are gonna be gone for 7 days so who are you gonna get to work our people?"

"Lisa been working Wimp and his crew," Kane said. "And y'all people already know Beck and Red so they'll handle them and make the drops. I'll do the pickups and Lisa can have Wimp make his drops here. Let your people know we ain't gonna tolerate no bullshit. We'll be at the club every night so you can keep in touch."

Chapter 17

Steve and Gina's wedding and reception went off without a hitch. The couple went on a cruise and 7 days later it was back to business. Four months later Kane and his family had a firm grip on the drug trade in Brooklyn, Mixon, Lackawanna, Kings Rd. and Myrtle, and also uptown. They had at least 2 dope houses in each area as well as trick houses, bootleg houses, and weed houses. They also had men on the corner serving in each area and were firmly entrenched.

They were pulling in nearly 3 million a week and with Frank supplying them there seemed to be no limit to what they could do. The legitimate businesses were prospering also. Crown Inc. had added 3 more pool halls but drugs were never sold from them. They had 2 more detailing shops, and Artess had proved to be very adept at business because he ran all 3 of the detailing shops. He had secured a contract with the city of Jacksonville and several car dealerships. They had opened 2 more Kings Crown night clubs one on Cesery Blvd. and the other across from Gateway Mall, and Big Chilly managed all 3.

7 Ladies had also prospered. They now had a Sandwich Shop in Regency Mall and one downtown. They had 2 more B.B.Q joints, one in Bay Meadows, and the other on Dunns Ave.

Anna and Doreen's Mom's Kitchens had blew up. They had them in Mandarin, Orange Park, San Jose, and Avondale. Leslie, Gina, Lucinda, and Jen had opened 4 more salons; one in Orange Park, Bay Meadows, Mandarin, and on Dunns Ave.

They all were doing exceptionally well. Their personal and business accounts were well stacked and they were paying off their loans on time. They could've done it all without the loans but to keep the I.R.S off their back it was all done through bank loans.

Kane had devised a system to flush the drug money thru all of the businesses at 3 million a month in fictional sales. Every hour in each place $200 was rang up in various ways. $13 here, $25 there and so on, so things looked legit. He had purchased a huge safe thru Pete at Arnie's Pawn Shop and he and the family put it in the garage at safe house. The safe was filled with millions of dollars.

By this time each of them were millionaires. All of their home safes had been traded in for larger models and they were filled with cash, a million or more in each place. Kane still worked at the first detailing shop at least 4 days a week and Tony at one of the others. Their base was still the original Kings Crown and Charles worked there 7 days a week. Naomi managed one of the new Kings Crown and Vanessa the other, but there was no doubt that Big Chilly was in charge.

Becky, Sherrie, and Lisa worked at The Sandwich Shop in Brooklyn during the week and at the original Kings Crown on Friday and Saturday nights.

Steve worked at the store in Lackawanna except for the weekend when he worked the club. Even though they all made a lot of money they still worked.

Kane was in the process of getting 7 Ladies and Crown Inc. into real estate. Their lawyers were trying to close a deal for 15 properties, 5 small apartments, 6 duplexes, and 4 big houses in Springfield. It was going slow and they needed 5 million to seal the deal but their companies only had 3 in liquid assets. They were waiting on the bank to front them a loan so they wouldn't have to deplete their resources.

They had the money but Kane knew it would be foolish to use untaxed income so they worked thru the banks. Things were really starting to look up.

*   *   *   *

Homicide detectives John Samuels and Evan Drummond were no closer to solving what they had dubbed the May Massacres. They had 20 or so dead bodies and more wounded, that they just knew had to be connected.

They had dropped in on vice and knew there was a drug connection but how it all tied together they didn't know. Vice couldn't tell them about any new players in the game so there was little information. To Samuels and Drummond who were working the case it was aggravating because all they got was zero. On the murders in Alderman Park they had zilch. No witnesses, no nothing, not a damn thread.

They had interviewed witnesses at the other crime scenes and there were discrepancies about the number of suspects in each case. Some said 6, some 5, and the numbers went as high as 8.

There were conflicts as to the make, model, and color of the vehicles but the description of the assailants was always consistent. Black ninja styles mask, black jumpsuits, boots, and gloves. There was also an intriguing twist; at least 3 of them were females and of one thing they were sure; they were all murderers. Well trained, and utterly ruthless. They fired on bystanders as well as their chosen victims and that spoke of danger. It had been quiet for a few months but how long that would last they didn't know. All they wanted was to take them down as soon as possible or at least before they struck again. It looked bleak this far, but they were beating the streets and had informants out in force.

*   *   *   *

Wimp sat in the pool hall on Myrtle Ave. surveying his little kingdom. He had damn near locked down the whole area from Beaver and Myrtle to Kings Rd., all the way down Kings Rd. to Flag St.; and he was starting to do business in Grand Park.

He felt good. He drove a Benz, had married his woman and they lived in Bay Meadows. She had a beauty salon on Kings Rd. and another on Moncrief and 33rd street. He had another pool hall on Kings Rd. and Fairfax but there was trouble brewing on the horizon.

Some dreads had opened up shop on Dot St. and were serving weed, powder, and rocks. He really didn't give a fuck because there was enough money for everybody, but he had a house on Dot St. that sold weed, rocks, and powder also.

The dreads had started making noise. They had beat down one of his workers and they in turn had shot up the dreads house. The dreads retaliated and at this time there seemed to be a tension filled truce. He never told Charles, Lisa, or Steve who he had gotten tight with about the incident.

Wimp wasn't slow mentally by a long shot. He knew Lisa dropped off his drugs. She always made sure it was quality and always there was something extra for him. He knew Charles and Steve were not the boss, but not that they couldn't be. And Lisa's man was a money getter but he wasn't the boss either. He had chilled with them on several occasions and if he had to make a bet it wouldn't be on Becky or Sherrie but on that nigga Kane.

It didn't matter that he tried to assume a low profile because all of the others looked to him. They tried not to but it was just natural. He was cool, friendly, and seemed to be genuinely caring but there was a quality about him that Wimp could find no words for. All he knew was that the nigga gave off something that said, "Don't fuck with me." Lisa had told him that if he had any problems to call her. At the moment shit seemed cool but he knew it was a powder keg and one spark would make shit explode.

He didn't want a drug war on his hands because too many bodies equal too much heat. He wasn't a coward by anyone's standards. He would fight, stab, or shoot but he wasn't a killer; that he knew. He could kill but he didn't want to, so he decided that he'd tell Lisa and the others about it before things got out of hand. He looked at his watch and saw that it was almost 12:00. He looked over at his brother Chuckie who he had running the spot and called him over.

"I'm going to The Kings Crown," Wimp said. "Beep me if you need me, if not just close up and I'll see you in the morning."

"Alright," Chuckie said. "You wanna take the bread that was dropped off? I got it in the safe."

"Yeah," Wimp said. "I might as well. It'll save me having to drop it off tomorrow. By the way, go check the other spot when you close and see if everybody is straight. If not, you know what to do. I'm going home from there so I'll see you tomorrow. Don't worry bout the spot on Dot St. let them bring their shit here alright?"

"That's cool bro." Chuckie said then went and got the money. Chuckie gave Wimp the money and Wimp drove to the original Kings Crown.

When he went in Janet was at the door. She never charged him because she knew he was down with the owners plus she liked him. The club had almost all new girls by this time since Naomi, Vanessa, and Teecy, who had taken Charles up on his offer were all gone. Teecy had moved to Miami with Lou and it seemed they got married in no time. Kane and his family had all flew down to attend the wedding. Alfredo and his camera crew had videotaped Steve and Gina's wedding and Lou wanted the same, so Alfredo and his crew flew down.

Alfredo and Kane were in the process of purchasing a gay bar and club in 5 points.

When Wimp stepped in the club he looked around and saw Kane and his crew at the big table that over looked the club and he walked over with the big tote bag slung over his shoulder. He spoke to everyone then just stood there until he was invited to have a seat.

He sat next to Kane who poured him a drink and he slid the bag on the floor. He looked around and pushed the bag to Lisa with his foot and said to himself, "Damn it's Wednesday and this joint is packed. These motherfuckers are clocking major bread."

They sat around and bullshitted for a while. They drank and kicked it until about 1:30 when things started quieting down and people started leaving. The club closed at 2:00 and Wimp waited patiently until the last patrons left then said, "Lisa we got a problem."

Lisa looked to Kane, caught herself then turned back to Wimp and said, "Wait until the employees leave and we'll discuss it then."

Wimp had noticed the way Lisa looked at Kane and said to himself, "I knew it! That nigga is the man." He got up and went to the bathroom. When he walked out he ran into Janet who asked, "What's up playa? I'm Janet."

"It's got to be you little momma," Wimp replied appraising her.

261

"I know you're down with the owners and shit," she said. "And I'm just an employee. I ain't a gold digger or trick bitch but I've been known to be bold. I've scared off some niggas I like because they thought I was too aggressive. I'm not the type of woman who sleeps around with a slew of niggas. I ain't got a man but I got a little friend, nothing emotional on either end. We just take care of each other when the need arises. I am the type that when I see something I like I go at it, and I like you! I ain't talking bout no one night stand either. I got my morals, so what's up playa?"

He looked her up and down and she was taller than him. She was at least 6' and she was slim fine. She wore a pair of tight, pink capri pants and there was a gap between her legs that he could slide his hand thru. Her cunt print was pronounced and she had slightly bowed legs. She had on a tight, pink sleeveless blouse, pink sandals, a big gold chain on her neck, and rings on every finger including the thumbs. One wrist had 8 or 9 gold bangles, the other a thin gold watch and a gold and diamond tennis bracelet. She was cute with a star symbol gold tooth on her left canine. Her hair was cut short, dyed red and finger waved. On a scale of 1 to 10 she was at the very least a 9.

"Damn girl," he said. "You sure know how to get your problems across but dig this I'm married, happily I admit," he flashed the wedding ring. "If you can deal with that without causing me or you any problems I'm cool with it."

"I been peeped the ring," she said. "And I don't mean your wife any disrespect, so if we hook up I'll respect your house and your time."

"It's on then," he said. "You got a car?"

"Naw," she answered. "I catch a ride to and from work but I got my own apartment."

"Wait on me," he said reaching in his pocket and giving her his car keys. "You'll know my car, it's the black Benz in the lot. In the morning we going to a car lot and change your status. Cool?"

"I'm cool with that," she said smiling. "One more thing what's your name?"

"Baby I'm Willie Wimp, the ladies pimp, so cool I walk with a limp."

She laughed and walked off. He watched the seductive sway of her ass then returned to the table.

They were all staring at him because guys had been trying to catch Janet and she batted them all down. She was all business.

"What's up?" Wimp asked looking at each of them. "I got a booger hanging out my nose or something?"

"Naw," Kane said. "But we were surprised as fuck when Janet rolled up on you. We know she did most of the talking; about what we don't know. Then you said a few words then gave her your keys. Man, Janet ain't fucked with a nigga since she has been working here and you just out of the blue got her. Lil bitty ass nigga tell me your secret."

They all laughed and Wimp said. "Nigga if any secrets need to be told you ought to be the one telling them the way Red and little momma be all over you."

They all burst out laughing. The employees had all left except for Janet and Big Chilly who walked over to the table.

"Y'all gonna lock up?" Chilly asked.

"Yeah," Charles said. "We got it big dog." Chilly turned and left. "Hey Jay check this out," Charles called out to Janet who came over. "You ain't got to go out and sit in the car. Go in the office for a few. We got some business to discuss so fix you a drink. We should be finished in 30 minutes or so."

She left and Wimp told them about the dreads and all that happened as well as all he thought would happen.

"Dig this," he said making eye contact with each of them. "Y'all run a tight ship. I see that cause when I stop by there is never anyone else that works for y'all on my level at this table. Now I don't know if I've got special privileges or what, if I do thanks, but I'm very observant. I've had to be all my life cause I've always been the smallest nigga, so I had to compensate. I developed my speed and keen observation so I would know how to react in any given situation. I understand the need for secrecy cause the game we in could end one of three ways, maimed, chain gang, or death! I discovered that this nigga here," he pointed at Kane. "Is the head of this shit and if anybody sat with y'all for a few hours it's plain to see. At least to me it should be. Now it ain't my business because y'all done showed me nothing but love and I'd never betray you. If I went to jail today my wife and kids would be straight for a long time, maybe forever. Y'all made it that way and I feel honored that y'all allow me to sit with the inner circle. That's all I wanted to say."

Kane looked around the table and burst out laughing. The others laughed too then Wimp said, "I ain't trying to say y'all ass kissers or nothing."

They all laughed again.

"Now y'all see my point, Kane said to his crew. "Now you see why I don't wanna meet your people. All of them may not be as observant as Wimp, but I don't want this shit to get out of hand."

"Naw nigga," Charles said. "Now you see my point when I told you who the leader should be. If a man from the outside looking in can see your leadership abilities then we on the inside surely can."

"Alright I dig where you're coming from," Kane said then turned to Wimp. "Yeah bro, I guess you're right. I am the leader of this shit as you say but that doesn't need to go past you. Lisa vouched for you, so did the others and they told me how you handled yourself in that situation y'all had. I trust these 6 with my life and if they vouch for you that mean something to me. Plus, I like you too. You're right that you're the only one we allow at this table, but by the same token you're the only one down with us that has his own shit. Being real you deserve to sit here with us. You're making us plenty of bread. When I say us that includes you. We may have been instrumental in getting the product, but you're the one that's moving it. Now, the situation with the dreads; do you know who leads them?"

"Naw I don't." Wimp answered in reply. "But I'm sure that if you give me a day or two I can find out."

"That's cool," Kane said. "Try to find out as much as you can about them. Who they are, who leads them, where they're from and swing thru here every night and keep us updated. We don't wanna wait too long before we get on this so you got to work fast."

"I got you Kane," Wimp said.

"Red, go get Jay." Charles said.

"Hold up Red," Lisa said. "I got it. I got to put this money away." She picked up the tote from under the table and sat it on the top.

"I need to borrow 8 or 10 grand," Wimp said to Kane. "I'll get it back to you in the morning. I don't keep that kind of cash on me."

"Give him 10 grand out of that there Lisa," Kane said.

Lisa opened the bag and started counting out the cash. She passed Kane a slip of paper with $130,000 on it. He got a pen and changed it to $120,000 and said to Wimp, "Count the 10 gees as a bonus. Are you alright on product?"

"Yeah I'm straight," Wimp replied. "But I been getting a lot of people coming thru that want boy cause them niggas in Durkeeville run out on a regular. Can you swing that?"

"That's done," Kane said. "Lisa will bring you enough so you can pass out samples to build up your clientele."

"That's cool," Wimp said as Lisa passed him the $10,000 and stood up to go to the office.

"Nigga if you paying 10 grand for some pussy you can take me to the motel," Steve said.

They all fell out laughing as Lisa clutching her side walked to the office.

Lisa and Janet came back and Wimp took Janet's hand and they left.

*   *   *   *

The next day at noon Charles and Kane walked into Arnie's Pawn Shop. Kane waved at the clerk who knew them and headed towards the back with his briefcase in hand.

Pete as usual sat at the back counter and he raised the gate when Kane and Charles approached. He gave them a hug and a kiss then led them to the office where they all took a seat.

"Okay Kane, what's the deal?" Pete asked.

"I need 7 vests, anything you got that's fully automatic, and some pineapples would be nice too," Kane said.

"This sounds heavy," Pete said. "Did you talk to Frank yet?"

"Not yet," Kane answered. "But I'm going to see him later and let him know what's up."

"Are they locals?" Pete asked.

"I don't think so," Kane replied. "They're rude boys so I don't think there are any family ties."

"I can tell you right now that they don't," Pete said. "But talk to Frank before you move. Do you need personnel?"

"Naw," Kane said. "We go it, but I've been meaning to try and find a doctor in case me or one of my people gets hurt. We can't go to a hospital and we'd never have time to pick up all the weapons on the scene."

"I see your point," Pete said. "Call me at 5:00 and I'll let you know something."

"That's cool," Kane said as Pete walked to the big safe and spun the combination

Pete opened the safe then pulled out a big drawer in the bottom. He pulled out 7 vests that were made by second chance, a company in Fernandina Beach that supplied vest and body armor to police forces around the nation. He picked up the phone and said a few words then hung up. A few minutes later one of the clerks appeared with a TV box. He left the box and walked from the room.

Pete put the vests in the box and sealed it then told Kane, "Frank said you get everything at cost, so that's 3500 for the vest. How many automatics do you need?'

"That depends on what they are," Kane said.

"I got 9mm Uzi's, and .45 caliber mac 11's," Pete said.

"Let me get 7 of each," Kane said.

265

"Alright," Pete said. "That's 7 gees and the pineapples are a grand a piece but I can probably get you 21 for 15 gees. Say $25,000 for all of it."

Kane popped open the briefcase and counted out the money and passed it to Pete.

"Sol will deliver it to the club," Pete said. "But only to you, Charles, Steve, or Tony so look for him in a couple of hours."

"That's cool," Kane said.

He and Charles stood to leave; they hugged and kissed Pete then left.

Kane saw a uniform store on the corner of 7th and Main St. Charles put the TV box in the van and they headed that way. Before they got there Kane saw another uniform store and said, "You go down the block and get jumpers for all of us and I'll do the same in this one."

They went and made their purchases and met back at the van.

"Let's go back and see Pete," Kane said.

They walked back into Arnie's then to the back counter where Pete sat.

"Pete I need 7 badges," Kane said.

Pete got up and left then returned with a box and said, "7 badges and 7 pairs of handcuffs. They're security guard badges so they won't stand up under close scrutiny."

"That's cool," Kane said taking the box.

He and Charles then went to the Pic-N-Save on 8th St. Charles bought the boots while Kane bought the gloves and skull caps. Charles bought 14 nylon black vests and as they were leaving he spotted a Glidden Paint Store and told Kane what they needed.

Kane went in and bought a stencil and fluorescent yellow paint, and then they dropped it all off at Post St. and drove back to the club.

Kane called the women and told them he was going to see Frank. They all wanted to go so he waited until they arrived then they got in the van and headed to Orange Park.

Crown Inc. had purchased 2, F150 trucks and a van. All were black with gold crowns airbrushed on both sides with their phone numbers underneath.

7 ladies had purchased 2 trucks and a van also, and all 3 were painted hot pink with silhouettes of 7 ladies holding hands painted on both sides; with 7 Ladies Inc. and their numbers on them.

*   *   *   *

Kane had called ahead to let Frank know they were coming so when they arrived they were met by Donnatella who had grown quite fond of the girls.

She and Frank stopped by the club at least once a month to go slumming as Frank called it. They all made sure to have a get together at least once a month, at someone's house with all the family in attendance. Even the kids had taken to calling Frank, Papa Frank, and Donnatella, Momma Donna. They loved it and would shower the kids with gifts.

Frankie, Shelia, Teecy, and Lou all came to town once a month which was also cause for celebration.

Jimmy sat outside and watched as they all hugged and kissed. It pleased him that the Kane's were once again in their lives. He constantly talked to Kane who he hadn't really had much contact with in years, and found him to be articulate, warm, witty, and intensely loyal. He always had fun when they came around. He went to the club frequently, often riding with Kane and the ladies who treated him like royalty.

Frank came out to greet him and the ladies screamed with glee and rushed to embrace him. It always amazed Kane when he saw them interact. Frank's chest seemed to swell with joy as he greeted them with fatherly affection. After all the kissing and hugging was done they went inside. Frank, Kane, and Jimmy strolled the grounds as Kane told them about the dreads.

"Do you need help manpower wise?" Frank asked.

"No," Kane said. "We can handle it."

"How are you set with product?" Frank asked.

"I got in touch with Frankie," Kane replied. "I'm expecting a shipment Monday or Tuesday."

Kane kept Frank abreast of his business dealings and it was Frank that guided him into expanding all of his operations.

"I talked to Leslie and the others about opening boutiques in the locations where their salons are," Frank said. "I already lined up the loans and we were just waiting until they discussed it with you before we moved on it. That was yesterday morning."

"Go on and get the ball moving on it," Kane said. "I haven't had a chance to talk with them yet, but if you see money in it let's get it done."

They talked business for a while then headed on inside where the ladies were, in the kitchen.

Donnatella was teaching them how to cook a traditional Italian Meal since Kane was truly Italian she claimed. They all laughed at that. Kane, Frank, and Jimmy sat at the table and watched as the women prepared the meal.

When it was done the ladies served it and they drank 2 bottles of wine that Frank said came from a vineyard he owned in Italy.

After the meal they all retired to the sitting room where Frank poured them all Cognac and produced 2 big blunts. Frank and Donnatella smoked weed on occasion so he fired up, took a few hits and passed it to Lisa who hit it then passed it to Donnatella who smoked daintily. The blunt went around and since it was excellent weed everyone was good and high.

Frank gave the ladies the other blunt to take with them. Kane and the girls had been there several hours and it was 6:00 p.m. when they got back to the club.

Pete had sent the hardware and, Charles got it and took it to Post St.

*   *   *   *

Later that night at the club around midnight Wimp showed up. He gave Janet a kiss at the door and she beamed. He walked over to the big table where the whole crew was already seated and slid the big tote under the table, and grabbed a glass. He poured himself a drink then sat down.

"Little nigga you just done made yourself at home," Steve said.

They all laughed and Wimp said, "I might as well, cause I know none of you niggas is gonna give me a drink. Shit I would've died of thirst waiting."

They all burst out laughing then sat around and bullshitted for a while. Wimp got up and went to talk with Janet for a few and the others danced.

A slow song came on and Janet said, "That's my jam right there. Hold the door down for me baby." She stuck her head thru the door and yelled, "Elaine! Elaine! Come here girl!"

Elaine came to the front to see what was up.

"Hold down my spot while me and shorty dance," Janet said.

"Girl Big Chilly gonna kill us both," Elaine said.

"He ain't gonna sweat it," Janet said. "Trust me on that."

"You know I need this job," Elaine said.

"Bitch I know that," Janet said. "Remember I'm the one got it for you. All this talking the record gonna be gone off by the time you finish."

Elaine sat at the desk as Janet took Wimp's hand and headed for the dance floor. She made a quick stop at the DJ booth and asked the DJ to play the song again when it ended. She got Wimp's hand and they got on the dance floor.

She wore a lavender tank styled mini-dress. It was form fitting and showed off her ass and long legs. She had apple sized breast that didn't need a bra as they stood up firm and full, with a flat stomach, and nice hips. She was draped in jewelry as usual and wore lavender gladiator styled sandals. Her hair was freshly pressed, her lips coated with glossy lavender lipstick. She wore no other makeup and she looked fantastic.

Wimp had paid cash for her a 90" Pontiac Trans Am. It wasn't new but it was still fresh.

They danced to the song and she went back to her desk after giving him a steamy kiss. He went back to the big table and sat down with the others. They sat and kicked it until the club closed.

Janet walked over to the big table and Wimp said, "Go on home slim, I'll come over when I finish." He stood up and pulled out a fat roll of bills. "This is 5 grand for you to move with," he passed her the money. "I don't like the area you live in. Too much shit going on over there, I know where some nice places are on Lanes Ave." He tiptoed and kissed her then she turned and left.

"Damn nigga!" Charles said. "You gonna go broke with a pussy bill that high." Everybody laughed.

"Black ass nigga it don't cost you a dime to mind your own business," Wimp said laughing.

"Y'all gonna lock up again?" Big Chilly asked when he came up.

"Yeah we got it dog," Charles said.

Kane notice that 2 girls that worked in the club, Bernice and Chrissy were lingering around. He looked at Charles and Steve then said in a low voice so the women couldn't hear, "Goddamn y'all fuck all the employees? We might need to start hiring nothing but niggas." They all burst out laughing.

Charles called the girls over and said, "Y'all go on in the office it's a bag of weed in my desk. Make yourself some drinks, smoke a few joints and chill; we'll come get y'all when we finish."

As the women walked to the office Sherrie pulled out the blunt Frank had given them and lit it.

"This is what I got on the dreads," Wimp said getting their attention. "They call themselves the Yardies. They have been moving in and taking over spots in several places. They got a spot on Dot St, over on 8th and Laura, and on 22nd and Pearl. The house on Dot St. is a single story 3 bedroom joint. No fence with abandoned houses on each side and behind it. There are usually 7 or 8 of them there all the time, 4 outside with weapons that they keep under the porch close at hand. I had the spot on 8th checked and they got 2 apartments side by side behind the blue front. The apartments are in the middle on the bottom floor and behind them is a bar. There's no way from the back except thru the windows. The place on Pearl seems to be their base. They got a club in the spot that used to be Banners

269

grocery store, called Montego Bay. They got a one story house behind the club that they serve from. I don't know how many rooms or how many of them are there, maybe anywhere from 8 to 12. The club is closed on Monday night but they hold a meeting there on Monday night at 10:00 or 10:30. Their leader's name is Lenwood Marcus. He's a big guy and they call him by his full name."

"Bet that up dog," Kane said. "That's just about all we need to know. We'll check the spots out over the weekend then decide a course of action. What I need you to do for me is get me 4 stolen cars. Preferably black or dark blue four door sedans. I want four stolen tags off of city vehicles, the yellow ones, and I need them by Sunday. Have you got a place to stash them?"

"I'm on it," Wimp said. "Yeah I got a good spot to stash them."

"Spare no expense," Kane said. "Let me know what you spend and I'll reimburse you."

"You ain't got to reimburse me," Wimp said. "Shit it's your bread I'm gonna use anyway."

They all laughed and Kane asked, "Is that it?" Everyone nodded and they rose to leave.

*   *   *   *

Wimp pulled up to Janet's place and parked next to the Trans Am. He got out and used the key she had given him to let himself in the apartment. The first thing he noticed was the smell, then the flickering light. It was a one bedroom apartment and there were scented candles arranged everywhere. They filled the air with a lovely fragrance.

Teddy Pendergrass softly crooned from the speakers as he looked at Janet who was perched on the sofa in a sheer, white negligee with matching bikini panties. Her legs were curled beneath her, a glass of wine in one hand, and a joint in the other.

He moved across the room and sat next to her. She passed him the joint then poured him a glass of wine and held it to his lips. He sipped the wine and glanced over the rim of the glass at her with a question in his eyes.

He finished the wine and she stood and took his hand, "Come on Shorty," she lead him to the bathroom, where it too was filled with scented candles. The tub was filled and on top of the water floated rose petals.

"Damn Slim!" Wimp exclaimed. "All of this for me?"

"Yeah Shorty," She said smiling. "It's all for you," then she start undressing him.

270

When he was naked she kneeled in front of him and stroked him until he was stiff, then sucked him into her mouth like he was a string of spaghetti.

As they lay in the tub she said, "Damn Shorty. I ain't been with you but 24 hours and you been so good to me. Can it be like this all the time?"

"It could if we savor the moments we share, but mainly it depends on you. See I ain't gonna be able to stay with you every night because of prior obligations. I can't promise that you won't get lonely cause certain times will bring that about." He said.

"If I feel it's getting to be more than I can bear believe me, before I trip I'll let you know what's up."

"I like the way you bring it slim," he said and kissed her. They bathed each other, rinsed and dried off then she carried him to the bedroom.

"Damn Slim," he said laughing. "What do you think I am a baby doll?"

"Hell naw!" She replied laughing. "You my fuck doll!" Then she gently laid him in the bed.

He lay back and she crawled between his legs and stroked, and sucked his penis. When he was hard she moved up his body and straddled him. He rose up and slid his cock in her and slowly eased down until he was all the way in, then slowly she started riding him making sure he penetrated her deep on every down stroke.

Slowly he pumped up into her his hands gripping the twin globes of her ass. She leaned forward so her breasts were hovering right over his face. He raised his head and sucked her breast into his mouth and powered his stiff penis up into her. She moaned, "Suck it....ummhmm....suck it baby."

He pumped up into her and bit her nipples lightly and she moaned out, "Ummhmm....just like that....like that..." She started riding him faster and faster.

"Fuck me...." She moaned. "Fuck me baby....." He released her ass and reached up and grabbed her. He pulled her down until she was lying on his chest then he rolled her over until he was on top. He threw her legs over his shoulders. Her cunt was cocked up at an angle and he started powering his cock into her with deep, rapid thrust and she screamed, "Oh yes! Fuck me harder!"

He pounded into her wet, slurping cunt swiftly and she moaned, "Faster Shorty....Fuck me....Faster...." And he drilled into her with blazing speed.

"Oh baby....oh baby....shit..." She moaned over and over as he drove his cock in her rapidly. "Oh shit ....I'm cumin now...Oh...I'm cumin baby...." She moaned. He felt her vagina clench his penis and he exploded, blasting his cum deep in her. He thrust into her a few more strokes then stopped.

He let her legs down and lay on top of her and kissed her. "Don't forget we gonna look at apartments tomorrow," he said softly.

"I won't baby," She said nuzzling his neck.

"I wanna make sure you're still close to your job," he said. "I would set you up with your own thing but I don't wanna take you away from my people. By the way, how much are they paying you?"

"I make $400 a week," she answered. "I work from 6:00 until 2:00 5 days a week. Monday and Tuesday I'm off. I go to work anyway most of the time if I don't have anything to do. They pay me even if they don't need me. They're good people baby."

"I know," he said. "I'll be swinging over to the club more often now, you can bank on that!"

She reached for his penis and slowly stroked it. "You ready baby?" She asked.

"For you slim all the time," he said laughing.

*   *   *   *

Sunday night at 12:00 they were all in the office at the club. Lisa had beeped Wimp and told him to come over.

They sat around the office giving their reports. Tony had checked the house on Pearl St. every night since they learned about it, and it was pretty much just as Wimp had said. He had bought dope from them 4 times and was let inside the house on all 4 occasions. Each time there was 5 or 6 dreads inside and 4 or 5 outside. Tony told them that the inside of the house was boarded up and they only used the front room, and a bathroom that was near it. He and Lisa had went to Montego Bay and spotted Lenwood Marcus who sat in a roped off section near the front of the club with his bodyguards flanking him.

"Me and Beck checked the spot on 8th St." Steve said. "They got a couple of men standing outside most of the time and I don't know where they keep their guns. I see a couple of possible places, trash cans and such but they let you right in."

"I asked them to use the bathroom," Becky said. "They let me and I notice that they had the back windows boarded up, so there's no way out. They've busted a big hole thru the wall so the apartments connect."

"They're about 8 deep," Steve said. "10 with the 2 outside."

272

"The spot on Dot St. is about 8 deep," Charles said. "4 outside, 4 inside. When I went in to cop, I noticed they had some of the back of the house boarded up."

"What's with that?" Kane asked. "Do you think they keep something back there or what?"

"I've dealt with a few dreads," Wimp said. "And I've seen a few of them do that. I don't think they keep shit back there. I think it's mainly to keep motherfuckers from hitting them from the back."

"That's cool," Kane said. "What about the rides Wimp?"

"I got 4 black cars, Taurus sedans," Wimp said, "swiped from 4 different areas and 4 city tags swiped from different areas. They're already on the rides parked inside the garage behind the pool hall. The shit so big you can park 4 or 5 more cars in it with no sweat. I was thinking chop shop but I don't have the connections in that area."

"That's a good idea," Kane said. "I'll get back with you on that later. Can anyone see you come and go in the garage?"

"Naw," Wimp said. "Ain't nothing back there but businesses. I think the garage was originally a small warehouse of some sort. I rented it because it butted up with the pool hall and I figured we might need some extra space."

"Good thinking," Kane said. "Now I know why I like you. I want you to personally check the spot at 8:00 tomorrow, and get all of your people off Dot Street. All of them, got it?"

"I got you boss," Wimp said.

"I want y'all to go home and get some rest now. Come on Beck and Red, let's roll Tee. You and Lisa need to be getting y'all asses on up right about now! Cee and Steve, if y'all rollin with Bernice and Chrissy tonight, give them the rest of the night off. If Chilly gives you shit pay him extra. Shit he makes damn near as much as me now. Wimp dig this bro; forget we ever had this conversation. We never talked about dreads; never saw any, no nothing! Cool?"

"I don't know what the fuck you're talking about," Wimp said. Both he and Kane smiled.

They left Wimp sitting in the office behind the big desk, feet up, joint in the corner of his mouth, and a glass of Cognac in his hand.

*   *   *   *

Monday at 7:00 pm they were gathered at the house on Post St. making plans. They had spray painted police on the fronts and backs of the vest and pinned the badges on them. They had all their gear laid out and ready.

"This is how we'll do this," Kane said. "We'll take the van to the garage and park it there. Get all 4 of the cars and leave 2 parked outside Durkeeville, then we'll hit the club and the house behind it at the same time. Me, Red, and Lisa will hit the club. Cee, you Steve, Tee, and Beck will hit the house. We going in hard screaming, "Police Freeze." You've got cuffs but we don't plan on using them so don't leave anyone standing. Destroy all threats immediately. Our main goal is to ice these motherfuckers but we want the bread and dope if we can get it. I'm not wasting any time trying to search the club. If we could go in on the Q.T. it would be cool but we're going in hard. Beck, you and Tee driving the first leg, after that Red and Lisa. Once we hit the club and house we're gonna hit 8th Street. Cee, you and Tee will kick down the doors and the rest of us will rush in. Always yelling, "Police freeze." Every dread that hits the ground stays there in every spot we hit. We don't need them to warn the others that we're coming, because we might get a hot welcome. After 8th St. we go straight to Dot St. and hit them. From there we take the back way to the garage, leave the cars get in the van and dip. We dump the weapons at the last scene. I liked that touch when y'all told me about it. Any questions?"

They all shook their heads then Kane started passing out weapons. He gave the 3 women Uzi's as their primary weapons and 9 mm's as backups. He and Steve got Mac 11's, and Glocks as back up pieces. Charles and Tony got sawed off riot guns; pump action 12 gauges loaded with double ought buckshot, and Glocks as side arms. He opened the small box that Pete had left and pulled out some olive green spherical objects and set them on the table.

"What the fuck?" Tony asked his eyes wide with surprise.

"Army issue grenades," Kane said smiling. "We use these to blow shit the fuck up. We won't use them on 8th St., we don't wanna leave innocents without homes. But, the club, the house behind it, and Dot St. them shits gonna be going up like it's the 4th of July," he reached in his pocket and pulled out 8 screw on clips. He grabbed one of the vests and inserted the clip thru a hook on the vest. He got a grenade and put the pin over the clip then screwed it closed. "Pull the grenade the pin comes out and this lever flies off," he pointed to the pin and the lever. "You got about 3 seconds before this shit explodes so when you snatch the shit off get rid of it. If not a funeral won't be necessary because there won't be much of your ass left to bury!" He got 3 more vest and put the grenades on them. He gave one to Charles, one to Tony, one the Sherrie, and he kept one. "Check your watches," he said.

It was 9:45 and Kane said, "Let's get ready."

They all cleaned and loaded their weapons, careful not to leave any finger prints. They grabbed the rest of their gear and 15 minutes later were dressed and ready to go. Each carried a small tote bag with their weapons inside.

They got in a black van with the crown logo on the side and headed to the garage.

When they pulled up to the garage Tony jumped from the passenger seat and swung one of the big doors wide, and Charles pulled in and parked.

They saw four gleaming black Taurus sedans with yellow tags. They put on their vest with police on them and put the skullies on their heads. Lisa collected the totes and threw them in the can then they loaded up in the cars and pulled out. When they parked on the side of Durkyville and loaded up in 2 of the cars they noticed the basers fleeing the scene; and they knew the 2 cars would be safe for a minute.

They drove to Pearl St.

Once they reached Pearl St. they drove past the club and stopped at the public library, and they all got out.

"Beck when I say stop the car, stop," Kane said. "Me, Red, and Lisa are gonna get out. Y'all got 3 minutes to go around the block and come up so your passenger side faces the house. Y'all know what to do then, so let's hit it!"

They drove back up Pearl and Kane spotted and empty doorway 2 doors down from the club and said, "Stop!"

Becky pulled to the curb and Kane, Lisa, and Sherrie slipped from the car and raced to the doorway and kneeled down. They pulled their mask over their faces and waited.

Kane had instructed them in the use of their weapons, "Safeties off," he said softly and heard two muffled clicks. They rose and walked swiftly to the club where Kane motioned them to stop. He caught their eyes and pointed to the grenade then had them to press their backs to the wall on the right side of the door.

He snatched the door open and glanced quickly to the right and left. He saw the area described to him to his left and snatched the grenade from the vest. He tossed it under hand toward the table. Quickly he closed the door and pressed his back to the left side of it. There was a deafening roar and the glass from the front door and windows exploded outward in a fire and crystalline shower. Smoke belched from the windows and doors along with screams, both male and female.

Kane and the women spun thru the door and fanned out then unleashed a hellish barrage of automatic weapon's fire throughout the club. Kane raced to the table where Lenwood Marcus was sitting and he sprayed the area. When he got there he saw there was no need. Mangled bodies were strewn all over the place. He signaled to the women and they stopped firing. In the silence all you could hear were pleas for help and moans.

Kane dropped the clip from his Mac an inserted another. The women followed his lead. In matter of 7 or 8 seconds they had turned a thriving nightclub into a slaughter house. They turned and ran for the door.

The dreads on the porch behind the club were listening to reggae and smoking a spliff when the back windows of the club exploded outward in a shower of glass. All 4 clutched their heads and closed their eyes.

Becky punched the gas and swung up on the curb then slammed on brakes. Tony was shouting, "Police freeze!" as were Steve and Charles. There was no need because as soon as Becky punched it the grenade in the club exploded. By the time she stopped the car the men were raising their heads.

Becky and Charles exited the car in sync and brung their weapons up. They riddled the four men with bullets and it looked like they were competing in some bizarre dance contest as their bodies jerked around from the impacts of the rounds. Blood, bits of tissue, shirt, pants and locks flew thru the air in a grisly miasma of color.

The front door flew open and a man rushed out with 3 men closely behind him. Tony and Steve fired at the same time and the first man's face disappeared in a shower of blood, flesh, and bone fragments. The men behind him were sprayed with the gory mess.

The impacts of the rounds halted his forward momentum and hurled him backward into the men behind him who then crashed to the floor in a tangled heap. By the time the men hit the floor Tony and Steve had rushed up the steps to the door and rained a hail of .45 calibers and double ought destruction on them.

Their bodies jumped and jerked as the rounds ripped them to shreds.

Kane, Sherrie, and Lisa rushed from around the building and Charles and Becky spun around with their weapons aimed. When they saw who it was they turned and raced up the steps. Kane motioned Lisa and Sherrie to the cars then ran to the house.

They did a quick search and came up with a garbage bag of weed, a tote filled with cash and another with rocks. They ran from the house. Charles stopped and snatched the grenade and tossed it in the house then raced to the car.

The grenade exploded and shredded the dead bodies and tossed body parts into the street. They drove sedately from the scene to 8th Street. They pulled in shouting, "Vice hit the ground!" And the men standing guard lay down with their hands clasped to their heads. Becky and Lisa stood over the 2 men with their weapons pointed at their heads as Charles and Tony kicked the door in. Kane was behind Tony, and Steve was behind Charles. As soon as the men kicked in the doors Becky and Lisa executed the men on the ground.

Kane and Steve opened fire and sprayed inside the house as they ran in with Sherrie hot on their heels.

A man attempted to raise a handgun and Kane hosed him with the Mac. Blood blossomed on his shirt as the .45 caliber slugs ripped into him. Sherrie saw a woman hiding behind a sofa and she rushed over and raised her weapon. She saw that the woman was really just a little girl, 15 or 16 at most.

"Please Mr. Police.... Don't hurt me...." The girl begged.

Sherrie could tell she wasn't Jamaican so she said, "lie down, be quiet and don't move!"

Becky and Lisa had come inside and Sherrie motioned to the girl. Lisa rushed over and kneeled beside the girl and asked, "Where do they keep the money and dope?"

The girl pointed to a cabinet across the room and Lisa showed Becky, who went over and opened the cabinet. There was a big garbage bag half filled with weed, a tote bag of money, and another filled with rocks. She grabbed the stuff and ran from the house.

Steve came out of the other side with similar packages and he and Becky got behind the wheels of the cars. They loaded up and drove to the other cars and switched then headed to Dot St.

Steve and Tony got out behind the target house, Kane and Sherrie on the opposite side facing the house. The four crept thru the alleys as Lisa, Becky, and Charles, sweated their watches.

Tony and Steve approached the front of the house from different sides. Stealthily they eased forward staying in the shadows. They halted a few feet from the front and kneeled with their weapons raised.

Kane and Sherrie knelt in the shadows across the street from the house and watched the dreads as they stood around. They watched the customers going in and out of the house as Kane saw head lights approaching. He touched Sherrie and they rose from the shadows and sprinted across the street with Kane shouting, "Vice! Freeze! Hit the ground!"

Tony and Steve shouting, "Vice! Freeze! Rose from the shadows beside the house.

The customers broke and ran in different directions. One of the dreads attempted to run and Steve cut him down with a quick burst from his Mac. The .45 caliber slugs smashed into his back and one neatly severed his spine. The impacts tossed him forward where he crashed bonelessly on his face.

Tony fired on one as he tried to run into the house. The shot gun blast took off the top of his left shoulder and the left side of his face. The force of the blow threw him sideways where he stumbled and flipped over the rail.

He fell towards Steve who caught movement from the corner of his eye and spun, firing a deadly and useless barrage of slugs into the dead man's chest. The .45 rounds seemed to stop the man in mid-flight as lungs, heart, and shattered breast bone sprayed from the exit wound in his back.

Sherrie fired her Uzi at the man who sat on the rail stunned. Her first round took him in the hip, the next the waist and on up until one round punched thru his left eye pulping it, and smashed into his brain. The slug exited the top right side of his skull and splattered the house with blood, bone chips, and brain matter.

Kane fired on his man as he was attempting to snatch open the screen door. His slugs marched up the man's back and exploded the back of his head like an over ripe melon. The man crashed thru the screen door ripping it down.

The cars had arrived and Charles ran up the steps, over the dead man's back. His shot gun booming out double ought death that sought a victim.

Kane rushed up onto the porch and fired thru the window. He swung the mac back and forth hosing the room then raced in behind Charles.

Tony and Steve rushed inside and saw that Kane and Charles had everything under control. Two of the dreads inside were dead and the other two were on their knees pleading for their lives, "Please don't kill we mon.... Jah please spare I."

"Where's the dope and the money?" Kane asked.

One of the men pointed to an area behind a sofa. Steve walked over and looked then nodded at Kane who shot both men in their fore heads. The .45 slugs ripped thru and pulverized their brains and blew the back of their heads off.

Steve and Tony had grabbed the drugs and left the house. Kane and Charles hurried out and the others were gathered by the cars in defensive positions. Kane pulled out his sidearm and threw his Mac on the porch. The others followed his lead.

Sherrie snatched the grenades from her vest and tossed both inside the house. They jumped in the cars as the grenades exploded.

They drove back to the garage and hurriedly dressed. They loaded everything in the van and pulled out.

At Post St. they called Wimp and told him not to go near the cars in the garage and to lock them up until further notice.

*　　　　*　　　　*　　　　*

Detectives Samuels and Drummond reported to the scene on Pearl Street. As they viewed the carnage Samuels said, "Drum my gut tells me that these are our boys again."

"I've got the same gut feeling Sam," said Drummond. "And damned if it doesn't seem like they've upped the ante. These boys are using the same type of explosive. I can smell it!"

"Yep," Samuels said. "You're right and we won't know what kind until forensics is finished. What's the body count so far?"

"12 and counting," Drummond replied.

"Damn Drum!" Samuels exclaimed. "We got to get these cowboys off the streets before they start wacking innocent people."

An officer ran over and told them about the murder scene on 8th St. and they rushed to their car. Before they could pull out they heard a call for all cars in the vicinity of Kings Rd. and Myrtle Ave., automatic weapons fire and what sound like explosions.

Samuels pounded the steering wheel and said, "Drum there's no need to rush now they're long gone and I wouldn't wanna be the one to run up on them while they're in the commission. They've got automatic weapons now, I can tell by the groupings in some of the victims. Automatic weapons and explosives. Plus they operate with military precision. I damn sure don't wanna catch them when they're armed like that. I believe we'll catch them slipping. That's the best way."

"I know you're right," Drummond said. "But I want these fuckers. They're way too dangerous to be left on the street."

"Let's work this scene from top to bottom, inch by inch. If our gut feelings prove us right it doesn't matter who gets to the scenes first because before the week's out the cases will be ours. Trust me; this is the work of one group."

"Sam we might need to start looking in our own house," Drummond said. "The witnesses reported seeing police vest and badges."

"God forbid we have to go thru that again," Samuels said. "I'd hate to be on that case."

"You got that right," Drummond agreed.

*　　　　*　　　　*　　　　*

Wimp sat in front of the T.V. at his wife Neicy's beauty salon contemplating the call he had received when a special bulletin came on. It reported on the escalating drug wars. It told of the gangland style slayings of more than 15 members of a Jamaican posse called The Yardies. No suspects were in custody, but the murders were believed to be connected to the execution style murders of alleged drug king pin Morris Jacobs and Theodore Burke several months ago.

Wimp sat and watched and thought, "That's around the time Lisa came up missing on the set for a while. Then she showed up with the others and that's when they put me on." He remembered Becky and Sherrie's words. "Poison."

"Man oh man," he thought. "All of them motherfuckers are stone cold killers." He thought they may have had Chico hit then remembered some of the talk going around that some of the killers were chicks. "Damn," he thought to himself. "I'm responsible for these last deaths. When I told that nigga Kane about The Yardies I signed their death warrants. Well, better them than me. I ain't gonna lose no sleep over it that's for sure, and I'm damn sure taking Kane's advice. We never discussed it." He smiled to himself then walked over and gave his wife a kiss and told her he would be busy and wouldn't make it home. He walked out and headed to the Kings Crown. When he walked thru the door he didn't see Janet on the front desk. There was a new woman there who demanded that he pay. When he told her to get the manager she got up and came back with none other than Janet. His mouth dropped open.

"Close your mouth Shorty and give me a kiss," Janet said holding her arms out to him.

He walked into her embrace and kissed her passionately.

"Angie," Janet said to the shocked woman. "This is my man Wimp and he's down with the owners. He's never paid to get in and probably never will. Remember his face and let him and any guest he has with him in, no waiting. Alright?"

"I got you Janet," Angie said finally smiling.

Janet took his hand and led him into the club.

"So you're the manager now?" Wimp asked.

"Assistant," she answered. "As well as hostess plus I got a $200 raise. Cee said that was to keep you from stealing me away."

He laughed as she led him to the big table where Kane and the others sat drinking and laughing like they had been there all night.

"Damn!" He thought. "These some cold blooded fuckers, I'm glad I'm on their team." Then he slid in the booth.

They kicked it until 2:00 a.m. then Kane said, "Wimp come with me," and headed for the office.

Once there he opened the safe, pulled out a big tote bag and gave it to Wimp. "$100,000, that's for you."

"Dog that ain't necessary," Wimp said sincerely.

"Nigga you're family," Kane said. "I don't give a fuck if you burn it or wipe your ass with it, but it's yours. Besides, you gonna earn it in the long run. In a month or two I want you to open up Montego Bay as a Jamaican night club. Same name just different management. Big Chilly will show you how to set it up and you can't take Janet. Chilly will find suitable people to run it for you. Find a Jamaican cutie to be hostess. If it was me I'd make sure all of the staff was West Indian, so suggest that to Chilly. I don't wanna make that big nigga mad with me," he smiled.

Wimp thought to himself, "That nigga don't wanna make you mad with him!" He said, "Alright boss I got you on that, so what you want me to do; hold this bread and use it towards the club?"

"Damn nigga," Kane said shaking his head. "As smart as you are do I still have to draw you a map? Listen, I'm gonna help you get a loan for the club you ain't got to spend a dime for anything. We got more money than we know what to do with and I ain't saying that to brag. It's gonna be a joint venture. I'm gonna get the lawyers to draw up the papers for you to get your businesses and your wife's businesses and incorporate them. Start looking for you a few more spots, legitimate. I'll get you the money for them. It's like I said, we've got too much surplus cash and I want all of my people to be set if this shit gets crazy. So look for stores or rental properties. I can get the loans so it all looks legit. I'll give you a million dollars to pay off all of your shit a little at a time and show you how to wash your money thru the businesses. But Montego Bay is to be a joint venture between you and Crown Inc."

"Damn Kane," Wimp said. "That's mighty white of you."

They both laughed then Wimp got serious and asked, "Why you willing to go out like that for me? What's the catch?"

"I told you," Kane said. "You're family! If someone fucks with you, they're fucking with me, and I play for keeps." He looked in Wimps eyes and went on. "Loyalty and trust bro, that's the catch. Be loyal and I promise you'll get rich. I like you, the others like you and that to me says a lot. Seldom do I misjudge character and I believe you got the right stuff. Family first dog. Always remember that because your life depends on it!"

Wimp stared into Kane's eyes and nodded his head. He knew Kane was a man that would abide by his word.

Chapter 18

A few months later it was near Christmas and Tony's workers were getting robbed at least once a week. None of the houses were hit, just the men he had on the street.

Tony's people seemed to be having a streak of bad luck. Besides the robberies they were taking busts all over, but it was never anything major.

Kane always took care of his people so if anyone took a fall he sent money to their families to bail them out and get them a lawyer. If they had to do some time he supported their families and sent them enough money to make it thru their sentence; so their workers were loyal to a degree.

They had workers who broke down their product and served it. When they found out they warned them. If it happened again they dismissed them and barred them from serving in any of their areas. Stealing was handled in a similar fashion except they beat them down. The second time they beat them down and dismissed them.

Montego Bay was up and running. Wimp had followed Kane's advice and had gotten 3 more businesses besides Montego Bay; another beauty salon, a Laundromat, and a dry cleaners. His company was called Lil Man Enterprises. He split 50/50 with Crown Inc. on Montego Bay as Kane had instructed. Montego Bay was enlarged so that in the daytime it was a restaurant and at night both a club and a restaurant. All of the employees were West Indian and they had opened a dope house, weed house, trick house, and a bootleg house down the street.

All of the principle people in Kane's crew maintained their same positions. They had to because Kane didn't want anyone else to know where their stash house was. The women still did the drops and pickups, even tough 7 Ladies had expanded by 2 more businesses. Crown Inc. had gotten the rental properties going. And Gina, Leslie, Jen, and Lucinda had six boutiques they joined together and formed their own company; SupHer Fashion Inc. Things were going just fine.

      *   *   *   *

Tracy, Sonny, and Tony sat at a booth in The Sandwich Shop trying to find a way to end the recent rash of robberies. They told their workers to never pack heat. If the jack came just give it up, but their workers were getting nervous so they needed to put a stop to it. Tony had brought it to Kane but unless they had more to go on it was a dead end.

They had basers beating the bushes because it seemed that one man was responsible for at least 8 hits. He wasn't hurting them financially but the morale of their workers was low so they planned to put a stop to it.

*   *   *   *

Billy Wallace was a jack man that lived on the east side. He robbed all over except for out east. Everyone that knew him called him Billy Guns and he had a reputation for being the wrong man to fuck with. Billy Guns felt that he was above the law and feared no man alive because he was a killer. The people that knew him knew that Billy Guns had been robbing in Brooklyn, Mixon, and Lackawanna for the last few months. He took the dope and money then went out east and sold the dope. He had saved up $50,000 from the robberies and every time he ran out of dope he'd just go rob them again. He didn't do coke in any form but he did smoke weed and drank.

As he headed towards Brooklyn he thought, "Damn them niggas over there are set. I think I'll hit one in all 3 places then cut this shit out and just serve. I got a nice nest egg so ain't any need to keep this shit up, cause eventually them niggas gonna step up to the plate. I know they ain't soft because if I would've tried this shit 9 months ago there would've been a shootout, and I'm Billy Guns not Billy the Kid."

*   *   *   *

T-Bone Jenkins stood on the corner of Spruce and Jackson with four other men; Sly, Shortarm, Monk, and Froggie. They all sold dope for Kane even though they didn't know it. They got the drugs form Sonny and Tracy. They were getting good money but were a little upset that sonny and Tracy didn't want them to tote guns. Kane had explained it to the inner circle that passed it on to the workers. A drug charge was alright but a drug and pistol case was some different shit all together.

They saw a blue Buick Regal pull to the curb and it was tricked out nicely. A tall skinny man got out and walked over to them. He was real slim so the men assumed he was a baser.

"What's up my nigga?" T-Bone asked.

"It's got to be y'all," Billy Guns answered. "Who serving?"

"All of us," T-Bone said.

"That's good," Billy Guns said and whipped out a huge .357 Magnum with a 12" barrel. "Give it up!"

They gave him their dope and money then he said, "Now y'all run across the park to that fence over there," he pointed to the fence with the big pistol.

T-Bone had been watching him closely, memorizing his face. They all turned and ran for the fence as Billy walked to his car laughing then headed for Mixon.

*   *   *   *

Tracy and Sonny used Sarah's as their base. After the robbery T-Bone and the others came to Sarah's and walked over to the table where Tracy and Sonny sat. They told them about what had just happened.

"Hold on a minute," Sonny said and went behind the counter and called Tony who was at The Sandwich Shop.

The Sandwich Shop and Sarah's were so close that Tony walked thru the door about 2 minutes later and came to their table.

"Tee, 15 minutes ago they got robbed," Tracy said pointing at the 5 men.

They told Tony what happened and gave him a description of the man and his car.

"Tee I think I know the nigga," T-Bone said. "But I can't put a name to the face yet, I'm sure it'll come to me."

"Alright Bone," Tony said. "Let me know what you come up with.

"I got you dog," T-Bone said smiling brightly.

Tony pulled out a fat roll of bills and gave the men $1,000 apiece and said, "That's for y'all. Take the rest of the day off and the ladies will bring y'all some work tomorrow."

*   *   *   *

An hour later T-Bone drove into the underground garage of The Police Memorial building and parked his car. He took the elevator to the vice department.

T-Bone Jenkins was actually Detective Terrance Bowens an undercover officer. He walked into a room and looked thru several big black books that contained mug shots. He was there for two hours until finally he spotted his man.

"Bingo!" He said out loud.

He pulled the man up on the computer. Billy Wallace, a.k.a. Billy Guns. He read the report on Billy Guns as it flashed on his computer screen and whistled. 3 convictions for armed robbery and suspected of several homicides.

284

"So Billy has been a busy little motherfucker," he said to himself. "He could be the key to me getting on the inside of this drug ring."

Detective Bowens had been getting all of the hustlers busted a few at a time to please the brass, but he noticed that each one was out the next day; and they all had the best lawyers. He had taken a fall or two himself, and had been bonded out promptly. He knew that one of the ladies always gave the bond money to a relative along with the name of a lawyer, and the cash to retain them. He also knew they dropped off the dope. Not to everybody but to Tracy or Sonny. Tomorrow would be the first time they will ever give him some directly and he'd have to turn it in as evidence. He had turned in enough cash to cover the price of the dope so he would wear a wire tomorrow. He wanted the transaction on tape so he had to use some of the money he hadn't been turning in. All of the money he made he kept a great deal of it, though he never spent it. It was rainy day money he kept stashed at his grandmother's house.

He knew there was more to this group then met the eye. They were too generous with their workers to be the rinky dink outfit they wanted to appear to be, and he wanted to be the man to bring them down. The whole kit and the caboodle.

His bosses had started pressing him to bring the case to a close so he looked at Billy Guns as his key to the inner workings of this organization. He knew he'd have to do something drastic to get in. Just telling them who Billy Guns was wouldn't be enough. He'd leave Billy Guns out of his reports because Billy Guns was about to bite the dust. He was gonna make sure of that.

*   *   *   *

Kane and Leslie lay in bed watching the news when she said, "Baby we're doing well, shit! We're multi-millionaires so where do we go from here?"

"Baby I don't really know," he answered. "When things started happening for us I had never mapped it out. I never thought it would develop and grow like it has. All I really wanted was enough for us to be secure and to keep our heads above water. But, shit just snowballed and exploded. Now I've got so many people depending on me, I'm afraid to let them down Les; this shit is much bigger than what you see. Think about this; SupHer Fashions has 12 businesses. Think of all the people you employ and their families. If SupHer Fashions closed down, think of what would happen to them. I've got twice the number of businesses and an equal amount of rental properties. Of course I don't do everything, but the family looks to me before they finalize any business deals. Hell, you and

285

your people do too. I don't have a problem with delegating responsibilities because I never asked to be the man in charge. I never chose this position. One incident happened and from that I'm now forced into a leadership role. It's one I didn't want and if everyone agrees that someone else is better suited for it, I would gladly step aside. Trust me Les, I would."

"I know you would," she said. "You don't even see that it's stuff like that, that makes you special. You're a reluctant leader but you're a good leader. Look at Tony, he was fucking up bad but now they've got fine cars, a big home, businesses of their own, and money in the bank. Baby it was you that gave us all of our dreams. I never knew that the things I said stuck in your mind. Shit I had long ago given up on the beauty salon. Why do you think I never mentioned it again? But you remembered. We are all where we are because of our dreams and the initiative you took to make them a reality."

"Are you happy Les?" He asked. "I mean really happy."

"Baby let me tell you something," she said. "No matter how ideal a life might seem; no matter how much money you have; there is always room for change as well as for complaints. You ask am I happy, damn right I'm happy and as long as I've got you I'll stay that way!"

She pulled him into her arms and said, "If only they should see you in your moments of insecurity they would know that the only chink in your armor is your care, love, and concern for yours. Baby am I the only one that sees this side of you?"

"I'd never reveal my weaknesses or indecisions to anyone else for fear they would attempt to exploit them," he said. "That doesn't just apply to my opponents but to family as well. But you, you have my heart and are my only true confidant."

"Baby I feel so special and blessed to know that there is a part of you that is solely mine!" Then she kissed him tenderly and they slowly made love.

*   *   *   *

About noon the next day Becky, Sherrie, and Lisa pulled up to the park on Spruce and Jackson.

When doing their drops and pickups they always rode three deep for protection. They were always armed and always watched each other's back.

Tony, Tracy, and Sonny were there talking with T-Bone and the others when they walked over and gave Tony a hug. Lisa hugged and kissed him deeply and passionately. She wore an Eagles jersey and long

286

white shorts, an Eagles cap turned to the left, and green hi top canvas Converse.

Sherrie wore long red shorts, a Miami Heat jersey, a Heat baseball cap turned backward, and hi top red Reebok Classics.

Becky wore a cropped Penny Hardaway jersey, and Orlando Magic baseball cap turned to the side, baggy jeans that sagged so you could see the waist band of her electric blue thong, and a pair of black and electric blue Nike Air Max sneakers.

They spoke to the men that sat on the hood of the car that was parked there. All of the men crowded around and Becky passed each of them a package.

"What's this Lil Momma?" T-Bone asked.

"The regular," Becky said. "But Tee told us to put a little something extra in for y'all."

"Yeah," Sherrie said. "That enough rocks there for y'all to get straight."

"Tony told us y'all got robbed yesterday," Lisa said. "And we like to look out for our people so we put 30 extra rocks in there for y'all."

"When y'all sell them Tracy and Sonny will contact us like always and we'll hit y'all up again," Tony said. "But don't wait until you run out to call us."

T-Bone stood the closet to them and he got every word on tape, enough to hang all 6 of them.

The women jumped off the car, went and got in theirs and drove off.

T-Bone walked to his car and turned the tape off, because he didn't want his next conversation on tape. He knew what he was about to do was cross the line. He was already dirty because of the money he had kept but what he planned to do next was a whole nother animal. He had busted quite a few people when he was on patrol and had kept several guns. He knew the men he took the guns from wouldn't say anything as they were all convicted felons. Some he let go scott free as he built up an arsenal of unmarked weapons, and he had on with him. He had gotten another car from the motor pool and stole a tag from a car at the impound, and put it on it.

"Hey Tee!" T-Bone called out. "Dig this!"

Tony walked over, "What up Bone?"

"I'm pretty sure I know who that nigga was that robbed us yesterday."

"You know him?" Tony asked.

"Not like that," T-Bone answered. "I done saw the nigga before if it's the same nigga. I think it was a nigga they call Billy Guns from out east."

Tony had heard of Billy Guns and was somewhat familiar with the man's reputation.

"Let's ride out east and if we see the nigga, I'll know if it's him or not," T-Bone said. "If I see his ride I'll know it for sure. I looked at the nigga's face real good so won't be no mistake if I see him."

"Bet that up Bone," Tony said. "Let's roll. Do you know where the nigga hang out at?"

"Either on the Ave, Franklin St. or 1st St. Apartments," T-Bone said. "So we ain't got to ride all over."

They got in T-Bone's car.

"Trace, Son!" Tony yelled. "I'll be back in a few!"

*   *   *   *

Billy Guns was in the back of 1st St. Apartments serving as he leaned against his car. The stunt he pulled yesterday had netted him nearly a 1,000 rocks, and they were big, fat ones. He could've made 3 nice dimes out of each one but he just cut them in half. He had nearly 2,000 rocks when he started serving and shit was jumping because he had the biggest rocks on his end. Cars were pulling in and out and he walked over and served them.

He had the big pistol in his hand so he wasn't worried about anyone trying to Jack him. His only flaw was that when he served a car he put the pistol under his arm and poured rocks into his hand for the customers to choose, thereby having both hands tied up. He saw a green Honda civic pull up and stop.

T-Bone saw Billy Guns leaning against a blue Regal. The same one from yesterday and he had the same big pistol in his hand. "That's him Tee," said T-Bone as Billy Guns walked towards the driver's side of their car.

Tony kept a gun on him at all times but he wasn't about to hit Billy Guns in broad day light without Kane's permission. All he wanted to do was identify the man, they would catch him later. So he reached in his pocket and pulled out $20.

Billy Guns leaned down and asked, "What up? What y'all need?"

"Serve this dub." Tony said and passed him the $20.

He took the money and put it in his shirt pocket then put the pistol under his left arm. He pulled his rocks from his crotch and poured some in his right hand. He leaned thru the window on the driver's side and extended his right hand.

T-Bone who was left handed reached into the elastic pouch on his door and pulled out a snub nosed .41 Magnum. He raised it and put it under Billy Guns chin.

Billy Guns reacted instantly by rearing back away from the car. As soon as his head cleared the car T-bone pulled the trigger. The roar from the .41 was muffled as the pistol was pressed tightly to Billy Gun's chin, but it was loud nonetheless.

The big slug plowed a path upward thru his chin, the roof of his mouth and pulped his brain before it exploded from the top of his head. It showered the midday sky with bits of, brain, blood, bone and hair.

The force of the shot stood Billy Guns up on the tips of his toes. His eyes bulged as smoke and blood spewed from his nose and mouth. He danced a little jig but was brain dead before his body got the news, then he crashed lifeless to the filthy asphalt. It was over in a matter of seconds and T-Bone pulled off.

As soon as Tony recognized what was going down he said, "Oh shit!" But he knew it was out of his hands. If he had stopped T-Bone, Billy Guns would've unloaded in the car so he sat and watched it unfold as if in slow motion.

T-Bone got on the 20th St. expressway and drove to Main St. and got off. He drove towards town then made a right on 13 Street. He pulled into the driveway of an abandoned house, got two big rags and passed one to Tony; who immediately started wiping his prints off of everything he thought he had touched. T-Bone did the same then they walked down an alleyway to 14 St. and got in the car T-Bone had parked there. A few blocks away T-Bone threw the pistol in a sewer and they headed to Brooklyn.

Tony hadn't said a word the whole time but occasionally he'd glance over at T-Bone.

"You alright with what went down back there?" T-Bone asked.

"Hell naw!" Tony said angrily. "I ain't alright with it. You could get me life in prison for that shit. What if somebody saw our faces? You planned this whole shit out, the least you could've done was to warn me."

"I ain't with a motherfucker robbing me," T-Bone said in his defense. "I don't believe you are either. I don't know how you would've handled it but I couldn't see that nigga walking around like we soft or some shit."

"I feel you bone," Tony said resignedly. "But it would've been handled properly, trust me on that. Since it's done ain't no need to sweat it, but we better lay low for a few days just in case.

"Alright Tee," said T-Bone. "So we straight on this?"

"Yeah we straight dog," Tony answered softly.

*   *   *   *

Tony called Kane and said, "Bro I need to see you, it's 911."

"Where and when?" Kane asked.

"At the Post," Tony answered.

"See you in 20 minutes," Kane said.

25 minutes later Kane and Tony were sitting in the house on Post St.

"Dig this bro," Tony said. "I told you about the robbery yesterday. Well one of the niggas that got robbed, a nigga named T-Bone said he thought he recognized the nigga that robbed them, but couldn't put a name to the face. All of them had described the nigga and his ride. An hour or so ago after the girls dropped them a package he pulled me to the side and said he remembered who the cat was. It was Billy Guns."

"I've heard of the cat," Kane said. "He got a serious rep as a jack man and a killer. He rarely slips, or so I heard."

"Bro not only did the nigga slip," Tony said. "The nigga fell and he won't be getting up. Bone said he thought he knew where the nigga hung out and suggested that me and him ride and check it out to make sure it's the right cat. We rode out east and hit a few spots. When we saw the nigga he was leaning on the blue Regal that they had described so we stopped. I was gonna cop a 20 just to get a close look at the nigga so we could roll on him later. When the nigga leaned in the car Bone put a big ass pistol under his chin. The cat tried to back off but before he could Bone scattered his brains everywhere then drove off. The nigga Bone had planned to kill the nigga all along and he did. He blew the cat's fucking brains out."

"Alright," Kane said. "This is the play. Lay low a few days and I'll try to see what's up. I'll get Wimp to put some ears out east and see what they hear."

"That's cool," Tony said. "What you wanna do about Bone? I didn't like the way he handled that shit but he saved us some wet work."

"That's true," Kane replied. "He did save us a job. Give him 10 gees and tell him to keep his head down for a few days."

"I already told him to lay low," Tony said. "I'll get Trace or Son to get the money to him since they know how to contact him."

"That's good," Kane said. "But I really don't need to meet that nigga now that he got a body on his hands. I wish you hadn't been with him when the shit went down, but that's a moot point now so where you gonna lay at?"

"I think I'm gonna Chill at the condo," Tony said. "Do you mind if I keep Lisa for and few?"

"Naw," Kane answered. "She can stand a few days off anyway." He hugged and kissed Tony then they left.

*　　　　*　　　　*　　　　*

Detectives Samuels and Drummond caught the body out East. By the time they got there the gun, drugs, jewelry, and any cash on the body was long gone. The crime scene was destroyed and they knew from the number of onlookers that this crime would go unsolved.

There seemed to be a festive air, like the crowd was at a circus or carnival. It pissed Samuels off to see that the death of a young black man seemed to be cause for a celebration rather than mourning.

Drummond felt the same and asked, "Sam is it so common place for us to die, that there's no longer a shock or feeling or lost?"

"Drum every time I see a young black man lying in the street dead it makes me feel as if I'm not doing enough. Regardless of what he's done I would rather see them all behind bars than in body bags." Samuels said sadly.

"My sentiments exactly," Drummond said.

They had come no closer to solving the other murders though they worked on them doggedly, even in their spare time. Their informants were either too afraid or simply didn't know anything. Of course they had their false alarms, snitches selling the wrong information or trying to get rid of competitors, but no solid leads. They had murder weapons that confirmed that the Yardies had been hit by one group, but there were no breaks in any of the cases so they were stuck at square one.

*　　　　*　　　　*　　　　*

Theo had opened a base house uptown and was serving for some men off of 45th Street. He was making good money but he smoked and tricked up most of his profits, so he lived from day to day.

He rented rooms to the tricks and charged $5 per person to come in and smoke; so it wasn't' like he wasn't making any money, he just couldn't keep any.

One night he sat in the house with an ounce and a half of rocks. He started out with 2 and business was rolling. He had only had the dope for about an hour and had already made a grand. The men fronted him the dope for $1,200 an ounce and mostly he kept their money straight. Of course he fucked up and was $200 or $300 short from time to time but he knew that if he had the cash he could get the same ounce for $700 or $800, so he didn't sweat it and neither did they. Theo didn't realize that he had served vice 10 or 12 times in the last 2 weeks, so it was a shock when they kicked his door in and arrested him and everybody else in the house. They got the ounce and a half of rocks, an array of pipes, stems, loose rocks, sacks of powder cocaine, heroin, needles, and a bunch of stolen property.

Since the place was in his name he was charged with armed trafficking, possession of a controlled substance, cocaine and heroin. Possession of a firearm by a convicted felon, use of a firearm during the commission of a felony, and sales and distribution of a controlled substance; of which he got 12 counts.

His bond was set at $500,000 and he knew he was in deep shit.

*   *   *   *

Frank had contacted Kane and made preparations to have a big bash at one of the Kings Crown clubs for Christmas.

Kane had told Frank that he didn't celebrate holidays but he could use either club and Frank decided to use the one on Cesery Blvd. He told Kane to attend because Frankie, Shelia, Lou, and Teecy would all be in town. So instead of thinking of it as a holiday celebration think of it as being a family reunion.

Kane agreed even though he had seen the others a week ago. He would never deny Frank anything, besides, Frank was totally without morals. He told Kane that he would break poor Donnatella's heart if he didn't show.

*   *   *   *

Donnatella with the help of Jen, Gina, Leslie, Lucinda, Lisa, Becky, Sherrie, Neicy, and Janet set the club up in a South Pole motif. And when Christmas Eve arrived all of the families came to the club.

Frank, Frankie, and Lou wore identical suits. They were red double breasted with dark green, silk shirts, red, green, white, and black tartan plaid ties, and black patent leather shoes. The only difference was that Frank wore a red and white Santa hat with white rabbit fur trim, and ball.

Donnatella wore a form fitting knee length dress in dark green, the sleeves came to her wrist and the cuffs were trimmed in white fox fur. She too wore a Santa hat, only hers was dark green with rabbit fur trim, and ball.

292

A pair of dark green patent leather pumps complemented her elegant legs. Donnatella still had a beautiful figure and she looked ravishing.

Sheila wore a plaid tartan dress whose overall color was dark green. It had red, white, and black lines, crisscrossing thru its form fitting fabric. It had white fox fur at the wrist, neck, and hem, plus she wore dark green satin pumps.

Teecy wore a red mini-dress with fur trimmed waist, wrist, and collar, red patent leather ankle strap pumps and a red beret with a fur puff on top.

Sherrie wore a red cat suit that fit her like a second skin, a wide black patent leather belt hung loosely at her waist, and a pair of thigh high black patent leather boots.

Becky wore a skin tight red mini-dress with fox fur turtleneck and wrist, a red cap cocked at a rakish angle, a white patent leather belt hung loosely at her waist, and white patent leather ankle strap pumps.

Lisa wore a dark green form fitting pants suit with a bolero styled jacket that showed off her fabulous curves, a red ruffled blouses, red patent leather wing tips, and a green fedora with a red band and green and red feathers.

Janet wore a red jumper, a green belt hung loosely at her waist, green ankle length boots, and a green beret.

Kane wore a snow white wool suit, blood red silk shirt, a white felt panama hat with a blood red band, and red gators.

Leslie wore an ankle length, red, fitted dress that showed her lush figure off, white ankle strap pumps, a short, white mink coat, and matching white mink Cossack styled hat.

Tony wore a dark green silk suit, a red silk shirt, and red gators.

Lucinda wore a green mini-skirt and matching blouse, green patent leather ankle length boots, and a white mink jacket.

Charles wore a crimson suit, black silk shirt, and black patent leather shoes.

Jen wore a crimson knee length dress, a wide black belt at the waist, short black mink coat, and black ankle strap pumps.

Steve wore a black silk suit, red silk shirt, and red suede dress boots.

Gina wore a black curve hugging cat suit, a wide, red leather belt hung loosely at her waist, red ankle length boots, and a short, red leather jacket.

When Wimp and his wife Neicy arrived the crowd roared their approval. Wimp wore a green velvet suit and the pants were knickers, coming just below the knee. He had on red stockings, green monogrammed velvet slippers, a red ruffled shirt, and a green Santa hat with fox fur trim, and ball.

Neicy wore a green velvet mini-skirt suit, a red ruffled blouse, red stockings, and green velvet pumps.

The whole family was there except for the kids and it was a party to be remembered. It was closed to the public and only family and employees of the legitimate businesses were invited. The place was nice and they danced, drank, and smoked until late.

Frank and Donnatella stayed until 2:00 a.m., which all of the elders left around that time. They had booked 2 floors, one at the Red Carpet Inn and the other at the Admiral Benbow Inn; so that those who were too deep in their cups to drive could go there and sleep.

Kane had reserved 6 rooms and all 6 were adjoining rooms. He gave Tony 2 keys, Wimp 2 keys, and kept 2. Becky and Sherrie would share one room and Lisa the other. Wimp and Neicy would have a room and Janet the other. When Kane gave them the keys they hugged him.

"Damn bro you think of everything," Wimp said.

Kane had told them to ply their wives with drink and weed then when they got to the room to love them up. Next feed them food to knock them out, and then make their move. Kane told Frankie to call his room an hour after they left the club under the pretense that they had business. They partied until 3:30 then they all left the club.

*   *   *   *

Tony and Lucinda went to their room and undressed.

"I had a good time tonight baby," Lucinda said slightly drunk and high as hell from the cigar sized blunts that Frank had supplied. He had 10 boxes and they were rolled and looked like cohibas down to the paper wrapper.

He pulled her into his arms and kissed her. They were both naked and he guided her back to the bed where they made love.

*   *   *   *

Wimp and Neicy lay in bed naked and she said, "I really enjoyed myself tonight and I really like these people. Since you hooked up with them we've been rolling. Baby when you were just a regular street nigga I always knew there was more to you than meets the eye. You took me from the projects to the penthouse. I feel like Weezy Jefferson."

"You finer though," he said laughing.

"Who was that guy taking all the pictures, with that red velvet suit on? He's a sissy isn't he?"

"That's Alfredo," Wimp said. "He's family. Yeah he's gay and that's probably the best term to use cause Kane and everybody else loves him."

Wimp didn't know that Kane and Frank were now partners with Alfredo and had backed him financially so he could branch out to Orange Park Mall, Gateway Mall, Dunn Avenue, Avondale, and 103rd St.

Neicy was feeling pretty good having been plied with champagne and weed. She climbed on top of him and kissed him, then she started kissing her way slowly down his body.

*   *   *   *

After the men got the calls they eased from the rooms with their sleeping wives and moved to the other rooms.

As Tony walked into the room Lisa threw the covers aside and said, "Just fuck me fast and hard baby." He hurried and undressed and dived between her legs.

As Wimp walked thru the door Janet lay there with her legs spread wide and her fingers planted deep in her wet vagina. She looked up at him and held a bunch of mistletoe over her pussy and asked, "Are you gonna kiss her under the mistletoe?" He laughed as he undressed then fell face first between her legs.

When Kane stepped thru the door the sight that greeted his eyes was Becky's perfectly shaped ass being spread wide by Sherrie's hands and Sherrie's tongue flashing in and out of Becky's cunt. They were in the 69 position and he smiled and slowly undressed.

*   *   *   *

On New Year's they had another big bash that served as the grand opening of the 4th Kings Crown Night Club on Dunns Ave. and the general public was invited.

Kane, Wimp, and Tony used the same method with the hotel only this time Steve and Charles got in on it.

By the beginning of 1993 they were making mega bucks and were contemplating branching out into other areas. They had feelers out to see if it could be accomplished without bloodshed.

They stuck to their plan of selling nickels, dimes, and quarters of their product and things were going great.

*   *   *   *

Detective Terrance Bowens had gotten no deeper inside the organization and he had been on the case for 6 months. His supervisors were pressing him to close the case even though he had gotten close to 40 busts. All were nickel and dime cases, and his superiors wanted something more substantial.

So the pressure to close the case came to a head and he coordinated with the task force and they made the busts at 4:00 in the morning.

They raided all of Kane's dope houses, bootleg houses, and trick houses in Brooklyn. They busted 10 of his street dealers.

Tony, Tracy, and Sonny were arrested at home. They didn't know where to locate Sherrie, Becky, and Lisa so they were still at large.

Kane received the news of the bust at around 5:00 that morning when Lucinda called ranting and crying hysterically, "Kane they done locked up Tony."

"Lu! Lu!" Kane said sternly. "Calm down! Everything's gonna be alright! Now calm down baby." She calmed down and sobbed into the phone. "Lu listen to me. All that carrying on ain't gonna help matters at all so chill out; hear me?"

"Okay," Lucinda said sniffling. "But what should I do? Should I go see him? Is he alright?"

"You don't need to run down there," Kane said. "He'll be out in the morning hopefully. Haven't I always taken care of things?"

"Yes you have," she said.

"Then leave it up to me," he said. "I got it. You just keep on doing like you been doing, and as soon as I find out what's happening I'm gonna get him out. I got everything, bond money, lawyers' fees the whole nine yards so you just chill out. Do you know what they got him for?" Kane asked hoping it wasn't the murder T-Bone committed.

"No I don't," she answered.

"Let me make some calls," he said. "I'll get with you later today. If he calls tell him to hit me up."

"Alright," she said and hung up.

As soon as she hung up the phone rang. It was Tony who explained to Kane the extent of the damage and told him they had warrants for the ladies but he wasn't in the picture. Tony told him what he was charged with and what their other workers were charged with. He told him the police were expecting to catch the ladies at The Sandwich Shop.

"Have they set bail for everyone yet?" Kane asked.

"We got to go to bond hearing tomorrow morning, and then we'll know what we need," Tony said.

"Get a list of all our people and their addresses after you find out what their bonds are. Give me yours first and be sure to tell our people not to worry we'll get them out tomorrow. That way they won't turn on you."

"I've got the list of names and addresses already and Susan, Red's sister got the women addresses. Are we gonna get the customers out that got busted too? I got their information as well and all we need now is the bond amounts.

"We might as well," Kane said. "It can only be good for business."

"I'll call the condo in the morning with the information," Tony said.

"Alright bro," Kane said. "Be easy until in the morning."

Leslie had woke up and was listening to the conversation. She looked at him but never said a word.

"Tony in jail," he said.

"Are they coming to get you?" She asked knowing that if Tony was into anything so was he.

"I don't think so," he said. "But it's better safe than sorry."

"Will everything be alright?" She asked.

"Yeah," he answered. "It's gonna be alright, no need to worry." She sat up and kissed him and he said, "I've got some calls to make." He got up put on his robe and walked to the den. He called Naomi to see if Charles was there. He wasn't so he called him at home.

Jen answered the phone and Kane said, "Put Cee on."

Charles got on the phone with sleep in his voice and said, "Damn nigga, I done told you bout calling me this time of morning. This better be important."

"Black ass nigga," Kane said. "You done forgot who you elected to be boss? When I say jump, get your ass in gear got me?"

"Yes suh boss," Charles drawled and they burst out laughing.

"Tee's in jail," Kane said seriously.

"Not that thing with bone?" Charles asked.

"Naw, ain't that." Kane said. "Get Steve and Wimp and y'all meet me at the club in an hour."

"Got you," Charles said and hung up.

Kane called the condo and Lisa answered the phone crying.

"So you already know?" Kane asked.

"Yeah," she said. "We know. Tee called and told us not to go to The Sandwich Shop."

"I'm coming to get y'all," Kane said. "So don't drive your cars. I'll be there in 30 minutes or so, be ready alright?"

"Alright," she said. "Wanna talk to Red and Beck they're standing right here listening to me?"

"Might as well," he said as Becky's voice came on the line.

"Daddy what should we do?" She asked.

"I'm coming to get you so don't sweat it," he said.

"Okay," she said. "Here's Red."

Sherrie got the phone and he could tell she had been crying by the sound of her voice, "Daddy should we pack to run?" She asked.

"Naw baby," he answered. "You ain't got to do that. Just chill and I'm on the way to get y'all. I'll tell you how we're gonna handle this so don't sweat it. I got everything alright?"

"Alright daddy," she replied and hung up.

*   *   *   *

An hour later Kane and the women pulled up to the club. They entered and the others were seated at the big table. The walked over and sat down.

"Our whole operation in Brooklyn fell," Kane said making eye contact with all 6 of them. "That tells me one thing, we got a mole. The way we designed this shit is in cells, each one independent. So a fall could only touch all of us thru the one thread that ties us all together and that's these 3," he pointed at the women. "I don't see a way around that but this is what we'll do. Cee, get your best female worker and she's gonna do deliveries to all of your people. Get two of your boys to trail her. Steve, you and Wimp do the same thing. From now on y'all are the only ones that will come in contact with them," again he pointed at the women. Our major concern now is getting our people out of jail and getting lawyers for them. We've got 5 lawyers already so I'll contact them and see if they can handle all the cases or refer us to others who can.

Y'all," he pointed to all 6 of them. "When we find out how much it cost you'll take the bond money to the families and give them the lawyer's name and fee. That won't happen until tomorrow which gives me time to get the lawyers lined up, and parcel out the cases. Tee, Trace, and Sonny are our first priority. Once we get that taken care of Beck, Red, Lisa, y'all are gonna turn yourselves in at 3:00 in the morning. The lawyers will be with you to make sure you're on the booklist for that morning, so y'all won't be in jail but a few hours alright?"

They all nodded their heads.

"I've got to make a call." Kane said and got up and walked behind the bar and grabbed the phone.

Jimmy answered and Kane asked, "Don't you ever go home?"

"I am home," Jimmy said laughing. "What's up son?"

"I need to see you and Frank," Kane said. "It's important."

"Let me get him on the other line," Jimmy said and clicked over. Frank picked up and Kane said, "I need to see you!"

"Nothing we can talk about on the wire?" Frank asked. "I've got some important things lined up for after lunch."

"It's important and I can't put it out over the wire," Kane said.

"Come on out," Frank said. "I'll set the business off until 1:00."

Kane looked at his watch it was 10:45 and said, "Let's go, we're going to Frank's."

*   *   *   *

It was 11:15 when they got to Frank's place. Donnatella was at the door and she rushed to the driveway when they pulled up.

Frank and Jimmy walked slowly from the house. They hugged the women who Donnatella lead into the house.

Kane, Frank, and Jimmy went into the study and Kane told them about the bust and his belief that there was a mole in that branch of his organization. He asked Frank to look into it.

"Berean if the mole is official or unofficial I'll find out," Frank assured him. "If it's official leave it alone. That kind of heat you don't need. If for some reason the mole is terminated and it's official, they'll leave no stone unturned. It could spiral out of control. If it's official just identify it and spread its identity so it's no longer useful. Do you understand?"

"I understand you fully," Kane said looking into Frank's eyes.

"You can't terminate it if it's official son," Jimmy said driving Frank's point home. "Do you need money or lawyers?"

"Naw," Kane said. "We got it under control."

"If you need us call or come out," Frank said. "You're family okay?"

"I understand," Kane said.

"How's business other than that?" Frank asked.

"It's good except for that little set back," Kane said.

"You designed a good system son," Jimmy said. "This proves it. Did it touch any of your legitimate spots?"

"No," Kane said. "They're all clear. I never do business from them though it was my intention at first but the houses and the street workers were more than enough."

"That's good," Frank said. "Anything else?"

"Naw that just about covers it," Kane said.

299

"Whatever you do don't tell Donna about the girl's trouble," Frank said. "She doesn't know they're in the business. You either for that matter."

"I won't even think about it," Kane said.

"I would never hear the last of it Berean," said Frank. "She would have me trying to pull strings in the White House."

They all laughed, and then Frank said, "Jim get the girls for me."

When Jimmy came back with the girls Frank came from behind his desk and said, "Please tell me you didn't tell Donna about our troubles."

"Poppa Frank we know that Momma Donna would scratch your eyes out if she knew," Sherrie said smiling. "And we love to see that sparkle in your baby blues so we'd never tell."

They all laughed. He hugged and kissed them all then said, "I love you all. You've brought so much joy to me and Donna. If you ever, I mean ever need anything don't hesitate to ask, understand?"

They all cried and nodded their heads.

"What's this, a funeral?" Frank asked sniffing. "Dry your eyes before Donna sees you. She's a smart old bird."

They all laughed and headed for the door.

*   *   *   *

After Kane got back to the club he sat in the office and made calls to the lawyers. He lined up 12 including the 5 he already had and they were all from the same firm. Kane estimated they would be working with 25 clients. They quoted him $7,000 per case and he did a quick calculation and came up with $175,000 to cover the lawyers.

He asked if they could get their business cards to him. They assured him a box would be delivered by messenger within the hour. They got the address and he hung up.

Now all he could do was wait. He called Jen and told her to go to safe house and get a million dollars and drop it at the club. He had checked the safe and there was about $600,000 in it, so they were set money wise.

The raid was early Sunday morning so things should be back on track by noon Monday. They all went to the condo, drank and smoked all day, and fell asleep in various positions in the living room.

*   *   *   *

The ringing of the phone woke them at 9:00 Monday morning. It was Tony, "Where's Kane?"

Becky gave him the phone, "What's up Tee?"

"Me, Trace, and Sonny are waiting to be released. I've got the list."

"Hold on," Kane said as he got a pen.

Tony called out the names, addresses and the amount of their bonds and he wrote them down. When he finished he did a quick calculation and came out with $500,000. He talked to Tony for a few and told him to tell their people they'd be getting out in the next few hours then he hung up. He called Set Free Bonding Agency which was Frank's, though his name wasn't on any of the papers.

A voice answered, "Set Free Bonding Agency, Carmela speaking. How may I help you?"

"Can I speak with Richie?" Kane asked.

"May I ask who's calling?" Carmela asked.

"Could you please tell him that Berean Kane is calling?"

"Thank you, could you hold please?"

The phone switched over and a voice said "Richie speaking"

"Do you know who I am?"

"Yes Sir Mr. Kane, I do."

"I'm gonna give you a list of names, please pull them all. They all have $50,000 bonds. Their families will bring the 10% before the end of the day is over. If anyone doesn't bring the money just beep me at this number." Kane gave him the number. "I'll have to you in 20 minutes. Can you handle this or do I need to make a call?"

No need sir. It's a done deal."

I'll call soon with the list of my female associates and their bail numbers. I'll need you to do the same for them."

"Will do Mr. Kane, just give me a call."

"Thanks for everything Richie," Kane said and hung up.

15 minutes later the phone rang. It was Susan. "I got the girls names and numbers."

"Give them to me." She gave him the numbers and names. "I got you baby and y'all should be out in an hour or so. Wanna talk to your sister?"

"Yeah, might as well."

Kane passed Sherrie the phone.

Kane did the math and calculated that he'd need at least $150,000. He called Richie and gave him the list of names then woke everyone up. They showered and headed to the club.

*   *   *   *

An hour later Tony, Tracy and Sonny walked in. Kane gave them some dap and a hug then said, "Listen up! I want y'all to open shop right back up. The ladies are dropping off the cash for the bonds. Steve, Wimp, and Charles are out there too but they should be back in an hour or so. What I need y'all to do," He looked at Tony, Tracy, and Sonny, "Is go check in with your families. Tee call Lu and she can come pick you up. Trace, you and Son go get one of 6 Ladies trucks just bring it back later and meet Tee at Sarah's. By then everything should be back in place, so get ready to roll. Tomorrow get your people to relocate all of the houses. We haven't lost any money because most of the customers been coming over here, so it's all good."

Tony picked up the phone and said a few words to his wife then hung up and turned to Kane, "Lu gonna pick me up in bout 30 minutes. What about the girls, they got warrants out on them?"

"Yeah they do but this the play. At 3:00 a.m. in the morning they're gonna turn themselves in. The lawyers are gonna make sure they get on the docket for in the morning so they won't be in jail but a few hours at the most." Kane looked at Tony and said," You know somebody from inside pulled you down right?"

"Yeah I know, but the only one who isn't on the list is T-Bone and that nigga smoked a muthafucka in front of me. I just can't see him as the one to do some shit like that."

"I see your point Bro, unless the murder was part of a ploy to get in deeper with us. But if the nigga a roller and willing to go to that extent to knock us off that nigga is real trouble."

A minute later Pete walked in and handed Kane an envelope. "Your mole. A photo is inside."

Tony got Pete a drink and stood over Kane's shoulder as he opened the envelope. Detective Terrance Bowens; the information included his entire career with the J.S.O as well as his background. Kane passed Tony the photo.

"That's Bone Bro."

"He'll surface again. Trust me; it wouldn't surprise me if he showed up on the set later today. What I want you to do is get a camera and take some pictures of this nigga and get flyers made. I want his name and who he is on them. I want them distributed on every side of town; not just ours but everywhere! I want this nigga posted in every one of our spots. We gonna get this nigga ass off the streets. I want pictures sent to the police memorial building addressed to vice also. Be sure to use a typewriter and wear gloves. Make sure you get pictures of the nigga that shows he's dirty. If the nigga as serious as I think he is, he's fucking up."

Pete laughed and said, "Wait until Frank hears this."

"Pete that fucker killed a man in front of Tee to try and get deeper in the family. If killing a man was enough for me we'd all be in deep shit right now. I've never met this dude, didn't want to, but he pulled a hell of a stunt. I don't trust people that try so hard to ingratiate themselves with me."

"I see your point." Pete said eyeing Kane and respecting him more for his mental prowess.

"Relay that to Frank for me and tell him I'll see him in a few days."

Pete nodded then hugged Kane and Tony and left.

15 minutes later Lucinda came in the club and ran straight to Tony crying. He held her in his arms and looked at Kane, "You need me for anything?"

"Not right now, but be at Sarah's by 3:00, we got a lot of work that needs to be done." He looked at Lucinda and said, "I need him so don't make him stay home."

"I got you Bro." Lucinda said as Tony held her waist and led her from the club.

After they left Kane sat there and thought to himself, "Shit is getting serious. I need to be thinking bout getting us out of this shit while we're ahead. I'll talk to Frank and get his point of view on this. He's semi-retired and still has his hands in a lot of pies. I'll see if there is a way for us to do the same thing."

Chapter 19

Later that day Tony stood on the corner of Spruce and Jackson with Sly, Shortarm, Monk, and another man named Moon. They were just chilling while the other men were all serving, but Tony was just watching the set. He saw the car that T-Bone drove pull up.

Tracy had paid the people that lived in the corner apartment on the end that overlooked the park to set up a camera on a tripod with a telescopic sight. When T-Bone pulled up Tracy started taking pictures. He took pictures of T-Bone serving dope to several customers as they had discussed it in advance. The play was that if Bone showed up they'd let him serve until he ran out. After Tracy finished he would leave from the back door, get in his car and head to Alfredo's where the photos would be developed.

When T-Bone got out of his car he walked over to Tony, "Man it was deserted on this end yesterday. I looked for y'all and word was that the whole set got knocked off." He reached in his pocket and pulled out a wad of cash and passed it to Tony.

Tony put the money in his pocket because he knew Tracy wouldn't take a picture of it. Tony pulled the money from his pocket and passed it back to Bone and Tracy took a picture of the transaction.

As Tony passed T-Bone the money back he said, "Here's the money Bone, thanks for looking out for us."

T-Bone stood there with a puzzled look on his face as he slid the money back in his pocket. Before he could get his mind in order the basers started coming. They all came straight to Bone because they had all been paid to do so.

When T-Bone sold out Tony went to his truck and got an instamatic camera. He took pictures of the fellows on the set then said "Let's take some." They took the photos and were passing them around when Tony said," take a picture of me and my dog Bone."

Sly took the photo and they stood around waiting for them to develop. Tony cuffed the picture of T-Bone and put more with it and turned to Sly and, passing him the pictures said. "Take these to Sarah's for me."

Tony hadn't told the men that T-Bone was heat. When Sly dropped the pictures off Lisa would get them and go to 5 Points and get flyers made. She would say that she was playing a practical joke on a friend. She would get 1000 copies as they had people waiting in the club from each side of town to pass them out.

After Sly had been gone for about 10 minutes Tony pulled T-Bone to the side and gave him the picture that he took with him. Then he pointed to the side window of the apartment that Tracy had took the pictures from. "See that window in that crib?"

"Yeah dog, I see it."

"Well dog, Trace been in that window taking pictures of you serving. Didn't you pay attention to details when you were in training? He got a picture of me giving you the money too dog. And that murder you pulled, you know; when you killed Billy Guns, the green Honda Civic; the sewer you threw the gun in. Oh yeah dog, I went back and got it. You didn't wipe the gun down. That was careless."

T-Bone looked around with wild eyes as Tony touched the center of his chest and felt the wire he wore." You got your people listening to us?"

T-bone shook his head, "No, the receiver is in my car."

The pictures we just took, a copy of them are going to your office. I doubt your supervisors gave you permission to sell dope and kill people. By 8:00 tonight your picture will be in every dope hole in the Bang'em. By morning you won't be able to bust a dog for turning over a garbage can. Oh yeah nigga. You fucked up bad when you fucked with us. Now my advice to you is this; we walk to your car and get the other part of this device you're wearing."

T-Bone turned and walked slowly to his car. He popped the trunk and reached in and gave Tony the receiver. Tony reached under his shirt and snatched the mic from his chest with the wire and box it was connected to, and threw them to the ground and stomped them then kicked them in the sewer. He pulled the tape from the spool and set it on fire then smashed the receiver.

"You are ruined as a cop in this town; if I was you I'd resign and get missing. I'm telling you this; if you get a job as a civilian anywhere in Duval County, and I see you I'm gonna break your fucking neck. By you being the type of nigga I think you are I'm sure you got a nice little stash. You need to get it and disappear. You gonna lose your job on the strength of the pictures, and when internal affairs get those pictures your ass is gonna be under the gun. You won't be able to save your cash then, so haul ass!"

With lightening like speed Tony's right fist rocketed forward and smashed into T-Bone's mouth, mangled his lips, and loosened his teeth. T-Bone fell to the ground and Tony kicked him in the ass then turned and walked off.

"Damn Tee! What Bone did to deserve that shit?" Asked Shortarm.

"That pussy nigga vice. He the one that got us knocked off. Bitch nigga was wearing a wire just now."

"Man let's finish his ass off."

"Naw, we can't fuck him up too bad."

The men stood there and watched as T-Bone got up and staggered to his car and drove off.

    *   *   *   *

Later that night the whole crew was at the condo as Tony told them about the incident with T-Bone. They were all rolling with laughter.

"Damn Tee, you might've blown their case out of the water with your idea," Kane said with a smile. "All we have to do is present some of those pictures to the lawyers and see how they can use them to our benefit. Hell, y'all might be able to walk away from this shit, I never would've thought of that. You got to tell Frank and the others this story."

Later that night Tony and Lisa lay in bed smoking a blunt. "Baby do you think we can walk away from this?" Lisa asked as she lay curled up on him.

"I hope so, but you know who we're dealing with. You gonna be alright?" Tony asked as he gently caressed her shoulder.

"Yeah, I'm cool. I've done time before so it's no sweat. Beck and Red done been to jail so we got this. All of us are strong so if it comes down to it, it's a cake walk."

"Yeah I done been that route but hopefully it won't come to that." He pulled her into his arms deeper and her hand slid between his thighs and grasped his penis.

    *   *   *   *

At 2:30 a.m. Kane, Tony, Becky, Lisa, and Sherrie met their lawyers at Set Free Bonding Agency. They went in convoy to the Police Memorial Building and asked for the shift supervisor.

The shift supervisor was a black female Sergeant named Atkins.

When the lawyers explained to her what was going on she personally booked them and made sure their names would be on the docket for later that morning. She informed them that if the bondsmen were aware of them being there they'd be out by 9:30.

The ladies hugged the men and were led off. Kane told the lawyers about the photos and the lawyers told him that if they could get them into evidence their chances of winning the case would surely increase. If not, then they had a fight on their hands. Even without witnesses the state had hours of tapes and material evidence against them. They would file a motion to see all of the evidence that the state had. It would surely be damning but the photos should open things up. If they didn't walk away scott free, then the time would be minimal and they would be out in a few months with good time.

Kane and Tony shook hands with the lawyers and went home.

*   *   *   *

Theo sat in jail trying to come up with a plan to get out. He had agreed with vice to set up the guys he had got the dope from, but all they would do is give him a bust bond and talk to the prosecutors to see if they could get him a reduced sentence. He wanted to walk, not do time. The only thing that he could come up with that might get him cut loose is the robbery that took place in his house when he lived in Brooklyn.

Kane was his homie but he would roll over on him to get free. He had lied to Kane the first time when Kane asked if he knew who Will was. He wasn't about to let a nigga serve out of his spot and not know who the dude was.

Will and Dave had come back that night with the police, but nobody talked that night. The police had a long list of witnesses to the crime so that just might be his ticket. He waited until the phone was free then he called vice and talked to the detective that was gonna get him the bust bond. He was switched to the robbery division where he talked to Detective Lewis, who told him that he'd be to see him in an hour. Theo hung up the phone with a satisfied smile. Kane hadn't been on the scene in months and he hadn't heard about him.

He had seen him a couple of times, but he knew his brother Tony was rolling in Brooklyn. He felt like Kane had his hand in it but his name wasn't ringing in the street.

*   *   *   *

An hour later Detective Lewis pulled Theo from his cell. They sat in an interview room that was used for contact visits and meetings with lawyers. "What've you got for me?"

"A robbery and shooting," Theo said nervously licking his lips.

"A murder?"

"An attempted murder." Theo said rubbing his hands together "But before I give it to you let's set the deal on the table. I'm working with vice on a few things and they're going to bat for me. If I can get you to step up with them I can walk on these cases. I get high man; I ain't a big time dope dealer. Hell, the majority of the shit y'all found wasn't even mine."

"You got to save all of that shit for the judge," Lewis said as he eyed Theo with distaste. "I ain't trying your case, and being honest if I was

I'd throw the book at your sorry ass cause you're a piece of shit! You break the fucking law, get caught, then you roll over on all of your so called friends. And just as sure as you get from under this case, your rotten ass will go out and do the same shit again. I hate it but I have to work with snakes like you. If your info is on the up and up I'll step to the plate for you. But trust me, you ain't gonna be able to snitch your way out of everything. The day is gonna come when you'll have to pay the piper; you just better hope the cost isn't too high."

Theo told Detective Lewis about the crime that Kane committed at his house in April, and Lewis taped the entire conversation.

After Theo finished Lewis said, "I'm gonna check on this right away. If I can get someone to corroborate your story, and with the help you'll get from me and vice, you could be out as soon as tomorrow."

Detective Lewis was a bulldog of an investigator. When he sank his teeth into a case, especially one where he could see closure; he worked with determination and passion. It took two days but he got what he needed. Both of the victims were in jail for sales and delivery and they identified Kane from a photo lineup. He talked to some of the other people that were there and he spread around a few dollars and some promises to help if he was needed.

He had enough to get a warrant for Kane's arrest. He got the warrant and went to pick up his man.

When he got to Kane's house he shook his head and thought, "There must be an error here somewhere. I can't see a man who lives in an area like this doing a petty dope robbery." He had checked Kane's record and saw that he had been to prison twice for the same type of crimes. He had been released from prison for armed robbery in 1990 and he had been quiet since.

There was no one there so he left his card where he knew someone would see it.

*   *   *   *

When Kane got home that evening Leslie was waiting on him and she passed him the card.

He looked at it and knew what would happen if he went to see the detective. He would be locked up. He looked out of the window and up and down the street. "Listen baby, I don't know what this is about but I plan to find out." He kissed her and left the house. Kane stopped at a phone booth and called Lewis at his home number.

"Lewis residence, Glenn speaking."

"This is Berean Kane you were at my home earlier. You left your card so I thought it would be in my best interest to give you a call. I'd like to know what's going on."

"I'm gonna shoot from the hip with you on this one Mr. Kane. I got a warrant for you for armed robbery, armed kidnapping, attempted murder, possession of a firearm by a convicted felon, use of a firearm during the commission of a felony, and discharging a firearm in the city limits. It's one continuous criminal episode. The charges stem from a robbery you allegedly committed in April of 92."

"You're joking right?"

"Mr. Kane most of those charges carry life sentences; believe me I'd never joke about such serious a matter."

"I appreciate your candor Mr. Lewis, the question is where do we go from here?"

"Since you know the nature of the charges against you and the penalty they carry that is a good question. You could get in the wind and I believe I'd catch hell finding you, but find you I would. Or you could do the sensible thing and turn yourself in. I'll tell you what I'm willing to do for you. It's been a year since the crime was committed and it seems you got your shit together. I want you to get you a lawyer and have him contact me in the next day or so, two days Mr. Kane, no later.

Today is April 19th so I'm gonna give you until May 4th to get your shit together, then I want you to come to my office got me?"

"I got you."

"I won't look for you, your paperwork won't be on the books if you get stopped for a traffic violation, but if you break the law I'm going to drop it on you so keep your nose clean. This is an agreement between you and me. My supervisors have no knowledge of it so do what you need to do. I'll cooperate with your lawyers to a degree. At least give them a chance to see what the state has against you and prepare themselves. Being honest with you the evidence suggests you're going down. For how long I don't know."

"I appreciate the break and I honor my word. I'll be at your office on May 4th. My lawyer will contact you tomorrow. What time would be good for you?"

"Anywhere between 9:00 and 10:30."

"Thanks again Mr. Lewis."

Kane went back home and Leslie saw the look on his face and asked," Bad?"

"Yeah Baby, it's bad," He replied. "I talked to the detective and he was straight up with me. He told me what they had against me, and what I was facing. He was cool though because he gave me time to get my shit in order, then he wants me to turn myself in. If I can bond out, I'll try to get the lawyers to stretch it out for as long as they can; the longer the better."

"Baby that's life as we live it, "She said and pulled him into her arms. "Come on let's go to bed, we don't have any time to waste and I know you're gonna be real busy in the next few days. I want you to promise that you'll make love to me at least once a day. I know you won't be home every night. You've got a lot of things to take care of in a short time, but I want you to promise me that we'll make love once a day no matter what."

"I Promise," He said as they headed to the bedroom.

*   *   *   *

Kane called Frank the next day and told him he was on the way. He got there at 9:30 and they went straight to the study. Frank looked at Kane with a question in his eyes.

"You got a problem son?"

"Yeah I do and it's a doozy."

Kane told Frank about the case he had.

"Witnesses?" Frank asked.

"I'm sure there are but how many I don't know. The lawyers are on it now and I should know something in a day or so."

"This is serious son. Do you want to fight it?"

"That's the only thing I can think to do. If I thought there was no way I could win it and the sentence was too long, I'd haul ass. I got enough money to do it, so that wouldn't be a problem. If I fight and get a few years I can live with that. That's the angle I'm looking at it from. I've got some of the best lawyers in the country, so if push comes to shove I'll cut a deal I can live with. What I need from you is this; keep an eye on the family. Advise Charles and do what needs to be done if he needs you."

"No problem. You just make sure you keep me up on things. There may be a loop hole we can work through."

"I'll make sure that you're aware of everything."

They hugged and Frank led him to the kitchen where Donnatella was, and she made them eat breakfast. After he finished he left, went to the club and called the crew.

When everyone arrived he told them about his case and explained to them their responsibilities in the organization.

"Cee if I fall you're the man. The rest of you know your places. Cee, Frank is gonna advise you. Don't be too proud to ask for help if you need it. If the others fall, you three," He pointed at Charles, Steve, and Wimp. "Y'all got to hold our shit together. Wimp that means you got to

310

find somebody to take your place on your end, and you take Tee's place in Brooklyn. Tee gonna show you the ropes. You don't take your cut from your end anymore starting today. You'll get yours from the overall profits like the rest of us. Trust me; it's a lot more than you're getting now. Tee I want you to show Wimp the whole setup. He needs to know.

If all of us that have cases fall don't add anyone else to the inner circle. Y'all will be enough. Every pay period keep taking out of our share for the defense fund. Make sure our bills are paid, and give our families generous sums every week. Remember this is a worst case scenario. Shit may not even turn out like that but if it does we'll be prepared. I believe my bond is gonna be a problem because the charges are mostly punishable by life."

The phone rang and Charles picked it up, said a few words then passed it to Kane.

Kane took the phone and it was Leslie who said in a seductive tone, "Once a day Baby."

"Where are you?"

"I rented a small place a few blocks from the salon. I got it furnished, lights and phone on, so it's set. It took me all morning to get it done but it's done. So when can you get free?"

"I'm free now. Meet me at the salon in 30 minutes and we'll test drive our lil love nest."

She laughed; he hung up and turned to the others. "I got some business to tend to. Beck, Red, take care of your business and I'll see y'all about 6:00."

*   *   *   *

The two weeks passed all too fast and it was time for Kane to turn himself in; being him he went alone. He grabbed all of the things he knew they'd let him have, met his lawyers, and they went to Detective Lewis' office.

He was represented by Rabinowitz and Goldstein, some of the best criminal lawyers in the country. Kane was spending mega bucks and had various business interests, and their firm had divisions that dealt with every aspect of the law; criminal, civil, and corporate. They gave him the rundown on his case two days after they got it.

They told him that they wouldn't be able to gauge the strength of the case against him until they took depositions, but that the evidence looked damning. They didn't sugarcoat it, and they didn't think the judge would grant bail but they were going to shoot for it anyway. They also had the motions to file if the judge denied the bail. They walked in Lewis' office and Kane introduced his lawyers to him.

Detective Lewis whistled and said, "I've looked over your case files and you've always had adequate representation on your previous cases, but boy you're in the big leagues now. Can you afford them?"

"Them, and 10 more as well qualified if I have to." Kane replied.

"I don't know what you're into Mr. Kane but I'm afraid you're wasting your money, because you're going down on this one. Trust me on that."

"I do. But their job," He pointed at his lawyers. "Is to try and prevent that or make the damage as bearable as possible. I'm sure you'll agree they're both well qualified to do either."

Detective Lewis nodded his head and said, "Well Mr. Kane let's get the ball rolling."

*   *   *   *

Kane went to bond hearing the next day and the judge denied him bail. The lawyers filed their motions with a long list of character witnesses, all of whom were reputable businessmen. The judge set another date for two weeks later. When the two weeks were up he went to the hearing and was again denied, but the judge set another date for 4 days away. When the day came he was given a bond of two million dollars, which his lawyers advised against paying because they were sure they could get it down in a few days. He took their advice and three days later walked out under an $800,000.00 dollar bond. Charles gave set free bonding $80,000.00 with portions of Crown Inc. as collateral.

*   *   *   *

Kane was out on bond for four months when he found out that Theo was responsible for his fall. There were other witnesses but they were nameless thus far.

Kane sat in Frank's study giving him the rundown.

"I know who rolled over on me."

"That's good," Frank said nodding. "Now what you need to do is give me the information and I'll take care of it. You get yourself a good alibi set up. I'll let you know when it's going down so you can cover your ass. This one has to be public because I wanna send a message to the other witnesses. Find out where he is and get word to Pete. Are the rest of the witnesses from Brooklyn?"

"I guess so I don't have any names on them yet."

"Well that's good because that's where his body will be dumped in broad day light!"

       *   *   *   *

Two days later Pete called Kane at the club. "We picked up that package for you. It's 12:00 now and we plan to deliver it in exactly an hour."

"Thanks," Kane said and then called Detective Lewis.

"Lewis here."

"This is Berean Kane. I was wondering if you had a few minutes because I'd like to talk with you."

"Sure come on down."

When Kane walked in Lewis' office he stepped to his desk and shook his hand. Lewis offered him coffee and he declined but took the seat he was offered.

"Why did you give me the break like you did, I sense you as being the type to go by the book?"

"Being honest I really don't know," Lewis said shaking his head. "You got me pretty much pegged right too, I don't usually do shit like that. Maybe it was the way the case came to me coupled with your house when I saw it. I never heard of you until the case came to me, so I thought you might deserve a break. After meeting you I know there's more to you than meets the eye. I'm a trained investigator Mr. Kane; I don't just rely on the physical aspects of a case. I also rely on my instincts, so I know you're much deeper than you appear to be on the surface. I know that you're cunning and wily, as well as a formidable opponent with vast resources. I say this because of who you have representing you. I checked up on you and I know about Crown Inc. and the loans you got to get it off of the ground.

The banks love you, and all of your notes are paid on time. You have a slew of businesses and they all started shortly after this caper. Your brother and some of his associates were busted on drug charges; the cases are still pending. You didn't fall with them but I believe in my heart that you're a part of it.

You've grown too wise to be out front, but you're running it. I can feel it in my bones. The only thing that makes me feel good about giving you the break is that I know you're going down.

Oh yeah, I made a mistake but the system will correct it for me. Your brother and the others might go down too, and if there are more of you, you can probably run it from behind bars but greed is a motherfucker and you can't oversee it. I don't expect you to confirm my suspicions;

you're much too smart for that but you know I'm right." Kane looked in his eyes and laughed.

*   *   *   *

At the same time that Kane sat in Detective Lewis' office, Pete and Sol had Theo in the back of a van parked on McCoy Blvd. Pete was in the back with Theo wearing a transparent rain suit, booties and surgical gloves. Theo was alive but hogtied with duct tape.

"Theo you should've just took the time and kept your mouth shut," Pete said standing over him. "But you just had to get back on the street. Kane's our brother and you betrayed him, that cost you your life. If by chance you're lucky enough to become an angel, you won't be doing any singing. I want you to know that after you're dead I'm going to cut your tongue out."

Theo's eyes bulged and he screamed behind the tape that covered his mouth, to no avail.

Pete wrapped a knotted rope around Theo's neck and slowly started applying the pressure. He leaned in and kissed Theo on the tape covering his mouth and whispered, "Ciao." Then he pulled the rope tight.

Theo struggled mightily against his bonds but it was useless. His eyes bulged even bigger as he pissed, then there was a loud fart as his bowels voided and he shit in his pants.

Pete stared in his eyes the whole while he strangled the life from him. He watched as the lights went out and Theo's eyes glazed over. "Roll it Solly," Pet said. Sol pulled off and headed down McCoy to Price and Elm where they stopped, and the doors of the van flew open.

Theo's body tumbled out of the back and a bloody piece of pink flesh was tossed next to his body. The doors closed and the van roared off.

*   *   *   *

Detectives Samuels and Drummond caught the case. The body still lay in the street which was roped off. They saw that the corpse was bound hand and foot with duct tape. They could plainly see the ligature marks on the neck and that told them the man had been strangled. His mouth was an open, bloody wound. Blood still seeped from it and puddled on the ground. Next to the body was a small piece of pink, bloody flesh which could only be the corpses tongue.

"Drum this boy was killed and sent as a message," Samuels said dryly.

314

Yeah, I know," Drummond said. "And everybody around here knows what the message is: keep your mouth shut!"

They shook their heads and started processing the scene.

       *   *   *   *

The message Theo's body sent worked both ways. Some of the witnesses clammed up, but others asked for protective custody. All of the cries were falling on Detective Lewis' ears. He went to the Prosecutor and begged him to revoke Kane's bail.

He told him about the death of his informer and the Prosecutor agreed and gave Lewis the okay to pick Kane up. Four days after Theo's death Lewis caught up with Kane at his detailing shop.

"Kane!" Lewis shouted, his face screwed into an angry mask.

Hearing his voice Kane turned and saw Lewis approaching with his gun in his hand.

"What's this?" Kane asked.

Detective Lewis, livid with anger stopped in front of Kane and said, "You slick son of a bitch, you used me! I'm your fucking alibi for the murder of my informant. I should just shoot your ass down like a dog but if I did that I'd be no better than you. Turn around and put your hands behind your back. He cuffed Kane and took him to the Police station.

They sat in an interrogation room and Lewis looked at Kane and said, "The witnesses said a white man drove the van and another threw the body out. The autopsy shows that he had been killed just minutes before he was dumped; at the same time that you were in my office. As much as I hate to admit it you're a cool customer. You knew he was being killed as we spoke. You have a history with the guy; don't you feel anything for him?"

"I didn't kill him, he killed his damn self! He didn't give a fuck about me; all he thought about was his self. Do you think I'd roll over on somebody just to get free of this shit? I answer, no. I wouldn't. When you play the game certain rules apply, and if you violate penalties apply. So he committed suicide, another man was just the instrument. Believe this Mr. Lewis; I would kill a million motherfuckers like him to be free, but I wouldn't snitch on one. Do you understand?"

"As distorted as your ethics are, I do."

       *   *   *   *

Tony and the others had been going to court every two weeks since they got the case. The judge wouldn't allow the photos of Detective

Bowens into evidence, and without them the case looked bad. They offered the ladies 18 months in the Florida department of corrections. The offer to the men was 2 years each. They discussed it with their lawyers who advised them to take it, because with gain time they'd be out in a matter of months.

They took the lawyer's advice and agreed to plead guilty to the charges on their next court date. The lawyers assured them that they could get them two weeks on the street when they pled to their case.

When Kane went to court the next day he pled guilty to armed robbery, armed kidnapping, and aggravated battery. He got 9 years for each charge, all to run concurrent.

The judge allowed him 2 weeks on the street to get his business in ordered with the stipulation that if he could not get his affairs in ordered, his lawyers could file for an extension. Kane agreed to the terms and was released from the courtroom.

*　　　　*　　　　*　　　　*

Ex-detective Terrance Bowens took Tony's advice and resigned from the force, and moved from Duval County.

He moved to St. Augustine and got a job as a security guard at a mini-storage. Three days before Christmas he was working the grave yard shift. Flashlight in hand and gun strapped to his waist, he made his rounds. Tony had judged him right because he had kept money from the drugs he had sold while working on the case against them. He had been at it since he was a patrol officer. By the time he resigned from the force he had saved up a nice little nest egg.

Because he was good at undercover work he slid right into the drug scene in St. Augustine, and was working with vice there. He was responsible for 7 or 8 decent sized bust since he had been in town. He had kept drugs and was moving them a little at a time as he worked his way inside of the largest drug ring in town.

He didn't take his security job serious as he was making money off of his drugs and the money for being a C.I. The security job was just a cover.

As he walked towards the back of the mini-storage he never saw the two men crouched in the shadows dressed in black. He never heard when one of them crept up behind him silently and smashed him in the back of his head with the large bolt cutters he held.

He fell to the ground unconscious and the man used the bolt cutters to break into a unit. The other man bent and quickly threw him over his shoulder and brought him into the unit. They tied his hands to an overhead beam, his feet barely touching the ground.

They taped his mouth cut his shirt from him, then slapped him until he regained his consciousness. His eyes fluttered open and he tried to speak but the tape over his mouth prevented it.

He shook his head to clear it as he tried to focus on the two masked men standing in front of him. One of the men was black the other was Spanish or either a very light skinned black. Both were muscular and looked to be in good shape. As he watched, the men took the masks off and he saw that the big olive complicated man was Italian.

"How are you T-Bone?" Frank asked with a slight smile on his face. "I'm Frankie Knuckles or at least that's what they used to call me; now it's just Frank. I know you don't know me it's been a while since I've been in the field. This is Jimmy my brother. You're probably wondering what this is all about so I'm gonna fill you in.

A few months back you weaseled your way into a drug operation in Duval County, and you got Tony Kane and his family knocked off. I'm the one that found out who you were, and if you had been on a police force anywhere in the country; this day never would've come.

You followed Tony's advice and became a civilian, if you had moved across the country I might've spared you. The move you made killing Billy Guns was ballsy but it was dumb. That never would've got you into the inner circle, but if you had just identified him and let us do the work we would've all been up shit creek. You fucked up Bone. You knew the shit was bigger than what you saw on the surface, but you could never know how far reaching this shit goes; and being honest I don't have the time to tell you.

Anyway Tony and the other fellows got two years and the girls got 18 months. Tony is my son and the girls are my daughters. I've been catching hell about those girls from my wife, but I'll take it out on you Bone. They called me knuckles in the old days because I used to beat my Vic's to death. It's been years since I did it but I guess it's like riding a bike. You'll be my test subject to see if I've still got it. I know I'm a little rusty but it's hours until daylight so I've got time."

T-Bone pleaded with his eyes as Frank reared back and smashed his nose with a wicked right. Frank systematically broke his cheek bones, blacked both eyes then methodically punched away at T-Bone's mid-section. With machine like precision he hammered away at him. T-Bone was conscious the whole while as Frank's fist shattered his ribs.

He pissed his pants as one of his ribs punctured his lung and it collapsed and started filling with blood. He had trouble breathing as blood gushed from his nose. His body twitched uncontrollably as his nervous system was overloaded with pain.

Frank bunched his knuckles in a hun-nukite strike and struck him in the throat with two quick blows that crushed his trachea. Frank stepped back and watched as T-Bone struggled for breath.

"I still got it huh?"

"Yeah, but you're still rusty. In the old days you only used the knuckle strike if you didn't have time to do a thorough job." Jimmy said with a smile.

"Always the critic. What do you expect from an old man?"

They threw the door up and walked off with T-Bone's body slightly swaying from the beam.

*   *   *   *

The two weeks passed all too fast again and Kane turned himself in. Two weeks later all of the others were in jail waiting to be shipped to prison.

A month later Kane was sent to Columbia Correctional Institution. He was given a job in the prison laundry and every Friday they gave him a list with the prisoners that were arriving that day. He saw that Tony and Tracy's name were on the list.

The women ended up at Lowell Correctional Institution for women.

Kane lay awake staring at the bunk overhead and listening as his cellmate snored. "I should be out in three and a half years if I walk a straight line. Fuck these pennies these muthafuckas chasing in here, there's millions to be made on the street and that's where I'm trying to get back to. I just hope murder and mayhem are not a part of the plan.

THE SAGA CONTINUES

A New Era
A New Regime

HoodWrittens Publishing
Presents

B.O.M Squad

Coming Soon!!!

A NOVEL BY BENYAHMIN DAVIS

Chapter 6

    ack heard the radio blare the theme to the Doug Banks Morning Show and looked at the digital read-out on the clock radio and saw that it was 6:01 a.m. He looked down and saw that Secret was stretched out against him. Her leg was thrown up on him and her gown had rose up to her waist. He could feel her soft pillowy breast pressed against him as he looked down at the smooth expanse of her hip and her creamy ass cheek. Her mouth was wide open and his shoulder was wet with her slob as she slept on. He smiled then shook her awake.

    She looked at him then smiled and wiped the slob from her mouth and looked down at his shoulder. Her cheeks blazed red with embarrassment and he burst out laughing.

    "Either I got to coat that spot in plastic or put a towel over it," he said then laughed again.

    Secret had her leg over his crotch and after her initial embarrassment she became aware of the fact that he had an erection. It pressed against her leg and she wanted to move her leg swiftly, but her face again blazed red.

    "Move, I got to go to the bathroom," he said and she moved away from him. Her leg travelled down his crotch area and she saw the big bulge there as he got out of the bed and walked pass her to the bathroom.

    "My God! That shit looks huge!" She said to herself as she watched him. He didn't close the door and she tore her eyes from him as he freed his cock. She heard the tinkling of his urine hitting the water, and she lay back in the bed and closed her eyes as the fire between her thighs ignited.

    "I'ma take a quick shower!" He shouted from the bathroom, "Get on up so you can cook us some breakfast!"

    She sat up in the bed and looked in the bathroom as he pulled off his pajama bottoms and boxers. She saw his muscled ass, as he moved to the plexi-glass shower doors and slid them aside. She had to pee so she got up and walked in the bathroom and pulled her panties down and sat on the toilet.

    "I don't eat breakfast!" She said it loud so he could hear her over the splashing water.

    "I do!" He shouted, "So tighten up!"

    She got off the toilet, washed her face and brushed her teeth.

    "What do you want?" She asked with a mouth full of toothpaste.

"Breakfast, woman!" He said loudly then turned off the shower and slid the door open.

"Good God man!" She said staring at his muscled body as he reached for a towel. She saw the water beaded on his chocolate colored flesh and her sex tingled with excitement. She looked down and saw his semi-erect rod and a thrill shot through her and she said, "You damn sho ain't shy are you?"

"Don't have any reason to be. You my woman and we're home so what I got to be shy bout?"

"You want the works for breakfast?"

"What do you call the works?" He asked drying off as she devoured him with her eyes.

"Grits, eggs, bacon, toast, orange juice, and coffee," she replied.

"That's what I want, but I know you gonna be late for work if you cook all that aren't you?"

"Yep," she said nodding, "But if that's what you want that's what you're gonna have. I worked late Friday so it ain't a big deal. You expect me to cook you breakfast every morning?"

"Damn sure do and I expect dinner too if you must know," he said seriously. "I'll do it for you on occasions, but it's your duty as my woman to make sure I eat properly. I realize you're a professional woman and aren't accustomed to that so I'ma exercise patience with you. I'ma be your man and you're gonna be my woman in every way. You my first priority and I expect me to be yours. There is nothing on this earth gonna come before you, and if it seems like something might I'ma cut it off. I ain't gonna be second Secret, I'ma be first! If anything proves to be a hindrance to you tending to my needs it's got to go, because I'ma do the same shit for you; understand?"

"What if I have to work late and because of that supper gonna be late?" She asked as he stood there naked.

"I got enough money for you to hire a cook, house keeper, or anything else you might need to make sure you handle your wifely duties. Give me your social security number and shit so I can get us a joint account set up. The money in the safe is for paying all the bills, the money in the account is for paying a cook or housekeeper. Most of the time I'll be getting in at 7:30 or 8:00, but you can contact me and I'll let you know. At that time I expect you to tell me where to go. If I'm not coming home I'll let you know then, because I won't have you waiting up if I don't come. I have to take trips out of town from time to time to do business and I'll probably take you sometime if you want to go.

By the way, all of them boxers and t-shirts and shit I bought; wash them cause I don't like the way that new shit feel on my skin. You gonna cook my breakfast or stand there looking at me all morning?"

She giggled and headed for the kitchen as he dressed. By the time he had put on a navy blue pinstriped suit, white shirt, red tie, black wing tipped shoes, and a crisp white pocket square she was finished cooking.

They sat down and started eating and he said, "I thought you didn't eat breakfast."

"I usually don't," she said, "But cooking got me hungry so I decided I might as well go on and eat."

"You gonna start working out with me too because you ain't bout to get all fat and sloppy on me, eating all that shit."

They burst out laughing and finished eating then put the dishes in the dish washer.

"So, you gonna show me yours since you done seen mine?" He said as they walked to the bedroom.

"Show mine since I done seen yours?" She asked puzzled.

"Yeah, your nakedness; you gonna let me see what I'm gonna be getting?"

"You serious?" She asked.

"Naw, I'm joking," he said sarcastically, "I just want to see you."

"You know what looking leads to Jack," she said looking in his eyes.

"I just told you that you gonna be my woman in every way; that means sexually too. Ain't no need in being all shy, because I want more than just pussy. I want your heart and mind, which I got a good head start on them already. So you gonna show me the goodies or you gonna go through the time phases?"

She shrugged then walked to the bathroom with him on her heels. She took off the gown and he saw her full perky breast, and the fully erect nipples that sat in butterscotch colored areolas. He saw the puffy print in her panties and when she pulled them off and stood up he saw her bush.

"Good God woman you got a Persian!" He said loudly.

"A Persian?" She asked puzzled by his comment.

"A hairy kitty," he said and chuckled as her face blazed red. "Turn around and let me see that booty." She turned and he looked at her curvaceous ass and whistled. "Damn that's a nice ass," he said and reached out and cupped her cheeks. He squeezed them and caressed them then he leaned forward and kissed the twin globes and a tingle went down her spine. He gripped her hips and turned her to him then he kissed her smooth stomach. He grabbed her breast in both hands and caressed them gently then flicked his thumbs over her stiff nipples. He kissed her passionately

322

then ducked his head and sucked her nipple in his mouth and flashed his tongue against it; then repeated the process on the other one. He could feel her body shivering as his tongue worked her nipple and he backed up and looked at her face. Her eyes were closed so he leaned forward and kissed her hungrily. She pressed her body to his and wrapped her arms around him, and he knew he could take her right then.

He broke the kiss and pushed her away and said, "I'll see you this evening. Call me on my cell bout 5:00 or 6:00, and let me know what's up," he kissed her again and headed out of the bathroom.

Secret shook her head to clear it then called out, "Jack! Wait Jack!" She walked out of the bathroom and went to a drawer that she kept most of her junk in and grabbed the extra ring of keys she kept there.

"What's up baby?" He asked as he walked back in the room.

"You gonna need these," she said walking to him naked and handing him the key ring. "These are to the house, Navigator, and the Benz parked next to it.

"I told you your actions give me my answers," he said as he took the key ring then pulled her in his arms and kissed her. He released her then left.

Secret was soaking wet when she got in the shower and fingered herself to an explosive orgasm.

*   *   *   *

It was 9:30 when Secret got to work and Henry Ross caught her before she walked in her office.

"Can I have a word with you real quick?" Henry asked.

"Sure," Secret said opening her door and walking in.

"You've got an appointment with Nichole Parsons at the Police Memorial Building for 10:30," Henry said. "She's the public relations officer for the department. If you want to go over the tapes they sent us; now would be a good time,"

"No," she said shaking her head, "I'll act as if they don't even exist, and I want Shani Edwards to work with me."

"You would pick the sole female from our group of rookies wouldn't you?"

"I know what it's like being a Black woman breaking into this line of work. The old boy system is still in effect so I'm creating an old girl network."

Henry laughed then said, "I'll send her to your office." He left Secret as she sat behind her desk and started loading the things she thought she'd need in her briefcase.

There was a knock at her door and she said, "Come on in."

Shani Edwards walked in the room with her head held high and said, "You wanted to see me Ms. Summers."

Secret had been watching Shani since she started working there and she liked her work ethics and the way she carried herself. Shani resembled a young Regina King with the same body and dimpled cheeks.

"Yes I did, and please call me Secret. There's no need for us to address each other formally. The company got a contract from the Sheriff's Department and you're gonna be working with me on it. Go on and have a seat because we don't have much time. What our job is; is to try to give the department a better look for the African-American community. You know their reputation has been long tainted in our communities and for good reason if I might say so. They have had a bunch of brutality cases brought against them in the last six months and the cases against the cops that robbed and killed that businessman only helped to cast a darker shadow over the department. Ethically, I don't want anything to do with making them look better in our communities until they actually start doing better in our communities; what I mean is stop targeting young black males because of social stereotypes. I know that's not about to happen because the shit is embedded too deep in some of them crackers and niggers on the force."

Shani's eyes grew wide when Secret cursed and said crackers and niggers.

"We got a job to do and there're no guarantees that we'll be successful. Even though my heart isn't in the project I believe in doing my best at whatever I set out to do. Who knows; we may be instrumental in making them change some of their policies. So, do you have any reservations about working on this project?"

"Not really because I hadn't really looked at it from your point of view," Shani said honestly. "I don't think that all police are bad though, I admit that just one can make the whole force look bad. I think the police presence in our communities is a good thing because it definitely discourages criminals. All of us aren't bad, but just like with the police; one of us can paint a picture for society at large. I'd very much like to work on this project because for one, its high profile and I can't see a better way to get my feet wet."

"Okay then," Secret said with a smile, "You might as well grab your purse and coat and meet me at the elevator."

"I'll be there," Shani said with a smile and hurried from Secret's office.

324

Secret got her briefcase and overcoat and walked to the receptionist desk.

"Hey Claudia, how are you today?"

"I'm fine Secret," Claudia said looking up at Secret with her big round eyes. Claudia looked like Alfred Woodard. She was forty-five years old and had been with Billings and Ross from the start.

"I need the keys to the company car," Secret said, "I've got an interview with Nichole Parsons the public relations officer for the Sheriff's Department. We've got a contract with them and I've got the assignment. Not that I really want it."

"It's a necessary evil," Claudia said, "Imagine what it would be like without them; total chaos!"

"I can understand that to a degree but I still see room for a great deal of change."

"That there is, but change is evident and with the political environment being what it is now I can't see much good change in the air, with the patriot act and so forth."

"So true," Secret said and took the keys Claudia passed her.

"I'll see you later," Secret said then headed to the elevator where she was met by Shani who carried a briefcase. "Where's your purse?"

"My briefcase serves as my purse during working hours," Shani said, "I'm not about to be bogged down with a purse and briefcase so I decided to leave the purse since my briefcase can serve as both, and it holds a whole lot more than a purse."

"I put my purse inside mine when I'm working," Secret said then laughed. "I basically refuse to take work home with me unless I have a deadline or something of that nature."

The elevator doors opened and Secret saw Jack standing there engaged in a conversation with an attractive middle aged white woman. He looked up and saw her and his face creased into a big smile.

"Excuse me a moment," he said to the woman then reached out and grabbed Secret's arm and pulled her to him. He wrapped her in his arms and kissed her lips lightly then asked, "Taking lunch early?"

Secret's cheeks were blazing red as she looked up in his eyes and said, "No I've got an appointment. I'll tell you about it tonight when you get home."

"Okay," he said nodding, "I'd like you to meet a client. Mrs. Toliver I'd like you to meet my fiancée Ms. Secret Summers; Secret please meet Mrs. Lorraine Toliver."

"It's a pleasure to meet you Mrs. Toliver," Secret said extending her hand with a big smile.

"Same here," Lorraine said smiling broadly as she assumed Secret was a white woman that had caught the handsome Black man.

"Jack, I'd like you to meet," Secret started, then looked at Jack and burst out laughing. Jack looked at her laughing eyes with a question in his, and she said, "R-red is de-definitely not y-your c-color," and Shani noticed what Secret was talking about and started laughing too. Jack and Lorraine looked at them puzzled as Secret composed herself then said, "You got on lipstick baby."

Jack moved to the polished steel doors and looked at his reflection then burst out laughing. Lorraine saw the red lipstick on his lips and laughed too. Secret opened her briefcase and pulled out some towelettes and wiped his lips.

"Thanks sweetheart," he said with a big smile. "Since you got those out I might as well get another one."

"Save it for later baby," Secret said smiling. "I'd like you to meet Shani Edwards; my co-worker. Shani, this is my fiancé Jack Bradshaw." They shook hands then Jack pulled Secret in his arms, and she said playfully, "Jack, no. Stop it."

"I told you that you'd admit it soon," he whispered in her ear. The elevator pinged and they walked out into the garage. "I'll see you later sweetheart."

"Okay baby," Secret said as she and Shani walked over to the company minivan and got in.

"Girl he's gorgeous! Shani said, "Any more like him?"

"Believe it or not there is and he's funny as Chris Tucker!"

"Oh my God!" Shani said loudly, "You do mean gay funny and not hilarious right?"

"Exactly!" Secret said. "He has a younger brother named Sherod who's beautiful with a capital B. He owns Ricardo's night clubs. You've heard of those, right?"

"Upscale for sure," Shani said loudly, "I've always wanted to check out the scene because I've heard they be jumping."

"Oh, that they do. Me and my girls going to Ricardo's this coming Friday night and you can roll with us if you want to. Trust me it's gonna be fun."

"I'd like that," Shani said smiling as Secret pulled off.

It didn't take them a good five minutes to get to the Police Memorial Building and they parked in the back lot and walked in. They walked to the desk where a sergeant sat and Secret introduced them and was told to have a seat.

They sat down and five minutes later a female officer with
sergeant stripes walked over to them and said, "Hello, I'm Sgt. Nichole
Parsons with the Jacksonville Sheriff's Office."

Nichole put secret in the mind of Philicia Rashad. She was finely
built in an excellently tailored navy blue uniform.

Secret stood and made the introductions and was led by Nichole to
her office where they sat.

"Would you ladies like some refreshments before we get down to
business?" Nichole asked. They both declined and Nichole sat down and
got to the business at hand. "I'm sure you're aware of the many complaints
we've received the last six months. It hasn't helped that two former
members of the J.S.O. are having a high profile trial or that two deaths
occurred recently of people that were in police custody. Needless to say,
the department is suffering greatly at this time. Things haven't been this
bad in all my years of service and I've been on the force for almost twenty
years. Public perception of the force hasn't been this low since the
turbulent sixties and you know the force was basically controlled by the
Klan and its affiliates."

"From my standpoint hasn't much changed and that's off the
record," Secret said, "Our people have suffered much by those who are
sworn to protect and serve," Nichole's eyes grew wide when Secret said
"our people" because she assumed from appearances that Secret was
Caucasian. "It's no wonder that we don't trust the department with the
heavy handed methods they use when they come into our communities.
The African-American officers are often no better than their counterparts
because they don't want the powers that be to think they're showing favor."

"Trust me when I say I understand your concerns," Nichole said,
"But the entire force isn't at fault. We're making strides, though I admit
that it always seems to be too little. With ideology aside we're here to put a
better face on the force. Do you realize how many cases we could solve
with more community involvement? I'll tell you; more that seventy-five
percent of the crimes perpetrated in our communities could be solved if
people cooperated with us instead of viewing us as the enemy. Quiet as it's
kept there are a lot of people on the force who are genuinely sincere about
upholding the public trust."

"That may be so, but those are the ones that should be policing
their brethren instead of putting up the blue wall of silence or covering up
then indiscretions," Shani said.

"Listen, I've suffered through the same things you two have and at
times I too get dismayed but in order for things to get better we have to step
forward. I joined the force young and idealistic and found out soon that
politics has its place in every organization. I've been on the force for

eighteen years and eight months and I've been a sergeant for nine years. I graduated with a degree in communications and political science, and I know for a fact that I could've had a less stressful, higher paying job. But, I choose to do this because even though I'm not the same idealistic young lady I was when I joined the force I believe I can make a difference."

Secret smiled then said, "You got work cut out for you girl. Come on and let's brainstorm and see what we can come up with."

They sat in Nichole's office kicking around ideas until 1:30 then broke for lunch. They sat planning until 3:30 then Secret and Shani left and drove back to Billing and Ross. As soon as they got off the elevator they saw Claudia's desk almost hidden by balloons and long stemmed roses.

"Somebody must really adore you," Secret said as her and Shani walked up to the desk and she passed Claudia the keys.

"I wish," Claudia said wishfully, "All of these are yours. You had a call from a Mr. Jack Bradshaw around noon. He didn't call back but he sent you this stuff and a small box," Claudia opened her drawer and pulled out a small box of chocolates that measure two inches by four inches and passed it to Secret.

Secret laughed and took the small box of chocolates then asked, "Y'all want one?" As she ripped the plastic from the box she flipped up the lid and shouted, "Oh my God!" She looked down at the big, pea-sized diamond surrounded by smaller diamonds in a platinum setting. It was an engagement ring.

Claudia and Shani looked in the box and Claudia said, "I want one," and the three women burst out laughing.

"Now that's a ring!" Shani said laughing.

"Come on because we got some work to do," Secret said with a big smile, "Help me take this stuff to my office please." They took all the balloons and flowers to Secret's office and she said to Shani, "Can you transfer everything from the tapes to a disk while I make a couple of phone calls?" Then she called her girls and told them to meet her at the condo at 5:30. She called Jack's office and his secretary answered,

"Bradshaw Realty, Nadine speaking, how may I help you?"

"Could you please tell Mr. Bradshaw that Secret Summers is calling?"

"He's been expecting your call; please hold."

Secret heard the phone ring then Jack's voice, "Jack here, may I ask whose calling?"

"It's me baby," Secret said seductively.

"Hello Me Baby," He said and she could hear the joy in his voice. "I take it you got the stuff I sent you?"

"How much was that ring?" She asked.

"None of your business, It doesn't matter how much it cost; what matters is whether you like it or not!"

"You can't be going out buying me expensive gifts like that Jack, besides it's not traditional to send the engagement ring. You were supposed to be on one knee when you presented it."

"If that's what you want I'll get another ring and do it. It's my money and I can spend it like I want to. Stop by my office before you go so I can give you our joint account number. The check books will be ready by Thursday and I need you to go get them. As for tradition I thought we had decided to dismiss it. I told you what my intentions were and thus far you followed my lead."

"That's true," she said, "But I'm not coming to your office before I leave because I got a lot of things that I need to get done. I'm going to the house tonight so I'll see you there. What time do you think you'll be home?"

"When I get there!" He said with laughter in his voice.

"Well I'll be there when you get there. What's your favorite food?"

"You, if that's on the menu," he said seductively.

"I'm serious Jack."

"So am I," he replied. "I don't have a favorite food; that's the truth. Whatever you put together will be good enough for me. I'll see you at around 8:00 but no later than 8:30."

"See you then," she said and hung up the phone with a big smile. She turned to Shani who was busy at the computer then grabbed a chair and sat next to her.

They worked on the project until 4:50 then started packing up their briefcases.

"I'm gonna take this home and work on it a little if that's alright with you?" Shani said.

"That's on you girl. I liked your input and I think you're going to be real good. What I'm gonna do is assist you on the project and you will get credit too, so put your best foot forward."

"Always," Shani said smiling brightly. "I really appreciate you trusting me with this."

"I've been watching you since you started working here and I liked what I saw. When I was asked who I wanted to have work on this project with me, I said you. I got confidence in you girl cause I know what you're trying to accomplish. It's a man's world and even though we're making strides we still got a long way to go. Do your thing and I got your back; trust me!"

"I do," Shani said, "I've been watching you too," they both laughed then they left the office and walked to the elevator.

"Follow me to my crib so you'll know where to meet me at Friday because we'll leave from there. Here's my card so you'll know how to contact me if you come across something that you don't think you can handle. Call only in an emergency tonight because I'm gonna be real busy if you catch my drift."

They both laughed then Shani said, "Big as that stone is I'd say don't call at all!" They laughed as the elevator pinged and the doors slid open soundlessly.

They walked to their rides and drove to Secret's condo. Secret thought Shani would just see where she lived, but she got out of her car and followed Secret inside.

"Damn this place is the bomb!" Shani said loudly as she looked at the condo. She walked around the living room checking out the décor.

"I own it," Secret said proudly. "Before I finished paying for it I was paying eight hundred. They've got a couple of units open but they're only two bedrooms and one and a half baths. They want at least seventy thousand and your payments would probably be about six or seven hundred a month. It's a good investment if you can afford it because it'll be yours when you finish paying for it. This is three bedrooms and it was seventy-five thousand when I started buying it, and if I sold it now I could get one ten for it easy."

"I got a few pennies saved up but the rent and utilities would damn sure have me tightening up my belt a little."

"It'll be worth it in the long run girl," Secret said, "The closer you get to paying off your mortgage the lower your payments. It's a plus any way you look at it, and if my instincts are right as they usually are you'll be getting a raise sooner than you think. The project we're working on will guarantee that. I'm gonna personally see to it that you move up in the company. All of the top people are men except for me, and I need some company."

They both laughed, then the doorbell rang and Secret walked over and looked out of the peephole and saw Tiana filling the frame.

She opened the door and Tiana barged in as was her custom with Gia and Atlantis pulling up the rear. "Alright bread you might as well come on out with it cause you was acting like the shit was super important," Tiana said as she headed for the sofa and plopped down on it.

Gia and Atlantis plopped down in the love seat as Secret opened her briefcase and pulled out the small box of chocolates and walked over to where her three friends sat. When Secret flipped up the lid and they saw the

big diamond ring their eyes grew wide and they said in unison, "Oh my God!!!"

"My words exactly!" Secret said as her friends stared at the big ring. "That ain't all; I want y'all to follow me. By the way, this Shani, she works with me; Shani that's Tiana, Gia, and Atlantis," as she pointed to each of them. "Them my girls. I got a whole bunch of shit to do so y'all come on," Secret led them out of the condo and in a convoy they followed her to Ortega Forrest where she pulled in the cobbled driveway of a big, beautiful house.

When the women got out, Gia walked over to the Maybach which was parked in front of the house and said, "I always wanted to see one of these up close."

The other women joined her as Secret pulled out her key ring and opened the door so they could all look inside.

"We pushing this to the club Friday night," Secret said smiling. "This Jack's car and he said I could use it anytime I want to. Come on let's check out the crib," Secret opened the door and led them on a guided tour of the house and the four women oohed and awed the whole while. She led them back to the living room and said, "I'd like to ask y'all to stay and chill for a minute but I got to get Jack's dinner ready. If y'all want to we can hang out here tomorrow."

None of her friends asked her if she thought she was moving too fast with Jack, because they all knew that if a man of substance came along and offered them all that Jack seemed to be offering her, they'd take the same chance. They knew Secret wasn't easily swayed by wealth or seeming wealth, so they knew she must be feeling something for Jack and they each kept their reservations to themselves. They truly loved her and were happy for her. They all had family that loved them but they were the only family that Secret had.

Shani didn't know that Secret and Jack had just met so she didn't entertain any of the thoughts or reservations that the others had.

Tiana, Gia, and Atlantis vowed to themselves that they'd be there for Secret if and when she needed them, just like she was always there for them when they needed her.

"Damn right we can chill over here tomorrow," Tiana said smiling, "You oughta get that nigga to build a swimming pool so we can really hang out!"

"I ain't got to get him to do it because he told me to do whatever I want to the house. He said I could redecorate or whatever, but shit this spot is already fly as hell. All it need is some pictures of my family, me, and Jack to set the shit off. I don't want you hoes to think for a minute that this nigga gonna fuck up our groove cause it ain't that kinda party, and he ain't

that kinda nigga. He told me he didn't come to change my life but to enhance it. So ain't but one thing gonna change and that's that I got a nigga to warm my bed at night!" They all laughed then she said, "I hope y'all don't mind if Shani roll with us cause she straight. I've had my eyes on her for a while and I'm going mentor her."

"If the bitch straight with you she got to be alright," Gia said, "She'll learn how we get down by hanging out with us."

"Damn sho will," Atlantis said, "See Shani, we been girls since college and ain't shit can come between us; no nigga, no other bitches, no money, no nothing! We fuss and fight but that's part of loving bitches like us."

"You ain't never lied!" Tiana said. "See you young and you probably done been in lil cliques with hoes that be tryin to outdo each other, fuck each other's niggas and all kinda crazy shit. We don't get down like that. If one of us needs some help for whatever, we drop whatever we doin and come handle that. We all professional women but we keep it "G" cause we done seen niggas come and go. If you got a taste for white dick, whatever you do, don't let that hoe there know," she pointed at Secret, "Cause the bitch pro Black! She the blackest bitch we know!"

They all burst out laughing as Shani looked at the way they interacted with each other and amazed at genuine warmth she felt in their presence.

"By the way, we going to Ricardo's this Friday," Secret said.

"Not the sissy club?" Tiana said.

"Yeah the sissy club," Secret said shaking her head. "I told y'all I had a fabulous time in there and Jack's brother owns it. A lot of straight niggas be up in there and if any of you hoes ever wondered what it's like to get your kitty licked by another chick it's on!" They burst out laughing then Secret said, "Y'all hoes can haul ass because I got to run to the grocery store right quick and get my man dinner ready."

"Bitch you done got all domestic on us," Tiana said as they headed for the door.

Secret locked the house and walked over to the Maybach and opened the door as Tiana said, "Flossin ass bitch!"

"Number one stunna hoe!" Secret said and got behind the wheel. She looked at the controls and saw that it was just like Jack said, "Just a car". She put the key in the ignition and cranked the car then adjusted the seat to her liking and pulled off.

NOTE FROM THE PUBLISHER

First and foremost I would like to give praise to Yahweh the true name of the creator of all things, without him none of this would be possible. I would like to give a shot out to every one of our readers out there, we love you all and thanks for your support. Duval county what's up you know we repp'en our city. All the hustlers and players out there who doing what they got to do to survive we feel y'all pain. All the people that are locked up in the U.S. and abroad we hope we can give you an escape from your current reality.

On another note, Kane Family Saga Series is the most intense, hardcore, urban street erotica faction in the game. If anyone has read something harder than this please let us know, because the crown belongs to us. Holla!!!!

Ausha Rogers C.E.O